# TO WIN THE THRONE OF KING OF KINGS!

It was a time when the world was large and dreams were small. Few ships strayed from the four great turtles who bore the mountains and plains across the seas. Humankind and demonkind alike brooded under the faded banners of kings who'd ruled too long. Borders were no more distant than a fast march could secure. All who dwelt beyond huddled in armed settlements to keep thieves and beasts at bay.

It was an uneasy time, a time crying out for change. Royal wizards studied the stars for signs to reassure their masters. Subjects gathered in secret to implore the gods to rid them of those same masters.

But the gods gave no clue of their intentions. The starry wheel where the gods slept in their ten holy realms churned onward year after year, heedless to all pleas.

Then the portent came. It was not from the slumbering gods but from the molten depths of the world itself. And it was a boy, not a master wizard, who first marked the sign.

That boy was Safar Timura.

## Other Cosmos Books

*No One Noticed the Cat*, Anne McCaffrey
*Science Fiction: The Best of the Year*, edited by Rich Horton
*Shadow Kingdoms*, by Robert E. Howard
*Fantasy: The Best of the Year*, edited by Rich Horton
*Little Fuzzy*, by H. Beam Piper
*The Spriggan Mirror*, by Lawrence Watt-Evans
*The Door Through Space*, by Marion Zimmer Bradley
*The Race for God*, by Brian Herbert
*If Wishes Were Horses*, by Anne McCaffrey
*Moon of Skulls*, by Robert E. Howard
*Star Born*, by Andre Norton
*Wolves of the Gods*, by Allan Cole
*The Misenchanted Sword*, by Lawrence Watt-Evans

# WHEN THE GODS SLEPT
# THE TIMURAS TRILOGY BOOK 1

by

**Allan Cole**

WHEN THE GODS SLEPT
*August 2007*

Published by

Dorchester Publishing Co., Inc.
200 Madison Avenue
New York, NY 10016

in collaboration with Wildside Press, LLC



Cover painting by Peler Elson and used by permission of the Sarah Brown Agency.

Typeset by Swordsmith Productions



ISBN-10: 0-8439-5909-6
ISBN-13: 978-0-8439-5909-3



Printed in the United States of America.

*For Kathryn*

*Think, in this battered caravansari*
*Whose doorways are alternate night and day*
*How sultan after sultan with his pomp*
*Abode his destined hour and went his way*

*The Rubaiyat of Omar Khayyam*
EDWARD FITZGERALD TRANSLATION

# WHEN THE GODS SLEPT

## THE TIMURAS TRILOGY

## BOOK 1

# Part One
## When the Gods Slept

# Prologue
# STRANGER ON A HILL

The villagers fear him.

They draw lots each day to see who must fill his beggar's bowl.

The loser creeps up the hill trembling and clutching a talisman. The stranger knows they fear the evil eye so he doesn't look when the approach is made. He makes no sound or movement until the deed is done and the villager flees as if there were a dervish at his heels.

The villagers think the stranger is a mad priest and curse the day he came to hide in these hills.

He's not mad and he is no priest. But he lets them believe what they like. If his true identity were revealed the village treasury would soon be bursting with gold. For the stranger is a fugitive from the King. Safar Timura, who was once Grand Wazier to King Protarus, is hunted by him now.

They were blood oath brothers. Safar sat by his friend's throne and gave him counsel and exorcised the devils troubling his sleep. Several times he saved the King's life. He was rewarded with lands and palaces and jewels and more honors than most men have ever dreamed.

When the history of King Protarus is written they'll say it was Lord Timura who betrayed him. They'll say Safar gambled and lost all for love.

To the first he pleads innocent. It's Safar's view it was the King who betrayed him. As for the second he admits guilt. And it is for that crime Protarus wants his head. But for the *King's* offense Safar demands more.

And he *will* have his payment—if the king doesn't catch him first.

Safar can see his enemy's city from his lonely post. At night, under the swirling Demon Moon, he can see the lights of Zanzair blur the stars. See the smoke from the foundries and kitchens rise up each morning to haze the day. And he can see the King's Grand Palace quite clearly, its windows a rosy glow in the dawn.

He models the palace in clay of the purest white—skillfully forming the towers between wet palms, etching the designs on the parapets with his silver witch's knife. He whispers potter's spells as he shapes the domes and pillars. Breathing his hate into the clay.

At night he wraps the model in wet leaves and sets it aside to await the new day. He empties the beggar's bowl, then wraps himself against the chill in a black mourning cloak. At dawn he begins anew.

When the palace is done and the great spell is cast Safar Timura's revenge will be complete.

Then he'll depart that lonely hill. He'll flee across deserts and grasslands and wide rocky plains to the mountains of his birth.

Where the snowy passes carry the high caravans to clear horizons.

The place he should never have left.

The place where this tale begins.

# 1

# VALLEY OF THE CLOUDS

It was a time when the world was large and dreams were small. Few ships strayed from the four great turtles who bore the mountains and plains across the seas. Humankind and demonkind alike brooded under the faded banners of kings who'd ruled too long. Borders were no more distant than a fast march could secure. All who dwelt beyond huddled in armed settlements to keep thieves and beasts at bay.

It was an uneasy time, a time crying out for change. Royal wizards studied the stars for signs to reassure their masters. Subjects gathered in secret to implore the gods to rid them of those same masters.

But the gods gave no clue of their intentions. The starry wheel where the gods slept in their ten holy realms churned onward year after year, heedless to all pleas.

Then the portent came. It was not from the slumbering gods but from the molten depths of the world itself. And it was a boy, not a master wizard, who first marked the sign.

That boy was Safar Timura.

He lived in the land known as Esmir, the Turtle of The Middle Seas. It was a land where demons faced humans across the Forbidden Desert. Only an ancient curse and constant internal warfare kept those ancestral enemies from overrunning and slaughtering the other.

In the demon city of Zanzair, however, King Manacia and his sorcerers plotted and waited for the right moment. Although humans were greater in number, Manacia knew their magic was weak and their leaders cowardly. And he yearned for the day when he'd make their corpses a staircase to a grander throne.

To achieve his dreams he pored over ancient maps and tomes and consulted many oracles. Then he created the greatest oracle of all, sacrificing five thousand human slaves in the process.

The human head was mounted on a metal post in the center of Manacia's courtroom. The eyes were closed. The mouth slack. The skin ghastly.

Manacia cast his most powerful spell and then commanded: "Speak, O Brother of the Shades. What is the key to my heart's desire? What road do I take, what passage do I seek, to win the throne of the King of Kings?"

The head's eyes came open, blazing in hate and agony. Stiff lips formed a word:

"Kyrania," the head croaked, sounding like an old raven with its mouth full of gore.

"What place is that?" the king demanded.

"Kyrania," the head croaked again.

The whole court looked on, demon jaws parting in anticipation, as the king jabbed a long sharp talon at an ancient wall map of the human lands.

"Where do I find this...Kyrania?" he asked.

"The Valley of the Clouds," the head answered. And then its eyes dulled and its mouth sagged back into death.

"Speak!" the king ordered, casting another mighty spell. But it was no use. The oracle was emptied of its power.

The Demon King turned to his assembled wizards and advisors. "Find me this place," he thundered. "Find me this Kyrania!...

"...This Valley of the Clouds!"

A thousand miles distant Safar Timura and his people toiled the land and tended their flocks in relative peace. They lived high above the troubles of the world and had grown to think they were of small concern.

Their valley was so remote it appeared on few maps. And those were jealously held by the merchant princes who transported their goods across the Gods' Divide, which separated the ancient human kingdoms of Walaria and Caspan.

The valley was known as Kyrania—meaning, in the language of Safar's people, "Valley of the Clouds."

It was a bountiful place and each spring and summer the valley became a bowl of blossoms and fruit cradled high in the craggy range they called The Bride And Six Maids. The name came from seven graceful peaks shaped like slender young women. From the south they appeared to march in an eternal procession. The tallest and most graceful promontory was in the lead and to all Kyranians this peak was The Bride because she was always covered with snow and veiled in lacy clouds. Although the valley was so high strangers sometimes found it difficult to draw enough breath, it was sheltered by the maidenly peaks and the weather was nearly always mild.

Filling half the valley was the holy lake of Our Lady Felakia and sometimes pilgrims traveled with the caravans to pay homage to that goddess of purity and health and to drink from the curative waters. They gathered to be blessed at the ancient temple, set on the eastern shore and so small and unimportant it was attended by only one old priest. Twice a year flocks of birds stopped at the lake to rest on their seasonal journeys. No one knew where they came from or where they went but they were always welcome visitors—filling the air with their song and the cooking hearths with their roasted flesh.

The people of Kyrania grew barley and corn and beans, irrigating the fields with water from the lake. Olive and fruit orchards also abounded, but the growing season was short so the Kyranians placed great value on their goat herds. In the spring and summer Safar and the boys would lead them into the mountains to graze on tender shoots. When winter came the goats huddled in stables beneath the people's homes, eating stored grain and keeping the families warm with the heat of their bodies.

All those things, which might seem trivial and even dull to city dwellers, were of prime importance to Safar and his people. They made up their talk, their dreams and all the rhythms of life.

In his own way—the way of Kyrania—Safar was royally born. He was the son of a potter and in Kyrania such men as his father were second only to the village priest in importance. His father's father had been a potter as well, and *his* father before him. It had always been so for the Timura clan and many generations of Kyranian women had balanced Timura water jugs on their heads as they made the hip-swaying journey to the lake and back. All food in the village was cooked in Timura pots or stored in Timura jars, which were sealed with clay and buried in the ground for winter. Spirits were fermented in Timura jugs, bottled in Timura vessels and it was said all drink tasted best when sipped from Timura cups and bowls. When the caravans arrived Timura pottery was more sought after than even the few fresh camels and llamas the villagers kept to resupply the merchant masters.

When the troubles came Safar was being trained to succeed his father as a practitioner of that once most sacred of all the arts. To accomplish this was Safar's sole ambition. But as a wise one once said—"If you want the make the gods laugh...tell them your plans."

The day that marked the end of those youthful ambitions began well before first light, as did all days in Kyrania. It was early spring and the mornings were still cold and one of his sisters had to bang on his sleeping platform with a broom handle to rouse him from his warm feather mattress.

He grumbled as he broke away from a dream of swimming in warm lake waters with nubile maidens. He was just seventeen summers—an age when such dreams are remarkably vivid and nearly as frequent as the grumblings at the unfairness of life.

Then he heard Naya, the family's best milking goat, complaining in the stable below. She was the sweetest of animals and he hated to think of her suffering. Safar leaped from the platform onto the polished planks that made the floor of the main living area. He dragged out the trunk where he kept his belongings and hastily pulled on clothes—baggy leather trousers, pullover shirt and heavy work boots. His mother was already at the hearth stirring handfuls of dried apple into the savory barley porridge that would make his breakfast.

She clucked her tongue to chide him for being tardy, but then smiled and gave him a hunk of bread spread with pear jam to tide him over until the milking was done. Safar was the middle child but the only boy of his parents' six children, so he was lovingly and deliberately spoiled by his mother and sisters.

"You'd better hurry, Safar," his mother warned. "Your father will be back for his breakfast soon."

Safar knew his father would be in the adjoining shop inspecting the results of the previous day's firing. The elder Timura, whose name was Khadji, preferred to have the family together at mealtimes. It would be especially important to him this morning. There had been a late-night meeting of the Council of Elders and Khadji would be anxious to report the news.

Mind buzzing with curiosity, mouth full of bread and jam, Safar thundered down the ladder and lit the fat lamps. He got out several pots made of his father's purest clay and glazed a dazzling white. As usual he tended Naya first. Her milk was delicious and his mother frequently accused him of squirting more into his mouth than in the pot.

"Why am I always to blame when something goes wrong around here?" he'd protest.

"Because you've got some on your chin, my little thief," she'd say.

Safar was always taken in, giving his chin a reflexive wipe and making the whole family howl at his embarrassment.

"Don't ever decide to become a bandit, Safar," his father would joke. "The master of the first caravan you rob is certain to catch you. Then the only thing we'd have left of our son would be his head on a post."

Naya seemed more anxious that morning than an overly full udder should warrant. When Safar removed the canvas bag kept tied about her teats for cleanliness' sake he saw several angry sores. He checked the bag and saw it was frayed on one side. The rough area had rubbed against her udder all night. The sores would fester quickly in the damp spring.

"Don't fret, little mother," he murmured. "Safar will fix you up."

He looked about to make certain there were no witnesses. His sisters had gone to fetch water from the lake so besides the goats and other animals the stable area was empty. Safar scratched his head, thinking.

His eyes fell on the lamp beside the stool. He dipped up thick, warm fat with his fingers and rubbed it gently on Naya's udder. Then he made up a little spell and whispered it as he dipped up more oil and coaxed it gently over the sores.

*Rest easy,*
*Little mother;*
*Safar is here.*
*There is no pain,*
*No wound to trouble you.*
*Rest easy*
*Little mother;*
*Safar is here.*

He looked down and the sores were gone. There was only a little pink area on her udder and that was quickly fading.

Then he heard his mother say, "Who are you talking to, Safar?"

He flushed, then answered: "I wasn't talking to anyone, mother. I was just...singing a song." In those days Safar felt compelled to hide his magical talents from others.

Satisfied, his mother said nothing more. Safar quickly finished the milking and his other chores and by the time he was done his father and sisters were sitting down to breakfast. There was one absent place at the table—the spot where Safar's oldest sister, Quetera had held forth all his life. Safar saw his mother give the seat a sad glance. His sister lived with her husband now and was pregnant with their first child. It had been a difficult pregnancy and the family was worried.

His mother swiped at her eye, forced a smile, and began to pass the food around. There was porridge and bread toasted over the fire, with big slabs of cheese from the crusted round Safar's mother always kept sitting near the embers. They washed their breakfast down with milk still warm from the goats.

"You were late coming home last night, Khadji," his mother said as she gave his father another slice of buttered toast. "There must've been much business for the council to discuss. Not bad news, I hope."

Khadji frowned. "It wasn't exactly *bad* news, Myrna," he said. "But it certainly was troublesome."

Myrna was alarmed. "Nothing to do with the caravan, I hope?" she said.

Caravan season was just beginning and the village had received word the first group of traders was making its way to Kyrania. It had been a long winter and the money and goods the caravan would bring were sorely needed.

"No, nothing to do with the caravan," Safar's father said. "It's not expected for a few weeks, yet."

Myrna snorted, impatient. "If you don't want a second bowl of porridge served on your head, Khadji Timura," she said, "you'll tell us right now what this is all about!"

Usually, Khadji would have laughed, but instead Safar saw his frown deepen.

"We agreed to accept a boy into the village," Khadji said. "He was presented to us by an elder of the Babor clan, who begged us to give him sanctuary."

The Babors were the leading family of a large and fierce clan of people who lived on the distant plains.

Myrna dropped a serving spoon, shocked. "I don't like *that*!" she said. "Why, they're practically barbarians. I'm not sure I like having one of their young ruffians among us."

Khadji shrugged. "What could we do? Barbarians or not, the Babors have kinship claims on us. It wouldn't be right to say no to our cousins."

Myrna sniffed. "Pretty *distant* cousins, for all that."

"He seems a likely enough lad," Khadji said in the stranger's defense. "His family is related to the Babor headman's wife. They live somewhere in the south. People of influence, from the cut of the boy. He's a handsome fellow about your age, Safar. And tall—about your size, as well. Very mannered. Good clothing. And well spoken. Seems the sort who's used to having servants to order about."

"He'll soon learn there are no servants in Kyrania," Myrna said sharply. Then, "Why is he being sent to us?"

"He's an orphan," Safar's father said.

Myrna was scandalized. "An orphan? What kind of orphan is he? No, I take that back. The Gods make orphans. It's no fault of a child's. It's the boy's kin I wonder about. What manner of people are they to push an orphan on strangers? Have they no feelings?"

Safar saw his father shift, uneasy. "It seems there's some sort of difficulty in his clan," Khadji said. "A quarrel of some kind."

Myrna's eyebrows rose. "With those sort of people," she said, "quarrel usually means violence and bloodshed. It's the only way they know how to settle an argument."

Khadji nodded, unhappy. "I suspect you're right, Myrna," he said. "The boy's uncle said as much. I think he fears for the boy's life. He's asked us to let the lad stay at the temple until the danger has passed."

Safar could have told his father he'd used the wrong words.

"Danger?" his mother exclaimed. "What danger, Khadji?"

"Only to the boy, Myrna," his father soothed. "Only to the boy."

"But what if *they* come here? What if *they* cause trouble?"

"Only his uncle will come," his father said. "And only when it is safe for the lad to return to his family. Be reasonable, Myrna. We have to explain this to the others and if you're opposed to it, why, we'll have to go back on our agreement.

"Besides, who would travel so far to Kyrania just to cause us grief? We have nothing they want. At least nothing that's worth so much trouble.

"And, as I said, how could we refuse?"

"Next time ask me!" Myrna said. "I'll show you all you need to know about refusal."

Then she relented as her natural Kyranian hospitality came to the fore. "We'll make the best of it," she declared. "Can't blame a boy for the troubles caused by his family."

"What's his name?" Safar asked.

"Iraj Protarus," his father said.

The name struck Safar like a thunderbolt.

He heard his mother say, "Protarus? Protarus? I don't know that family name.

But Safar knew the name quite well—much to his sudden discomfort.

He'd experienced a vision some days before while working in his father's shop. Whether it meant good or ill, he couldn't say. Still, it had disturbed him deeply.

The vision had seized him while he was cleaning pebbles and roots from a new batch of clay his father had dug up from the lake.

Besides the lake, there were many fine clay beds in Kyrania. The lake clay was pure and therefore gray. But as any potter knows pure clay needs to be mixed with other kinds or it will not fire properly. Within a week's stroll in any direction the Timuras could find clay of every color imaginable—red, black, white, a yellow ochre, and even a deep emerald green. Clay was long considered a holy substance and the clay from Kyrania was considered the holiest of all because it was said that Rybian, the god who made people, once spent much time in the Valley of the Clouds wooing the beautiful goddess, Felakia. The tale was that she spurned the god's advances and during the long lovers' siege Rybian became bored and pinched out all the races that make up humankind and demonkind. He used the green clay, it was claimed, to make the demons.

As Safar worked his thoughts were far from heavenly speculation. Instead, his imagination was fixed on the hiding spot he'd discovered overlooking the pool where the village maids liked to bathe.

Then he found an unusual stone in the clay debris. It was a broad pebble—smooth and blood red. Examining it, he turned the pebble this way and that. There was a clear, thumbnail-size blemish on one side. The blemish was like a minuscule window and he was oddly drawn to look into it.

Safar jumped back, thinking he'd seen something move...as if trapped in the stone. He looked again, blinking. The image blinked back and he realized he was looking at a reflection of his own eye. He peered closer, wondering the idle things people contemplate when they are alone and staring at a mirrored surface.

Suddenly Safar found himself falling. But it was unlike any sensation of falling he'd experienced before. His body seemed to remain kneeling by the clay bucket while his spirit plunged through the window.

His spirit self plummeted through thick clouds, then broke through. Safar felt oddly calm, looking about with his spirit eyes. Then it came to him he was floating rather than falling. Above was a bright sky, with clouds that were quickly retreating. Floating up at him was a wide vista of fertile lands with a broad highway cutting through.

At the end of that highway was a grand city with golden spires.

The last of the clouds whisked away, revealing a mighty army marching along the highway to the city, banners fluttering in a gentle wind. It was a dazzling array of troops and mailed cavalry—both horse and camel. Two graceful wings of chariots spread out on either side. In the lead was a phalanx of elephants Safar recognized only because of the illustrated books at school. The elephant heading the column was the largest by far. It was white and carried an armored howdah on its back. A large silk banner flew over the howdah, displaying a comet moving across a full moon.

The comet was silver, the moon harvest red.

Then he saw the city gates thrown wide and a crowd poured out to greet the army. Safar spread his spirit arms and flew toward the crowd. No one saw him as he sailed over a forest of spears and lances and he took a boy's immense pleasure in doing what he liked amongst so many adults and yet remaining unobserved. Then he overshot his mark and nearly flew through the city gates. Correcting his course, he hovered over the crowd and looked down.

Milling beneath him were hundreds of screeching monsters. He knew instantly they were demons. He should have been frightened. Demons were humankind's most ancient and deadly enemies. But there was an opiate blur to his trance that allowed him to feel nothing more than amazement.

The demons had yellow eyes and were fiercely taloned; horns jutted from their snouted faces. Sharp fangs gleamed when they opened their mouths and their skin was scaly green. All were costumed in the finest of cloth and jewelry, especially the tall slender demons in front, whom Safar took to be the city's leaders.

The tallest of them held a pike. And stuck to the top of that pike was a head. Safar had never seen such a grisly sight and it disturbed him far more than monsters boiling about beneath him. Still, he couldn't help but move closer. It was a demon's head on that pike. Huge—twice that of a human's. Its snout was fixed into a wide grimace, exposing two pairs of opposing fangs the size of a desert lion's. It had a jutting armored brow and long bloody hair. Perched on the brow, as if in mockery, was a golden crown.

The demon king's dead eyes were open and staring. But Safar imagined he saw a small spark of life in their yellow depths. This unsettled him even more than the gory display of death. He stretched his arms and flew away.

Seeing the great white elephant approaching, he flew toward it to investigate. Sitting in the howdah was a large man with long gold hair, flowing mustaches and a thick military beard. His features were so fair he appeared strange to Safar, although not as strange as the demons.

Below dark, moody eyes was a strong beaked nose, which added to his fierce looks. His armor was rich and burnished; the hilt of his sheathed sword was finely worked ivory bound with silver wire. Encircling his head was a thin band of gold embedded with rare stones.

Safar knew he was looking at the new king—come to replace the one who had his head mounted on a pike. The demon crowd was shouting to their new king and he waved his mailed hand in return.

They grew wilder still, chanting: "Protarus! Protarus! Protarus!"

The king looked up and saw Safar. Why this man alone could see him, Safar didn't know. Protarus smiled. He stretched out a hand, beckoning the hovering spirit closer.

"Safar," he said. "I owe all this to you. Come sit with me. Let them praise your name as well."

Safar was confused. Who was this great king? How did he know him? What service could Safar have possibly performed to win his favor? Again Protarus beckoned. Safar floated forward and the king reached out to take his hand.

Just before their fingers touched Safar again felt the sensation of falling. But this time he was falling *up!* The movement was so swift he started to feel sick. Then city, army and finally even the green fields vanished and he was enveloped by thick clouds.

The next he knew he was crouched over the bucket, turning away as quickly as he could to avoid fouling the clay with the contents of his belly.

Luckily his father was absent. Safar hastily cleaned up the mess, finished his other chores and crept up to his bed. The experience had exhausted him, unnerved him, so he pleaded ill when the dinner hour arrived and spent a troubled night contemplating the mysterious vision.

That uneasiness returned as Safar sat listening to his family chat about the young stranger who had come to stay in Kyrania—a stranger whose name was also Protarus. He fretted until it was time for school. Then he dismissed it as a coincidence.

In his youth Safar Timura believed in such things.

It was a clear spring day when he set out for the temple school with his sisters. Men and women were in the fields readying the muddy land for planting. The boys whose turn it was to tend the goats were driving their herds into the hills. They would stay there for several weeks while Safar and the others studied with the priest. Then it would be his turn to enjoy the lazy freedom of the high ranges.

The small village marketplace was already closing for the day, with a few late risers arguing with the stall keepers to stay open a little longer so they could make necessary purchases.

The Timura children walked along the lake's curve, passing

the ruins of the stone barracks which legend claimed were built by Alisarrian The Conqueror who crossed the Gods' Divide in his campaign to win a kingdom. That kingdom, the Kyranian children were taught, had once included all Esmir and demons as well as humans bowed to Alisarrian's will. But the empire had broken up after his death, disintegrating into warring tribes and fiefdoms. It was during that chaos humans and demons had sworn to the agreement making the Forbidden Desert the dividing point between their species—a "Nodemon's" as well as a "Noman's" land.

Outsiders claimed it would've been impossible for the Conqueror to have driven his great army over the Gods' Divide. But Kyranian tradition had it that Alisarrian settled some of his troops in the valley and they married local women. Kyranians were mostly a short, dark skinned people while Alisarrian and his soldiers were tall and fair. Occasionally a fair skinned child was born in Kyrania, bolstering the claims.

Safar saw his own appearance as evidence that the local tales were true. Although he was dark, his eyes were quite blue and like the ancient Alisarrians he was taller than most. Also, his people tended to be slender, but even at seventeen Safar's chest and shoulders were broadening beyond the size of others and his arms were becoming heavily muscled. Any difference, however, is an embarrassment at that age and so Safar saw his size and blue eyes as a humiliating reminder that he was different from others.

As the Timuras passed the stony inlet where the women did the wash one fat old crone happened to glance up. Her eyes chanced to meet Safar's and she suddenly gobbled in fear and made a sign to ward off evil. Then she cursed and spat on the ground three times.

"It's the devil," she shrieked to the other women. "The blue-eyed devil from the Hells."

"Hush, grandmother," one of the women said. "It's only Safar with his sisters going to school at the temple."

The old woman paid no heed. "Get thee gone!" she shrieked at Safar. "Get thee gone, devil!"

He hurried away, barely listening to the comforting words of his sisters who said she was just a crazy old woman and to pay her no mind. But there was no solace in their words. In his heart he believed the woman spoke true. He didn't know if he actually was a devil. But he feared he'd become one if he didn't abandon the practice of sorcery. Each time he performed a magical feat or had a vision he swore to the gods he'd never do it again.

The older he became, however, the harder it was to resist.

Safar had possessed the talent even when he was a toddler. If a glittering object caught his eye he could summon it at will. He'd pop it into his mouth and start chewing to soothe his tender gums. His mother and aunts would squawk in alarm and drag the object out, fearing he'd swallow it and choke. Safar drove them to distraction with such antics, for no matter how well they hid the things he'd sniff them out and summon them again.

When he grew older he turned that talent into finding things others had lost. If a tool went missing, or an animal went astray, he could always hunt them down. He was so successful that if anything was lost the family would instantly call him to retrieve it. Safar didn't know how he was able to do such things but it all seemed so natural his only surprise was that others lacked the facility.

That innocence ended in his tenth year.

He was in his father's workshop one day, pinching out little pots he'd been taught to make as part of his apprenticeship. Safar's father was engaged in an errand, so the boy quickly became bored. One of the pots had a malformed spout which he suddenly thought looked like the village priest's knobby nose. The boy giggled and mashed the pot between his hands, rolling it into a ball. Then his hands seemed to take on an intelligence of their own and in a few minutes he'd formed the ball into a tiny man.

He was delighted at first, then thought something was missing. In a moment it came to him that the clay man lacked a penis, so he pinched one out where the legs met. He put the man down, wondering what he could do with him. The man needs a friend, Safar thought. No, a wife. So he rolled up another ball and made a woman with pert breasts like his oldest sister's and a little crease where such things should go. Once again he wondered what he could do with his new toys. Then it came to him that if they were man and wife they should have children. The sexual act is no secret to children who live close to nature, much less in homes such as Kyrania's where there is little privacy. So Safar put the two figures together in the proper position.

"Make babies," Safar said to them. But nothing happened.

A childish spell popped into his head, although at the time he didn't know that was what it was. He picked up the figures and held them close together while he chanted:

*Skin and bone*
*was all clay once*
*until Rybian made people.*
*Now Safar makes people,*
*so clay be skin,*
*clay be bone.*

The clay dolls grew warm, then they began to move and the child laughed in glee as they twined together like the young lovers he'd once spied in the meadow.

Then Khadji came in and Safar cried, "Look what I made, father!"

When Khadji saw the figures he thought his son was making the sexual motions and he stormed over and cuffed the boy.

"What filth is this?" he shouted.

He snatched the dolls from Safar's hands and they became lifeless again. He shook them at the boy.

"How could you do something so disrespectful?" he snarled. "The gods blessed us with these pleasures. They are not to be mocked."

"But I wasn't mocking anything, father," Safar protested.

His father cuffed him again just as his mother came in to see what was happening.

"What is it, Khadji?" she asked. "What has our Safar done?"

Angrily he showed her the dolls. "This dirty little boy has been making these obscene things," he snarled. "Behaving like one of those depraved potters in the city instead of a gods-fearing Timura."

Safar's mother eyed the dolls, her expression mild. His father became embarrassed, threw them into a bucket and reared back to give the boy another cuff.

"That's enough, Khadji," Safar's mother warned. "You've made your point. He won't do it again...will you, Safar?"

The boy was crying, more in humiliation than pain. His father hadn't hit him that hard. It was the act of being struck by someone Safar thought a hero that hurt worse.

"No, mother," he blubbered. "I won't do it again." He turned to his father. "I'm sorry, father," he said. "I promise I won't be a dirty little boy anymore."

The elder Timura grumbled, but Safar saw him nod. The boy prayed to all that was holy his father was satisfied. He swore to himself he'd never again give him cause to be scornful of his son. Then Myrna led Safar away. She took him up to the kitchen where she put him to work scrubbing the hearth.

Safar bent to the task with a will, sobbing as he scoured the stone with all his little boy's strength. Eventually the sobbing stopped. He chanced a look at his mother and saw she was eyeing him. But she didn't look angry, or ashamed.

"They were very pretty, Safar," she murmured.

The boy said nothing.

"So pretty, I doubt you meant anything wrong. Is that true?"

Safar nodded. Another great sob threatened, but he fought and won control.

"Well, then," she said, "if you meant nothing wrong, don't let it bother you. Just be careful from now on. Would you do that for me?"

She held out her arms and Safar ran into that warm harbor, escaping the emotional storm. But from that day on he associated magic with something shameful—an act performed by dirty little boys. And that shame grew along with his powers and his inability to stop committing such sins. He felt apart from others, the good people of Kyrania who had almond eyes and were properly small.

So when the crone cursed Safar as a blue-eyed devil, she'd unwittingly found a gaping wound for a target.

When Safar and his sisters reached the temple their priest, Gubadan, was already lining the children up for their exercises. He was a cheery little man—with that great knobby nose which had inspired Safar's earlier shame. The priest's ample belly stretched the material of his yellow robes and he had a habit of gripping the sides when he was talking and thumping it with his thumbs. He also had a shaven head and a long white beard he kept in immaculate condition.

As Safar joined the others in the slow, sacred motions and deep breathing Gubadan had taught them to rid their minds of trifles that hinder learning, he looked about for the new boy. He was disappointed when he didn't see him.

Gubadan noted his inattention and snarled: "Put your spirit into it, Safar, or I'll take a switch to you."

The others laughed, which drew more threats of switchings. But that only made them giggle more for Gubadan was a gentle soul who'd no more beat them than he'd defile the altar of Felakia with an unclean offering. Although the exercises were the motions of warriors taught from the time of Alisarrian, Gubadan meant them to be soul cleansers—a means to examine the inner self. Once a week all the boys would use those same exercises on the drilling field. There they were overseen by a fierce old soldier whose duty it was to train them to defend Kyrania in case of attack.

The laughter soon stopped and they all fell into the dreamy motions of the exercise.

When Gubadan was satisfied, he led them through the ancient portals, graced by etchings of Felakia in all her forms—from graceful swan to gentle mother to the beautiful armored maid who protected Kyrania. The temple was a crumbling place that kept the village busy repairing it when the stormy season passed. The classroom was a small room next to the chamber where the incense was stored so it was always filled with godly odors that made even the most unruly child feel serious about his work.

Although Kyrania was remote and the people made their living by hard toil, they were not ignorant. They held learning to be a sacred duty and took pride in their ability to read weighty texts, figure complex sums and write a hand as fair as any taught at the best schools in Walaria. Kyranians were particularly proud of their ability with languages and all could speak half-a-dozen or more. The tradition of scholarship dated back to the legends of Alisarrian, who was reputed to be a learned man as well as a mighty warrior king. Legend had it that the first Kyranian school was founded by the Conqueror for the men he left behind. True or not, all those skills learned in at the temple school were not put to idle use. Kyranians required agile minds and an understanding of foreign tongues to deal with all the caravans that came through. Otherwise the shrewd traders would have skinned them of all their goods long before. Instead, the Kyranians were the ones who profited most from the hard bargaining sessions that always followed the llama trains into the valley.

That day, however, Safar couldn't keep his mind on scholarship. He earned several stern warnings from Gubadan and stumbled when he was called on to name the brightest constellation in the spring heavens. He knew it was the Tiger but when asked the answer fled his mind.

"Is this a game you are playing with old Gubadan, boy?" the priest scolded. "You are my best student. All know this. Your family pays me dearly to spend extra hours with you so you can learn even more. And yet you mock me, boy. And by mocking me, you mock the gods who gifted you. Do you think you are better than others, Safar Timura?"

"No, master," Safar said, ducking his head in embarrassment.

"Then why do you pretend ignorance of the obvious?" the priest roared. "Tell me that!"

"I honestly couldn't think of the answer, master," Safar said.

"Then you are lazy!" the priest shouted. "Which is a worse sin than mocking. Mocking I could excuse to high spirits. But laziness! Inattention! Unforgivable, boy. You should be setting an example to the others."

Safar wanted to say he couldn't help it, that his mind was fixed on the absent boy whose name was Protarus—the name of the king in his vision.

Instead he said, "I'm sorry, master. I'll try to do better."

He did try, but the day progressed slowly and not well. Finally he was free and he dashed out, trying to ignore Gubadan's fierce looks in his direction.

Safar was relieved he had a task to perform for his father and didn't have to walk with his sisters and listen to them tease him about his performance in school. He headed immediately for the clay beds where his father had left buckets for him to fetch home a fresh load. His path took him beyond the temple through a fragrant wood, where he dawdled in the clean air and sighing breezes.

He was just emerging from the wood and turning toward the clay beds on the lake's edge when he heard angry voices. The voices had a familiar ring to them and he wasn't surprised when the angry words became shouts and then sounds of fighting erupted. He hurried up the hill to investigate.

When he reached the summit he looked down and saw a tangle of flailing and arms and legs.

Four brawny youths had another pinned to the ground and they were pummeling him unmercifully.

The attackers were the Ubekian brothers, considered the greatest bullies in Kyrania. They came from a rough, unclean family that'd wandered starving and half-frozen into the valley one winter and begged charity. The Ubekians had claims of kinship, which although distant were strong enough to make their appeal undeniable under Kyranian tradition and law. To everyone's dismay the family settled into a cave near the main village and set up permanent housekeeping. They also got busy making general nuisances of themselves.

Safar had more reason than most to dislike the Ubekian brothers. They'd fixed instantly on his odd, blue-eyed appearance and had mocked him unmercifully. In fact, until the arrival of the family no one had commented on his looks at all. But now others, such as the old woman at the lake, had become bold enough to torment him.

One by one, Safar had caught the brothers alone and thrashed them. Now they no longer mocked him—at least not in his hearing.

Safar had no doubt the brothers were to blame in the fight he saw below. His dislike of the brothers plus the unpleasant events of the day made his blood sing in furious joy as he ran down the hill and threw himself into the fray.

Cries of pain and surprise greeted his attack. But the brothers quickly recovered and turned on him. Safar was hard-pressed for a moment, catching a blow to his nose that made stars brighter than those that formed the Tiger.

Then the brothers' victim jumped up and barreled in. Everything became a fury of fists, knees, elbows and butting heads.

Suddenly the fight ended and the brothers scampered away, pausing at the top of the hill to hurl empty threats to salve their pride. But when Safar and his companion moved forward the brothers dashed off, shouting obscenities over their shoulders.

Safar turned to see who he'd rescued. The youth was about his height and weight. But then shock hit when he saw that the boy was fair skinned with blonde hair, moody eyes and a strong beaked nose.

The features were disturbingly familiar.

The strange boy grinned through bruised lips, showing bloody teeth. "You arrived just in time," he said. "In a moment I would have lost my temper and risen up to break their heads."

Safar recovered his wits. "From where I stood," he said, dryly, "you didn't look like you'd be getting up soon."

The strange boy laughed. "That's because I have such a peaceful nature," he said.

The comment broke the ice and Safar laughed with him. "Next time you meet the Ubekian brothers," he said, "lose your temper as quick as you can. Or it'll be *your* head that's broken."

The strange boy stuck out his hand. "I'm Iraj Protarus," he said.

Safar hesitated, remembering his vision. But the young man's face was so friendly he couldn't see any harm.

He clasped the offered hand. "I'm Safar Timura."

Iraj looked at him oddly. "Safar, eh? I had a dream about a fellow named Safar."

Safar didn't reply. The coincidence froze his tongue.

Iraj noticed, thinking, perhaps, that Safar was only being shy. He shifted his grip into the handshake favored by brothers. "I think we're going to be very good friends, Safar," he said. "Very good friends, indeed."

# 2
# THE DEMON RIDERS

Badawi shifted in the saddle, seeking a more comfortable position for his haunches. His gray mare chuffed in complaint, stumbling as she moved to accommodate his bulk. The fat man nearly fell, grabbing wildly at the saddle to save himself.

He lashed the mare, growling, "Watch how you go, you fly-blown daughter of a dung beetle."

The animal was used to such treatment and, other than a painful grunt, showed no reaction as she picked her way across the rocky ground. It was not yet midday and although the worst hours were still ahead the high plains sun was hot enough to make the overburdened gray miserable. The ground was hard on her feet, the brush dry—offering little relief for her growing hunger and thirst. But Badawi had no pity and raked her with his spurs and cursed her again to prod her on.

The mare's breathing quickly became labored, nostrils foaming, coat darkening with sweat. Badawi ignored her plight. He wasn't worried about grinding the beast down and leaving himself afoot. His final destination was in the rolling foothills to the south, no more than five or six miles away. Towering above those foothills were the snow-capped peaks of the mountain range he knew as the Gods' Divide. To his east was the dusty wasteland that marked the border of the Forbidden Desert.

Badawi rode the gray hard a few score paces then suddenly remembered—sawing hard on the reins to slow the mare. "You are a fool, Badawi," he chastised himself. "An unfeeling fool."

He turned, chins descending in a cascade of sorrow, to look at the animal trailing behind. It was a graceful young camel, padding easily across the rocky ground. A rope lead looped from its neck to Badawi's wood-framed saddle.

"Forgive me, little one," he called. "For a moment I forgot you were with me." He lashed the mare. "Blame the foul temper of this ugly daughter of a bonegatherer's ass. She tested my kind nature and I had to teach her a lesson."

Badawi gave the rope a gentle tug and the camel obediently quickened its pace to come to his side. His greedy little heart warmed and he smiled fondly at the animal, who presented him with dark pleading eyes framed by long, upswept lashes. The camel was pure white—white as the snows, Badawi thought in a rare moment of romantic reflection, powdering the peaks of the Gods' Divide.

He pulled honeyed figs from a pouch and the camel's head swept out for the treats. "I can deny you nothing, Sava," he said, shivering as the camel's tender lips nibbled at his fat palm. "Not even the food from my very mouth." He sighed. "What a lucky man I am. The gods must truly love one such as I. To have a thing of such beauty."

Badawi was a man much pleased with himself. Any who knew him would've instantly realized his enjoyment came at the expense of another. They would have guessed, correctly, that he'd ground another man into the dust to win the pretty white camel. He was a man of low cunning who'd made his fortune farming and breeding fine horses and camels in a region no one else would approach. The land he owned was rich, but cost him nothing because of its proximity to the Forbidden Desert.

Years ago his first wife had reacted first in fear, then in rage when he'd announced the news of the place he'd found for their new home. After he'd beaten her into submission he'd given her a good husbandly talking to.

"Don't be such a stupid cow," he'd advised. "The only reason people are frightened of that place is because it's close to the Forbidden Desert. I say, bah to that! Pure foolishness. So what if the demon lands are on the other side of that desert. I mean, it *is* called Forbidden, after all. The demons can't cross it any more than humans can. Besides, there hasn't been a demon seen for hundreds of years. And the only reason there's land for the taking is because people are not only stupid but have no vision.

"I, on the other hand, am not stupid. I see fortune where other see fear. And wife of mine, if you don't have the household packed and ready to move before the week is out I'll whip you within an inch of your life. Then I'll send you back to your father. Let him see if he can knock some sense into such a silly cow."

Badawi's lips curled into a sneer as remembered that conversation of long ago. He'd prospered mightily since then, raising his herds on the lush grass of the foothills and selling them for fat profits to the settlements and nomad encampments in the so-called safer regions. He'd worn out the first wife and three others in the process, as well as many children, all of whom labored on his land like slaves.

Then his grin suddenly became a growl as his mare snorted in alarm, head jerking back and almost striking him in the nose.

"What's this?" he shouted, slashing its flanks with his whip.

This time the gray reacted. It shrilled fear, rearing onto its two hind legs. Badawi plunged to the ground. He struck hard, breath whooshing out, but was remarkably unscathed. He was just coming to the realization the mare had been frightened by something other than himself when he heard his beloved Sava bawl in fear.

The camel attempted to bolt away but became tangled with the rope and the plunging mare. The two animals screamed and fought the rope, trying to escape.

Badawi, who could be agile when called upon, rolled about beneath them, shouting for his maddened animals to stop. Then the rope parted and the mare and camel raced off toward the familiar foothills and the safety of home.

Badawi leaped to his feet crying, "Come back my Sava! Come back, my sweet!"

But his pleas went unheeded and soon both the camel and the mare vanished over a hill.

Badawi cursed the fates. Then he sighed, resigned to the long walk home. It was the gray's fault, he reassured himself. He swore that low creature would suffer miserably for causing him such trouble.

Then a sudden chill gripped him. Danger wormed about in his belly and his hackles rose, stiff and bristly as a desert hedgehog's spines. Instinct made him turn to look out across the Forbidden Desert.

He shaded his eyes but nothing was immediately apparent. Then he saw a dust cloud churning up and wondered if it might be an approaching storm. His wonder turned to dismay as the dusty veil parted and a long column of dark figures emerged.

They were coming toward him fast and he tried to turn and run. But fear turned his feet to stone and he found himself standing there gaping at the approaching figures, trying to make out who they might be.

Then the figures took form so swiftly and with such startling clarity Badawi's bowels broke.

Demons!

Monsters in battle harness, with broad snouts and mottled green skin. The steeds they rode were more horrible than their masters—not horses, but creatures vaguely looking like horses—with long curved fangs to tear flesh and great cat's claws instead of hooves.

Badawi came unstuck and whirled, stubby legs carrying him forward. He'd taken no more than a few steps when his spurs tangled and he pitched face forward to the ground.

Then the monsters were all around him, howling spine-chilling cries. Weeping and crying to the gods, Badawi curled into a ball, trying to avoid the snapping fangs and slashing claws of the demons' mounts. Spear points jabbed at him and he screamed like a pig and jumped each time they pierced his skin.

He thought he heard shouted orders and suddenly there was silence and the torment stopped.

A voice said, "Get up, human. I wish to look upon you." The voice was cold and harsh and quite alien.

Badawi remained curled, but whined, "Please, master. Don't hurt me. I am only a poor horse merchant who means no harm to anyone."

Then he heard another inhuman voice say, "Let's just kill him and cook him, Sarn. I'm hungry! We're *all* hungry!"

The remark brought growls of agreement from the other demons and chants of, "Eat, Eat, Eat!"

Fear sparked inspiration. Badawi uncurled, scrambling to his knees, arms raised to plead for his life.

Sarn, the demon who'd spoken first, and another smaller monster stared down at him from their steeds, drooling amusement.

"Please, master," Badawi wailed. "Spare the life of this undeserving insect. I have daughters, master. I have sons. I have a wife. Take pity, master! Spare old Badawi!"

His pleas brought howls of laughter from all but Sarn. He peered at Badawi with immense yellow eyes. Then he raised a taloned claw for silence, which he got.

"You ask pity of *me*?" Sarn said, scornful. "Sarn pities no one. Much less a human."

"You misunderstand, master," Badawi babbled. "I don't want you to spare me for my own sake. But yours."

"My sake?" Sarn said. "What can you possibly do for Sarn, human?"

"Why, ease your hunger, master," Badawi answered. "If that is what pleases you. However, if I may be so bold as to point out...there's only one of me. And many of you. It grieves me to say that ample as I am some will still suffer the pangs of hunger when there's no more of me left. However, master, at my home—which isn't far away—there's more than enough to satisfy every single one of you."

"The daughters and sons you mentioned?" Sarn asked, scaly lips curling back.

"Yes, master," Badawi replied. "And my wife as well. A tender morsel, if I do say so myself. Fed her only the best since she's come to live under my roof."

Giff, the other demon, snarled disgust. "You're offering your family, human? To save your own life? What manner of creature are you?"

Sarn made an ugly noise—a chuckle to demon ears; a horror to humans. "He said he was a horse merchant, Giff," he said. "That should explain everything."

Badawi ignored this, saying to Sarn, "Let me lead you to my home, master. You'll see that all I claim is true."

Sarn stared long at the ugly mound of flesh that was Badawi.

Any other time he'd have quickly dispatched this cowardly human to the cooking pot. They could find Badawi's household on their own. Sarn and his band were one of many bandit clans who stalked the lawless regions in the demon lands. Until recently he had no more ambition than to raid and kill at will. Then King Manacia had sent an emissary to offer a bargain. Sarn would be granted royal permission to strike across the Forbidden Desert, seeking human riches and prey. The King wanted nothing in return but information. Sarn was to sweep west along the Gods' Divide, mapping all major byways. Manacia was particularly interested in a particular place—a route that legend said would lead over the mountain range. Sarn didn't ask why King Manacia wanted such information. Whatever the reason, Sarn was certain it'd be soldier's work—dangerous, with little hope of booty—and therefore of no concern to Sarn and the other bandits. When he was done Sarn would return across the desert, saddlebags and pack animals laden with treasure.

As he weighed Badawi's fate it occurred to him his foray might be made easier if he had a willing human guide. And Badawi certainly appeared willing.

"Tell me, human," he said, "do you know of a place called Kyrania?"

"Kyrania?" Badawi cried. "Kyrania? Why, Master, there isn't another man within a hundred leagues who knows the way to Kyrania better than this, your most desolate slave."

Sarn nodded in satisfaction. He turned to Giff. "Let him live for now," he said. "It seems this human swine may be of use to us."

Badawi wept in relief. He came to his feet, bowing and blubbering. "Oh, thank you, kind master," he wailed. "May the gods smile on all your efforts."

But even then—life still hanging in the balance—Badawi's greed reared up.

He dried his eyes, saying, "I'm, uh, reluctant to bring up a small matter, master. A boon, if you please, for serving you. When we arrive at my farm do what you like." He waved his arms. "All that's mine is yours, master," he said. "Except...well, there's this white camel, you see. It isn't much, master. No breeding at all. Worthless to anyone. But I've grown fond of her, master. And if you'd only—"

Sarn's claw shot forward and Badawi's jaws snapped shut, cutting off the rest. The demon beckoned and Badawi's mouth became a parched desert when he saw the length of the demon's razor talons. He took an obedient step forward, then was rocked as a great smothering force enveloped him. It fell over him like a fisherman's net, dragging him toward the demon chieftain. His throat clogged in fear and he couldn't speak, much less breathe. He staggered forward, drawn by the demon's spell.

Badawi trembled as his chest touched the longest talon, jutting like a curved blade. And still he couldn't stop. The spell made him press forward until the talon pierced first his robe, then his flesh. Blood flowed, staining his robes. The pain was unbearable but no matter how hard his mind struggled he couldn't regain his will. He felt the talon cutting deeper. Then he heard Sarn laugh and suddenly the spell was gone and he was free.

Badawi fell to the ground clutching his wound, too frightened to do more than groan.

"If you want to live, human," Sarn said, "you will do *all* I command. Without question. And you will never ask anything in return."

"Yes, master, yes," Badawi wailed, knocking his forehead against the ground in obeisance. "I was a fool! Please forgive such a stupid one."

"Rise, human," Sarn said.

Badawi did as he was told, standing before the demon trembling and wondering what would happen next.

"Here is my first command to you, human," Sarn said. "You will immediately lead us to your home. And when we arrive..."

"Yes, master?"

Sarn grinned, exposing a double row of stained fangs. "You will lead us to the camel first."

Badawi wisely buried his dismay, nodding eagerly in case the demons couldn't read his expression of wild agreement.

"And then, human," Sarn said, "when we are done..."

"Yes, Master! Anything Master!"

"...When we are done with your family you will lead us to Kyrania!"

After the demons finished with Badawi's homestead, they raided along the Gods' Divide for nearly six hundred miles. Scores of homes and settlements were overrun and many humans were killed. Some were granted a honorable death as worthy enemies. But many were killed for the pot, or jerked for flesh to feed them on the road.

Badawi led the way, picking out the fattest settlements, betraying the human leaders, and generally making himself useful. And whenever the subject of Kyrania came up, the horse merchant would say, "Just a little further, Master. Just a little further."

In truth, Badawi hadn't faintest idea where Kyrania might be. He knew the legendary caravan route over the Gods' Divide was in the general direction he was leading the demon bandits. But he didn't have the faintest idea where the passage was. Only a few merchant princes knew the route and Badawi, despite his success, was a treasury or two short of actual wealth. So he did what any decent horse merchant would do.

He lied. "This way, Master. Only a little further along..."

At first the bandits had been satisfied, gathering up pack animals to carry off their growing booty. In the beginning they'd also taken many young men and women captive for later sale in the demon slave markets. They chained them together, fixing them to long posts which the slaves carried on their shoulders—and made them march along with the baggage animals. But the number of slaves and baggage weight became unwieldy, slowing the demons' progress to a crawl.

Then the day came when the demons had enough and once again Badawi faced the roasting spit.

They'd hit another settlement typical of the human villages scatted through the remote foothills regions. It was rich in bountiful fields and bursting storehouses, but, as Sarn's chief lieutenant complained, there was barely a copper or two for a decent bandit to rub together.

Sarn and Giff took their dinner that night in a wide pavilion pitched above the main encampment. Below them they could see the main roasting pit where their brother demons were gathered about a shrieking victim, slowly turning over a slow fire.

Crouched among them was Badawi, daring many talons to snatch a piece for himself.

Giff sneered at the sight and turned to his leader, saying, "That is the most disgusting mortal to have ever fouled the land. He even eats his own."

Sarn laughed. "It wasn't as if we gave the human a choice," he said. "He's been allowed to eat nothing else."

"Still!" Giff said. "Still. You'd think he'd have more pride."

At that moment Badawi made the mistake of looking up from the fire and staring at the pavilion. Giff growled as their eyes met and the horse dealer quickly ducked to avoid the demon's glowing yellow eyes. He muttered a prayer to himself, beseeching the gods to not let Giff take offense. That prayer went unanswered as in the pavilion Giff gnashed his teeth in anger and turned to Sarn.

"The human was looking at us," he said.

Sarn shrugged. "What does it matter where the human looks?" he asked.

"It matters to me," Giff said. "I hate that lowly creature. I feel filthy in his presence. His very gaze makes me want to scour myself with dust."

Sarn laughed. "That would indeed be a sight, my good but unclean fiend," he said. "Considering that nearly four seasons have passed since you last bothered to bathe."

Giff saw no humor in this. "That's not my point," he said. "This human offends me. His presence disturbs my demonly serenity. Let me kill him so I can have some peace."

"Be a good fiend and try to learn patience," Sarn said. "Peace comes with patience, or so say our priests. This human offends me as well. They *all* offend me. Their odor is worse than the shit of any beast I've ever encountered. And their looks are as bad as their odor. So soft and wriggly they remind me of worms. But worms with hairy heads and bodies. And their small mouths and flat teeth with only four puny fangs make me think of blood suckers." Sarn shuddered. "Two headed demon children have been known to be born to mothers who have looked upon things half so frightening."

"Then why must I be patient, Sarn?" Giff asked. "Let's make the gods happy and kill that fat slug."

"We still have need of the human," Sarn said. "That's why you can't kill him now."

Giff snorted in disgust. "Oh, I forgot what a valuable slave he's been to us," he said, voice dripping with sarcasm. "Why, tomorrow he may lead us to a village rich as this. Once again we'll seize stores of useless grain, poor quality cloth, tools we can't carry, old rusted weapons, and maybe, just maybe—the gods willing—two silver coins for a lucky thief to jangle in his purse."

"I admit the take hasn't been enough to make our enemies gnash their teeth with envy," Sarn said. "We've found only small villages and farming settlements to raid. Most of their wealth has been in their crops and animals. Some also might bring a pretty price at the slave market. But we're too far from home to make that sort of thieving very profitable."

Giff gnashed his teeth. "*Very* profitable!" he said. "You don't see any of us doing a demon dance for joy over the weight of our purses, do you? Why, even if you count the little gold and few paltry gems we've taken, I doubt we'll make any profit at all. And we've missed nearly a whole season of raiding at home."

"It's not the human's fault," Sarn said, circling back to the discussion of Badawi's fate. "The terms of the warrant we hold from King Manacia bade us to stay close to the mountains where the population is small. We can steal what we want, do what we like with anyone we find. But we must leave no witnesses. We must not allow any human to live who might carry the news that we've strayed across the border.

"And, most important of all to our king—and the only reason he even gave us this warrant—was that we were to seek a passage over these mountains. To a place called Kyrania."

Giff snorted, gesturing with his talons at the distant figure of Badawi. "And that human was supposed to lead us to the bedamned place. Well, he's been leading, and leading and so far we've nothing of it. Bah! He's a horse trader! Therefore he's lying."

Sarn gazed out at Badawi, scratching his horny chin with needle-sharp talons. "Perhaps he is," Sarn mused. "Frankly, I was a little too overcome with raidmust to think about it."

He shrugged. "If he is we'll have to find another. It shouldn't be too much of a bother. Humans are such a traitorous lot."

"Why do need to find another?" Giff argued. "To the Hells with Kyrania." He snorted. "Valley of the Clouds, indeed. I think Manacia is suffering from a royally cloudy mind."

"Without Kyrania," Sarn reminded his henchdemon, "we have no warrant. We must at least make an attempt."

"Your precious warrant from the king will be our ruin," Giff said. "What use is it to dare the curse of the Forbidden Desert when we get so little in return? The others feel the same way, Sarn. They were frightened to make this journey to begin with. All know a black spell was cast on that desert long ago. Any demon or human who crosses is becursed."

"King Manacia is a most powerful wizard," Sarn pointed out. "The warrant he gave us will protect us from any curse."

"How do you know?" Giff pressed.

Sarn gave him a blank look. "What do you mean?"

"You told us all about Manacia's curse-defying warrant," Giff said. "That's what convinced us. But now I'm beginning to wonder. How do we know Manacia didn't lie? And he has no power to shield us from such a curse?"

"What reason would he have to lie?" Sarn responded. "The king seeks information from us. Information I suspect his armies will one day follow up on. Why else would he want us to find a way over this mountain range? Why else would he be so particular to even name a place he suspects might be the key?"

Giff scoffed at this. "What's a damned name?" he said. "Kyrania? Humania? Dismania? Hells, he could have picked any name he liked and we'd never be the wiser!"

"Might I remind you, my faithful fiend," Sarn said, "that the king has promised us much gold for these efforts. Over and above any loot we seize. And there will be a particularly handsome bonus if we find a pass that leads through the mountains."

"Let him keep his bonus, Sarn," Giff pleaded. "Listen to me. We've been good fiends together since our youth. You lead. I advise. That's why we've been so successful. You know you can trust my advice. So hear what I'm saying. I speak from my heart like a brother.

"Let us leave this hellish land. Let us return home and breathe good demon air. If we make haste there's just enough raiding time remaining in the season to make all our purses heavy. We've searched every gully, every trail for nearly six hundred miles, Sarn. I don't believe there *is* such a place as Kyrania. Or any way at all over the Gods' Divide. And if there is, it's so well-hidden we'll never find it in a hundred years. We'll wander these hills the rest of our days. It'll be our ghosts who earn the king's bonus. And gold is no good to a ghost."

Sarn thought a moment, then nodded. "If that's what you and the others want," he said, "I won't stand in your way. I'll tell you what. We'll cast lots in the morning. If the majority wants to return home, that's what we'll do. You'll hear no argument from me. I'll add one more thing. No matter what the vote, at least ten of our fiends should return home with the goods and slaves we've already gathered. That's all I can spare, although it ought to be enough. The slaves are quite docile with the spell I cast over them. Then the rest of us shall proceed as quickly as we can, taking no more slaves and carrying away only gold and silver and other easily-transportable goods."

Sarn stretched out a paw. "Agreed?" he asked.

Giff nodded, rasping talons against his leader's claws. "Agreed," he said. "With one provision. If the vote is for our return I want the pleasure of killing the human."

Sarn laughed. "Do what you want with him," he said. "But do it in public. It's been a long time since we've enjoyed a really good entertainment."

Sarn was an artful chief. Giff's protestations of brotherhood didn't fool him. Giff always had his eye on the main chance. But Sarn knew his lieutenant represented a point of view among his band that must be dealt with. For a bandit chief Sarn had a unique ability to appear to shift with the prevailing winds and still get his way in the end. More importantly, he had magical powers much greater than the normal talent for sorcery all demons possessed.

In the morning he gathered his band together and carefully spelled out the two choices. He weighted no side heavier than the other. But he'd prepared well for the vote, casting a mild spell none of his demons would notice that would temporarily make the dangers and unpleasantness ahead seem of no consequence.

Badawi watched the proceedings from a distance, knowing his fate hung in the balance. For the whole time Sarn spoke Giff stared at Badawi, hate and hungry longing in his demon eyes. The night before Badawi had suspected something was up because of the intensity of the conversation between Sarn and Giff. The horse dealer had gone on a frantic, all night search for something, anything, to assure his survival.

Now he held what he prayed was that item in his hand and after the demons had cast their lots—voting to continue on King Manacia's mission—he was waiting with it at the pavilion when Sarn returned.

"What do you want, human?" Sarn demanded.

Badawi stilled his trembling limbs, doing his best to ignore Giff's stares of unrequited hate.

He held out an old firepit-encrusted bowl for Sarn's inspection. "I found this, master," he said.

Sarn struck it away. "Rubbish!" he said. "You present me with rubbish!"

Badawi grabbed the bowl up again, which had remarkably had not shattered. "Please, master," he said. "This isn't rubbish at all. Look at this bowl. See the rich glaze beneath all the filth? Touch the clay, Master. Feel the quality. And old as this bit of pottery is, notice the artfulness of the design. Why, if this were new and we had its twin, we could get a pretty bit of silver indeed at any marketplace."

"Don't insult me with silver, pretty or not," Sarn said. "I'm through with pots and jars and bolts of cloth. That's no way for a decent bandit to make a living."

"Ah, but master," Badawi said, "I'm not suggesting we look for more of this. But I am suggesting we find out where it came from. I've seen this type of pottery but once in my life, master. It's very rare. And therefore highly prized in human markets. The place this pottery comes from is secret to all but the richest caravan masters.

"The story is told in the marketplaces that there is a family of master potters who live in a valley high in the mountains. And in those mountains is a holy lake surrounded by beds of the purest clay. Clay that is used to form pots and dishes and brewing jars fit only for kings and their most royal kin.

"That family of potters, Master, is know as the Timuras. And this is a Timura pot, Merciful One. It could be no other!"

"My ears are growing heavy just listening to you, human," Sarn said. "Say what you came to say and be done with it. What do I care about this tale of lakes and beds of clay and grimy potters who grub in the earth?"

"Yes, master, I'll hurry, master," Badawi babbled, but frightened as he was, he stuck to his point.

"That valley I spoke of, master," he said, "sits on a caravan route that leads over these mountains. At least that's what the stories say. And those same stories also claim the caravan route is the same ancient trail Alisarrian took when he invaded Walaria. It was said that to his enemies it seemed Alisarrian and his entire army suddenly appeared, pouring out of the mountains. They said it was magic, master. Sorcery. However, it wasn't magic that was their undoing, but a secret passage across the Gods' Divide."

Badawi waved the bowl in front of the demon. "The same place this bit of pottery was made."

Sarn used a talon to pick a bit of food from between his fangs. "If you aren't speaking of Kyrania, human, find a good dull knife and slit your throat for me. I grow wearier by the minute."

"Yes, Master, immediately, Master," Badawi said, scrapping and bowing. "I am indeed speaking of Kyrania. This bowl is proof that Kyrania is near."

"You've said that more than once, human!" Giff snarled.

Badawi shivered, but held his ground. "Forgive me, master," he said to Sarn. "This low worm you call your slave admits he stretched the truth a bit when he had the immense honor of first meeting you. I don't know *exactly* where Kyrania is. But I do know how to find it."

He saw the two immense demons exchange a look that did not bode well for him. So he hurried through his logic.

"Listen to me, please," he said. "I'm a merchant. I know things. I know you can't hide something as large as a caravan route. So we must assume it is still to our west. How far I can't say with certainty. However, I can *guess*, master. The route would by necessity go from Caspan, the largest city on this side of the mountains, to Walaria. Which, as you know, is the most important kingdom on the southern side."

Badawi crouched down and scratched a map in the dust.

"Caravan masters are secretive, but they wouldn't waste time covering their trail. Time is money and money is time and the length of the shadow between is feared by all men of business. So I think we can assume the route is fairly direct."

Badawi kept scratching until he had the mountains sketched in and the two cities of Walaria and Caspan. Then he drew a circle. "It's only reasonable to assume, master," he said, "that the place you seek is within this circle. Perhaps two or three hundred miles distant at the most."

Sarn turned to his lieutenant, snout stretched in what demons considered a smile. "You see, Giff," the bandit chief said, "this human has been some use to us after all."

Giff peered at the greasy little human, measuring..."A vote is a vote," he said with some reluctance. "I'll let him be for now. But remember your promise."

Badawi was alarmed. "Promise? What promise, O Merciful Masters?"

"Just find us Kyrania, human," Sarn commanded. "And know that your miserable swinish life depends on it."

# 3

# THE VISION AT WORLD'S END

Despite Iraj's prediction Safar didn't immediately embrace him and call him milk brother.

They had little in common. One was the son of a potter, the other that of a warrior chieftain. Safar's people were peaceful and generous to strangers. Iraj's were fierce plainsmen who trusted no one. Safar was contemplative by nature. Even as a child he had tended to think before he acted. Iraj, on the other hand, tended to be ruled by the heat of the moment. He was as intelligent as Safar, but impatient with learning. If he couldn't grasp a thing immediately he became bored and disdainful. Safar was willing, on the other hand, to labor long hours until he could command knowledge as easily as Iraj later commanded men.

There was one great similarity which formed the glue that eventually bound them. Both young men thought of themselves as outsiders—apart from the others in the village.

Safar's reason was magic.

Iraj's was a blood feud.

Much time passed, however, before either boy learned the nature of the other's mystery.

It was an idyllic spring. The sun was warm, the first crops bountiful and the herds were blessed with many offspring. During those lazy days Gubadan was hard pressed to hammer learning into the thick skulls of his charges. The young people of Kyrania drove their teacher and their families to distraction as mischief and youthful high spirits lured them from their duties.

Safar soon forgot about the troubling vision and Iraj seemed to have forgotten his dream as well, for he did not mention it again. Although Safar didn't consider him the "best of friends," Iraj *was* his constant companion.

As a stranger, and an object of worry for the trouble he might bring from the outside, Iraj was shunned by all but old Gubadan. On the other hand as an obvious prince everyone was warm and sweet as one of Mother Timura's peach pies when in his presence. Royalty rubs off, as the old grannies said, and sometimes in rewarding ways. So no one was willing to say "begone" to his face. And a few were so bold as to wonder if they could make a good marriage with one of their daughters.

Fleeing these pressures, Iraj went everywhere with Safar. He accompanied him to the clay beds when Safar went to fetch new supplies for his father. Out of boredom he even helped Safar with his most common chores, suffering dirt on his hands and clothing, for instance, while cleaning up after the goats. In repayment, Safar was moved to show Iraj the place near the lake where they could spy on the girls bathing naked in a hidden cove.

The two boys became such a pair they eventually combined their wits at school to bedevil poor Gubadan and divert him from the lesson at hand.

One day that game took a turn Safar found to be most revealing.

Gubadan's subject of the day was once again the starry constellations. It was just after the midday meal and it was all the students could do to keep their eyes open in the overly warm little chamber.

"We can all see how the Lion Cub suckles at his mother's breast during the spring," Gubadan was saying. "But in the winter the Cub must hide while the Hunter is lured away by the Lioness. So it follows that if you are born under the sign of the Cub you are affectionate by nature, but in the winter months you are timorous and hesitate to make decisions. Those of us with the Hunter as our major sign tend to be aggressive, fearless, but easily fooled by stealth when we encounter the Lioness."

Bored, Safar raised his stylus for attention.

"Pardon, Master," he said after he was acknowledged. "I'm having difficulty understanding."

Gubadan's heavy brows furrowed about his odd-shaped nose. "What is it, Safar?" he asked suspiciously.

"Why do we call the Wolf Cub timorous when he hides?" Safar said. "Isn't this actually a sign of wisdom? The Cub has no defense if the Hunter finds him."

Iraj broke in. "Safar has a good question, Master," he said. "I was also wondering about the Hunter. Why is he a fool to pursue the Lioness? She's in plain sight. I'd chase her myself and ignore the Cub. She'd make a much better skin to drape about my shoulders and stave off the cold."

Gubadan thumped a fat volume on his lectern. The leather cover was etched with stars and planets.

"The answer to both of you," he said, "is in this book. It was written by wise men many centuries ago. Stargazers have followed those laws for many years, predicting grand events as well as the future of great men."

"These Stargazers," Safar asked. "Are they never wrong?"

Gubadan harumphed. A sure sign Safar had found a weak spot. "Well," he said, "I can't honestly say there have never been errors. But they were due to faulty interpretation. Not by the laws themselves. All Stargazers are not equally blessed by the gods."

"I suppose, Master," Iraj said, "that some might even purposely make mistakes."

Gubadan flushed in anger, gripping his beard. "That would be sinful," he growled. "Why would a Stargazer commit such a godless act?"

Safar quickly saw Iraj's course. "For gold," he said. "Men *have* been known to sin to possess it."

"Not Stargazers," Gubadan said, horrified. "They are holy men. Why, one might as well doubt the honesty of Dreamcatchers."

"One might indeed, Master," Iraj said. "If enough gold were offered, or bloody threats."

"Master," Safar said, "was not Alisarrian's grandson—King Ogden—betrayed by a Dreamcatcher?"

Gubadan brightened. The Conqueror Alisarrian was his favorite subject.

"You've made my point exactly, Safar," he said. "King Ogden was born under the sign of the Hunter. And the Jester was his lesser sign as well so he was easily taken in by the rogues and charlatans of Zanzair. The demons were at the heart of the conspiracy, of course. Alisarrian, on the other hand, had the Demon Moon for his sign with the Comet ascending. So he was fierce and wise at the same time."

He began pacing, excited by the diversion the boys had caused. Safar wasn't fool enough to mention Gubadan really hadn't made his point at all. There was no disputing a Dreamcatcher had played Ogden the fool. History said so. Which had been *Safar's* point.

"Who was this man, Alisarrian?" Gubadan said. "Was he a monster as his enemies claimed? A monster who bent us to his will with his mailed fists, or was Alisarrian a blessing from the gods who cut the curtain of ignorance with his sword? We were dim-witted savages when he blew over these mountains like the last storm of winter. But when the spring of his enlightenment came, what a lovely field of learning bloomed. What a mighty..."

Safar settled back to doze as Gubadan waxed eloquent on the Conqueror. He noticed, however, that Iraj hadn't follow suit. Instead he was intent on Gubadan's every word. Safar examined

Iraj, then suddenly remembered the banner with the red moon and silver comet he'd seen in the vision—the Demon Moon with the Comet in ascension! As Gubadan had just reminded him, it was the sign of Alisarrian.

Then Safar heard his friend interrupt Gubadan with a question. "Tell me, master," Iraj said, "do you think a man as great as Alisarrian will ever rise again?"

The priest shook his head. "Impossible," he said. "The gods blessed him with more qualities than is ever likely to be repeated." Gubadan shrugged. "There will be other conquerors, of course. Esmir has always been a divided house and it cries out for unification under one throne. There were conquerors before Alisarrian and others will follow. But they'll always rule under his great shadow."

Safar noted Iraj seemed upset at this answer. But the youth shook it off and pressed on. "May I ask you this, master?" he said. "Do you think any of those future conquerors will rule the demon lands as well? They were once part of Alisarrian's kingdom."

"Empire, not kingdom, lad," Gubadan corrected. "But to your question...once again I must answer with a negative. Only a human such as Alisarrian could rule the demons. To begin with, besides being a mighty warrior and leader, Alisarrian was a powerful wizard. Powerful as any demon sorcerer. As you know, few humans possess magical ability."

Safar shifted uncomfortably in his seat.

"And this ability tends to be weak compared to that of the demons," Gubadan continued. "The greatest human wizard I know of is Lord Umurhan who heads the university in Walaria. And powerful as he is, even Umurhan would admit he'd be hard pressed in a match with a demon wizard. Humans have always used superior numbers to defend themselves against the demons. Just as the demons have used their great magic to stave off humans.

"But Alisarrian was strong enough to break that stalemate and conqueror the demons. Why he didn't slay them all is in my opinion one of his great mysteries. He could have rid all Esmir of their foul presence, but he chose not to. For what reason, no one knows. His empire might have lasted to this day if he had done otherwise. It is the one area of his character that has disappointed me."

For Gubadan to admit his hero had a flaw of any kind was a remarkable event. It so disturbed the old priest he quickly ended the diversion and to the groans of all the students, he returned to the boring lecture on the distant constellations.

A few days later Safar and Iraj were strolling by the ruins of the old fort, stopping to watch younger boys playing soldier on its last remaining wall.

Remembering the interest his friend had shown, Safar pointed to the fort, saying, "Supposedly Alisarrian himself ordered this built when he came into our valley."

Iraj shook his head. "I don't think so," he said. "Look at how poorly it's placed." He pointed at a hill a short distance away. "If an enemy took that hill the fort would be within even a poor archer's bowshot. Alisarrian would never build such a thing. He was too good a general."

Safar looked at the rising ground stretching out from the ruins with new eyes and saw how vulnerable any force gathered inside would be.

"It's more likely," Iraj continued, "some fool tried to oppose Alisarrian from that fort. And was easily overwhelmed."

"There are tales that say you're right," Safar admitted. "Those same tales claim he made the whole valley his fortress, with strong guard posts in the passes and hidden caves where supplies and additional weapons were stored."

Iraj looked at Safar, eyes glittering. "Have you ever seen such things?"

Safar nodded, saying, "Many times. While grazing my father's goats in the mountains. There's one place in particular—very high up where you can see a great distance." The boy shrugged. "The grass is poor, but I like to go there and think."

"Take me!" Iraj urged. "I must see this for myself."

Safar was sorry he'd spoken. The place he had in mind was a private retreat where he went to nurse the wounds of youth. Many a tear had been shed there in solitude and many a dream conjured.

"Maybe later," he said. "The snow is still too deep just now."

He hoped his friend would forget, but each day the sun shone warmer, the streams swelled with the melting snow and Iraj pestered Safar to take him to his secret place. Finally, the next time it was Safar's turn to watch the herds he agreed to take Iraj with him.

At first Gubadan fussed about letting his charge out of sight for the weeks the boys would be gone.

"What will Iraj's family say, Khadji," he protested to Safar's father, "if something should happen to him?"

"They'll be just as angry with you if he drowns while swimming in our lake," Safar's mother broke in. Despite her first suspicions—natural to the cloistered people of Kyrania— she'd warmed to Iraj and now even defended the orphan prince to the others.

"The mountains are as natural to Kyrania as that lake," she said. "Let the boy go, Gubadan. Herding goats is not so dangerous an adventure."

"It's knowledge, not danger I'm after, Master," Iraj put in. "I want to see for myself where the great Alisarrian crossed these mountains."

This argument won the day and soon the two young men set out for the high pastures. They were overly laden with supplies, thanks to Gubadan's concerns, and they had to take a llama to carry all the clothing, blankets and food stuff pressed on them. Stirred, no doubt, by romantic dreams, Iraj took along the scimitar his uncle had given him when he left home. He was also laden with a short bow, an ample supply of arrows and an ornate dagger he said his father had bequeathed to him.

Safar carried his sling, a small shot bag of clay missiles made in his father's kiln and a sturdy staff—all he'd need to stave off the occasional pack of hungry wolves intent on goat flesh. He laughed when he saw Iraj struggling under the burden of so many weapons. "There's only trees and rocks up there," he said. "But if they should attack we'll be ready."

Iraj grinned, but his eyes were serious. "You can never tell," was all he said.

The skies were sparkling when they set out, the lower ranges green with new life. Safar picked up handfuls of fallen cherry blossoms to brighten their tea when they camped that night. The boys tarried for awhile at some of the higher huts, clustered among a grove of arrow trees, exchanging gossip for almonds and fat pheasants. The people were glad to see them and it was apparent to Safar that from the way they stared at Iraj they were more interested in this strange youth than in news from below.

One of the girls walked with them for a time, eyes shimmering in admiration of Iraj's tall sturdy figure and handsome looks. She turned back when they reached the trail leading to the pasture where the goats were grazing. She called after them to stop by her home when they returned, promising her mother would feed them well.

"I think she loves you," Safar teased. "If you had asked she'd have crept into the bushes with you and let you pull up her dress."

"I was tempted," Iraj admitted. "It's been too long since I hip-danced with a woman."

Safar was surprised. The other village boys boasted frequently of their conquests but he knew their claims to be lies. He'd heard his sisters and mother joke about young men who were foolish enough to think any well-raised Kyranian girl would lessen her bridal price by dallying with them—unless marriage was the intended result. Sometimes a caravan would be accompanied by prostitutes bound for distant pleasure halls. But their carnal interest was stirred by fat men with fatter purses, not poor, skinny-legged boys.

But when Iraj spoke Safar knew it was no empty boast.

"Are your unmarried women in the habit of bedding anyone who asks them?" he asked. "No offense intended. It's just that such things are frowned upon in Kyrania. The only reason that girl would have gone with you is she thinks you're rich, as does her father. And if you'd opened her legs her father would soon be talking to Gubadan about a wedding date."

"I suspected as much," he said. "That's why I kept my sword in its sheath. And no, our women are not of easy virtue. It's just that I've always had serving maids around to tend my needs. My mother saw to it there were always a few comely slaves about. Among my people it's considered unhealthy for a young man to be denied such pleasures."

"I wish my mother were so concerned for *my* health," Safar said.

"But what if there are children? What do you do then?"

Iraj shrugged. "After they're weaned we usually sell them," he said. "It's cheaper to buy new slaves than to raise one to a useful age."

Safar was shocked. "How could you sell your own child?" he asked.

Iraj looked at his friend as if he'd gone crazy. "I've never thought of them as my own," he said. "I might as well claim the blanket lint in my bed as children every time I make love to my fist. Besides, even free women have no more of a soul than say, a camel or a horse. They were put here by the gods for our pleasure and to birth more of us. I'm only making the use of them that the fates decreed."

Safar bit back a heated reply. To hear someone say his mother and sisters were nothing more than brood mares and whores angered him. But he said nothing, thinking Iraj couldn't help how he was raised.

The two continued climbing and soon came to the vale where the herds were grazing. Safar relieved the boys tending them, gathered the goats and drove them higher into the mountains.

The hills were in full springtime bloom, flowers and tempting grasses rising from every flat spot and crevice so he set a slow pace, letting the goats and the llama stop and nibble whenever they liked. The young men made camp early, setting the herd loose in a small meadow and bedding down in a grotto shielded from the night winds. They roasted the pheasants and filled the left over hollows in their bellies with toasted almonds, cheese and hard bread—washed down with milk from the goats. The sunset was brief but spectacular, turning the meadow and grotto into a dreamy, golden landscape. Then the moon and the stars winked into life. Safar and Iraj gazed at them for a long time, silent as acolytes at a temple ceremony.

Then Iraj said, "Did you know my star sign was the same as Alisarrian's?"

Safar shook his head, although it suddenly came to him that he'd known all along. He tried to make a joke of it, saying, "Does that mean you have sudden urges to go a' conquering?"

Iraj didn't laugh. His eyes glittered as if the remark had struck an unintended target.

"I'm sorry if I offended you," Safar said. "It was a silly thing to say."

Iraj nodded. After a moment he asked, "Don't you sometimes imagine you have a destiny to fulfill?"

"Only as a potter," Safar said.

Iraj pierced him with his gaze. "Is that what you truly think, Safar?"

"What else would I be? I'm a Timura. Timuras make pots."

Iraj shrugged as if to say, claim what you like but I know better. Then he said, "I told you I dreamed of a fellow named Safar, did I not?"

"When we first met," Safar answered.

"I was surprised you never asked me more about it. Most people would."

Safar didn't reply, remembering the vision of the king on the white elephant.

Iraj stared at him for a long moment. "If I tell you a secret, will you promise not to reveal it?"

Safar promised, relieved that the conversation seemed to have taken a less dangerous turn.

"If you break the vow," Iraj warned, "I will most certainly be killed."

Safar was taken aback. At that point in his young life he'd never encountered a secret with such a penalty attached.

"It's the reason I'm living here with you," Iraj continued. "My father, you see, was lord of our tribe and I was to succeed him."

"Did your father die recently?" Safar guessed.

"He caught a fever a little more than year ago," Iraj said. "It took six months for it to suck out his life. During that time my family quarreled and became divided—with some favoring me as a successor, while others backed my uncle, Fulain. When my father died the break became permanent."

Iraj went on to explain that at first the tide was in his favor because more family members supported him. One of his cousins—a much respected older man who was rich in land and horses—was to be appointed regent until Iraj came of age and could take up the ruler's staff.

"But Fulain made a bargain with my father's most hated

enemy," Iraj said. "An evil man named Koralia Kan who slew my grandfather when my father was a boy. And my father revenged the family by killing Kan's first born. So there is much spilled blood between us."

Iraj said one dark night Fulain gave Kan and his horse soldiers free passage through his land, joining him in a series of surprise attacks. Many died, including the cousin who would have been regent. When Fulain had the rest of the family under his heel he demanded Iraj's head so there would be no one to dispute his claim as clan lord.

"My mother begged one of my uncles—her sister's husband—to help," Iraj said. "I was forced to flee my own home and hide out with his people—the Babor clan. But there were so many spies about it wasn't safe to remain long. My uncle was ashamed to send me away. But he has his own wives and children to look after so he sent me here to hide from Fulain and Kan."

To Safar the tale had the ring of legend about it. He felt like a child listening to his father tell stories of old days and wild ways.

"Will you never be able to return?" he asked.

Iraj jammed a stick into the fire and flames leaped up to carve deep shadows on his face. He looked older in that light. And quite determined.

"The war in my family continues," he said. "But it is a silent war of spies and night raids. When it's safe my uncle will send for me. And then I will be tribal lord."

"How can you be sure?" Safar asked. "What if Fulain and Kan keep the upper hand?"

Iraj went silent. He stabbed moodily at the fire. Then he said, "I must believe it, don't you see? Otherwise I might as well take my own life now."

Safar didn't see. Why should Iraj die because he couldn't be lord of his tribe? Why not stay in Kyrania where no danger could touch him? He could live a long peaceful life. Marry one of the village women and be happy with all the beauty and bounty of Kyrania. But he said none of those things because he could see from Iraj's agitation it would only upset him more—although Safar didn't understand why. Instead, he asked him about the customs of his own people.

"It's nothing like here," Iraj said with unconscious disdain. "We don't farm. We aren't slaves to the land. We fight for what we want. And we fight more to keep it. For I tell you, Safar, I learned at my father's knee that men will either love you or fear you. There is no in-between."

He said his family had roamed the broad Plains of Jaspar for centuries. They were the fiercest of the tribes that remained after Alisarrian's kingdom broke up. They lived by raiding weaker tribes and looting villages and cities in distant lands. In recent years—even before his father became ill—things had not gone well.

"Our horse herds are not so numerous as before," he said. "And a plague took many of our camels. Other tribes have made bargains with the kings of the cities who once paid us tribute. We became surrounded by powerful enemies who are envious of our lands.

"My Uncle Neechan—the one who supports me—blames my father for what's happened." Iraj sighed. "I suppose he's right although I hate to admit it. I loved my father. But I think he was born too rich. His father was a great war lord and perhaps this weakened him. We used to live in yurts, tarrying until the grazing grew sparse, then packing up and moving on. Sometimes we took to the plains just because the notion sparked us and we traveled whichever way the winds blew. Now we live in a grand fortress my grandfather built."

Iraj said life was luxurious in that fortress. There was gold to buy whatever the family cared to purchase—tapestries and carpets and slaves to tend every need. They supped on food made lively with rare spices, some so deliciously hot that the meal was followed by iced sherbets made from exotic fruit gown in distant lands. There was a garden with an ornate fountain in the courtyard of Iraj's home and his father had liked to take his ease there, musing on the antics of the fish, munching on honeyed figs while sniffing at gentle breezes carrying the scent of oranges and roses.

"I think such rich living lessened my father's will to fight," Iraj said. "When he'd drunk too much wine—which was often in his later days—he'd curse those riches and swear that on the morrow he'd pack up our household and take to the Plains of Jaspar again.

Living in yurts and going a-raiding like his father had as a young man. But in the morning life would continue as usual.

"I know he felt guilty about it. He even admitted it several times, warning me about the hidden dangers of so many riches. I think this is why he made me take the sword vow. So I might accomplish what he could not. Now the honor of my family is on *my* head."

"I'm sorry," Safar said, thinking this was a burden *he* wouldn't want to carry.

"Don't be, Safar," Iraj said. "This is what I want. The gods willing, one day I shall restore my family to its former greatness." His voice fell until Safar could barely make out his next words. "And more," he murmured.

Just then a flaming object shot through the heavens and the boys' heads jerked up in awe. It hung above them, a vast swirling ball that chased the night from the hills. Then the ball exploded, bursting into a fiery shower.

Safar gaped as the glowing particles floated down until they filled his whole vision with dancing light. There were so many it was like snow from a rainbow and then they were drifting over him and he instinctively stuck out his tongue to catch one like a child marveling at snowflakes. To his surprise one floated into his mouth, which was immediately filled with a taste like warm, honeyed wine. Safar's whole body tingled with pleasurable energy and he suddenly felt above all mortal things.

He heard laughter and looked at Iraj. A glowing blanket of particles swirled around him and his features seemed comically twisted like a pot collapsing in a kiln. He was pointing at Safar, laughing, and the young man knew he must look the same. Then the particles vanished and all was normal again. For some reason Safar was left feeling somber, moody, while Iraj was still chortling.

"You *are* lucky for me, Safar," he said. "I tell you my deepest secrets and immediately we are blessed by a sign from the heavens."

"But a sign of what, Iraj?" Safar asked. "How do we know it has to do with us?"

"It was too wonderful to be anything but a blessing," Iraj replied.

That night, while Iraj slept peacefully, Safar remained awake, wondering what the heavenly display had meant. Was it a sign? If so, what did it portend? His senses were acute and every sound stood out clearly from the usual night muddle of chirps and frantic scurrying. He heard a cricket sing and at first he thought it was a spring song to its mate.

Then he heard, "It's coming! It's coming!"

Another cricket said, "What's coming? What's coming?"

And the first answered, "Better hide! Better hide!"

Then a soft wind blew up and the crickets fell silent. The silence came so abruptly it seemed to have substance, an object Safar could feel and turn about and examine if only he could touch it. In his mind he made a bucket of fresh clay. The silence, he thought, was in that bucket and he began to clean the clay, washing out twigs and pebbles. And then he found it. He fumbled it up—a broad, unusually shaped pebble. Blood red.

His spirit self looked into the stone's polished surface, saw his eye reflected back, and then he was falling...falling...

He stretched his arms and let the spirit winds carry him. At first he thought he was returning to the conquered city he'd seen before. But the winds bore him up and he was speeding across plains and deserts and then seas. He flew for what seemed an eternity, shooting from dark horizon to dark horizon until those horizons became gray and then startling blue as night turned to day and emerald seas churned beneath him.

Surely, he thought, I must have flown far enough to be on the other side of the world. The place Gubadan's books called "World's End." Just as he wondered when he'd stop he came to a mountainous isle in the middle of a vast ocean.

He heard chanting and drums and strange horns bellowing mournful notes that drew at him like a great tide washing to shore. Safar let the tide of notes carry him to a great grove of towering trees all heavy with ripe fruit.

Among those trees handsome people danced to the beat of big drums with skins made of thin bark. Several men blew through huge shell horns, making the mournful sound that had drawn him here. The people were naked and their sun bronzed bodies were painted in glorious colors. A tall woman danced in the center, high breasts bobbing to the wild, joyous rhythm. Her shapely hips churned and thrust in the ancient act of mating. Safar's young body reacted and he became powerfully aroused.

Suddenly she stopped, eyes widening in such terror that Safar's lust vanished, to be replaced by a feeling of immense dread.

The woman shouted in a language Safar didn't understand—pointing fearfully into the distance. The other dancers froze, their eyes seeking out whatever it was that had frightened her.

Safar looked with them and saw smoke puffing out of a coned mountain top. The people began to shriek and run about in mad confusion, like ants caught in a sudden thunder shower. Safar felt their terror as if it were his own. His heart pounded and his limbs twitching with an hysterical desire to take flight.

There was a blinding flash, followed by an explosion that hammered at his ears. Huge rocks and trees were ripped from the ground by the force of the blast and he instinctively ducked, although he knew he couldn't be harmed. Boiling smoke obscured his view.

Then his vision cleared and he saw a pile of dead, including the dancing woman, crumpled among the uprooted fruit trees. He saw the survivors stagger up and run toward the shore where a line of canoes waited.

There was another explosion, more forceful than the first. Fiery debris crushed the runners and Safar saw the canoes burst into flames from the intensity of the heat.

Molten rock poured out of the mountain, which was split nearly in two. It reached the sea and the waters began to boil. Thousands of dead fish bobbed on the surface, mingled with the blackened corpses of the few people who had made it that far. A yellow acrid smoke streamed from the mountain, filling the sky until the sun was obscured.

And there was a taste of ashes in his mouth.

The vision ended and Safar jolted up and found that he was weeping. He wiped his eyes, then glanced over at Iraj and saw he was still asleep.

Safar wished his friend would awaken. He felt lonely and a tremendous sense of loss had wormed a hole in his gut. There was also dread crouched there. Dread for the future, although he couldn't make out what he ought to fear. He tried to imagine himself ten years from now, a mature potter crouched at the wheel, hands forming wet clay into a perfect vessel. But each time a vague image formed he couldn't hold on to it and it would vanish. Safar struggled to imagine any sort of future at all. Not for himself, but the world. What would it be like if he lived a full span? But his mind seemed to become clouded with a yellow, biting mist.

Miserable, he gave up. He was cold and pulled his blankets close and stretched out on his leafy bower. As he waited for sleep to come he saw the first rays of the rising sun spilling over the ridges. They were the color of blood and so powerful that a distant promontory pushed out from that portion of the range as if it were alive.

Safar closed his eyes, whispering prayers for the souls of all the people who had died in his vision—the handsome people who'd once danced under fruited trees on an island at world's end.

And then he slept a dreamless sleep.

# 4

# ALISARRIAN'S CAVE

When Safar opened his eyes again the sun was higher, casting a peaceful glow on the morning scene. Iraj was bustling about, poking the fire into life and getting things out for breakfast. But when he saw Safar's face he spotted the misery there and asked what was wrong. Still shaken by the vision, Safar blurted out the whole tale.

Iraj made no sign of surprise the whole time Safar spoke and when the story was done he said, "Don't trouble yourself, Safar. It was only a bad dream. Some of those almonds we ate were probably green."

"It was no dream," Safar protested. "But a vision of something that actually happened. It was the cause of the fiery shower we saw last night."

Iraj gave his friend an odd look. "Why do you think that? Have you had visions before?"

"Yes," Safar said in a low voice. "Sometimes about things that are going to happen. Sometimes about things that are happening."

"Do they always come true?"

Safar shrugged, miserable. "Mostly."

Iraj squatted down beside Safar. "I've thought since we met you were keeping something from me," he said. "Is that all of it?"

Safar shook his head. "No."

"Do you want to tell me the rest?"

"Not yet."

Iraj nodded. "We have time."

Safar sat numbly as Iraj did all the necessary work, packing their things, gathering up the animals, and loading the llama. When it was time to go Safar's mood had improved. Everything seemed so normal in the light of day. Visions and sorcery had no place amid such brightness. The morning air was cool and soul cleansing. The birds were out, pecking among the dewdrops for breakfast. Butterflies perched on broad leaves, drying their wings in the warming sun. Fat sleepy bumblebees peeped from the blossoms.

Iraj whistled a merry tune as they set out and he kept it up for most of the morning, although Safar saw him glance in his direction every now and then, eyes hooded, as if measuring. After a time Safar pushed the vision away and made it into the mere nightmare that Iraj had suggested. He began to feel foolish for even mentioning it. He remembered his father's caution that the mountains could create a melancholy, distrustful mood, and finally he decided that what he'd seen was no vision, but the result of a fevered imagination brought on by melancholy's chill.

In a short time his own youthful spirits rose naturally to the fore and he joined in Iraj's tune. As they whistled their eyes met and their lips twisted into grins that turned the notes into airy bleats and they both exploded with laughter. The laughter was followed by much giggling over silly boys' jokes. They staged mock fights and wrestled, behaving like the striplings they were.

The day was half gone by the time the two friends reached their goal. The ground was covered with hard-packed snow, marked here and there by green shoots struggling out to greet the spring sun. The day was warm and windless and as the trail steepened they began to perspire from the effort of their climb, forcing them to shed their coats. The narrow path curved and swooped over the snowy rocks, carrying them to the summit. Progress was impossible to mark. In many places broad overhangs and outcroppings blocked their view of everything but the rocks around them and the path under their feet. The goats and llama scrambled ahead, disappearing around a sharp bend.

Even though Safar knew what to expect when he rounded that bend, the view leaped on him as suddenly and delightfully as the first time he'd come this way.

They emerged into bright light, finding themselves on a broad ledge looking out across the northern side of the mountain range. Just below was a small, grassy hollow where mountain berries abounded. A spring burst from the rock beneath their feet, plummeting down to gather in a crystal pool in the center of the hollow. The goats were gamboling among the berries, bleating with joy. The llama ignored his less-than dignified cousins of the wool, his snout already buried deep in one of the berry bushes.

Falling away from the green hollow was a wonderland of white-capped crags that tumbled down to the great desert wastelands of the north. Fat columns of towering clouds drifted across the blue skies, islands of layered browns and grays and cottony whites. The desert sands caught the sunlight, casting it back at the skies and the whole appeared to be formed of glittering, multi-colored gems.

Beyond the desert there was nothing to stop the eye. Safar's vision sailed swiftly for the horizon's rim, a dark blue line where the vault of the sky mated with the earth. He heard Iraj gasp and knew that even he—born to the vast southern plains—had never looked such a great distance. The view was overwhelming but everything also seemed enlarged in the thin air so the horizon somehow appeared close—although Safar knew from the caravan masters that it would take much time to travel so far.

He glanced at his friend, who had a foolish grin on his face. Iraj reached out—hesitantly—as if trying to touch the horizon. Safar laughed for he'd done the same thing the first time he found the place.

"Follow me," he said. "There's more."

Safar shed his light pack and clambered down the rocks running along the rushing spring. About half way the water sheeted over a cave mouth. Safar pointed it out to Iraj, then showed him how to edge his way between the falling water and the rock face and duck into the cave.

He'd left materials for torches there on his last visit and he quickly assembled several, then struck sparks with his flint tool to fire one. Instantly the cave was flooded with an eerie light. The walls and floors and ceiling were carved from smooth, green stone that captured all light and flung back a ghostly glow.

When Iraj had recovered from his initial amazement he fired a torch of his own and peered about, noting the place where Safar sometimes made a fire when the weather was cold. Then he saw a mass of pentagrams and magical symbols and star signs—some old, some newer—inscribed on one wall and the floor.

"A wizard's den," he said.

Safar nodded, not mentioning that the clumsier and newer symbols were his attempts to copy and learn from ancient masters. He'd yet to make magic with them, hampered as he was by youthful doubts. But in the back of his mind he knew it was only a matter of time before he succumbed to the temptation to cast a real wizard's spell.

Safar pointed to a series of faded red symbols etched on the floor. They led deeper into the cave, as if indicating a path. Iraj gaped as he recognized the symbols—the demon moon and comet of The Conqueror.

"Alisarrian came here?" he gasped.

"I don't know," Safar said. "But I think some of those who knew him used this place."

He motioned Iraj forward and they followed the path through the several chambers that made up the cavern. One room had a stone shelf with ancient jars still sitting on it. Although some of the magical symbols identifying them were still plain, the contents of the jars had dried up long ago. Another room featured a small pile of weapons and armor so rusted they'd bonded together. Iraj examined them with much interest, commenting with authority on their purpose and former quality.

The final room was empty, save for brackets mounted on either side of the far wall. Safar lit two more torches and placed them in the brackets.

"This is what I brought you to see," he said, pointing to the broad space between the two torches.

Iraj peered where he pointed but at first saw nothing remarkable.

"Look closer," Safar said. "It takes a minute to see the first time you try. After that it's easy because you know what you're looking for."

Iraj's eyes narrowed with effort and he turned his head this way and that, trying to make out what Safar was pointing at. Then the young potter smiled when he saw the stare turn into a look of wonder as the image between the mounted torch brackets leaped out.

A large painting had somehow been created just beneath the translucent surface of the stone. It was barely visible until the torches were lit—and only then if it were looked at a certain way.

The picture was of a tall, handsome warrior dressed in the archaic armor of a prince. He was fair skinned and had long light hair and fierce eyes as blue as the waters of Kyrania's holy lake. The warrior carried a helmet under his right arm and about his brow was a simple gold band of kingly authority. He had a sword in his left hand, held high as if greeting or challenging another warrior. Safar had never decided which.

Above the warrior king was the symbol of the Demon Moon and ascending comet.

"Alisarrian," Iraj hissed.

"None other," Safar said.

Iraj laughed in loud delight and clapped the young potter on the back, thanking him profusely.

"A secret for a secret," he said. "Although I got the better bargain, my friend."

At that moment Safar realized that sometime between the

moment they'd set out on the journey and their arrival, they *had* become friends. The knowledge made him feel somehow more adult. He'd never had a real friend before.

Iraj gazed at the portrait again. "I've studied everything about Alisarrian," he said, "but I've never seen such a likeness before. He looks every inch a conqueror. A man fated by the gods to rule a great empire."

He drew his sword, flourished it, then struck a pose like that in the painting—sword held high, head lifted and eyes far-seeing.

With a jolt, Safar noticed something for the first time. "You're left-handed," he said, "just like Alisarrian."

Iraj nodded, face sober. "And tall and fair as well," he said. "But my eyes are dark. His eyes are blue...like yours."

Safar blushed. One of the many reasons he treasured this secret place was that here was another blue-eyed person like himself. It made him feel not only less strange, but superior—if only for a little while.

Iraj turned, holding his pose. "Tell me, Safar," he said quite seriously. "Do I look like a king?"

Safar studied him carefully. No vision followed, no great bolt from the skies, but realization boiled up from within. And he just suddenly...*knew*.

His mouth was dry and his voice came in a croak. "You *will* be king, Iraj," he said.

"What?" Iraj said, startled. "I was only—" he broke off. Then his voice became fierce, harsh.

"What are you telling me?"

"You will be as great a king as Alisarrian," Safar answered. "I see it..." he tapped his chest "...here."

Iraj's sword hand fell, the blade scraping against the stone. "Don't mock me," he warned.

"I'm not."

"You're speaking of my greatest dream," he said. "To create a kingdom as grand as Alisarrian's."

"I know this," Safar said.

"You don't think I'm crazy?"

"Perhaps." The young potter shrugged. "You'll probably have to be."

"You've seen this in one of your visions?" Iraj asked.

"Just before you came," Safar said. "I saw you...wearing a crown."

"Was I sitting on a white elephant?" Iraj asked, chin jutting forward in surprise.

"Yes," Safar said. "You were leading a great army. In my vision you beckoned me."

Iraj came closer, as if drawn by a magnet. "And I told you to sit beside me," he said. "And that you—Safar—were responsible for what I'd won."

"It seems we had the same vision," Safar said, numb.

"I'd believed it was just a dream," Iraj said. "I only thought it might be more than that when I met you and heard your name."

"Somehow," Safar said, "we got into each other's minds."

Iraj shook his head. "It was *your* vision," he said. "Such things never happen to me."

"Well they do to me," Safar sighed.

"You act like it's a curse."

"You don't know how much of one," Safar answered.

"But...if what you say is true—"

"It is," Safar broke in. "I'm not often wrong."

Iraj put his arm around Safar's shoulders, pulling him closer. "Then, when I am king," he said, "you will be my most trusted advisor. You will be Lord Timura from the moment I take my rightful place on the throne."

Then he withdrew his arm and stepped away, raising his sword with much ceremony. He gently tapped Safar on the head with the blade, saying, "I, King Iraj Protarus, do so decree."

His face shone with youthful zeal. Emotion made his voice waver and crack and his eyes welled with tears. There was a smear of dirt on one cheek and standing there in his rough boyish clothes attempting to strike an heroic figure, he might have even looked a bit ridiculous.

But Safar didn't laugh.

After the impromptu ceremony Iraj investigated the chamber further, taking special note of all the magical symbols and jars.

"What do you suppose was the purpose of the cave?" he asked.

"My guess," Safar replied, "is that it was used by a Dreamcatcher to cast Alisarrian's future."

Iraj grinned hugely, saying, "How fitting for me to have my own future told in this place. And by my own Dreamcatcher as well."

"I'm no Dreamcatcher," Safar protested. "I'm just an apprentice potter."

"A potter who has visions," Iraj laughed.

Oddly, Safar was stung by his comment. "Being a potter may not be as great as becoming a king," he said. "But it is an honorable craft. Some even say it's an art—an art blessed by gods."

"I'm sorry if I said anything to upset you," Iraj said. "The only craftsmen I've ever known were sword and armor makers. But as you say, it's well known that potters are blessed because they work with the same stuff the gods made us from. Did you ever think that could be why you have visions? Maybe you got a double portion of blessings when you were born."

"It could be," Safar said. "Although my father has never had anything like that happen to him."

"How do you know?" Iraj asked.

"From the way he acted when—" Safar stopped.

"What happened?" Iraj pressed. "What did he do?"

Safar shook my head, refusing to answer. "I'd rather not say."

"We shouldn't have secrets between us," Iraj said. "Especially after what's happened."

He's right, Safar thought. But instead of confessing all, he became angry. "Nothing's happened!" he snapped. "Just one stupid boy told another stupid boy a silly tale. That's all."

Safar stormed away, ducking between the watery curtain at the cave's mouth and clambering over the rocks until he reached the meadow where the goats were grazing.

Wisely, Iraj took his time in following. Safar raged about the meadow, kicking innocent rocks, tearing up offending plants by the roots and slapping at the llama when he approached and nuzzled him to see what was wrong. When he struck out at the animal it sprang back in shock. Safar had always treated him gently. It stared at him with accusing eyes, then turned and ambled off in that overly casual way llamas have when they don't want to show they've been offended.

A goat got in its way and it charged the animal as if it were the greatest nuisance that had ever crossed its path. The goat dashed off, then revenged its humiliation by butting a smaller animal, which did the same and before Safar knew it the whole field was full of angry animals, butting each other and hopping about like fakir's apprentices attempting their first walks across a bed of hot coals.

By the time Iraj showed up Safar was laughing so hard he'd forgotten the argument. Iraj didn't bring the subject up and the two were soon engaged in the rough play and adventuring of boy goat herders alone in the mountains.

But it hung there between them, an uncomfortable presence.

When Badawi saw the wide caravan track leading into the mountains he fell from his donkey and dropped to his knees. He thumped his breast and shouted huzzahs to the heavens for saving his life.

That morning when Sarn sent him out to scout the way the horse dealer knew this day would be his last—unless he came up with a miracle. Badawi's luck had seemed to desert him after he'd discovered the old Timura pot from Kyrania. They'd traveled over four hundred miles since then and hadn't even found a goat path, much less a full blown caravan track leading over the Gods' Divide.

As he sang praises to all the holy presences he could think of, Badawi suddenly spotted a mound of camel dung a few feet away. His heart leaped with greater joy and—still on his knees—he scrabbled over and broke the sun-crusted mound open, revealing a still-moist center.

Just then Sarn came riding up, his column of demon bandits not far behind. When Badawi saw him he scrambled to his feet. "Look, Master!" he shouted, displaying two big handfuls of dung as if they were a great treasure.

"What's that in your hands, you filthy human?" Sarn growled.

"Camel dung, O Master," Badawi said, doing a little dance of joy, spilling the stuff on the ground. "The gods have guided your unworthy slave across a thousand miles of wilderness to find the very thing you have been commanded to seek."

"Have you gone mad, human?" Sarn said. "What do I want with camel dung?"

Badawi didn't seem to hear. He'd seen still more of the droppings and he raced over to them, leaping from mound to mound like a fat toad, scooping up dung and throwing it into the air, crying, "Praise the gods!"

At that moment Giff came up. "What's wrong with the human?" he asked.

"I think I've pushed him too hard," Sarn said. "He's seems to have lost his senses from the strain." He sighed. "I suppose he's of no use to us anymore. You can kill him if you like, Giff. Just be a good demon and don't say 'I told you so.'"

Giff grinned and started to draw his sword. But Badawi had overhead them. He hurtled over to the two demons, anger momentarily overcoming his fear.

He shouted, "Kill me? Why would you do such a stupid thing? I've found your route over the mountains, haven't I?" Badawi pointed to a wide track winding up into the hills. "There lies Kyrania!" he shouted. "There lies the Valley of the Clouds!"

Badawi became overly excited from his discovery. Excitement bordering on dangerous hysteria. "You'd never have discovered this on your own!" he cried. "Only I, Badawi, could manage such a thing.

"Furthermore, haven't I also just shown you evidence that a caravan passed this way not more than three or four days ago?" He indicated the dung-strewn trail with a stained hand. "Or do you suppose all these animals were out wandering in the middle of nowhere looking for a comfortable place to shit?"

As soon as his outburst ended Badawi realized what he'd done. His nerve collapse and he fell to the ground. "Forgive me, Master," he begged. He beat his head against the ground and threw dust over his head. "This insignificant beetle of a slave has offended you, Master. Cut off a hand, if it pleases you. Pluck out this miserable tongue that wagged without thought when the brain became overly excited by discovery. Only spare me, Master. Spare me. And I shall serve you faithfully, content with crumbs for food and lashes for praise for so long as I live."

While Badawi begged, Giff kicked his mount forward to examine the signs.

"I hate to admit this," he said when the horse dealer was done and reduced to a weeping wreck, "but the human is right. A caravan did pass this way not long ago."

Badawi wiped his eyes and blew his nose on his sleeve. "You see, Master," he said, "I spoke the truth. Even Giff says so. And we both know how much he hates me. I deserve it, of course, although—"

"Shut up, human!" Giff said. "If you dare foul my name again by speaking it aloud I'll cut off your head to make a pisspot!"

Badawi bowed, trembling. "Please, sir," he said. "I meant no harm."

Sarn ignored the exchange. He was noting the width and depth of the trail—more of a wide road, now that he really looked at it. A road worn into the very rock from centuries of use. He stared up at the snow-capped mountains, wondering how rich a prize the caravan would make.

As if reading his thoughts, Badawi said, "My guess is that it's out of Caspan, Master." He pointed northwest, roughly indicating where Caspan would be. "The caravan master is no doubt heading across the Gods' Divide to Walaria." He pointed south across the mountains. "It's a journey of several thousand miles—going there and back, of course. As you no doubt have already supposed, Master, no merchant would travel so far if he weren't expecting to make a handsome profit for his efforts. Seize that caravan, Master, and you will possess a fortune."

Giff had been listening closely, realizing all the horse dealer had said was true. Added to these glad tidings was another fact that delighted him even more.

He clacked his talons to catch Sarn's attention and when he had it he said, quite simply, "Are we done with him now?"

Badawi gawped. "What do you mean, 'are we done with him now?'"

The two demons ignored him. "Actually, I really don't see any further use for him," Sarn said. "We've found what King Manacia wanted, plus what *we* wanted. And soon as we take the caravan we can return home."

"Done with who?" Badawi pressed. "Who do you mean, lords?"

"You promised I could kill him," Giff pointed out.

"Do you mean me?" Badawi said. Then he began to weep again. "Not me," he sobbed. "You *can't* mean me!"

Sarn pulled a huge, gem encrusted ring from a taloned hand. He tossed it to Giff, who plucked it out of the air.

"I'm buying my promise back," Sarn said. "I've had to put up with him more than you. I had to pretend I didn't completely loathe him." He gnashed his fangs. "It's not good for a demon's health to keep things inside that way."

"I'll do anything, Master," Badawi sobbed. "Anything."

Giff growled laughter and jammed the ring on his finger. "Consider the promise retrieved," he said.

Sarn kicked his mount closer to the sobbing Badawi. His steed's snout curled back in disgust at the human's smell. The beast snarled in fear, but Sarn steadied him by digging a heavy heel into his ribs.

"Look at me, human," the demon said.

"No, no, I won't look!" Badawi cried, trying to scrabble away.

"I said look!" Sarn roared.

Badawi sagged to the ground as if the demon's shout had been a blow. They he slowly looked up. Huge yellow eyes stared down at him. Sarn gestured and the horse dealer's body suddenly stiffened. Badawi had no will of his own, but he still had thoughts and he still had fear.

"Don't hurt me, Master," he shrieked.

"I don't intend to, human," Sarn answered. "I wouldn't foul my hands with your cowardly blood. No, you shall have the death you deserve, human. The death the gods must have decreed, or the idea would not have come so quickly into my head."

"Please, Master!" Badawi begged.

"Silence!" Sarn shouted.

Badawi was struck dumb.

"Take this knife," Sarn said, handing over an ornate dagger. Badawi's fingers, acting against his will, stretched out and took the knife.

Sarn pointed to the ground. "Dig your grave there. Make it deep, so no unsuspecting jackal will poison itself with your rotted corpse. And make it wide to contain your bloat."

Like a clockwork machine Badawi came to a crouch and started digging.

"When you're done, human," Sarn said, "climb into the grave and cut your guts out. I want you to do it slowly. To cause yourself as much pain as if I were doing the cutting."

He rode off laughing.

Badawi's mind screamed, "No, no, I won't do it!"

But he kept digging, gouging the hard ground with the knife, scooping up dirt and rock with bleeding fingers. He couldn't slow down, much less stop. And he knew once he did stop he'd have no choice but to carry out the rest of Sarn's sentence. As commanded, he'd take his own life—as slowly and painfully as a spirit possessed could manage.

A mad thought came to him. It was all because of a camel. That's when his luck first left him. When he fell in love with a camel and stole her for his own.

And he thought, but she was such a pretty animal, my Sava. And white, so white…

As white as the snows on the Gods' Divide.

Iraj returned to the cave several times over the next few days. He went alone, never announcing his intentions when he left or speaking about it when he returned. Although he never said what he did there, each time he emerged he seemed to stand taller, his bearing more confident and his eyes more commanding.

Safar only returned once and he also went alone. Late one night he relived the nightmare of the dancers who died in the volcanic eruption. After he calmed himself and his mind became clear he remembered something he'd found in the cave several visits ago. After checking that Iraj was asleep he went into the cave to the room with the stone shelf and old jars. In one corner was a shattered pot that had caught his interest because of all the ancient magical symbols painted on it. He'd laid out the shards on the floor in a vague attempt at reconstruction.

Safar held the torch high to get a closer look at the nearly completed puzzle. This time his interest wasn't drawn so much to the symbols, but to what the pot once represented. Which was a round jar shaped like the world with a small opening that had once held a stopper. The major features of the world had been displayed on the jar, consisting mostly of the oceans and the four turtle gods that bore the lands. Here, in the Middle Sea, was Esmir—which in the ancient tongues meant simply the land, or the earth. To the north was Aroborus, the place of the forests. To the south was Raptor, the land of the birds. Last of all was Hadin, land of the fires. Safar studied this arrangement in greater detail, remaking the pot in his mind. On the globe Hadin was on the other side of the world—directly opposite Esmir.

He bent to get a closer look at the large piece of shard that contained Hadin, actually a huge chain of islands rather than a single land mass. The largest island had a picture of a cone-shaped mountain with a monster's face. The monster was breathing fire. The memory of this piece of painted pottery was what had drawn Safar into the cave. He wondered now if the large island in Hadin was the place he'd seen in his vision. If vision it was.

He felt ignorant. He'd always prided himself on his mind, but now all his knowledge of the world and what made it seemed so insignificant he might as well have been an insect contemplating the heavens. He hungered to know more, which made him sad because he realized he'd reached the end of what Gubadan could teach him. And as Safar looked at the shattered glove it occurred to him that much of what he'd learned might be in error, or based on Gubadan's stirring myths. Even the old priest admitted, for instance, that there were no turtle gods carrying the continents. The lands floated on the oceans without assistance, he said. The turtle gods were symbols, not science, he said. Although he cautioned symbols sometimes hid inner meanings that might make science.

Safar determined the next time he traveled Walaria with his father he'd find books to broaden his knowledge—although he didn't have the faintest idea what types of books those might be. To start with, however, he could look for something that could tell him about the four continents. Particularly Hadin.

He reached for the shard containing Hadin and as soon as his fingers touched it his body tingled all over with that warm, honeyed sensation he'd felt the night when the fiery particles had rained from the sky. The feeling quickly vanished and all was normal again. He shook himself, wondering what had happened. He stared hard at the pot shard with its fiery mountain. No answer came. After a time he gave up and tucked the shard away into his shot pouch to be examined later.

He returned to the campsite and his blankets. He slept and this time he didn't dream.

Over the next few days he became uncomfortable in the grotto. Although he didn't show it, there was a buzz of magic and danger in the air that disturbed him. Finally he made an excuse for the two of them to get away for awhile. He told Iraj they needed to find meat for their cooking pot. Always eager for a hunt, Iraj agreed.

Leaving the goats and llama to graze, they wandered along snow-patched trails for hours. Safar felled a few mountain grouse with his sling and Iraj shot a hare with his bow. Safar teased him because he'd brought heavy arrows better suited for bear than rabbits and the creature was so torn up by the missile it was useless.

Iraj pretended to be hurt. "I just saved our lives, you ingrate. Didn't you see that mean look in its eyes? A man-eater if I ever saw one!"

"Eeek!" Safar shrieked. "A man-eating hare! Run! Run!"

And they both bounded down the path as if a tiger were after them.

An hour or so later they came to a promontory that overlooked the main caravan route. Passage through the Bride and Six Maids wasn't easy. It consisted of a complicated series of trails and switchbacks winding up from the desert to the first pass. The pass led to a rickety bridge—built, some claimed, by Alisarrian's engineers—that crossed to the next mountain. More passes and bridges joined into the final route, which traveled over the broad summit of the Sixth Maid, then dipped to catch the trail across the Bride herself and then down into Kyrania and beyond.

Safar had spent many an hour perched on that promontory watching the caravans. At the height of the season, when as many a dozen might be traveling, it was a wondrous sight. He'd once spotted four caravans moving along four different peaks at the same time. He'd never seen an ocean, but to Safar the caravans looked like a small fleet of ships sailing over a sea of clouds and snowdrifts. The Kyranians called the region the High Caravans, for it was said that in all the world there were no higher mountains that traders crossed.

As the two young men stood there that day gazing out at the snow-covered peaks, Safar felt sudden joy when he spotted a caravan, the first of the spring, moving down toward the Bride's Pass. He pointed it out to Iraj, who hadn't been in the mountains long enough to distinguish distant objects easily. As he marveled at it they could both hear the sound of jangling bells echoing strangely in the cold, dry air. Soon they could make out the small figures of people, some on foot, some mounted on horseback—following the heavily-laden llamas and camels that padded over the snow. A few large ox-drawn wagons completed the caravan.

"All the places they must have been," Iraj said dreamily, "and all the places they've yet to see. The very sound of those bells makes you want to join them, doesn't it Safar?"

"Why should it?" Safar said, a little sharply. "I'm happy here. Why would I want to live among strangers?"

Iraj gave him an odd look. "You have visions," he said, "but you don't dream?"

"Not of things like that," Safar answered. "I'm perfectly happy where I am. Oh, I've visited the city once or twice. My father sometimes goes to Walaria to sell his best pots. But whenever I went with him I was always anxious to get back as quickly as I could."

Iraj waved his hand at the caravan and the vista beyond. "But that's the *real* world out there, Safar, " he said. "Where great men determine events. And there are all sorts of mysterious people and things to see. Your valley is beautiful, I admit. But nothing happens here, or will ever happen. Don't you feel left out?"

"Never," Safar declared. "I have all I want here. And all I shall ever want."

Iraj shrugged, then said, "Let's go down to meet them. I've never talked to a caravan master before."

There was plenty of time left in the day so Safar had no reason to deny him. Also, as every Kyranian child knew, the first to meet a caravan were always rewarded with treats and small gifts. Safar's eyes swept the terrain, picking out a route that would intersect with the travelers at the edge of the Bride's Pass. He pointed the way and the two young men charged down to meet the caravan.

They were skirting a jumble of rock when motion caught Safar's eye. He grabbed Iraj's arm to stop him and looked closer.

A line of figures moved swiftly out of a ravine toward the caravan. They were traveling in a wide loop that kept cover between them and the caravan and Safar knew they were doing this purposely so they wouldn't be seen.

At first he thought they were bandits. He cupped his eyes so he could see better and the lead group jumped into view so clearly and so frighteningly that he cried out.

"What is it?" Iraj asked. He was peering at the figures, still not able to make them out.

"Demons!" Safar shouted. "They're going to attack the caravan!"

# 5
# A WIZARD IS BORN

As Giff watched the caravan crawl along the snowy pass, camel bells chiming, oxen grunting, horses blowing steamy blasts into the chill air, a sudden feeling of foreboding descended on him. He glanced at the other nine mounted demons waiting with him in ambush. They were tense, but professionally so, as they made last-minute inspections and adjustments to their weapons and gear. They were the best of Sarn's fiends with scores of successful raids to their credit.

Giff was not reassured.

He couldn't put a talon on it but it seemed to him that something wasn't quite right. He thought, I should have killed the human myself. It had been bad luck to let Sarn do it. He should have insisted on his rights. But then he thought, don't be so superstitious. You've always made your own luck. Besides, what could go wrong?

He studied the mounted soldiers guarding the pack animals and covered wagons that made up the caravan. The humans were well-armed and seemed skilled enough to cause alarm but this wasn't the source of Giff's worry. Sarn had sent their best scout into the caravan's encampment the night before to steal small items from each of the sleeping human soldiers. Sarn had used those items to make a spell that would confuse the soldiers and turn them into cowards when attacked.

The only defender who wouldn't be affected was the caravan master, a big brawny human Giff would dislike to meet in anything but an unequal fight. He slept apart from his men in a pavilion the scout couldn't approach without being discovered. Even so, Giff thought, when the attack came the caravan master would be quickly overwhelmed without his soldiers to support him.

The plan was simple enough: a double ambush. Giff and a small force would attack the caravan first. It would be a fierce, no mercy attack, designed to frighten the humans as much as to harm them. "Be as bloody and horrific as you can," Sarn had said. "Soften them well for me."

At that point Sarn, striking from another vantage point, would hit full force. The entire action shouldn't take more than a few minutes, Giff thought. Yes, it was a good plan. An artful plan that seemed to guarantee success. But why was it he still felt so uneasy?

As if he were being watched himself.

"They can't be demons," Iraj said. "You must be mistaken. It's forbidden for them to be here."

"Well, I guess nobody told them!" Safar snapped. "Look for yourself." He pointed at the monstrous figures hiding in ambush below. "What else could they be?"

Dazed, Iraj aped Safar, funneling his hands so he could see more clearly. His head jolted back as the full realization sunk in. Then he swiveled, taking in more of the scene.

"Hells!" he said. "You're right. And look! There's more! A second group—moving through that ravine."

Safar spotted them immediately. It was a much larger group than the first—possibly thirty demons or more. He watched them snake through a ravine with high, snow-packed walls. The ravine narrowed at the mouth and Safar saw the leader pull in his mount and signal the others to stop. The group paused there to reform its lines.

"I think I see what they're going to do," Iraj said. His tone was oddly casual as if he were commenting on an interesting tactic in a military text. "The first bunch will jump the caravan, while the others hold back. Then when the caravan soldiers are fully committed the rest will charge out of the ravine and roll them up."

Iraj dropped his hands. "It's a good trick," he said. "I'll have to remember it."

Sarn made certain his demons were ready, deploying them in short-winged cavalry ranks so the ravine's narrow mouth wouldn't diminish the force of his attack. Giff's position was opposite the ravine in a clump of frozen boulders. When the caravan moved between them Giff would strike first and then, when the panicked soldiers turned their backs to confront him, Sarn would leap out and close the pincer's jaws.

The bandit chief unlimbered his sword and made a few practice passes in the air. His blood sang as his demon heart pumped battle lust into his veins. In a few moments all the riches his scouts had told him were on the caravan would be his. Then he'd speed up the mountain, following the pass to Kyrania. He doubted it would difficult to eliminate everyone in such a remote village. Sarn surmised that the humans in Kyrania might be expecting the caravan. Some could even be on their way now to meet it, which meant he might not have enough time to wipe all traces of his demonly presence from the snows. King Manacia had commanded that no witnesses be left behind. So Sarn had to make it appear that bandits—human bandits—had hit the caravan. He'd do the same with Kyrania, perhaps even picking up a bit more booty in the process. Then he and his fiends could make their way home with nothing at their backs to worry them.

Sarn was already imagining the greeting awaiting him on his return. A hero ladened with so much loot that other bandit clans would clamor to join him. Better still, the king himself would be in his debt. Sarn was by now convinced King Manacia was planning an invasion of the human lands. An invasion this mission had just proved was possible.

He was wondering if he ought to press the king for some sort of noble-sounding title when a sudden uncomfortable thought occurred to him. Wasn't it Giff who'd asked if perhaps Manacia had lied about the shield he'd conjured to protect them from the curse of the Forbidden Desert? What if Sarn had been too quick to dismiss Giff's supposition? After this mission Sarn would be a much more important demon than before. For daring the Forbidden Desert and striking out at the hated humans he'd be a fiend to be reckoned with. And the king hadn't held his throne so long by being stupid, or by allowing potential rivals to live. He might consider Sarn as one of those rivals. In fact, King Manacia, who was a mighty wizard, might have foreseen such a possibility in his castings. In which case he'd want Sarn to be weakened from the start. One way to accomplish that would be to lie about the potency of his shield. Sarn might have done the same himself if he were in Manacia's place.

Another thing: what if the curse didn't kill right away? What if it allowed him to live long enough to return home with the information the king wanted? And afterwards he'd die a horrible, lingering death, made worse by the knowledge Manacia had never intended to reward him for his faithful service. It was not unlike the way Sarn had treated the human, Badawi. For the first time he felt a touch of empathy for the horse dealer.

Then he thought, you're being a fool, Sarn. Pre-battle jitters, that's all. If royal betrayal had been in the wind he would have sniffed it out at the start. The bandit chief considered himself a most devious demon who could show even a king a trick or two about the art of treachery.

Nerves steadied, all self-doubt conquered, Sarn peered out and saw the caravan nearing the mouth of the ravine.

The attack was about to begin.

His yellow eyes glowed in anticipation.

Safar watched the smaller group of demons brace for the charge.

His mind was numb, his limbs oddly heavy and when he spoke his voice came in a croak.

"What will we do?"

There was nothing numb about Iraj. The tragedy about to unfold below seemed to have the opposite effect, charging him with an inner fire.

"Warn the caravan," Iraj said, eyes dancing. "What else?"

Before Safar could fully register the answer, Iraj burst out of their hiding place and bounded down the hill. His action swept away all of Safar's caution. Hot blood boiled over and without a second's hesitation he leaped forward to follow.

But as he scrambled down the steep hillside in Iraj's wake he thought, "My father's going to kill me."

It was a small caravan, spread out and weary from hard travel. As Safar drew closer he heard the harsh voice of the caravan master urging his men on.

"Your fathers were brainless curs," he was shouting. "Your mothers were lazy mongrel bitches. Come on, you dogs! Listen to Coralean! Only one more day's travel to Kyrania, I tell you. Then you can bite your fleas and lick your hairless balls all you like."

Safar heard a camel bawl and a driver curse its devil's nature. He also thought he heard the high-pitched voices of angry women. That was impossible, he thought. Women rarely traveled with the caravans.

He strained his aching lungs for air and in a burst of speed caught up to Iraj. They reached the caravan just as it crossed the mouth of the ravine. Three outriders spotted them first. Safar and Iraj raced toward the soldiers.

"Ambush!" Iraj shouted. "Ambush!"

The soldiers were slow to react. Their eyes were dull, their mouths gaping holes in frosted beards. But when Safar and Iraj ran up they suddenly came to life, drawing their horses back in fear. Safar realized with a shock they thought he and Iraj were the threat.

Safar desperately grasped the reins of the nearest horse. "Demons!" he screamed into the face of a dull-faced soldier. "Over there!"

He turned to point and saw monstrous figures storm out of the mist, sweeping in to crowd the caravan defenders closer to the ravine where the main force waited. Safar heard a demon war cry for the first time—a piercing, marrow-freezing ululation.

A series of images jumped out at him. He saw swords and axes raised high in taloned paws. Crossbows lifting to aim. Black bolts taking flight.

The soldier kicked at him—reining back sharply at the same time. The horse reared and Safar leaped aside to avoid its lashing front hooves. A heavy crossbow bolt caught the animal in the throat. It toppled over and Safar heard the soldier scream as the horse's weight crushed him. He'd never witnessed such agony before.

The other two soldiers turned their horses and raced away.

"Stand and fight!" Iraj cried after them. "Stand and fight!"

But his shouts only seemed to add to their panic.

"Ambush!" Safar heard them scream. "Ambush!"

The soldiers piled into the main caravan, knocking over men and animals alike. Then the air was shattered by the shrieks of what Safar realized *had* to be women. Their screams mingled with the bawling of beasts and the desperate cries of men fleeing death.

Safar and Iraj ran into the center of the chaos. Pack animals charged about dragging their drivers and strewing their loads into the snow. Camels careened into wagons, tumbling them over. Oxen tangled their traces. A half dozen soldiers milled around, striking hysterically at anything that came near, as if llamas and camels were the enemy.

A huge man—the caravan master—thundered up on his horse, waving his sword and shouting orders. Then, from behind, Safar heard the demons howl closer and then the distinct meaty thunk of steel cutting into flesh. Followed by the screams of wounded men.

It was his first battle and an odd calm descended on him. Everything seemed to move slowly and yet quickly at the same time.

He saw gore stain the snow.

He smelled fear's foul musk mixed with the powerful odor of demons gone berserk.

He heard men choke and die.

Then a demon loomed over him, rising high in the saddle to

strike with his sword. The image seemed more dream than real and Safar became intensely curious, noting the pale green of the demon's skin, the studs on his leather armor, the short snout and sharp fangs and the small, pointed ears. As Safar studied him Gubadan's training took hold. His mind became clear, his breathing slow.

He slipped to the side as the sword sliced down. He heard the demon grunt in surprise as he missed.

Safar jabbed at him with his staff, but the demon's blade swept in and back and Safar found himself holding nothing but a mass of splinters. He gaped at his now useless weapon, dumbfounded. The only reason he didn't die then was that the demon kicked his mount forward to meet a charging caravan guard. He cut the man down, whirled to find another and plunged out of Safar's view.

Safar heard shrill human cries and turned to see two demons attacking an ox-drawn wagon. They reared their mounts and the beasts' claws ripped away the canvas, revealing a writhing tangle of frightened women. They screamed and tried to fend the demons off.

One creature grabbed a girl by the hair and charged away, howling gleefully as he dragged her through the snow by long black tresses. Frozen rocks shredded her garments and for the first time Safar saw the naked limbs of a young woman who was not of his village. She cried out as a rock tore her leg and Safar found himself running forward to face the demon with nothing more than a shattered wooden staff.

Safar was not a killer by nature. He was raised to believe all life was precious, including that of the animals killed for the table. But at that moment he was stricken with a murderous fury—triggered as much by the young woman's humiliation as the threat to her life.

As he charged forward words came to him—the words of a spell. And he chanted:

*I am strong.*
*You are weak.*
*Hate is my spear.*
*May it pierce*
*Your coward's heart.*

In his mind the ruined staff became that spear. It was perfectly formed—heavy, but balancing easily in his hand. He reached back, then hurled the staff with all his strength. Before his eyes he saw the splintered wood reform itself in mid-flight.

And he had caused it to happen. Somehow he caused the splintered wood to become hard black metal. He caused the tip to broaden and become killing sharp. He caused the weapon he'd made to fly straight and true. And he caused the spear to pierce the leather armor and thick demon skin and then burst that demon's heart.

The demon fell, releasing the girl. His mount veered wide but the force of the charge carried her body forward and she slammed into Safar. His breath whooshed out. As the two tumbled into the snow together the girl flung her arms around him, fastening him in a grip made strong by fear.

Safar's breath returned and he tore away from her grasp and leaped up. The scene was madness. Demons were hewing left and right, killing men and animals without discrimination. But in that madness Safar saw the caravan master had managed to rally a small group that was beginning to fight back. His immense body weaved this way and that as he dodged blows and kicked his horse toward one of the demons. Safar gasped as another demon charged in from the side, bearing down on the caravan master with a battle ax. Before the demon could strike Safar saw a tall figure leap from a felled wagon.

It was Iraj!

His legs scissored open as he vaulted onto the saddle behind the demon, then closed to grip the mount's flanks with the ease of a practiced plains rider.

Iraj flung one arm around the demon's head, heaving to draw it back—and he plunged a dagger into the exposed throat.

It was then Safar learned that demons die hard.

The creature gouted bright red blood, but reached for Iraj, talons scything out. Iraj somersaulted off the saddle just in time, landing on his feet and drawing his scimitar as he came up. The wounded demon rolled off and rushed at Iraj, fouling the snow with his bloodspray.

Iraj stepped forward to meet him but his foot slipped and he fell face forward. The demon was on him, raising his ax to kill his fallen enemy before his own life drained away.

Once again all time slowed for Safar. This time it wasn't only magic that came to his aid. His sling was suddenly in one hand. With the other he was withdrawing a heavy clay ball from his shot pouch.

Then time jumped and the demon's ax was descending.

Time froze again as Safar loaded his sling and swung it about his head.

He let loose just before the demon's blade struck. The ball caught the beast full in the mouth and Safar cursed, for he'd aimed at the killing spot between the demon's eyes. His fingers suddenly turned numb, betraying him as he fumbled for another clay ball. But it wasn't necessary.

The monster sagged back...slowly, so slowly...then toppled over into the snow.

The demon tried to struggle up on one elbow. Safar drew his knife and raced over to finish him off.

But then the demon looked at him, freezing him with his strange yellow eyes.

"I should have killed the human myself," the demon said. "Bad luck all around."

Then blood burst from his mouth and he fell back, dead.

Too fired by the battle to wonder what the creature meant, Safar rushed over to Iraj to help him to his feet. As he bent down, back unprotected, a huge shadow fell over him. He looked up, thinking he'd see the face of death. Relief flooded in when he saw a bearded human face peering at him instead of a demon's. And it was an ordinary horse the man sat upon, not a monster with fangs and claws.

The caravan master's gaze went from Safar to Iraj.

"Thank you for my life, young fellow," he said to Iraj. "If the gods are kind and Coralean survives this day you will learn just how much I value my skin."

Then he spurred his mount back into the action. But now the winds of fortune had shifted and it was the demons who were being routed and slain.

Safar's relief lasted only the length of time it took for Iraj to leap to his feet.

"There's more, Safar!" he cried. "It's not over yet!"

And Safar remembered the other—much larger—force waiting in the ravine.

No sooner had memory wormed its cold way through the mud of his confusion then he heard the shrill ululation announcing the second attack. His head shot up and he saw the demons beginning to pour out of the mouth of the ravine.

"Stop them!" Iraj shouted.

Safar gaped. Had his friend gone mad? How was he supposed to accomplish that?

"You can do it!" Iraj said. "I *know* you can!"

Then all questions and fear dissolved and he saw quite clearly that Iraj was right. He could stop them.

Once again he gripped his sling. Once again he reached into his pouch. But instead of a heavy ball his fingers touched the pot shard he'd taken from the cave. The shard that bore the picture of Hadin, the land of fire. A shock of magic clamped his fingers closed.

Instinctively letting the moment rule, Safar didn't fight the magic. He drew the shard out and carefully inserted it into his sling. He swung the weapon about his head, eyes searching for a target. He saw an immense demon leading the charge out of the ravine. But it wasn't that demon he wanted. One death would accomplish nothing.

He had to kill them all.

His eyes were drawn up and once again he noted the heavy snow clinging to the sides of the ravine. In his mind he also saw the rotten slate beneath that snow. And then the mass of boulders hanging above the frozen incline the ravine bisected. He knew what to do.

Whirling the sling, Safar pictured the pottery shard in his mind, chanting:

*You were made in fire*
*And within you fire*
*Yet remains.*
*It grows from spark*
*To finger flame*
*To kiln fire.*

*And now I release you...*
*Fly free!*
*Fly free!*

And he let loose the missile.

When Sarn led his demons out to fight he knew he'd already failed.

Moments after Giff had attacked a sudden blast of sorcery had seared the air. It wasn't directed toward him, but it was so strong it rasped his senses. Fear iced his heart and he thought, there must be a wizard with the caravan. How could I have missed him?

Then he'd seen Giff go down and a human—a mere stripling at that—standing over him. Sarn goggled. This was the wizard?

But there was no mistaking the aura of raw power radiating from the stripling. It was so strong it had swept away Sarn's spell of cowardice and the human soldiers were already rallying. One part of him insisted this was impossible. No human was capable of such magic. The other part took stock, recognized that impossible or not there the boy stood with all the magic he needed at his command.

Sarn saw instantly his only hope was to strike while an element of surprise still remained. Any moment now the caravan master and his soldiers would realize a threat still remained in the ravine. With the young wizard's help Sarn and his demons would be trapped in this all-too-perfect ambush.

If he were lucky he'd merely be killed. If not, he'd be captured. And he'd be damned if let himself fall into the foul hands of a human.

So he made the signal. Heard his fiends shrill their battle song. And he booted his mount forward into the attack.

As he charged from the ravine Sarn saw that the stripling wizard was already in action, whirling a loaded sling about his head and searching for a target. Just then the boy looked directly at Sarn. A chill scuttled up the demon's spine. It was as if he were being measured for the grave.

Then the human let lose and Sarn laughed because he saw immediately that the human was off his mark. The missile was arcing high into the air instead of towards him. Wizard or not, he thought, the boy was a coward. Fear had spoiled his aim.

Then the missile sailed over his head, a strong current of sorcery rippling the air, and his laughter was choked off.

The boy was no coward. His aim had been true.

Sarn's last thought was that Giff had been right. The king *had* lied.

Now that lie was about to cost Sarn his life.

Safar smiled as the shard sailed over the lead demon's head.

Then, in midflight it exploded into a ball of flame. The back-blasting heat was so intense it scorched his face. But he didn't shrink away. Instead he watched the fiery ball loft upward toward the big snowy brow that frowned over the mouth of the ravine. It sailed farther than he normally had strength to fling any object. He noted this with casual interest, not amazement.

Safar felt as if he were standing several feet away from his own body, calmly studying his own reactions as well as the course of the flaming missile. His separate self found it oddly amusing to see the ball of magical fire slam into the frozen ridge. It was even more amusing to note the wild joy in the boy's eyes who had made it.

A explosion shook the ridge and with calculated interest Safar pondered whether the force of the blast would be enough.

As the frozen mass began peel off, he thought, Hmm. Yes, it was....But will it have the effect I desire?

The mass crashed down onto still another ridge below.

And Safar thought, The snow and ice will shatter. But what of the shale? And if so, will the weight of the whole create a still larger force?

An avalanche was his answer.

Shale and ice and snow thundered down on the demons, moving so fast it overtook them in midcharge.

The boiling wave of snow and ice and rock swallowed them from behind, gobbling them up with an awful hunger. Then all was obscured by an immense white cloud.

Safar stood there, waiting. Then the avalanche ended and a silence as thick as the cold blinding cloud settled over him.

The mist cleared and the only thing Safar could see in the sun's sudden bright light was a broad white expanse running to the edge of a blank-faced cliff that had once been cut by a deep ravine.

Safar nodded, satisfied. The experiment had gone quite well, he thought. Then, still in his mode of the cold observer, he began to wonder about himself. The boy who'd just killed all those living beings. They were demons, of course, and deserved to die. Still.

Still.

Then someone was pounding his back and he turned to find Iraj, pounding, and was babbling congratulations of some sort. The first emotion that thawed Safar's numb interior was annoyance.

He pushed at Iraj's arm. "Quit that," he said. "It hurts."

Iraj stopped. Safar was surprised to see awe as well as joy on his friend's face.

"You did it, Safar!" Iraj shouted. "You killed them all!"

The numbness thawed more and Safar was suddenly frightened. "Quiet," he said. "Someone will hear."

"Who cares?" Iraj said. "Everyone should hear!"

Safar clutched Iraj's arm. "Promise you will say nothing," he pleaded.

Iraj shook his head, bewildered by the request.

"Promise me," Safar insisted. "Please!"

After a long moment Iraj nodded. "I promise," he said. "You're insane to ask it, but I promise just the same."

Then Safar was struck by a wall of weariness that seemed as great as the avalanche. Iraj caught him as he collapsed and then darkness sucked him down and he knew nothing more.

Terrible nightmares inhabited that darkness.

Safar dreamed he was pursued by demon riders across a rocky plain. He ran as fast as he could, leaping ravines and even canyons, dodging falling boulders, bounding over thundering avalanches. The sky was aboil with storm clouds and the sun dripped on the landscape, turning it blood red. And no matter how fast he ran the demon riders were faster.

Suddenly he was naked. He was still running, but now shame mingled with his fright. The demon riders converged on him, cutting in from the sides. Their shrill ululations drove every thought from his head until only fear remained. The demons hurled their spears and Safar saw they were spears of crackling lightning. They struck, burning and jolting his body with awful, painful shocks.

Then the demons were gone and Safar was running on soft grass and the sun was a cheery yellow, the breeze gentle on his naked flesh. He came to a hollow where Naya and the other goats gamboled and drank from the sweet waters of a spring. His mouth was suddenly dry and he knelt among the goats to quench a burning thirst.

And Naya said to him, "What have you done, boy?"

"Nothing Little Mother," Safar answered.

But she stuck a lightning bolt in his heart and the lie hurt almost more than he could bear.

The other goats gathered around, baying accusations.

"He's been out killing," one said.

"Our Safar?" another asked.

"Yes," said another. "*Our* Safar has been killing."

"Is this true, boy?" Naya asked, disgust in her tones.

"They were only demons, Little Mother," he answered.

"Shocking," the other goats said.

"But they were attacking the caravan," he protested.

"Oh, Safar," Naya said. "I'm so ashamed of you." She butted him, knocking him down. Sharp stones jabbed into his buttocks. "I suppose you used magic," Naya said.

"I couldn't help it, Little Mother," he confessed. "Honestly I couldn't."

Then Naya rose on her hind legs and became Quetera, his pregnant sister. She was wearing a long white gown, swollen at the belly with new life.

"Naya says you've been out killing," his sister said. "And using magic to do it."

He didn't answer.

"Look at me, Safar," his sister said.

"I can't," he said. "I'm ashamed."

He pointed down. There was a demon's body at her feet.

"Did you do this, Safar?" she asked.

"I had no choice, Quetera!" he cried. "They were killing people." He pointed at the demon. "He was going to kill the girl."

Quetera's face suddenly turned kindly. "Poor Safar," she said. "Such a gentle lad. But now violence and death have found you. And they may never let you go."

Safar groaned and collapsed on the ground. He heard his sister come closer.

He smelled her perfume as she knelt down to comfort him. "Let me take you home, Safar," she said.

He tried to get up but he couldn't rise. His limbs were numb and all he could do was groan.

Then cool water touched his temples. A soft wet cloth wiped his face and he felt as if all his sins were being sponged away.

And he was thirsty. By the gods he was thirsty! He opened his mouth. Not water, but cool milk dribbled in and he lapped it like a hungry kitten.

"Safar," a voice said. It was gentle and as soothing as that milk. "Safar," it said again.

He floated out of the blackness to find a lovely face peering down at him. Dark, almond-shaped eyes full of sweet concern. Long black hair tumbling down like a silken scarf. Lips red and ripe, smoothed into a smile displaying teeth as white as the Snow Moon.

"Who are you?" he mumbled, weak.

The smile became sweeter still. "I'm Astarias," she said.

"Do I know you?" he asked.

She laughed. It sounded like distant music. "You do, now," she said. "I'm the girl whose life you saved."

"Then you're not my sister," he said.

More laugher. Puzzled laughter. "No, I'm not your sister. I'm Astarias."

"Well, thank the gods for that," he said.

And he slipped into a deep, peaceful sleep.

# 6

# THE COVENANT

When the caravan rolled into Kyrania Safar learned what it was like to be a hero.

He and Iraj rode in the lead with Coralean, mounted on the caravan master's finest horses. They were high-stepping steeds with painted shells and beads woven into their manes and tails. Behind them, guarded by the surviving soldiers was the caravan itself, bells jouncing, colorful banners waving. The air was pungent with the odor of precious goods from far away places. A boy ran in front carrying a demon's head mounted on a stake. The creature's yellow eyes were open and staring, snout gaping to display many rows of bloody teeth.

Safar felt like a participant in a strange, barbaric dream. The battle seemed distant, unreal. Yet there was the gory head bobbing in his view. His memories of the fight were vague, adding to the dreamlike quality. He felt as if it were not him but another who had cast the great spell that brought the avalanche down. There was no sign of the power he recalled coursing through his body. That morning, before the caravan set out, Safar had quietly attempted to tap some of that power. But it was either denied him, or, he'd thought, perhaps it had never existed at all. Maybe the avalanche had been a coincidence. Perhaps it was an accident of nature that killed the demons and not Safar Timura.

They rounded the last bend and excitement rushed in and all introspection vanished. Safar saw one of the Ubekian brothers posted at the old stone arch marking the village entrance. With much satisfaction he saw the bully's eyes widen in fear when he spotted the demon's head. Then he whirled and sprinted out of sight, crying the news of the caravan's arrival.

Iraj cantered close to Safar, face beaming with pride and he pointed to the gay ribbons festooning all the trees that lined the road. He started to speak but then the sound of glad music caterwauled from up ahead.

Coralean's smile was a bow of pleasure in his beard. "It is good," he boomed, "that your friends and family are giving you a proper reception. A true welcome for young heroes."

In the two days since the battle the people in the caravan had tended their wounded, repaired the damage and had bathed and wrapped their dead in white linen sheets. The bodies were loaded into a wagon for later funeral ceremonies. While Safar slept off the effects of the battle, Coralean had sent word to Kyrania, assuring everyone their young men were safe and unharmed. Iraj had been clear-headed enough to tell Coralean of the herd left in the mountain meadow and the messenger had carried that news with him as well so a boy could be sent to fetch the goats and llama.

When Safar had finally awakened there was no sign of Astarias. Iraj reported she'd been returned to the wagon with the other women. Safar had pined for her, although he'd been shocked when Coralean had informed him the women were being taken to the brothels of Walaria where they'd be sold.

"If it were not for you and your brave friend," he'd told Safar, "Coralean's wives would not only have lost their loving husband, but would have been impoverished as well—without even the price of a bowl of barley and rice to stave off starvation. As for the fair Astarias, she and her sisters in seduction squabbled so heatedly over who would care for you they gave poor Coralean a headache that could only be treated with a large jar of brandy."

He'd rubbed sore temples, groaning. "But the cure, as always, has afflicted your humble servant anew. I fear Coralean must apply yet more brandy to treat this malady." Then he'd winked at Safar. "Astarias surprised us all with her fire," he said. "She may be small, my boy, but she's as fierce as a desert lynx."

Then he'd leaned closer to confide: "Coralean was worried that after they'd survived the demon attack with little harm, the gods would mock me. And the women would then be damaged in a silly harem fight. I have a large investment in those women, you know. Not only their purchase price, mind you, but I spent much Coralean silver assuring they were fresh and free of all diseases. And I gave a witch a fat purse to cast spells that will make them inventive and full of passion for any man who pays to be taken into their embrace."

Safar had flushed, angry at such treatment of Astarias and her sisters. Coralean mistook his angry coloring for a village boy's blush from hearing of such worldliness.

"You'll learn of these things soon enough, my boy," he'd said. "As a matter of fact we should consider furthering your education soon. I'll make your schooling in such matters my personal responsibility. I, Coralean, do so swear. And there is not a man who knows me who will dispute that the word of Coralean is sounder than any coin a king has minted."

His promise echoed in Safar's thoughts as they approached Kyrania. What the caravan master intended, he didn't know. He had several guesses, however, that had him squirming like a fly in a honeyed dilemma. If Safar was right, one part of his nature was insulted that Coralean thought so little of him. The shameful human side of him was powerfully intrigued.

Then all thoughts were swept away when Safar saw the huge gathering at the outskirts of the village. All of Kyrania had turned out. The musicians played horns and bagpipes and drums and the whole village cheered when they saw the caravan. Safar's family was in front with Gubadan and the village headman and elders. Everyone was dressed in their best costumes. Boys stood tall, chests puffed out, trying to look like men. The girls wore flowers in their hair and blew kisses as Safar and Iraj came near.

All goggled and pointed excitedly when they saw the gory head. "It's true, then," a man said, "that the demons got out!"

"Too bad for them they met our lads, eh?" said another. "This'll teach them to stay where they belong."

Coralean called a halt. He raised his hand for silence and the crowd hushed. He rose up in his stirrups so all could hear.

"Greetings, O gentle people of Kyrania," he said. "I am Coralean of Caspan. We meet in circumstances filled with both joy and fear." He pointed at the head. "There is the fear. But you will notice, no doubt, that this particular demon is taking a long rest on a stake made of good Kyranian wood." There were chortles in the crowd. "This one and his companions," Coralean continued, "defied the curse of the Forbidden Desert. Now they have their reward. To dance in the Hells for all eternity."

Laughter and nods followed that statement.

"And now I will speak of joy. And it is joy, not fear, that fills Coralean's heart. For more years than it is comfortable to consider Coralean has heard other caravan masters speak of the warmth and hospitality of the people of Kyrania. My brothers of the road are notorious liars, as I'm sure you all know. But the tales were so frequent and seemed so little exaggerated that Coralean came to believe they were true. So it was with much anticipation of meeting you all that I undertook this trading journey. The

Coralean business has never taken him to this side of the Bride and her Maids before.

"During the long, hard months of travel Coralean thought of your peaceful valley many times. When we were thirsty, Coralean dreamed of the sweet waters of your lake. When we were hungry, Coralean took comfort in visions of your fat lamb kabobs and beds of barley spiced with oil from your olive trees and garlic from your gardens. When my men despaired, Coralean cheered them with tales of your charming village. 'All will be well,' I told them, 'when we reach Kyrania.' Yet how was Coralean to know that not only were the tales true, but Kyrania had more than mere hospitality to offer?"

He indicated Iraj and Safar. "She also has brave young men of whom she can rightly boast. Young men whose like I've never had the thrill to see. And Coralean, you should know, has seen much in his long life. Others I've met are more full of bluster than true courage. Such men would most certainly have kept their silence and slipped away when they saw the demons creeping up on a party of strangers. And Coralean and his companions would have been doomed.

"But these two gave not a thought for their own safety. They risked their lives when they charged out to give warning. Then they turned to fight the demons as they rode down on us. Why, none of us would be alive today if they had not taken such a brave course.

"This one"—he pointed to Iraj—"saved Coralean's life with an act of bravery and skill rarely witnessed. While this one"—he pointed to Safar—"joined in the fray as if he were warrior born, instead of a gentle village lad. And then, wonder of all wonders, the gods of Kyrania personally intervened. They caused a great hill of snow and ice to fall on our attackers. Proving that these mountains and this valley are the most blessed in all the world. For it is here that the curse brought these demon interlopers down.

"After we have honored our dead, sending their souls back to the gods who made them, it is Coralean's fondest wish to reward these young men. And to reward Kyrania, as well. The gods willing, we will have a feast tomorrow night. A feast like no other

Kyrania has ever seen. And all that is eaten and drunk shall be my gift to you. I, Coralean, do so swear!"

The crowd roared approval and crowded close to praise him and wish him well. In the confusion Safar slid off his horse and into his family's arms. His mother cried, patting him all over to make certain he was uninjured. His father clasped his shoulder in the strong grip men of Kyrania reserve for those they honor. His sisters wept and crowded around him.

Quetera slipped in to hug Safar when his mother stepped away. As he leaned over her child-swollen belly to kiss her she laughed at the awkward embrace.

"I'm so proud of you, Safar," she said.

Safar was surprised at her reaction. His dream had been so real he'd been braced for a scolding. Instead of thanking her, he blurted out that he was sorry.

"Why should be you be, Safar?" she asked. "Why should you be sorry for bringing such honor to our family?"

Iraj heard the exchange and pressed through to join them. "He's just tired." He chuckled. "Spearing demons is weary work."

Everyone laughed as if this were the greatest jest they'd ever heard. His words were passed along through the crowd of well-wishers and soon everyone was roaring.

That was another lesson Safar learned that day: that success could turn a man's every word into the purest gold. Which was something no wizard, living or dead, could accomplish.

The next day everyone gathered at the temple for the funeral ceremonies. Gubadan wore yellow robes of mourning, while the villagers tied yellow sashes around their waists and streaked their cheeks with hearth dust tears. The bodies of the seven dead caravan soldiers were laid out on a raft decorated with the red streamers favored by Tristos, the god who oversees the Kingdom of the Dead.

While a drum hammered a slow beat, Gubadan prayed over the poor strangers who had come among them and sprinkled their white-wrapped bodies with holy oil. When the sun reached its highest point, Coralean—dressed in the flowing golden robes with the scarlet fringe of his kinsmen—stepped forward to light the oil-soaked kindling piled around the corpses. Then Iraj and Safar used long ribbon festooned poles to push the raft out into the lake. The current caught it, carrying it into the middle. Everyone prayed as thick smoke made a dark pathway in the sky. There was no wind that day and the smoke was carried high, curling under a bank of glowing white clouds, then streaming away in pale gray ribbons. Later, all said that this was a lucky sign.

As Safar bowed his head in prayer he chanced a look and saw the women from the caravan gathered in a quiet group. They wore heavy robes and their faces were veiled, so at first he couldn't make out Astarias. Then he saw a small figure slip her veil aside and a single eye peeped out. The eye found him. It was dark, with long flowing lashes. Safar smiled. A slender white hand fluttered at him. Then the veil was drawn back. Safar turned away, heart hammering, loins burning from the promise he thought he'd seen in that eye and fluttering hand.

Gubadan nudged him. It was time to lead the others in the funeral song.

The musette player set a slow tempo and one by one each instrument joined in. Safar lifted his head and let the clear, sad notes pour forth:

*Where are our dream brothers?*
*Gone to sweet-blossomed fields.*
*Where are our dream brothers?*
*Asleep in the Gods' high meadow.*
*Our mortal hearts*
*Yearn to follow their souls.*

The words carried far on the balmy air. And when the last notes fell, all were weeping.

Later, Coralean and the village leaders met to discuss the mysterious appearance of the demons. Safar and Iraj were allowed to attend the gathering in the large, colorful tent the caravan master had erected in the caravanserai.

Safar had never seen such luxury. The floor was covered with many layers of thick, expensive carpets. Pillows and cushions were spread around a central fire, where a servant tended a pot of steaming brandy. All manner of fruit bobbed on top and as the servant stirred the pot it gave off an odor so heavy Safar felt a little drunk from breathing the air. Curtains divided the tent into rooms and on one side Safar saw the shadows of the courtesans moving behind the thin veil, coming close so they could listen in.

"Here is Coralean's view of the situation," the caravan master said. "The demons who attacked us were outlaws of the worst and most foolish kind. Their actions may even end up being a favor to us, for when they fail to return all demons will know the price that must be paid for defying the laws of the Gods."

There were murmurs of agreement from the elders.

"Then what shall we do about it?" Coralean said. "What is our next step? Coralean asks this, believing it would be best if we acted in concert."

"Alert the authorities, of course," Gubadan said.

Coralean's bushy brows lofted. "Do you really think so, holy one?" he asked. He looked around at the others. "And who, after all, are these authorities? Coralean owes no king his allegiance. He is his own man."

Buzal, the headman, who at eighty was the oldest of the group, said, "Kyrania makes its own laws. No one rules us." He indicated Gubadan. "Our priest has superiors, which is only natural." Buzal grinned, displaying dark, rock-hard gums. "But I don't think they talk together much. I'd guess that they barely remember if he exists."

Gubadan stroked his beard, then nodded in unembarrassed agreement. "We're far away," he said. "And the temple isn't considered important. Still, don't we have a duty to warn others?"

"That's a load of goat droppings," Foron, the village smithy, broke in. "Meaning no offense, of course. What's to warn? The demons are dead and stinking. No more are likely to come. And that's that. The tale is told."

"But why shouldn't we tell others?" Gubadan asked. "What would be the harm?"

Coralean harrumphed and all turned to see what he had to offer. "I do not know these parts," the caravan master said. "This is the first time the Coralean business has carried me over these mountains to the markets of Walaria and beyond. It cost me much to buy the necessary maps from my brother merchants. Even if this first journey proves profitable beyond my wildest estimates, it will take many such journeys before Coralean's initial investment is repaid."

He shook his great, shaggy head. "Even so," he said, "if Coralean were a lesser man this incident might give me pause. I might never dare such an undertaking again. And I know my brother caravan masters well enough to say with some confidence that they would feel the same if they suddenly thought these mountains had become unsafe."

There were murmurs among the men. It would be disastrous if Coralean reported such a thing. All trade over the Gods' Divide would cease. And more than just Kyrania would suffer. Life could become very bleak.

"Not only would there be no more caravans crossing," Safar's father said to Gubadan, "but there'd be no more pilgrims."

The old priest winced. Everyone knew how much he depended on the donations of the faithful who visited the Goddess Felakia's temple and holy lake.

"Yes," he said, "I can see the wisdom in your words, Khadji. However, what if we are mistaken and these demons are not the only ones? We are cut off here from the rest of the world. News travels slowly. What if others have been plagued by demons? Our silence could end up being an unnecessary and dangerous decision."

Iraj cleared his throat. All looked at him. He flushed at the attention, then emboldened himself to speak before the elders.

"Forgive me, sirs," he said. "As you know, I made a long journey not many months ago, passing through Walaria on the way. And I heard nothing in the market place of demons...or any other dangers, for that matter, other than the usual tales of marauding bandits."

The men listened to Iraj quite carefully and with deep respect. Safar thought it ironic that only a few days before many villagers had gone out of their way to avoid Iraj, fearing the trouble he might bring from the outside world. Now he was a hero because he'd turned back a threat from the outside.

Gubadan gently broke in to explain Iraj's background—carefully skirting the issue that he was hiding out from some of his own tribe. However, Coralean immediately caught on that although demons might not be riding about at will, there were other troubles to be considered.

"May the name of Coralean be bandied about in the company of swine, if I'm wrong," the caravan master said, "But from what your wise priest just said, it sounds to me like the south is about to become a permanent battle ground for warring clans. This would almost be as bad for trade as the demons."

"Not if *I* have anything to say about it," Iraj blurted. Then he turned as red as a ripe apple for making such a seemingly foolish statement.

Coralean studied him for a long moment. Then he smiled. "After hearing of your background I now fully understand where you got your fire," he said. "You didn't learn it here, that's for certain."

He made a soothing gesture to the rest of gathering. "I cast no doubts on the courage of the men Kyrania," he said. "Your own Safar has proven there is steel in your spines. But I know you do not claim to be warriors. Which this young man—" he indicated Iraj—"was surely bred to be." There were mutters of agreement from the men. "It's also my guess," the caravan master said, "that you are the son of a chieftain."

Iraj bowed his head, not saying anything, while Gubadan tried to leap in to save his secret. But Coralean only laughed and shrugged his shoulders. "You needn't reveal more," he said. "Something is going on, or you may call Coralean the son of an ass who mated with a dog who doesn't know from one minute to the next whether he will bray or bark."

He leaned closer to Iraj. "I'll tell you this, my brave young warrior. If you should ever need the help of Coralean, you have only to ask."

When he said that Safar learned it doesn't necessarily take a magical vision to see through the disguise of a future king. A canny merchant can do just as well—and without disturbing the serenity of his dreams.

Iraj lifted his head to return Coralean's curious stare. His lips lifted slightly for a brief smile and then he nodded. This was a promise he would long remember. A silent understanding passed between the two. When the time came—and there was no doubt it would—not only would Iraj ask, but he would repay the caravan master many times over for any assistance he gave.

Coralean turned to others. "Is it agreed, then?" he asked. "We say nothing of this incident. Correct?"

There was a whispered discussion among the elders. Then Buzal said, "What of your men?" He pointed at the curtain that divided the room from the harem. "And the women? Can you assure us of their silence?"

"My men obey me in all things," Coralean said. "There's no need for worry in that quarter. As for the women, well, Coralean will tell you a little secret of the courtesan trade. Before I deliver these girls to their new masters each will drink a Cup of Forgetfulness. They will have no memory of their past. No reason to pine for home and family and friends. This makes for a most pliable and happy bed slave. No weeping to dampen the ardor of their masters. And in this case, no tales of demons to disturb their dreams."

The men snickered and then relaxed. Carnal jests were exchanged and there was much manly guffawing and knee-slapping. Only Safar was horrified at this casual dismissal of Astarias and her sisters. He glanced over at his father and saw that Khadji had the same knowing look in his eyes as the others. The same flushed and swollen features.

Then Coralean had his servant dip out hot bowls of brandy punch to be passed around. They were quickly emptied and refilled several times. Soon the talk became louder, the men's voices deepening as they recounted the bold adventures of their youth. Coralean held forth for more than an hour, telling every detail of the fight that he'd witnessed. The men murmured in appreciation when he told of how Safar had fought the demons—slaying the beast who took Astarias with a splintered staff that he'd wielded like a war spear. But there were loud gasps at Iraj's courage when he'd rescued Coralean, leaping on the demon's steed like the greatest of plains warriors, testing his strength against a more powerful enemy and finally cutting a path in his throat so the demon's soul could flee.

Safar looked over at Iraj and smiled, grateful he'd kept his promise. But Iraj frowned and made a motion, asking if it were finally time to tell the tale as it had really happened. Safar shook his head—a firm no. Iraj's eyes flickered, wondering why Safar was happy to allow him the greatest praise when Safar deserved much more.

Iraj leaned close, whispering, "Are you certain?"

Safar's answer was a lifted brandy bowl and a loud call for a toast to honor the deeds of his brave friend. It was the first toast he'd ever made in adult company. And all hailed Iraj Protarus, the young man Safar knew would someday be king.

After that everyone became a little drunk. It was another first for Safar. Relief mixed with fuddlement and he was suddenly very happy. He became happier still when Coralean began handing out the gifts.

First he told the elders that he would pay double for any goods, services or animals he purchased during his stay in Kyrania. Then he had his servants bring out heaping baskets of gifts. He asked the men if they would be so kind as to distribute them to the villagers. For each of the elders he had a purse of silver. For every man in the village there were small sacks of tobacco and a single silver coin. For every woman there were vials of perfume and little baubles to string as jewelry or to sew on their clothing. For every child there were ginger sweets as well as a copper coin.

Finally he came to Safar and Iraj.

"Coralean has thought long on this, my young friends," he said. "I have other presents I will give you both a bit later." He snorted. "Money, of course. But what is money, lads? Coins have value only because we all agree to give them such. I have a few pleasures in mind—yet you will have pleasures aplenty in the long lives before you. But I wanted to give each of you something special. A gift you will always remember Coralean by.

"First, my friend Iraj..." He took out a black velvet pouch. Iraj's eyes sparkled as Coralean withdrew a small golden amulet. It was a horse—a wondrously formed steed dangling from a glittering chain. "Some day," Coralean said, "you will see the perfect horse. It will be a steed above all steeds. A true warrior's dream, worth more than a kingdom to men who appreciate such things.

The beast will be faster and braver than any animal you could imagine. Never tiring. Always sweet-tempered and so loyal that if you fall it will charge back into battle so you might mount it again.

"But, alas, no one who owns such a creature would ever agree to part with it. Even if it is a colt its lines will be so pure, its spirit so fierce, that the man it belongs to would be blind not to see what a fine animal it will become." He handed the horse amulet to Iraj. "If you give this magical ornament to that man he will not be able to refuse you the trade. But do not fear that you will be cheating him. For he only has to find another dream horse and the man who owns *it* will be compelled to make the same bargain when he gives him the amulet."

Tears welled in Iraj's eyes and they spilled unashamedly down his face as he husked his thanks and embraced the caravan master. "When I find that horse," Iraj said, "I promise that I will ride without delay to your side so you can see for yourself what a grand gift you gave me."

Coralean, whose emotions were as large as his frame, harumphed to cover the sob in his throat.

Then he turned to Safar. The first thought the young Timura had was that he hoped Coralean wasn't going to give him a horse as well. What use would such a rare creature be to a potter? It was a foolish thought and he was immediately ashamed of himself for thinking it. He vowed to accept whatever gift he received with loud—although pretended—delight, so as not to spoil the pleasure of such a generous man.

"They tell me, young Safar," Coralean said, "that you are very wise. Some say you are the wisest child ever to have been born in Kyrania." Safar started to protest but the caravan master raised a hand to stop any foolishly modest statements that might burst forth. "For you Coralean has two small gifts. Together they may more than equal the gift I made to Iraj. That depends on whether you are as wise as they say and make good use of them."

He took a scroll from his robes. "This is a letter to a friend in Walaria. He is a rich man, an educated man. A patron to the all the artists and thinkers in Walaria. It asks him to present this to the chief priest at the temple school. He will entreat them to grant you entrance and once you join the great scholars there Coralean will pay all your expenses until you are the wisest man in all the land."

Safar's fingers shook as he took the rolled up scroll. It was heavier than he expected and he nearly dropped it. Then a small silver dagger slipped onto his lap.

Coralean stroked his beard. "That is my second present to you," he said. Safar lifted the knife, knowing it had some hidden purpose and wondering what that purpose might be. "Since you will be among so many wise men," Coralean said, "that knife may prove even more valuable than the education you will receive. Listen to an old merchant. When a thought is too weighty it's probably not to be trusted. When a man's words are thick with the fat of hidden meaning it's doubtful they have as much value as the speaker implies. That knife will cut through those weighty thoughts and fatty words. And you will come to the true answer with little struggle."

He looked at the other men, heavy eyebrows lifting high with humor. "At least that's what the witch Coralean bought it from promised."

Everyone chortled. Safar was stunned, not knowing what to make of either gift, especially the mysterious properties the knife supposedly held. He picked it up, felt a trickle of power and knew it to be as magical as the witch had warranted.

His father's voice came to him from far away, as if in a dream. "Aren't you going to thank Coralean, my son?" Khadji asked. "Otherwise he'll think you were raised without manners."

Safar fumbled thanks, as graceless as any youth of seventeen years, but Coralean seemed to understand the shyness. He embraced the young man, nearly smothering him with his great strength. Safar hugged him back.

"Come, now," the caravan master roared as he pulled away. "Coralean promised the people of Kyrania a feast! Drink up, my friends, so we may all stumble out with a good cargo of spirits in our bellies to begin the celebration."

The men shouted, bowls were emptied in mighty swallows, then refilled to the overflowing.

And there were few in the village who were not of tender years who did not spend the following days in a stupor so blissful that it was spoken of for much time to come.

That first night the sky was filled with fiery smoke balloons and kites with long flaming tails. There was drunken song and music everywhere and lovers slipped off into the darkness. Many a betrothal was sealed that night and many a child conceived in sighing embraces and barely-stifled cries of pleasure.

Coralean drew Safar and Iraj aside before they'd imbibed too much. He took the brandy bowls from their hands, saying: "You'll have need of *all* your senses tonight, my young friends." He chuckled. "Besides, you're both certain to end up in the arms of a village lass if you become too befuddled."

He wagged a finger. "No sense spoiling your futures with a too early marriage. Coralean is blessed with a passionate nature himself. Ask any of his wives and serving girls." He winked. "They call me their beloved bull. I have swarms of children to prove it. I tell you, if Coralean had been born into a poorer family my father wouldn't have been able to afford to save me from my youthful indiscretions."

Then he threw his arms about their shoulders and led them through a series of curtained rooms to the women's quarters. The main area was filled with pillows piled as high as their knees. Coralean plumped down and patted the pillows for the young men to sit on either side of him.

"I promised to show you a thing or two about pleasure, my boys," he said. "And I, Coralean the Bull, know more of such things than most men. It isn't a boast but a simple statement of fact concerning the Coralean nature."

He clapped his hands and a wide curtain parted. Safar heard high, pleasing voices and the courtesans filed through, parading before the men in a silky, perfumed line.

Safar never seen so much beauty—and certainly not so seductively displayed. He was no stranger to the feminine shape. He was raised with sisters, after all. And he'd spied on the village girls when they went to bathe in the lake. But the women he saw that night were so...available. His for the taking. What little they wore was sheer and artfully draped to entice, not conceal. Some were tall, some were small, some were dark, some were light, some were slender, some were plump. And they all displayed practiced smiles and movements. But more than just professional skills were on display. The courtesans were enchanted by the two handsome young rescuers. And eager to show their thanks.

"Pick one," Coralean said. "Or even two or three if you like."

Safar hesitated, but not from indecision. What he was being offered, some might think, was the answer to every young man's greatest dream. All those hot, uncomfortable nights filled with perfumed sirens were about to be exorcised. Such fiery imaginings and desires are as much a part of a youth's nature as the downy beard beginning on his face. Safar knew from listening to his sisters that young women are afflicted with similar feelings. And here was his chance to realize his most lurid fantasies. But a different although related emotion boiled up from that youthful cauldron. And that was sudden blind, unreasoning love. Which at that age is the same as lust, only most mistake it as having a more noble purpose.

So as Safar's eyes swept the line of courtesans, they ignored all that jiggling pulchritude. He was searching for one woman and one woman only. Astarias.

He didn't see her among the group. He glanced around, heart thundering, mind swirling. And his thoughts became...pure? At least in his imagination, they were pure. And he determined at that moment that he wouldn't shame Astarias with his embrace. Foolish youth that he was, he thought this would be his gift to her. Furthermore, he'd somehow release Astarias from what he believed was her enslavement. She'd live with his sister Quetera and be as chaste as any maiden in the village. And she'd be free to choose any youth she wanted for a husband. But somehow her love for him—and her admiration for his kind gesture—would overcome any feelings she might have for any other. They would be wed and have many children and live happily forever in each other's arms. All these things were running through his drugged mind. And he heard:

"You should choose first," Coralean said to Iraj. "After all, you saved my life."

Safar looked at Iraj. His friend's face was red with lust. Then he saw Safar and smiled. The redness vanished to be replaced with feigned bored interest. Iraj's eyes returned to the courtesans. He looked each one over slowly, shook his head, then passed on to another. Sudden realization clotted in Safar's belly then rose to become a lump in his throat. He *knew* what Iraj was up to. And then he became angry, certain that for some reason Iraj was about to cheat him of what he desired above all things.

"There seems to be one missing," Iraj said to Coralean. "A dark-haired wench."

Those last four words fell like weighty stones into Safar's well of despair.

Coralean frowned. "You mean Astarias?" he said.

Iraj covered his mouth, hiding an elaborate yawn. "Is that her name?" he said. "Very pretty."

Coralean shifted in his pillows, disturbed—and a bit embarrassed. "I held her back," he said, "because she is still a virgin. I have a dear friend—a very rich dear friend—I was keeping her for."

Iraj raised his eyebrows as if surprised. Then he shrugged. "Well, I suppose that's too much to ask," he said. "I wouldn't want to lessen your profit." He gazed at Coralean, his face mild. "However it was she—Astarias, you say?—I really wanted. But...if it's too much *trouble* for you..." He rose as if to go.

Coralean grabbed Iraj by the arm and drew him back down. "Is it not known to all that Coralean is the most generous of men?" he said. "Especially to one who preserved his most precious possession, his very life? If it is Astarias you desire most, my good friend, then Astarias you shall have." And he clapped his hands and called her name, commanding her presence.

Astarias came into the room, seeming to float through the curtain. Her dark hair was tied back with a white silk band. Unlike the others she wore a robe that covered her from slender neck to ankle. It was also made of white silk and as she walked it flowed over her body—chaste, but still highlighting all the delicate parts of her. She looked at Safar and the most delightful smile graced her features. She took a step forward, thinking she was meant for him.

"No, no," Coralean barked. "Not Safar! It's Iraj I promised you to."

Her face fell for an instant and in that moment Safar hated Iraj so much he would have gladly killed him. Then her smile returned, although Safar didn't think it was as bright as before...and she went to Iraj. He laughed and clasped her around the waist, roughly pulling her down.

The caravan master got up. He grinned hugely at the young men. "Coralean must attend to his duties as host," he said. "Take who you like, Safar. And if you can't make up your mind, let me suggest these two." He pointed at a pair of dark-skinned twins. "They've given me more pleasure, I'll warrant, then any other woman here." He clapped Safar on the back and exited.

The twins moved toward the young potter, expectantly. Safar started to turn away, so full of hateful thoughts that he wanted nothing more than to escape.

"Wait," Iraj said.

Safar swiveled, anger plain on his face. Iraj ignored it, pulling away from Astarias' shy embrace.

"Go to him," he ordered.

Safar was bewildered. "But, I thought..."

Iraj laughed. "I know *what* you thought," he said. "I was testing you, don't you see?" He grinned at Safar. "You didn't do too well with that test, my friend," he said. "But maybe it was unfair. So I forgive you for it."

He gave Astarias a gentle push. "Go, on," he said. "If you stay much longer I'll be helpless to let you leave."

Astarias pealed glad laughter and scurried over to leap into Safar's arms. All his noble intentions vanished as he crushed her to him. Then Safar heard Iraj call his name and broke away, gasping. His friend was standing at the curtain opening, arms around the dark twins.

"Thank you," Safar husked. "Coralean might not have agreed if *I* had asked."

Iraj shrugged. "No thanks needed," he said. "After all, we both know who the true hero of this night is." He started to exit, pulling the twins with him. Then he stopped. "Know this, Safar," he said. "From this day forward, all I have is yours."

Safar grinned. "And all that is mine, and all that shall be mine," he said, "will be yours for the asking."

Iraj grew quite solemn. "Do you mean that?"

"I swear it," Safar answered.

Iraj nodded. "Remember this night well, Safar," he said. "For someday I may come to ask an equal favor."

"And you shall have it," Safar vowed.

"No matter what it is?" Iraj asked, his eyes suddenly hard and probing.

"Yes," Safar said. "No matter what. And if you should ever test me again, I will not fail you."

And with that covenant he sealed his fate.

# 7

# DREAMS OF KINGS

Sarn was wrong—King Manacia hadn't lied. If the gods had still been watching they'd have been highly entertained by his error. Sarn's final torment, when he believed himself undone by royal betrayal, was a heady-enough brew of misery to satisfy any god's tastes.

In truth, King Manacia waited many anxious months for news of the bandit chief's return. As time dragged on the king became increasingly impatient, paying little attention to the business of state. He even ignored his harem and his wives and courtesans became fearful their master had wearied of them. To combat this they sought out the most beautiful and seductive demon maids to stir his lust. It was to no avail, for the king remained in his throne room until late every night wondering what had become of Sarn and drinking himself into a stupor.

It was difficult for King Manacia to admit failure—a condition he'd rarely experienced in his long reign. From the beginning he'd worked patiently, gradually extending his borders until all but a few of the wildest regions had been subjugated. The others had been forced into alliances weighted so heavily on Manacia's side it meant the same thing. Soon all would recognize him as supreme monarch of the demon lands. But this was not enough. The king wanted more.

"It's not as if I do these things for myself, Fari," the king liked to say to his Grand Wazier. "The future of all demonkind rests upon my shoulders."

And Lord Fari, who never reminded the king he'd heard these words before, always answered, "I thank the gods each eventide, Majesty, they made your shoulders wide and strong enough to bear that holy burden."

The Grand Wazier was a wise old demon of nearly two hundred feastings. Skillful flattery and ruthless intrigue had allowed him to keep his head through four bloody successions to the Zanzair throne.

The king took heart from Fari's reassuring display of fealty, greeting the oft-repeated praise as if it were freshly coined. Then he'd frown, as if overtaken by yet another bleak thought. And he'd sigh, saying, "Still, Fari, I'm sure there are *some* misguided ones in my kingdom who disagree. A few might even think me insane."

He'd sigh again, stroking his long curved horn. And shake his mighty head in sorrow.

"Only speak the names of these heretics, Majesty," was Fari's routine answer, "and I shall have their lying tongues plucked from their mouths and their throats filled with hot sand."

"If only they understood as well as you, my dear fiend," was the king's formulaic response. "Peace and plenty will always be denied us so long as more than one king commands the demon lands. It's only natural that there should be a single ruler for all."

And Fari would agree, saying, "How else, O Great One, can we ever rid ourselves of chaos? Or end the years of war and banditry? One demon must rule. And that one, the dreamcatchers portend, is you, My Lord."

"But that isn't enough, Fari," the king would remind him. "The humans must recognize me as well. I must be King of Kings. Ruler of all Esmir."

"I have dedicated the remainder of my humble life to that end, Majesty," Fari would answer. "Demon history has long been awaiting one such as you. What other fiend has had your wisdom? Your strength? Your benevolence? Your sorcerous power? The gods have gifted us with your august presence, Majesty. There's no denying it. It's as plain as the mighty horn on your royal brow."

With that, Fari would knock his old head against the stone floor, then rise with some difficulty, gripping his great dragon bone cane and heaving himself up with much cracking of aging joints and tendons. Then he'd withdraw, his bone cane tap tap tapping against the stone, fainter, ever fainter, until he reached the distant doors to the vast throne room and disappeared beyond. He always left a contented king in his wake, a king with renewed vigor to dream his dreams and plot his plots.

There had only been one King of Kings of Esmir—the human, Alisarrian. It was Manacia's deeply held belief the time was ripe for another such historic occurrence. He was determined this time a demon would hold that scepter. There was no question that demon should be him. Manacia's entire reign had been dedicated to that goal. Yet as the years passed he began to fear he wouldn't be ready in time. That somewhere in the human lands another Alisarrian may have been bred. A conqueror with an army at his back who'd soon come knocking on his palace doors.

One night, as he prowled his Necromancium wondering if the answer to his troubles was hidden in the blackest of magical arts, there came the tap tap tap of Lord Fari's cane, the ghostly herald of the Grand Wazier's approach. When he heard the tapping Manacia turned away from a large jar containing a human head floating in brine. As he looked up Fari came through the portal, the air shimmering like the surface of a vertical pool.

"What news, Lord Fari?" the king asked with exaggerated cheer. "Has our wayward bandit finally returned?"

Fari, whose mind was deeply engaged in another matter, jolted up, scaly jowls rolling in a wave of surprise. "What, Majesty?" he asked. Then, "Oh. You mean, *Lord Sarn*, Excellency. No, Majesty. There's still no word. I'm here on another matter, Excellency. One that requires your urgent attention."

But Manacia abruptly turned away, plunged into as foul a mood as he'd ever experienced. "I've reviewed it from every side, Fari," he said. "And I still don't see where I went wrong."

"Wrong, Majesty?" Fari said. "How can you think that? Give it more time. He'll appear any day now, loaded with spoils, bearing the maps you sought and demanding an enormous reward in that swaggering manner of his." Fari snorted. "As if he were the only *real* fiend in the land."

"It's been nearly a year, Fari," Manacia said.

"So long, Majesty? I hadn't realized..."

"I might as well face it," the king said. "I've wasted enough time and energy that could be put to a more positive use. Despite all our efforts, all our experiments and labors, the shield we built to protect Sarn from the curse wasn't good enough. And somewhere in the Forbidden Desert, perhaps just out of sight, his bones and his fiends' bones are bleaching in the sun."

Fari thought, quite correctly, that perhaps the shield hadn't failed at all. Some natural misfortune might have befallen the bandit chief. But he hadn't lived so long by telling his monarchs what he truly thought. So when he saw which path the king was taking he quickly stepped in that direction.

He made a mournful face. "I fear you are right, Excellency," he said. "The shield *has* failed. I'll find out at once who is responsible for this appalling state of affairs and have them suitably tortured and put to death."

The king bared his fangs in what was meant to be a kindly smile. "Spare them," he said. "I too share the blame. And you as well, my dear friend."

Fari gaped, revealing whiter and sharper teeth than he had a right to own at his advanced age. "Me, Majesty? What did I—" He wisely clipped that off. He rapped his bone cane and bowed. "My name should top that list of failures, Excellency," he said. "Tonight my wives will sing your praises when I tell them how you so generously spared this noble fool. Of course it was my fault! I take the whole blame, Majesty. A blame you should never dream of sharing."

Manacia waved a claw, silencing him. "You know who this is, Fari?" he asked, pointing at the human head floating in the jar.

The Grand Wazier stared at it. The human was a young adult. Possibly handsome once—by human standards. "No, Excellency, I don't know him."

"This is the first creature I used to test the shield." Manacia chuckled. "We tied a rope to his waist and used whips to drive him out into the Forbidden Desert. He'd taken not more than a dozen steps when he suddenly screamed, clutched his breast and fell to the ground. When we dragged him back he was dead, although there wasn't a mark on him to hint of the cause. He was a healthy creature straight from the royal slave pens. Clean. Well fed. I examined him myself. There was no reason for his death, other than the curse."

"I recall the incident, Majesty," Fari said, "but not the human."

"How could you?" Manacia said. "There were so many. Demons as well. They were the worst kind of felons, of course."

"Of course, Majesty."

Manacia stared at the head, remembering the four years of experiments. He'd labored hard, delved into every nook and cranny of the magical sciences, casting spell after spell to create a shield strong enough to defy the ancient curse. The curse had been created hundreds of years before by a Treaty Council composed of both demon *and* human wizards. Its purpose was to permanently sever all contact between the two species, permanently ending the years of bloody strife and war-ravaged harvests that followed the fall of Alisarrian's empire. It was believed by all the curse would be impossible for even the greatest sorcerer to render harmless.

Manacia believed otherwise. He was not only a powerful wizard—stronger than any other in the demon lands—but he had a mind for such puzzles and had attacked the curse full force with all the sorcerous resources at his command. Hundreds had died in those experiments. Body after body was dragged back at the end of a rope. But Manacia had hope because each time the victims crept a little further into the desert. The last group made it so far the king's archers had to fire arrows at them to force them to go deeper. Finally, all who were sent out returned unharmed. The shield appeared to work so well Manacia had to have the survivors killed so they couldn't use his spell to escape across the desert.

It was then he made his bargain with Sarn. The king had personally attended the bandit's departure. He'd praised the thief greatly, cast a special spell of blessings and watched Sarn and his friends thunder off into the desert for the human lands to seek

Kyrania—the passage through the "Valley of the Clouds" that the Oracle had spoken of. The passage that was the key to forging the two great human regions into a great kingdom.

Manacia's hopes had been high that day. He was already dreaming of the time when his armies could follow. He had visions of swift and easy victories over the humans. Once he had a dream of a grand court ceremony, with human ambassadors bowing before his throne, bearing treaties that declared him King of Kings. Ruler of all Esmir.

Manacia peered into the human's dead eyes. He was certain it was the human side of the sorcerous equation that had foiled him. A side he somehow had not been able to penetrate. It was for this reason, not sentimentality, that Manacia had the head of his first victim displayed in his Necromancium. It was here in this vaulted chamber of watery light that his collection of black arts and books and materials were kept. There were jars and vials of the most evil liquids and powders and unguents. There were scrolls detailing horrid practices and spells. There were strange objects and idols with shapes so menacing they'd haunt the dreams of the most callous and uncaring demon.

Manacia rapped his talons against the jar. The liquid stirred and the head bobbed about. "We'll begin again, my friend," he said to the skull. "And once more you shall have the honor of being first."

He turned to the Grand Wazier. "We'll start in the morning," he said. "Have my wizards meet me here at first light. I'll solve this riddle no matter how long it takes."

"That's the spirit, Majesty," Fari said. "Never admit defeat. Consider it an unpleasant setback, nothing more. I'll send word to the royal wizards at once!"

He turned as if to go, hesitated, then turned back, saying, "There's still that other matter, Excellency. The matter that forced me to come here and disturb your thinking."

The king's mood had brightened now that he'd formed a course of action. He said, "Yes, yes. I'd almost forgotten. What is it?"

"Many months ago, Majesty," Fari said, "not long after Sarn and his friends left for the human lands, a strange event occurred which has only just come to my attention. A celestial disturbance, Majesty, that went unnoticed by our stargazers because Zanzair was heavily overcast that night. But a shepherd, far to the north where the skies were clear, reported seeing an immense shower of fiery particles. Other reports have trickled in since then, confirming the shepherd's sighting. As near as we can determine the display was in the human lands, over the Gods' Divide."

Manacia shrugged. "What of it?" he said. "There's nothing unusual about fiery particles falling out of the sky. Rarely do such occurrences have anything to do with our affairs. If it were a comet perhaps there'd be cause for concern. Or deeper study."

"Quite true, Majesty," Fari said. "And if that were all there was to it I would not be here troubling you with news of such a minor event."

The king rapped his claws against the glass jar, impatient. Fari hurried on. "Once the event was dated with some certainty," he said, "your wizards recalled other signs that occurred at, or near, the same time. The water from our wells suddenly tasted foul and bitter, a condition that lasted for some weeks."

Manacia nodded, remembering that trouble.

"The day after the sighting," Fari continued, "it was noticed that the liquid in the water clocks turned in the opposite direction. And one of the temple acolytes claimed when he rose that morning his reflection in the mirror was backwards, or, that is to say, he looked just like one demon sees another, left claw on the true left, right to right. Neither anomaly lasted long, Majesty, but there *was* concern at the time. Since then it has been observed that the ground has settled dangerously under some of our older buildings, causing them to sag. Moreover, bees have been swarming out of season, birds have appeared of a kind never seen before. And there has been an unusual number of birth oddities, two-headed swine, limbless dogs, fish with no eyes."

"This is indeed disturbing news, Fari," the king said. "You were right to report it to me. Does anyone know what these things mean? Could it have anything to do with our attempt to defy the curse?"

Fari jolted in surprise. He thought a moment, tapping his bone cane against the floor. Then he said, "I don't know, Excellency. It's a thought that hadn't occurred to me."

"But it *is* possible," the king said.

"Yes, Majesty. I suppose it is."

"What would you advise?" the king asked.

Fari saw the danger at once and sadly shook his head. "I'm ashamed to admit, Excellency," Fari said, "that I am at loss. Not enough is known to form an opinion."

"We must find out," the king said. "It might be dangerous to begin my experiments until we do."

Fari nodded. "I can see how that could be so, Majesty," he said. "This is a most unfortunate situation. Your Excellency's plans for invading the human lands will most certainly suffer a delay."

"It can't be helped, Fari," the king said. "Curses have a way of spreading beyond their original intent. There are so many links, some not even known to the original spell casters, that it's impossible to account for all the effects a curse might trigger. That's why I first sent bandits instead of our own soldiers across the Forbidden Desert.

"As much as it grieves me to say this, Fari, it would be wise for us to proceed cautiously. But I want you to spare no expense. I want all my stargazers working on this. All my dreamcatchers. And I want daily sacrifices to the gods at the main temple, with weekly ones for the lesser houses of worship."

"Yes, Excellency," Fari said, bobbing his head and rapping his cane. "Without delay." He hurried off, relieved that he'd once again shifted all possible blame and responsibility onto the backs of others, while still being assured of winning praise and honors for any successes.

For a change, however, he did not leave a happy king in his wake. Manacia was deeply troubled as he turned back to examine the head. The old fear of a rival oozed up to torment him. A shiver ran up his long bony spine.

Manacia suddenly wondered if even now his enemy was thinking of him.

If so, did that enemy have a human face?

And if he did, was it possible he had already discovered the way through the Gods' Divide.

Had he found Kyrania?

***

Not long after Manacia's eve of disappointment, Safar and Iraj said farewell. They made a ceremony of it, returning to Alisarrian's Cave and the snowy pass where they'd battled the demons. Storms had further buried the evidence of the carnage and as they pushed across the snows on rough wooden skis there was nothing to hint of the events that had occurred there.

"Maybe it was just a dream," Safar said. "Maybe it never happened at all and any moment now we'll wake up to an ordinary day in ordinary two ordinary lives."

Iraj barked laughter. "I've never been ordinary, Safar," he said. "And, admit it or not, neither have you. You'd save yourself a lot of bother if you just accepted it." He grinned. "If you dreamed Astarias," he said, "then you have the greatest imagination of any man in Esmir—a courtesan, young, beautiful, virginal and trained in all the arts to please a man. That was no dream, my friend. To make her one would be the greatest sin any god could imagine. When you're an old man it'll be memories of women like Astarias that will make your life seem well spent."

Safar made a sour face. "I'd just as soon forget about it," he said. "I'm afraid I embarrassed myself with Astarias."

Iraj clapped him on the back. "Don't be ridiculous," he said. "So you fell in love with a courtesan. You're not the first man. Nor will you be the last. So you professed undying love. So you promised her the moon and the stars and all the heavens contain, if only she'd remain in your arms. I said that to both of my twins. Separately. And together."

"You didn't mean it," Safar said. "I did, I'm ashamed to say."

"Of course I meant it," Iraj replied. "At the time, anyway. Especially when I had one curled up in my left arm, the other my right."

"That was lust talking," Safar said.

Iraj snickered, then wrapped his arms around himself in a comic embrace. "And yours was undying Love, right? A Love that *could not* be denied. Come, my friend!"

"She laughed at me," Safar confessed, blushing.

"What of it?" Iraj answered. "You rode her all night and half the next morning. And then, in a moment of weakness, you asked her to be your wife. She tells you, charmingly, I imagine, and with a few tricks to arouse you some more, that she has no intention of making bread and babies for a village boy the rest of her life. She's a courtesan with as much beauty as ambition. You persist. Climbing between those lovely thighs once again, I expect." Another blush from Safar told Iraj he'd guessed right. "And then she laughed. You should be the one laughing. You got what you wanted. *I* saw to that. And now you're done with her and she's the loser for spurning you. You are Safar Timura! A man meant for great things. The very sort of man she prays every day is in her future."

"I can't look at things as coldly as you," Safar said.

"Don't then," Iraj said, shrugging. "But I suspect you'll come around to my view soon enough. Bed your women when you can, whenever you can. A courtesan's scornful laugh—*after* the deed is done—is no price at all. The truth is the next man who rides Astarias will be old and fat and it'll be your memory she'll cleave to when she's forced to pretend her fat old master is a handsome god."

Iraj's callous words of comfort, although spoken in friendship, did little to soothe Safar's wounded spirit. So he was grateful when Iraj gave a sudden shout of discovery.

"Look at this!" he cried, dropping to his knees and digging in the snow.

Safar crowded close to see. A demon's face emerged beneath Iraj's scraping fingers. The corpse's features were a pale, bluish green. Dagger-size fangs hooked out from the grimacing mouth. Although Safar and Iraj had no way of knowing it, the demon was Giff and the look on his face was as surprised in death as it had been when Iraj had drawn his blade across his throat. Safar turned away.

"This is the demon I killed!" Iraj said. "I can tell from the wounds." With a finger he traced the gaping red gash beneath Giff's pointed chin.

"Cover him up," Safar urged.

"I will," Iraj said, but first he unsheathed his knife.

Safar glanced over and was horrified when he saw his friend digging out the fangs with the blade point. "What are you doing?"

"Taking his teeth," Iraj said. "I want to make a necklace of them."

Safar, who had never become used to his friend's plains' savage ways, kept his eyes averted. "I thought we'd agreed to keep the whole thing a secret," he said. "So people don't become unnecessarily alarmed."

Iraj snorted. "I'll keep my promise to Coralean," he said. "But in my own way."

He held up the bloody fangs and Safar couldn't help but look. "I'll make a chain of these to wear around my neck when I greet my enemies. They'll won't know what they are, exactly. But they'll be dripping green slime from their arses wondering what kind of a beast it was I killed."

Despite his revulsion, Safar understood. Iraj's kinsman had just arrived in Kyrania to inform the young prince it was safe to return home. Apparently Iraj's turncoat uncle—Lord Fulain—had fallen ill. His soldiers had become dispirited and his ally, Koralia Kan, had been forced to sue for peace. As part of that peace Iraj was permitted to return and take his place as hereditary leader of the clan. There were provisos, of course, intended to keep him weak—leader in name only. But Iraj was already planning how to get around them.

Iraj put the teeth in a leather pouch and tucked it into his belt. Then he covered up Giff's corpse, smoothing the snow until all looked as before.

"I wish I could convince you to stay in Kyrania," Safar said. "This could all be a lie to entice you out of the mountains."

"At least part of it *is* a lie," Iraj said, rising to his feet and brushing snow from his knees. "But they'll pretend otherwise for awhile. When Fulain becomes well the blood feud will start again. But I intend to be ready when that happens." He touched the leather pouch containing the demon fangs. "I'm young, they'll claim. Untested in battle. These teeth will say otherwise. I'll keep where I got them a mystery, which will only add to their power."

Safar, wanting to avoid further discussion of the matter, said, "I'm getting cold. Let's go back to the cave."

A half hour later they were crouched in the cavern, warming their hands over a small fire. The painting of Alisarrian hung over them, glowing eerily.

"You haven't mentioned your own plans," Iraj said, digging

out some dried goat's flesh. "What will you do after I leave? I still can't imagine you being content as Safar Timura the potter."

"I don't know why," Safar said. "It's easy enough for me to envision."

"You know as well as I do," Iraj said, "that you're dodging the truth. You're a wizard, Safar. The teeth I collected are nothing compared to what you have a right to. How can you possibly refuse Coralean's gift of an education at the finest university in Esmir?"

Safar sighed. "I wish I could," he said, "but I don't think my family is going to let me."

"Or Gubadan," Iraj pointed out.

Safar nodded. "He's worse than they are," he said. "He claims I'll be shaming all Kyrania if I refuse the chance. That there's much good I'll be able to do when I return home with all that learning."

"He's right about the first," Iraj said. "It *would* shame your people. In the whole history of Kyrania it's unlikely any of its sons had such an opportunity. But Gubadan's wrong about the second part. You won't return, Safar. I'm no Dreamcatcher like you, but I know once you leave Kyrania you'll never return. Because you'll be with me, remember?"

"That was a false vision," Safar said.

"Are you sure?" Iraj asked, smiling.

"Absolutely," Safar answered. "You're the ambitious one. Not me."

"What of your other vision?" Iraj said. "The dancing people and the volcano? Do you think that's wrong as well?"

Safar hesitated, then, "No, I don't. And that's the main reason I'll probably end up giving in to my family and Gubadan. The only place I can find out what the vision meant is Walaria."

"Whatever your reason, Safar," Iraj said. "I beg you to make up your mind as soon as possible. Learn as much as you can. As fast as you can. For I promise that someday, when you least expect it, I'll show up to plead with you to join me."

"And I'll refuse," Safar said. "You are my friend. But I'll still say no."

"Why don't we test it?" Iraj asked. He hauled out the leather pouch and shook Giff's bloody teeth into a palm. Then, in a mock intonation, he said, "Cast these bones, O Master Wizard, and pray tell us what the future holds."

"Don't be silly," Safar said. "I'm no bone caster."

"Then there's no reason to be afraid," Iraj said. "Here, I'll even clean them up for you."

He rubbed some of the blood off on the leather pouch and held them out. Safar didn't move, so Iraj grabbed his right hand, pulled it forward and dropped the four fangs into Safar's outstretched palm. Safar didn't resist, automatically closing his fist over them.

"What do we do now?" Iraj said. "Make some kind of chant and toss them, I suppose?"

"I don't want to do this," Safar said.

"I'll tell you what," Iraj said, "to make it easier, I'll chant and you toss. Okay?"

Without waiting for an answer Iraj drew a breath and then intoned:

*"Bones, bones, demon's though you be,*
*Tell us what the future holds,*
*What roads shall we see?"*

As Iraj chanted the demon's teeth suddenly grew warm in Safar's hand. Instinctively he loosened his hand and shook the fangs like dice.

"Chanting was never one of my best subjects," Iraj said. He laughed. "But if I can chance making a complete fool of myself, so can..." and his voice trailed off as he saw Safar rattle the bones, blue eyes glowing in concentration.

Safar cast them on the cave floor and instead of a dull clatter, the sound was like the ring of steel against steel.

Red smoke hissed up, rising like a snake and the two lads drew back in alarm. The smoke was thick, smelling of old blood, and it swirled in front of them like a miniature desert dervish—a slender funnel at the bottom, billowing into a fist-size head on top. Then a mouth seemed to form, curving into a seductive smile.

The lips parted and they heard a woman speak—*"Two will take the road that two traveled before. Brothers of the spirit, but not the womb.*

*Separate in body and mind, but twins in destiny. But beware what you seek, O brothers. Beware the path you choose. For this tale cannot end until you reach the Land of Fires."*

The smoke suddenly vanished, leaving the two young men gaping at the four small gray piles of ash where the demon fangs had been. It was as if they'd been consumed by a hot flame.

Iraj recovered first. "You see?" he chortled. "We heard it from the mouth of the Oracle herself." He threw an arm around Safar's shoulders. "'Brothers of the spirit, but not the womb,'" he quoted. "What a pair we shall make! The King of Kings and his Grand Wazier!"

"That's not exactly what the Oracle said," Safar replied. "Hells, whoever she was, we don't even know if she was speaking about us."

Iraj made a rude noise. "I don't see anyone else here in this cave with us," he said. "Who else could she mean?"

"There was also a warning," Safar said. "Don't forget the warning."

"Sure, sure," Iraj said, impatient. "I heard. And I'm forewarned. It's settled then. I'll return home with my uncle and start building my forces. And you'll go to Walaria and learn as much as you can until it's time for us to be rejoined."

"I'm not convinced that was what the Oracle was predicting," Safar said.

"Of course she was," Iraj replied. "But it doesn't matter what either of us think. We'll find out for ourselves in the days to come. Just think of me sometimes. When you're in Walaria up to your elbows in dusty books and scrolls, think of me riding free across the southern plains, an army of horsemen at my back carrying my standard. It will be the banner of Alisarrian that I fly as I charge from victory to victory."

He tapped Safar's chest. "And it will be the banner of Alisarrian you will be carrying in your heart," he said. "We'll make a better world before we're done, Safar. A better Esmir for all."

It was then that Safar finally made up his mind. He'd leave his beloved Kyrania and go to Walaria. He'd enter the university at the Grand Temple, pore over every tome, soaking up all the knowledge he could hold.

The decision had nothing to do with Iraj's impassioned speech. Safar was remembering the Oracle's final words about the land of fires. Hadin was known as The Land of Fires! Hadin, where the handsome people of his vision danced and died and a mighty volcano raged, spewing flames and poisonous clouds into a darkening sky.

"You *have* decided to go, haven't you?" he heard Iraj say.

Safar looked up and saw his friend's eyes ablaze with joy as he read Safar's intentions on his face. "Yes," he answered. "I've decided."

"Then let us say farewell now, brother mine," Iraj said. "A great dream awaits us. The sooner we get started, the sooner that dream will come true."

And so the two young men embraced and swore eternal brotherhood and friendship.

Iraj took one road. Safar another. But neither doubted—for entirely different reasons—the roads would someday converge.

And that they'd meet again.

# Part Two
# Walaria

# 8
# THE THIEF OF WALARIA

Nerisa watched the executioner sharpen his blade. It was long and broad and curving and he stroked the edge with such tenderness one might have thought his sword was a lover.

And maybe it was, Nerisa thought. She'd heard of stranger things.

The executioner was a big man, naked torso swelling out of baggy silk pantaloons of the purest white. He had thick arms, a neck squat and strong as an oak stump. His features were hidden by a white silk hood with two holes for his dark gloomy eyes to contemplate his victims' sins. Masked or not, everyone knew who he was—Tulaz, the most famous executioner in all Walaria. Five thousand hands had been severed by his legendary sword. One thousand heads separated from their shoulders. And he'd never needed more than one cut to accomplish his task.

There were seven condemned to test his record that morning. The plaza, set just inside the main gate, was packed with gawkers, hawkers, purse snatchers and pimps. Gamblers were betting heavily on the outcome for Tulaz had never attempted so many heads before. The odds were in his favor for the first six—a mean lot who hadn't learned their lesson from previous mutilations. The seventh, however, was a woman charged with adultery. She was said to be beautiful and there were many among the crowd who wondered if Tulaz might falter when confronted with such a tender and record-breaking neck.

Nerisa had an excellent vantage point to view the proceedings. She was crouched atop a high freight wagon just returning from market and had a clear view of the six felons chained to the dungeon cart. But the adulteress was hidden by a tent pitched on the cart. It wasn't out of humanity her jailers had provided such privacy. They knew a featured attraction when they saw one and were among the heaviest bettors. They were also, Nerisa noted, selling quick glimpses of the woman to all who'd grease their palms.

Nerisa didn't have slightest interest in the executions. In her twelve summers of life she'd witnessed many such things. For as long as she could remember she'd been a child of the streets. She'd awakened in alleys next to fresh corpses—corpses not so cleanly slain as Tulaz was wont to do. There were worse things, she'd learned, than being executed. She'd spent her whole young life dodging those things with a skill matched by few young denizens of Walaria. Her only fear of Tulaz was she might someday make an error that would cost her a hand—the traditional penalty a thief paid for a first offense. Nerisa was a thief intent on keeping all her parts.

It was professional purpose, not entertainment, that had drawn her to the plaza; although she'd experienced an added thrill when she realized she'd be breaking the law under the executioner's nose. She peeped out of her hiding place to check on the stall keeper - her intended victim. She buried a giggle as she watched him step up on a box so he could see over the crowd. He was a fat old turd, she thought. The crate would never hold such a skin load of grease.

True to her estimate the crate collapsed, sending the stallkeep sprawling. Nerisa hugged herself to keep from laughing. The joke was especially delicious because the crowd was so intent on the executions that she was the only one to see his humiliation. There was nothing that Nerisa—by circumstance and nature a solitary person—enjoyed more than a private joke. The merchant grumbled up, found a heavy barrel and rolled it over to the edge of his stall. He leaned on the trays bearing his wares and clambered gingerly onto the barrel. It held and he looked around, a yellow-toothed smile of victory dissolving when he realized no one was watching. With a belch, he turned to see Tulaz prepare for his legendary work.

Nerisa examined the trays set up under the tented stall. They were overflowing with all manner of poor quality merchandise; old lamp parts, broken toys, tawdry jewelry, spoiled cosmetics, healing powders and love potions of doubtful quality. The wares were typical of the stalls lining the old gray stone city walls inside the gates. Amid all that trash was an object that had great value to Nerisa. She'd spotted it while foraging the day before. But when she'd tried to examine the object closer the stallkeep had leapt from his wide chair and rushed her, driving her away with a thick stick, shouting, "Begone boy!"

Nerisa, who was tall for a girl and slender, was frequently mistaken for a boy. It was a mistake she'd made a habit of not correcting. She'd even adopted a male urchin's raggedy costume of breeches and baggy shirt. Until recently she'd worried that the bumps and curves of womanhood would soon appear, making it more difficult than ever to avoid the evil-eyed men who preyed on young women with no home but the streets. If they ever did catch her there was no one to care about her fate, except the old bookseller who let her sleep in his shop. It was there she'd met the handsome youth who'd turned her thinking upside down. Now she worried that she wouldn't grow up soon enough.

A vision of the young man who'd awakened this interest floated into her mind and her heart knocked hard against her ribs. She pushed the image away. Don't be such a stupid cow, Nerisa thought. Keep your mind on that fat dog turd of a stallkeep. He'll get you if he can.

The crowd roared and Nerisa swiveled to see the jailers unchain the first felon and lead him to Tulaz's stone platform. Indentations in the stone marked the place where many a poor soul had been forced to kneel on hands and knees and the stone surface was stained black from all the centuries of spilled blood. The sudden realization that the gory platform would be the condemned's last view of the world sent a shiver down Nerisa's spine.

The crowd laughed when the first felon mounted the platform, heavy chains rattling. The man was a thief, a poor thief at that—he was already missing his ears and nose, as well as both his hands.

"Not much left to aim for, Tulaz," some wag shouted above the din. "Already cut most of him off!"

The crowd roared laughter.

"What'd he use to steal with?" someone else cried. "His toes?"

Immediately an crone piped up, "Not his toes, you blind shit. His prick! Can't you see it peepin' out at us?"

Nerisa couldn't help but look. Sure enough she saw a long, very male part of the thief, dangling from his dungeon-rotted costume. The thief was a good natured fool and went along with the game. To the immense pleasure of the crowd he held up the two stumpy things that were arms and jerked his hips back and forth, humping the air. The crowd howled delight and rained coins onto the platform to bribe Tulaz to make the thief's agony short for rewarding them with such fine entertainment. Tulaz saw the copper mount up and dispensed with his usual ceremony, which consisted of ominous cuts in the air and much stance and grip shifting.

"Get him down," he shouted to the jailers.

Instantly the thief's guards threw him to the ground and jumped out of the way. Tulaz took one mighty pace forward and swung just as the thief's head bobbed up.

It was so swift there wasn't a cry or a gasped breath. Just a snick of resistance then blood fountained from a suddenly empty neck. The thief's head, broken-toothed grin still fixed to his face, sailed into the crowd where pigs, dogs and children quarreled over it.

"Oh, well done, Tulaz! Well done!" Nerisa heard the stallkeep cry. He'd obviously had a wager on the first cut of the day.

Nerisa thought she saw her chance when they led out the second victim. The stallkeep was highly interested, raising himself on his toes to get a better look. Nerisa started to slip off the wagon. All she needed was a single moment of inattention and she'd snatch her prize and disappear into the crowd before anyone was the wiser. A barrel shifted under her and she had to grab to steady herself. Although there was little noise, the stallkeep sensed something was amiss and jolted around. Nerisa swore and ducked back into her hiding place just in time.

The girl settled down to wait. She'd have to be patient to get the better of this sow's breath of a stallkeep. Nerisa prided herself on patience and stubborn intent. Put a goal in her head and she'd achieve it no matter how long it took. The best time, she thought, would be when they brought the adulteress out. The jailers most certainly had been paid to strip the woman before she was killed. The stallkeep, along with the rest of the viewers, would be so fixed on all that doomed nakedness he'd never notice Nerisa's bit of business.

As she crouched there waiting for the moment to come, Nerisa thought of the poor woman waiting in the tent. The terror she had to be feeling made Nerisa's heart pang in empathy. What a price to pay for something so natural as being in your lover's arms. The unfairness of it clawed at her. For a moment it was painful to breathe.

Stop it, Nerisa, she commanded herself, fighting for control. It's not like you haven't seen it before.

Safar sat in a small outdoor cafe, shaded by an ancient broad-leaf fig tree, counting coins piled in a sticky puddle of wine. A pesky wasp made him lose count and he had to tot it all up again. A little drunk, he rubbed bleary eyes and decided that he had enough for another jug of the *Foolsmire's* best. Which is to say it was the worst and therefore cheapest wine in all Walaria.

It was late afternoon and the summer heat lay thick over the city, stifling thought and movement. The streets were empty, the homes and shops shuttered for the hours between the midday meal and evening call to prayer. It was so quiet that in the distant stockpens the bawl of a young camel, lonely for its mother, echoed across the city. The people of Walaria dozed fitfully in shuttered darkness, gathering their energies to face the day anew. It was a time for sleep, for lovers' trysts. A time for self reflection.

Safar rapped politely on the rough wood of the table. "Katal," he cried. "My strength is fading. Fetch me another jug from the well, if you please."

There was a muttering from the shadowy depths of the book-shop abutting the cafe and in a moment an old man emerged, carelessly dressed in worn scholar's robes. It was Katal, proprietor of the *Foolsmire*, an open air cafe and bookshop tucked into the end of a long dead-end alley in the Students' Quarter. Katal had a book in his hand, index finger pushed between the pages to keep his place.

"You should be resting, Safar," he said, "or tending to your studies. You know as well as I that the second level acolyte exams are less than a week away."

Safar groaned. "Don't spoil a perfectly good drunk, Katal. I've invested a week's room and board to reach my present condition of amiable insobriety. It's drink I need, sir. So dig into your holy well for the precious stuff, my dear purveyor of bliss. And dig deep. Find me as cold a jug as these coins will buy."

Katal clucked disapproval, but he set his book on the table and hobbled to the old stone well. A dozen ropes were strung around the rim, tied to heavy eyebolts imbedded in the stone and disappearing into the cool black depths. He hauled on one of the ropes until a large bucket appeared. It was full of jugs made of red clay, all the width of a broad palm and standing a uniform eight inches high. Katal took one out and fetched it to Safar.

The young man pushed coins forward, but Katal shook his head, pushing them back. "I'll buy this one," he said. "My price for you today is talk, not copper. A *Foolsmire* special, if you will."

"Done," Safar said. "I'll listen to your advice hour after hour, my friend, if you'll keep my cup full."

He sloshed wine into a wide, cracked tumbler. He stoppered the jug then held it up, studying it. "Three years ago," he said, "I helped my father make jugs like these. They were much better, of course. Glazed and decorated for a fine table. Not turned out in factories by the scores."

Katal eased his old body into the bench seat across from Safar. "I could never afford such a luxury," he said. "If I had bucketsful of Timura jugs in my well I'd pour out the wine and sell the jugs. Think of all the books I could buy with the price I'd get!"

"I'll tell you a secret, Katal," Safar said. "If you had Timura jugs you could make your own wine, or brandy or beer, if you prefer. My father makes a special blessing over each jug he produces. All you need then is some water, the proper makings for whatever brew it is you desire and you'll have an endless supply of your favorite drink."

"More pottery magic!" Katal scoffed. "And this time water into wine. No wonder your teachers despair."

"Actually," Safar said, "there's no magic to it at all. My father would dispute that. But it's true. Part of the spell, you see, is that we pour spirits from an old tried and true brewing bowl into the new jug. We shake it up and pour it back. And the little animals left in the clay will produce spirits until the end of time—as long you don't wash the jug."

"Little animals?" Katal said, bushy gray eyebrows beetling in disbelief.

Safar nodded. "Too small for the eye to see."

Katal snorted. "How do you know that?"

"What else could it be?" Safar said. "As an experiment I've made several such jugs. Some I chanted the spell over, but failed to use the brewing bowl liquid. Others got the liquid, but not the chant. The latter produced a good wine. The former nothing but a watery mess."

"That still doesn't explain the small spirit making animals," Katal pointed out. "Did you see them?"

"I told you," Safar answered, "they're too small for the unaided eye to behold. I theorized their existence. What other explanation could there be?"

Katal snorted. "Be damned to theory," he said. "When will you learn that supposing doesn't make it so."

Safar laughed and drained off his cup. "Then you don't know anything about magic, Katal," he said, wiping his chin. "Supposing is what sorcery is all about." He belched and refilled his cup. "But that answer is a cheat. I admit it. It's scientific observation you were speaking of. And you were right to chastise me. I've never seen the little animals. But I suspect their presence. And if someone gave me money I could grind a glass lens so powerful I might be able to see them and prove their existence."

"Who would give you money for such a thing?" Katal said. "And even if your proved your point, who would care?"

Safar was suddenly serious. He jabbed a finger into his chest. "I would," he said. "And so should everyone else. If we are ignorant of the smallest things, how can we know the larger world? How can we guide our fate?"

"We've had this argument before," Katal said. "I say the fate of mortals is the business of the gods."

"Bah!" was Safar's retort. "The gods have no business but their own. Our troubles are no concern of theirs."

Katal glanced about nervously and saw no one in earshot, except his grandson, Zeman, who'd come out while they were talking and was brushing fig leaves off the tables on the other side of the patio.

"Be careful what you say, my young friend," Katal warned. "You never know when one of the king's spies will be about. In Walaria the penalty for heresy is most unpleasant."

Safar ducked his head, chastened. "I know, I know," he said. "And I'm sorry to be so outspoken in your presence. I don't want to get you in trouble because of my views. Sometimes it's difficult to remember that I must guard my tongue here. In Kyrania a man of twenty may speak his mind about any subject he chooses."

Katal leaned close, a fond smile peeping out from his untidy beard. "Speak to me all you like, Safar," he said. "But discreetly, sir. Discreetly. And in well modulated tones."

The old man had been a kindly uncle to Safar since he'd arrived in Walaria some two years before. In that spirit Katal dipped into his robe and fished out a small cup. He cleaned it with a sleeve, then filled it with wine.

He drank, then said, "Tell me what this is all about, Safar. If your family were here they'd be worried. So let me worry for them. I'll tell you what your own father would say. Which is that you've been drinking heavily for nearly a month. Your studies must be suffering as much as your finances. You've had no money for food, much less books. I'm not complaining, but I've been feeding you for free. I'd even be willing to forgo my usual rental fee for any books you required, if only I thought you'd make some use of them. There's an exam coming up. The most important in your career as a student. All the other second level candidates, except the sons of the rich whose success is assured by the fact of their wealth, are studying hard. They don't want to bring shame to their family."

"What's the use?" Safar said. "No matter how well I do Umurhan will fail me anyway."

Katal's eyebrows shot up. "How can that be?" he said. "You're the best student Umurhan's had in years." Umurhan was Walaria's Chief Sorcerer. As such he supervised the temple and attached university where scholars, priests, healers and wizards were trained. He answered to no one but King Didima, ruler of the city and its environs.

"He's going to fail me just the same," Safar said.

"There must be some reason," Katal said. "What did you do to earn his wrath?"

Safar made a sour face. "He caught me in his library," he said, "making notes on a forbidden book."

Katal was aghast. "How could you take such a chance?"

Safar hung his head. "I thought it was safe," he said. "I've slipped into his study before without being caught. I knew the risk I was taking. But I'm on the trail of something important, dammit! And I thought one more trip might turn up what I needed. I slipped in well before first light. Everyone knows old Umurhan likes his sleep, so there shouldn't have been any danger. But this time I'd barely entered the room and lit a candle when he suddenly appeared from the shadows. As if he'd been waiting there for me."

"Did someone alert him?" Katal asked.

"I don't see how they could," Safar said. "It was a last minute decision. No one knew. My only guess is I left some clue on my last visit. And he's been waiting all this time to pounce."

"You were fortunate he didn't expel you at once," Katal said. "Or, worse, report you to Kalasariz as a dangerous heretic." Lord Kalasariz was Didima's chief spy. There were so many in his employ the joke was that in Walaria even the watchers were watched.

"Umurhan said the same thing," Safar replied. "He said he could have me thrown into one of Kalasariz' cells where I could rot for all eternity for all he cared. And the only reason he didn't call one of Kalasariz' minions right then was because I was such a good student."

"You see?" Katal said. "There *is* hope. You've completed four years of work in two. No one else your age has ever qualified to take the second level acolyte exams in so short a time." He indicated the wine jug. "Now you're destroying the chance he's giving you to make amends."

Safar grimaced, remembering Umurhan's wrath. "I don't think that's possible," he said. "The only reason I wasn't thrown out immediately is because my sponsor is Lord Muzine, the richest merchant in the city." Muzine was Coralean's friend, the man he'd said he'd call on to help get Safar admitted to the university. "Umurhan doesn't want a scandal and he certainly doesn't want to offend Muzine. He'll fail me, then report the sad news to Muzine. It's the cleanest way to be rid of me."

"Well I for one won't be sorry," came a voice. The two turned and saw that Zeman had worked his way across the patio and was now cleaning the table next to them. Zeman was about Safar's age and height. But he was so thin he was nearly skeletal. His complexion was bad, his face long and horse-like, with wall eyes and overly large teeth.

"It's leeches like you who keep my grandfather poor," Zeman said. "You all eat and drink on credit, or for nothing at all. You rent books and scrolls and keep them as long you like without paying for the extra time. And it isn't only the students. What of that bitch Nerisa he's taken under his wing? A thief, of all things. No, I fear my grandfather is too charitable for his own good. And for mine. I go without as well because of your sort."

He indicted his costume—tight brown leggings, green thigh-length smock, slippers with curled toes—a cheap imitation of what the fashionable lads wore. "I'm forced to clothe myself in the alley markets. It's an insult to a young man of my class and prospects."

Katal was angry. "Don't speak to my friend like that! Safar only receives what I beg him to take. He is a friend and he possesses one of the finest young minds I've met in many a day."

Safar intervened. "He's right, Katal. You are too generous. I'll wager you haven't raised the prices since you opened the *Foolsmire* forty years ago. That's why we all come here. You have a right to a decent profit, my friend. And at your age you deserve to live a life of ease."

Zeman pushed in. "I'll thank you to let me defend myself to my own grandfather," he said to Safar. "As if I need defending. I'm only being sensible, not mean."

"Both of you speak with the arrogance of youth," Katal said. "Neither has the faintest notion of why I live my life as I do."

He pointed at the faded sign hanging from a rusty iron post over the door of bookshop. "The name speaks it for all to see—'*Foolsmire.*' I was a young man when I hung that sign. I planted that tree at the same time. It was just a stick with a few leaves then. Now it shades us with its mighty boughs." His old eyes gleamed in memory. "I was a bright young fellow," he said. "Although probably not as bright as I thought. Still, I had a mind agile enough to compete at the university. But I had no money or influence to gain entrance. Yet I loved books and knowledge above all else. And so I sought a fool's paradise and became a seller of books. I wanted the company of the most intelligent students to discuss the ideas the books contained. I created a place to attract such people, offering my wares at the lowest prices possible. You see before you a poor man, a foolish man, but a happy man. For I have achieved my dreams at the *Foolsmire.*"

Safar laughed and nodded in understanding. Zeman frowned, more unhappy than before. "What of me, Grandfather?" he protested. "I didn't ask for this life. I didn't ask for the plague that killed my parents. My mother—your daughter—was comely enough to attract a man with prospects for a husband. But he died before he could prosper and see that I had a chance to prosper as well."

"I gave you a home," Katal said. "What more could I do? Your grandmother died in the same plague, so I lost my whole family, except for you."

"I know that, Grandfather," Zeman said. "And I appreciate the sacrifices you've made. I'm only asking that you try a little harder. Don't give so much away. And when I inherit this place someday you can go to your grave in peace, knowing I've been cared for." Zeman glanced about, noting the shabbiness of his inheritance. "It *does* have a good location, after all. Right in the heart of the student quarter. It should fetch me a decent sum."

Safar had to fight his temper. In Kyrania it was unheard of for a lad to speak so coldly and rudely to his grandfather. But to leave Zeman's comments completely unanswered would bedevil his dreams.

"If it were me," he said, "I could never sell all these books. To misquote the poet—What could you possibly buy that was half so precious as what you sell."

"A brothel, for one," Zeman said. "With a well-planned gaming parlor attached." He gave the table an angry swipe and stalked off.

"You shouldn't let him get away with that," Safar said, hotly. "He shows no respect."

"Never mind him," Katal said. "Zeman is what he is. There's

nothing to be done about it. It's Safar Timura I'm worried about just now."

"There's nothing to be done about that either," Safar said.

"What possessed you to take such a chance with Umurhan?" Katal asked, giving his beard a tug of frustration.

Safar lowered his eyes. "You know," he said.

Katal's eyes narrowed. "Hadin, again?"

"Yes."

"Why are you so obsessed with a place on the other side of the world?" Katal said. "A place we're not even certain exists. 'The Land of the Fires,' it's called. For all we know it might really be 'The Frozen Lands.' Or 'The Lands of the Swamps.'"

"I know what I saw in the vision," Safar said. "And I know deep in my bones it's vital that someone find out what happened."

"I gather you think the trail leads into Umurhan's private library," Katal said, dryly. "Among his forbidden books."

Safar nodded, then leaned closer. "I've run across a name," he said, low. He gestured in the direction of the book shop. "It's repeated many times in some of your oldest scrolls. Scholars refer to an ancient they call Lord Asper. A great magician and philosopher. He measured the world and also the distance from Esmir to the moon. He made many predictions that came true, including the rise of Alisarrian and the collapse of his empire."

Katal looked interested. "I've never heard of such a man," he said.

"I don't think Asper was a man," Safar answered.

"What else could he be?"

"A demon," Safar answered.

Katal was so startled he nearly came to his feet. "A demon?" he cried. "What madness is this? The demons have nothing to teach us but evil! I don't care how wise this Asper was, he was most certainly wicked. All demons are. That's why there's a barrier between our species. The curse of the Forbidden Desert."

"Oh, *that*," Safar said. "It's nothing."

"How can you call the greatest spell ever cast in history nothing?" Katal said, aghast. "The finest minds—and, yes, some were demon minds—composed that spell. It's unbreakable."

Safar shrugged. "Actually, I suspect it can be broken quite

easily," he said. "I really wasn't looking for the details, but I do know the curse is based on Asper's work. He had many enemies, many rivals, and to protect his most powerful magic it's said he created a spell of complexity. It made the most simple bit of sorcery appear so tangled and difficult that it would confound even the greatest wizard. If I wanted to break the curse I'd attack the spell of complexity, not the curse itself. I don't think that would take much effort to solve. I'm sure I'd find the key if I could lay my hands on one of his books. Which is exactly what I was looking for when Umurhan surprised me."

"Would you really do such a thing, Safar?" Katal asked, shocked. "Would you really try to lift the curse?"

"Of course not," Safar said, to Katal's vast relief. "What purpose would that serve, except to endanger us all? I have no greater opinion of demons than you."

As he'd promised Coralean, Safar had never mentioned his own experience with demons to anyone, even Katal. So he didn't add he had even more reason to fear the creatures than the old book seller could imagine. And it had occurred to him more than once that despite Coralean's rationalizations, the demon raiders might have found a way to cross the Forbidden Desert. If so, it was his frequent prayer the knowledge had died with them in the avalanche.

He said nothing of this to Katal. Instead, he said, "I'm only interested in what Asper had to say about Hadin. I think it goes to the origins of our world. And all of us. Humans and demons alike."

"This is all very intriguing, Safar," Katal said. "But merely for intellectual discussion among, I might add, the most select few. For it's dangerous talk. Please, for your sake and your family's sake, let it go. Forget Asper. Forget Hadin. Study hard and pass the exam. Umurhan will relent, I'm sure of it. You are capable of great things, my young friend. Don't stumble now. Look ahead to the future."

"I *am*, Katal," Safar said passionately. "Can't you see it? In my vision..." he let the rest trail off. He'd been over this ground with Katal many times. "I never wanted to come to Walaria in the first place," he said. "My family insisted I take advantage of Coralean's generous offer." Safar had told various vague tales of why the caravan master felt beholden to him. Katal, realizing it was a sensitive area, had always avoided pressing him for the details. "Old Gubadan wept when I first refused. It was as if I were robbing him of his pride."

"I can see that," Katal said. "You were his prize student, after all. Not many young people like yourself come before a teacher, Safar. It's an experience to be treasured."

"Still, that's not what shook me from my resolve," Safar said. "I love Kyrania. I never wanted to leave it. I loved my father's work. And yet I haven't touched a bit of wet clay in nearly three years. But I was haunted by the vision of Hadin. I couldn't sleep. I could barely eat. The more I thought about it, the more ignorant I felt. And the only way to relieve that was to go to the university and study. So it was Hadin that drove me from my valley, Katal. And Hadin that drives me now."

Safar's blue eyes were alight with the holy zeal of the very young. Katal sighed to himself, only dimly remembering his own days of such single-mindedness. It seemed likely to him, however, that Safar's tale was much more complex than the one he told. There were other forces at work, here. A bitter experience. Perhaps even a tragedy. Could it be a woman? Unlikely. Safar was much too young.

He was forming the words for a new plea of caution when loud voices and the sound of running feet interrupted.

The both looked up to see a small figure in bare feet and raggedy clothes sprinting down the alley towards them.

"What's wrong, Nerisa?" Safar cried as she approached.

Then he heard voices just beyond the alley mouth shouting, "Stop thief! Stop thief!"

Nerisa ran past him and shot up the fig tree like a bolt fired from a bow, disappearing into the thick foliage.

A moment later the fat stallkeep, trailed by several hard-looking men, lumbered into view. They slowed, panting heavily.

"Where is he?" the stallkeep demanded when he'd reached them. "Where'd he go?"

"Where did who go, sir?" Katal asked, face a mask of surprised innocence.

"The thief," one of the rough men said.

"He's a big brute of a lad," the stallkeep broke in. "A real animal, I tell you. I don't mind saying I was in fear for my life when I caught him stealing from me."

"We've seen no one matching that description," Safar said. "Have we, Katal?"

Katal made a face of grave concern. "We certainly haven't. And we've been sitting here for hours."

"Let's check around," one of the rough men said. "Maybe these two good citizens were dipping in the wine too deeply to notice."

"I assure you no one looking like the one you described has come this way," Katal said. "But feel free to look all you like."

Nerisa gently parted a branch to peer at the scene below. While the rough men searched, Safar and Katal engaged the stallkeep in casual conversation to soothe suspicion.

The young thief was not pleased with herself. She'd let her emotions spoil her timing and then she'd reacted in a panic when things went wrong. The execution, to the dismay of many of the heaviest gamblers, had gone off without a hitch. Tulaz's reputation was intact. The adulteresses' head was not. And the plaza crowd had gotten a good show. The victim had been as beautiful as advertised. And she'd wailed most entertainingly when the jailers stripped her, trying pitifully to hide her nakedness with chained hands. Tulaz had played the showman to the hilt, pretending to hesitate several times over the lovely curls bent beneath his blade. Then he'd whacked off her head with such ease that not even a blind fool could doubt the minuscule size of his stony executioner's heart.

But just before he'd struck, the woman had let out a mournful groan that had echoed across the hushed plaza. It was a groan of such anguish, hauled up from the darkest well of human misery, that Nerisa had been wrenched from her emotional moorings. For the first time in her life she'd burst into tears. An uncontrollable urge to leave that place of horrors, and leave it quickly, had overwhelmed her.

Then Tulaz's blade severed the woman's head. The crowd thundered its approval. Nerisa leaped off the wagon, landing with her face to the stall. The object she'd come for gleamed at her from the trays and instinct took over. She scooped it up, heard the stallkeep's alarmed howl of discovery, and dived blindly into the crowd.

"Thief!" the stallkeep had cried.

Despite the after-execution chaos the plaza guards had heard the stallkeep's cry and had come running. The blackest of fates must have made the crowd part before them. One of the men had even managed to get a grip on her arm, but she'd clawed him and he'd yelped and let go. Nerisa ran as hard as she'd ever run in her life. But the plaza guards were street-smart pursuers and so they knew all her tricks, blocked all her avenues of escape. And Nerisa, to her present immense shame, had taken the panicked route of least resistance and had led her pursuers directly to the *Foolsmire*—her only place of refuge where anyone at all cared about a skinny little girl thief who had no memory of mother, father, or even the slightest touch of warmth.

She patted the small object hidden under her shirt. It was a gift for Safar. She peeped through the broad leaves of the fig tree and saw him shove coins forward to buy the stallkeep a jug of wine. She hoped Safar would like his present. Stolen or not, it had been purchased at a greater price than he could ever know. Nerisa saw the rough men return, shaking their heads and saying their quarry had escaped. Safar called for more wine. Katal obliged. And while the tumblers were poured and the first toasts drunk, Nerisa slipped off the branch onto the alley wall.

Then she shinnied up a drain pipe to the roof and then to an adjoining building and was gone.

# 9

# GOOD MEN AND PIOUS

The Student Quarter was the oldest section of Walaria, an untidy sprawl between the rear of the many-domed temple and the western most wall. The western gate had been built many centuries before. It was so little used it had fallen into disrepair and the king had it permanently sealed to avoid the expense of fixing it. The Quarter itself was a warren of broken cobbled streets so narrow that front doors opened directly into traffic. The residences and shops were among the poorest in the city and were stacked atop one another with no particular plan, leaning crazily over the streets.

Safar lived in the near ruins of the one remaining gate tower on the western wall. He'd rented it from an old warder who considered himself the owner because in his view the king no longer had any use for it. He also offered board—one meal a day cooked by his wife. The gate tower consisted of two rooms, one without a roof, and strolling rights along the wall. It wasn't just the cheap price that had attracted Safar to his accommodations. He was a child of the mountains, the gate tower gave him an unimpeded view of the entire city on one side and the broad empty plains on the other. At night the tower also made a marvelous observatory where he could study the heavens and check them against his Dreamcatcher books.

It was also good for sunsets and on this particular day, some hours after he'd left the *Foolsmire*, Safar was sprawled across the broad stone windowsill, toasting the departing sun with the last of his wine. From the other side of the Quarter he was serenaded by a priest singing the last prayer of the day from the Temple's chanting tower. It was magically amplified so it resounded across the city. The song was a daily plea to the gods who guard the night:

*We are men of Walaria, good men and pious.*
*Blessed be, blessed be.*
*Our women are chaste, our children respectful.*
*Blessed be, blessed be.*
*Devils and felons beware of our city.*
*Blessed be, blessed be.*
*You will find only the faithful here.*
*Blessed be, blessed be…*

When the song ended Safar laughed aloud. He was still a little drunk and found the song's sanctimonious lies amusing. The prayer was a creation of Umurhan's, coined in his youth when he was second in command of the temple. It was considered by many—meaning Umurhan's most fervent political supporters—to be the mightiest spell against evil in the city's history. Umurhan had used the acclaim to help topple his wizardly superior. Once that had been accomplished he'd joined with Didima and Kalasariz, both ambitious young lords at the time, to make Didima king and Kalasariz the chief wazier. The three ruled Walaria to this day with brutal zeal.

To Safar the nightly spellsong had become an ugly jest, a riddle that would be a worthy creation of Harle, himself, that dark jester of the gods. Was the evil outside the walls of Walaria? Or within?

He'd heard the song the first time only a short two years before. The setting sun had been in his view that day, just as it was now...

It was a small caravan, a poor caravan, carrying castoffs from the stalls of distant markets. The finest animal was the camel Safar sat upon, a fly-blown, bad-tempered male he'd hired for the journey. He'd made the jump from Kyrania—more a wobble, actually—in three stages. The first was a traveling party to the river towns at the foot of the Gods' Divide. The second was with a group of drovers herding their cattle across the dry plains to new grazing grounds. He'd come across the caravan during that leg of the trip. It was heading directly for Walaria and so he'd joined it, saving many days and miles.

The sun was falling fast as he approached the city, rolling in his camel saddle like a fisherman in troubled waters. Walaria was backlit by a rosy hue casting the city's immense walls into shadow so they looked like a forbidding range of black mountains. Palace domes and towers of worship glittered above those walls, with high peaked buildings steepling the gaps in between. The night breeze brought the exotic sounds and scents of Walaria: the heavy buzz of crowded humanity, the crash and clang of busy workshops, the smell of smoke from cooking fires and garbage heaps—good garlic and bad meat. The atmosphere was sensuous and dangerous at the same time—as much was promised as was threatened.

Guarding the main gate was a squad of soldiers bearing

Didima's royal standard—gilded fig leaves, harking back hundreds of years to when Walaria was nothing more than a small oasis for nomads. The gate was menacing—looking like the cavernous opening of a giant's mouth. The gate's black teeth were raised iron bars thick as a man's waist and tapering to rough spear points. The caravan master, a vaporous little man with shifty eyes, bargained with the soldiers for entrance. But he couldn't, or wouldn't meet the bribe price and so the caravan was ordered to camp overnight outside the walls—just beyond the enormous ditch encircling the city. The ditch was as much for waste disposal as it was a defense and it was filled with garbage and offal and the cast-off corpses of citizens too poor for a proper funeral. Smoke-blackened figures scurried along the ditch, tending the many fires kept burning to dispose of the waste. These were the city's licensed scavengers, so low in station it was considered a curse to stare at them overlong, much less suffer their touch.

Safar, hoping to avoid an unpleasant night, shyly approached the sergeant in charge of the squad and presented him with Coralean's letter of introduction. It was written on fine linen and bound by thick gold thread and so impressed the sergeant that he waved Safar through the gate. Safar hesitated, peering into the huge tunnel bored through the walls. It was long and dark with a small circle of dim light—looking like the size of a plate—announcing the exit on the other side.

It was then he first heard the spellsong, a wailing voice from far away, and seeming so close...

*"We are men of Walaria, good men and pious.*
*Blessed be, blessed be..."*

It filled him with such dread he tried to turn back. But the sergeant shoved him forward. "Get your stumps movin' lad," the sergeant said with rough humor. "I've had a long day and there's a flagon of Walaria's best missin' me down at the tavern."

Safar did as he was told, treading through the darkness to the gradually widening circle of light, the spellsong wailing in his ears:

*"...You will find only the faithful here.*
*Blessed be, blessed be..."*

It was with immense relief that he exited the other side. The spellsong had faded, boosting his spirits. He looked about to see which way he should go, but the night had closed in and he was confronted with dark streets glooming in every direction. Here and there light leaked through heavily-shuttered windows. Only the hard cobbles beneath his feet hinted there was a path through that darkness.

Then torches flared and he saw the sign of a nearby inn. Beneath it the inn's crier extolled its virtues for all to hear: "Soup and a sleep for six coppers. Soup and a sleep for six coppers..."

Safar hurried toward the crier, a wary hand on his knife hilt. Cheap as it was, the inn proved to be a cheery stopping place for travelers and he spent the night in comfort. The following day he presented himself at the house of Lord Muzine, letter of introduction clutched in his hand.

The Lord's major domo was not so impressed by the fine linen and gold thread as the sergeant. His face was stone as he took the letter, glanced boredly at Coralean's wax seal.

"Wait here," he said in imperious tones.

Safar waited and he waited long—pacing a deep path in the dusty street outside Muzine's gated mansion. For a time he marveled at the passing crowds and traffic. Although he'd been to Walaria before, he'd been in his father's company and seen things through a child's eyes. Now he was an adult on his own for the first time. He eagerly searched the crowds for signs of the decadence Gubadan had warned him against. He wondered what he'd missed during the previous visits besides the evening spellsong. But if there was anything to tempt a young man in that neighborhood it was kept hidden behind the walls of the mansions lining the avenue. He became bored and hungry but he didn't dare leave his post and miss the major domo's return.

Finally, when the day was nearly done and the time approached for the nightly spellsong, the man emerged. He sniffed at Safar as if he smelled something bad.

"Here," he said, limply handing Safar a rolled up tube of paper bearing Muzine's seal, so recently dripped it was still soft to the touch. The linen was of poorer quality than Coralean's letter of introduction and there was only a black ribbon binding it instead of gold thread.

"The Master directs you to present yourself at the Grand Temple tomorrow. You will give this to one of Lord Umurhan's assistants."

The major domo brushed empty fingers together as if they'd previously held something offensive, then turned as if to go.

Safar was confused. "Excuse me, friend," he said. The major domo froze in his tracks. He looked Safar up and down, wrinkling his nose in disgust. Safar ignored this, saying, "I was hoping for an appointment with your master. I have gifts to give him from my father and mother who also send their wishes and prayers for his good health."

The major domo sneered. "My Master has no need of such gifts. And as for an appointment...I will not insult my lord with such a request from someone of your station."

Safar felt his temper rise and quickly doused it. "But he *has* agreed to sponsor me at the university, hasn't he?" he asked, indicating the letter.

"My Master said that was his intent," the major domo answered. "Funds will be deposited for your care. He has the Lord Coralean's promise of repayment for any necessary expenses." The major domo paused for emphasis, then said, "But he said to warn you not to take advantage of his good nature and friendship with Lord Coralean. My Master's charity will only extend so far. So do not return here for more. Do I make myself clear?"

Safar wanted to throw the letter into the man's sneering face. But he'd made promises he couldn't break and so he swallowed his pride and turned away without comment. The next day, after a night of angry teeth-grinding, he made his way to the Grand Temple of Walaria.

The route took him through the heart of the great crossroads city and the sights and scents and sounds were enthralling. The crowds were thick, barely making room for cursing wagon drovers ladened with market goods. Except for irritated grunts when he bumped into them, the people ignored him—keeping their heads low so as not to meet another's eyes. The traffic flow carried him past beggars crying "alms, alms for the sake of the gods," and open windows framing scantily clad women who called for the "blushing boy" to come tarry in their arms. There were shops with luxurious carpets and rich jewelry mixed with coffee houses and opium stalls. Thieves of all ages and sexes darted in and out of the crowd, snatching at opportunity.

And all the while cart pushers sang out their wares and with the drums and bells and whistles of the street entertainers it made a thrilling song: "Pea-Nuts! Pea-Nuts, Salted And Hot! " Or, "Rose Pud-Ding! Rose Pud-Ding. Sweet As The Bud!" And, "Sher-Bet Iced So Nice! Sher-Bet Iced So Nice!"

The Grand Temple and University was so vast it made a walled city of its own. It had a wide gateless archway for an entrance with fearsome monsters carved in the stone. There were no guards and men dressed in priestly togas or rough student robes poured in and out with the single-minded purpose of bees tending a forest hive. Safar asked directions and soon was making his way through the confusion of temple buildings to the busy office of the High Clerk. There he presented his sponsor's letter and was again commanded to wait.

This time he was ready. He'd brought food and drink and an old stargazer's book to while away the hours. His supplies as well as the day were gone and he'd memorized the book by the time a skinny priest with prunish lips and a rushed manner returned with an answer.

"Come with me, come with me," he said. And he turned and raced away without waiting to see if Safar was following.

Safar had to hurry to catch him. "Have I been accepted, Master?" he asked.

"Don't call me master. Don't call me master," the priest chided. "Holy one will do. Holy one will..."

"Pardon my ignorance, Holy One," Safar broke in. "Have I been accepted to the school?"

"Yes, yes. This way, now. This way now."

Safar was led to a large empty dining hall with stone, food-encrusted floors.

The priest said, "Scrub it down. Scrub it down." He pointed at a wooden bucket of greasy water with a brush floating on top.

Safar looked and by the time he raised his head the priest had darted off. "Wait, Holy One!" he shouted after him. But the little priest had already gone out the door, slamming it behind him.

Safar fetched the bucket and brush and got on his knees and scrubbed. As a village lad he saw no shame in necessary labor, no matter how mean the task. He scrubbed for hours, making little headway because the water was as filthy as the floor. At spellsong an older acolyte came to take him to a huge dormitory, crammed with first-year students. He was given a blanket, a place to stretch out on the bare floor and a rusty metal pail containing a cold baked potato, a hard wheat roll and a boiled egg.

While he wolfed the food down the acolyte gave him a quick summery of his duties, most of which seemed to involve scrubbing dirty floors.

"When do my studies begin?" Safar asked.

The acolyte laughed. "They've already started," he said. And he left without further explanation.

Safar had learned long ago from Gubadan that teachers liked to make obscure points. Very well, he thought, if floor scrubbing is my first lesson, so be it. He scrubbed for a month, lingering as he toted buckets of water past foul-smelling workshops and lecture halls that echoed with the wise orations of master priests.

Then Umurhan summoned him and he never had to scrub another floor again.

Safar drifted out of his reverie. He rubbed his eyes, noting the view through the window had been replaced by glistening stars. He saw a comet tail just near the House of the Jester and became absorbed in the astral meaning of the occurrence. Then he heard a sound—a scratching at his door. Through a fog of concentration it came to him that he'd heard this sound only a moment before. And he thought, Oh, yes...I was thinking about Umurhan and something interrupted me. And that something was a noise at my door.

He heard a voice call, "Safar? Are you awake?"

It was a young voice. Safar puzzled, then smiled as he realized who it was. "Come in," he said.

# 10
# NERISA

On the other side of the rough plank door Nerisa hastily combed fingers through her hair and straightened her clothes. She wore a short loose tunic that showed off her long legs, belted tightly about her small waist to draw attention away from her boyish figure. The gray tunic and pale leggings were castoffs, but the cloth was of such good quality that the patches barely showed.

"That *is* Nerisa, isn't it?" came Safar's voice. She heard him laugh. "If it's some rogue instead, you're wasting your energies, O friend of the night. For I've spent all my money on drink and other low pursuits."

Nerisa giggled and pushed the door open. Safar was grinning at her from the other side of the room, lolling on the windowsill, white student robes hiked up over his strong mountaineer's legs. Nerisa thought she'd never seen such a handsome young man. He was tall and slender, with wide shoulders and a narrow waist, accented by his red acolyte's belt. His skin was olive; his nose curved gracefully over full lips. His dark hair was cut close, with a stray curl dangling over eyes so blue they had melted her heart when she first looked into them.

He beckoned her to the window. "I've just sighted a comet," he said pointing out at the star-embedded heavens.

She came to him, leaning over his sprawled out legs so she could see.

"Right there," he said, directing her. "In Harle—the House of the Jester."

She saw the long, narrow constellation of Harle, with its distinctive peaked hat and beaky-nosed face. Crossing at about chin level was the wide pale streak of a comet's tail.

"I see it," she said, voice trembling from being so close to Safar. Troubled, she drew away, turning her head so he wouldn't see her blush. "I hope I wasn't bothering you," she said.

"Nonsense," Safar replied. "I'm lonely for my sisters. If you ever meet them don't you dare say I told you that. They'd never let me forget it." He chuckled. "But I do miss them. There, I've said it. I grew up surrounded by my sisters and now I pine for them. I hope you don't mind being a substitute."

Nerisa *minded* very much! She wasn't quite sure exactly what reactions she wanted from Safar but she could say most definitely brotherly feelings were not among them.

She put a hand on her hip, trying to look as adult female as possible. "If you miss women so much, Safar Timura," she said, bold as she dared, "why don't I ever see you with one? Except *me*, of course." She unconsciously touched her hair. "The other students spend all the time they can chasing women at the brothels."

To Nerisa's enormous delight Safar blushed and attempted a stumbled answer—"I...uh...don't go in for...that sort of thing." He recovered, saying, "I made a fool of myself once. I hope I know better now."

Nerisa nodded, thinking, I *knew* it was a woman! A bad experience, obviously. She hated the woman who'd made Safar suffer. But she was also delighted that her rival, although probably beautiful and certainly more mature, had made a bad job of things.

"What happened to her?" she asked.

"Who?"

"The woman in the bad experience."

Safar made a wry face. "I didn't know I was being that obvious," he said. Then he shrugged, saying, "Her name was Astarias. A courtesan I was fool enough to fall in love with. But she made it plain she had no intention of making a life with a potter's son. It seems she had grander plans which didn't include me."

As Nerisa was mulling this over Safar motioned for her to sit on the pile of old pillows and rugs that were the room's sole furnishings. She sank down and he joined her. She made herself look away as he sat, robes carelessly riding up over his long limbs.

"I suppose Katal gave you a bad time," Safar said, sliding away from the previous subject.

"What?" said Nerisa, in a bit in a daze.

Safar smiled saying, "After the, ah, large gentleman and his...friends left I believe you called the entire thing a, ah...'misunderstanding?'"

"Well it was!" Nerisa said. She saw with relief—and some disappointment—that his robes had been properly tucked over his lap. "I was *trying* to pay for it. But he thought I was a thief. Guess he didn't see the money in my hand."

"You must admit, Nerisa," Safar said, "you have been known to engage in, shall we say, long term *borrowing?"*

Nerisa shrugged. "It's how I live," she said. "I know old Katal can't understand it. Maybe he thinks I've got a family someplace. And any day they'll come back and I can stop sleeping at the *Foolsmire* and be with my family again. But that isn't *ever* going to happen. So I steal. I'll stop when I don't have to anymore."

"I understand that," Safar said. "It wasn't how I was raised, but I can see how things can be different in Walaria. I wish I could do something to help you. But I have a hard enough time helping myself."

"Oh, but *you have* helped me," Nerisa said with unintended passion. She calmed herself, took a breath, then, "I mean, you show me your books. And teach me things out of them. It's almost like I'm a student myself. The only gir—I mean, woman student at the university."

Katal had given her reading and writing lessons, but her interest hadn't really been sparked until Safar had taken her under his intellectual wing. Nerisa was so bright and eager to please that she quickly caught on to everything he introduced her to.

Safar sighed. "I've also tried to teach you logic," he said. "Let's go back to your basic defense. Which was that as a poor orphan child you're forced to steal in order to live."

"That's true," she replied firmly.

"Very well," he said. "I'll accept that. But pray tell me what did you find at that fat old knave's stall that was so important?"

"This," Nerisa said, softly, shyly pushing forward a small paper wrapped package. "It's for you. It's a...present."

Safar's eyebrows shot up. "A gift? You *stole* a gift?" There was an edge to his tone, indicating that such an act was anathema to someone of honest rearing. But he was unwrapping the package just the same, saying, "This isn't right, Nerisa. You shouldn't steal a gift. Hells, you shouldn't steal at all. But to think that I was responsible for..."

His voice trailed off as the wrapping fell back and the object was revealed.

It was a small stone turtle, black with age, stumpy legs arching from its shell. Its head stretched to the end of a long wrinkled neck, beaked jaws open as if the turtle were chasing a fish. All in all a charming toy for a child in some long ago day.

Safar's first jolt came as he realized the little object was no toy, but an ancient idol representing one of the turtle gods. Great care had been exercised in carving it—the detail so intricate the turtle seemed alive, as if it were in motion instead of a piece of stone at permanent rest. His second and decidedly greater jolt came when he saw the painting on the turtle's back. It was of a large green island, a jagged line of blue surrounding it to mark the seas that washed its shores. On that island was a huge red mountain, with a monster's face spewing painted flames from its mouth.

"Hadin," Safar breathed.

"You're always going on about it," Nerisa said, pleased at the awe she saw in his face. "And you've shown me pictures in your books. When I spotted it I knew right away it was something you'd want." She shrugged. "So I got it."

Safar was smiling and nodding, but from the absent stare in his eyes she doubted he'd heard a word. She fell silent, watching in fascination as his hand seemed to be drawn to the turtle as if it were a powerful lodestone. He twitched when his fingers met the stone, and his eyes widened in surprise.

"It's magical," he whispered.

He lifted the idol up, turning it about to study it from every angle. "I wonder where it came from," he mused "And how it got here."

Nerisa said nothing, realizing that Safar was only speaking his thoughts aloud. He was so absorbed in the turtle god she felt as if she were peeping through a window at a private moment.

His face cleared and he lit up the room with his smile. "Thank you, Nerisa," he said, quite simply. "I can never repay you for such a gift."

Then to her enormous, heart-stopping thrill he leaned over, put an arm about her shoulders and pulled her close. He kissed her lightly on the lips and she shuddered, excited and frightened at the same time. Then the moment ended and he drew away and she hated the tender brotherly look in his eyes.

To revenge herself she pointed at the turtle, saying, "I stole it, remember? Are you sure you want to dirty your hands with it?"

"It doesn't matter," was all he said, voice so loving she forgave him.

And so she asked, "What's it for?"

Safar shook his head. "I don't know," he said. "Whatever its purpose, it's definitely magical. I can feel it!" He hesitated, thinking, then went on, "I think it must be like a harp feels when a musician plucks a string. A sound resonates all through me."

"How do we find out what it does?" she asked, casually including herself.

Safar frowned. "I have to cast a spell to find out," he said, "and I really shouldn't do anything with you here. Lord Umurhan doesn't approve of his acolytes performing magic in public." Actually, the penalty for discovery was immediate dismissal, but Safar didn't mention that.

"Oh, please! Please!" Nerisa said. "I've never seen magic done before."

Safar hesitated and she leaped into the gap. "If you *really* want to thank me," she said, "let me watch what you do. Please, it's important to me. I see the spells and stuff in the books you show me. And sometimes you explain it to me. But if I could see it for myself I'd understand it better."

Her lips curled into a twisted little grin. "And you *know* I won't tell anybody. There's probably nobody in the world better at keeping their snapper snapped than me."

Safar was watching her closely the whole time she spoke. He'd liked her the first time they'd met at the *Foolsmire* nearly two years before. She'd have been ten summers old then, he thought. He'd been shocked to see a little girl living alone on the streets. Nothing like that would ever happen to any child in Kyrania. She was also amazingly bright. She had only to look at a page and she could turn away and recite every word exactly. Katal had told him she'd learned to read and write in less than two weeks. And whenever he corrected her speech she never made the same mistake again. Safar had not only found her easy to converse with but sometimes used her to test news ideas. No matter how complex the subject, he'd soon learned, if Nerisa didn't understand the fault was either because he didn't truly understand it himself or because he was putting the matter poorly.

To the Hells with Umurhan, he thought. He's going to throw me out anyway. What do I have to lose?

So he said, quite formally, "Your wish, Ladyship," he said, "is my command."

Nerisa clapped her hands and cried, "Thank you, Safar! You won't be sorry. I promise."

Overcome with her delight she threw caution to the winds and hugged him and dared to kiss him on the lips. Then she pulled back, blushing furiously. She ducked her head and concentrated on a stray thread as if the task were one that required immense concentration. For the first time Safar noticed she wasn't wearing her usual urchin rags. There was no sign of boyish pretense in the Nerisa sitting beside him. She was feminine through and through, from the tilt of her chin to the graceful arc of her wrist as she plucked at the thread. He saw she'd also dressed with care in a costume that set off her best womanly features—long legs beginning to find shape despite their slenderness. Soft slippers defining her small, well-formed feet. A narrow waist with a broad belt pulled tight over budding hips. From the experience of a large but close family he guessed her bosom—hidden under the loose material of her tunic—was just beginning to develop. He remembered his sisters' embarrassment at Nerisa's age. And how that embarrassment had quickly become something else entirely when they started looking at the village lads differently and the age of long romantic sighs began.

Nerisa recovered and raised her head to look at him. She was smiling, but her lower lip was trembling. Her eyes were unguarded and he could see emotion boiling just beneath their dark surfaces. He realized that if he said the wrong thing just now she'd burst into tears—and suddenly he knew the reason for those welling tears. Nerisa was in love with him. He'd seen his sisters fall in love with much older lads and suffer the same torment. It was a quickly passing illness, he knew. A malady of the very young—although just as painful as anything an adult endured. It would be even harder on Nerisa, he thought, because she was so alone—so unloved. Safar, who still wore scars from his encounter with Astarias, knew that anything he did to hurt Nerisa would wound her deeply. He wondered what he ought to do about the situation. Then he thought, why do anything at all? Give her a chance to grow out of the crush, like his sisters had. He'd just have to tread carefully from now on.

Safar cleared his throat and picked up the turtle. Nerisa tensed for words of scornful dismissal.

"This spell will be much easier if you help me," he said calmly.

Nerisa's reprieved heart soared. She leaped to her feet. "What do you want me to do?" she asked eagerly.

He pointed to a battered trunk across the room. "You'll find a wooden case in there," he said, "with most of the things I need. Then, if it's no trouble, you might start a fire under the brazier."

"No trouble at all," she said, adopting Safar's casual tones.

She fetched him the case, and while she got the fire going he poured different colors of scented oils into a wide-mouthed jar. Then he sprinkled packets of mysterious powders and strong-smelling herbs into the oil, mixing it all together with a stone mortar. Nerisa heard him chanting as he worked, but his voice was so low she couldn't make out the words. When he judged the fire hot enough, he carried the large jar and turtle to the brazier. He set the jar on the grate and while it heated he drew colored chalk marks on the floor, making an elaborate, many-sided design that enclosed the fire.

When he was done he said, "Now, if you'll sit right there..." He motioned to a spot well inside the design.

She did as he directed, scooting in as close as she could to the brazier. Safar sat across from her. His image appeared watery through the heated fumes rising from the jar.

"Are you comfortable?" he asked.

She nodded.

"We'll get started then," he said. "But you have to promise me you won't laugh if I make a mistake. I'm just a student, you know."

Nerisa giggled. She was sure that, student or not, Safar just had to be the best wizard in all Esmir. Then she realized how relaxed she'd become since he'd asked her to help. She wondered if his request had been a ploy to put her at ease. If so, she loved him even more for it.

Safar sniffed the fumes. "It's ready now," he said.

"What do I do?" she asked.

Safar handed her a long-handled brush with a narrow blade made of boar's bristles. "Dip this into the jar," he told her. "Stir it around and get a good load on the bristles."

She stirred the brush through the thick, bubbling mixture. She wrinkled her nose at the fumes, although later she couldn't have said if the scent was foul or fair, sweet or sour. Safar signaled with a nod and she withdrew it. He picked up the stone turtle, centered it in his flattened right palm, then extended it over the fumes.

"Now paint the turtle's back," he said.

Nerisa gently stroked the brush across the green image of the island. Although the mixture from the jar was tarry black, it left only gray streaks on the green.

"Lay it on thick," Safar said. "This isn't a job for a timid hand."

Nerisa furrowed her brow and daubed with a will until the goo spread all over the stone and spilled into Safar's hand.

"That's exactly right," he said. "Now dip up some more and do another coat. Thicker than the last, if you can. But this time we need a chant to help things along. So listen closely to what I say and repeat it exactly."

Nerisa nodded understanding, loaded the brush again, and as she laid the mixture across the idol's back they chanted together:

*"Light dawning through the night,*
*What pearls hide beneath the stone?*
*All that is dark emerge into bright,*
*Give flesh to rock and marrow to bone."*

Nerisa's pulse quickened as she saw a faint light emanating from the stone idol. She swore she saw the turtle's legs move and then she gasped as the idol twitched into life and scuttled across Safar's palm. He whispered for her to be still and laid the turtle on the floor. Instantly the light died and the idol sank down, freezing into its former lifeless pose. Safar swore, then looked up to give Nerisa an abashed grin.

"This is going to be harder than I thought," he said. "We could chant all night and still not come up with the right spell.

From his sleeve he withdrew a small silver knife, double-edged and etched with elaborate and mysterious designs. It was the witch's knife Coralean had given him to unravel difficult problems.

"Fortunately," he said, indicating the knife, "I have a way to cheat."

Again he signaled for Nerisa to be silent and he laid the knife against the idol's stone shell—point touching the red painted mountain with the monster's face. He chanted:

*"Conjure the key*
*That fits the lock.*
*Untangle the traces,*
*And cut the knot..."*

Safar's voice dipped lower and the rest of the chant was lost to Nerisa. But she was so struck by his intensity that she probably wouldn't have heard the words even if they'd been shouted. She'd never seen such concentration. Safar's eyes seemed to be turned inward, smoldering with smoky blue fire. A soft light formed about his whole body, a rosy band shot with pinpricks of color. His long face shone with perspiration, making the hollows seem deeper and the edges sharper. Nerisa smelled the faint musk rising from his body and felt a great calm settle around her like the softest of blankets. Her eyes, as if they had a will of their own, fixed on the monster's painted face and became riveted there.

Safar gave the stone a final sharp rap with his knife and suddenly the monster's face broke free from the stone, floating up and up, and then the painted eyes blinked into life and its mouth moved, forming words:

"Shut up! Shut up! Shut up!" Nerisa heard it say.

A body formed beneath the face, and Nerisa pulled back in surprise as a little creature, perhaps three hands high, hopped off the turtle's back and stood on the floor. It had the visage of a toad, with huge eyes and a mouth stretched wide to reveal four needle-sharp fangs. But the rest of its body was that of an elegant little man, richly clothed in a form-fitting costume covering it from toe to neck. The creature seemed angry, hands perched on narrow hips, ugly toad head turned toward the stone turtle.

"If you don't shut up," it said to the idol, "I'll make you! Just wait and see if I don't!" Then the creature looked up at Safar, complaining, "He gives me a headache! Always talking. Never listening. Sometimes I can't even hear myself think!"

"I'm sorry you're forced to live with such noisy company," Safar said, as natural as could be. "But in case you haven't noticed you've just been summoned. And if you'll pardon my rudeness, whatever quarrel you have with your companion is of no interest to us."

The creature glared at Safar, then at Nerisa. "That's the trouble with humans," he said. "No concern for others." He cocked his head at the idol as if listening, then nodded. "I couldn't agree more, Gundaree, " he said to the idol. "For a change you speak wisely." Then, to Safar, he said, "Gundaree says all humans are selfish. And you've certainly done nothing since we met to disprove it."

"Who is Gundaree?" Safar asked.

The creature snorted, tiny flames shooting from its nostrils. "My twin! Who else?" He spoke as if Safar were the most ignorant mortal in existence.

"And you are?"

Another fiery snort. "Gundara, that's who!"

"Why hasn't your twin also appeared?" Safar asked. "Tell him to come out so we can see him."

Gundara shrugged, the gesture as graceful as a dancer's. "He never appears to humans," he said. "It's not in the rules. I take care of your sort. He does the demons."

"Then you *do* understand you've been summoned," Safar said. "And that you must do my bidding."

Gundara hopped up on a three-legged stool, perching there so he was eye-level with Safar. "Sure, sure. I understand. Bid away, O Master of Rudeness. But would you mind getting to it? I haven't eaten my dinner yet." He gestured at the idol. "That damned greedy twin of mine will get it all if I don't get back soon."

He turned to Nerisa, perhaps hoping to find more sympathy there. "You won't believe how hard it is to come by a decent meal when you live in a stone idol."

"I can see how it might be," Nerisa said. She rummaged in a pocket and came up with a sweet.

Gundara's eyes lit up. "Haven't had a taste of sugar in a thousand years," he said. He held out a tiny hand for the treat.

Nerisa hesitated, looking at Safar. He nodded for her to go ahead and she extended the sweet, which was immediately grabbed by Gundara and popped into his mouth. He chewed, closing his eyes as if he were in paradise. Then he gave a delicate flick of his long red tongue, picking off any stray sugar crumbs from his lips.

When he was done he turned Safar. "What do you want, human? And don't make it too difficult. You don't get the world for a sweet, you know."

"First I want to know something about you," Safar said. "Where are you from? And what is your purpose?"

Gundara sighed. "Why do I get all the stupid ones?" he complained. "Three times out in five hundred years and each one dumber than the other."

Safar proffered the silver knife and the creature shrank back, petulant look turning to one of fear. "I've had just about enough of your smart talk," Safar said. "I'm the one in command here."

"There's no reason to get so excited," Gundara replied.

"Answer my questions," Safar demanded.

"I'm from Hadin, where else?" Gundara said. "My twin and I were made there long ago. How long, I can't really say. A few thousand years, at least. We were a gift to a witch on her coronation as queen."

"And your purpose?" Safar asked.

"We're Favorites," Gundara said, rolling his eyes at such a stupid question. "We help wizards and witches with their spells."

"You said you and your twin's duties were divided between humans and demons," Safar said. "Why is this?"

"How do I know?" Gundara said with barely disguised disgust. "That's how we were made, is all. Those are the rules. I do humans. Gundaree does demons. Simple as that."

"Is your twin exactly like you?" Safar asked.

Gundara laughed, and the sound was like glass breaking. "Not in the slightest," he said. "I'm beautiful, as you can see. Gundaree, on the other hand, has a human face." The creature shuddered. "What could be uglier than that, no offense intended, I'm sure."

"How did you come to be in Esmir?" Safar asked.

"Now that," Gundara said, "is the saddest tale in the whole history of tragic stories. We were being transported in the Queen's treasure chest and pirates attacked our ship. From that time on we have been the property of the foulest creatures you can imagine. Traded from one filthy hand to another. Then we got mixed in with worthless goods about fifty years ago and were lost. We've been living in market stalls ever since. Ignored by everyone."

He gave Nerisa a fond look. "That was quite a trick you pulled at the market place," he said. "I've always thought females made the smartest humans." Nerisa blushed, but said nothing.

Gundara turned to Safar. "I suppose my twin and I are stuck with you for awhile," he said. "Until somebody kills you, or you trade us to someone else, that is."

"If you don't show some manners soon," Safar replied, "I'll make you and your brother a gift to the oldest, dirtiest, wartiest witch in all Esmir."

"Okay, okay," Gundara said. "Don't get so upset. I was only making conversation."

"What can you do," Safar asked, "besides act as my Favorite?"

"As if that wasn't enough," Gundara grumbled. "I guess no one's satisfied with good, sound sorcerous enhancement these days. Why, in the old—" he broke off when he saw Safar's warning look. "Never mind. Forget I said anything. Apparently a poor Favorite doesn't even have the gods-given right to grumble around here. If you want more, more you shall get. I can fetch and carry things that would be fatal for a mortal to touch. I can also spy on your enemies, if you like. Although that's kind of limited since I can't get more than about twenty feet from the turtle. So you'd have to hide me in your enemy's quarters, or whatever else your feeble human imagination can come up with. I'm also pretty good at giving warning if evil-doers are about."

Gundara snickered at some private joke. "As a matter of fact," he said, "if I were you I'd command me to get busy with that job right now."

"What do you mean?" Safar demanded.

Another snicker. "Never mind," Gundara said. "My loyalty can only be tested so far, you know. If you can't take a hint, O Wise Master, sod off!"

"Favorite!" Safar barked. "Post guard! Immediately!"

The creature laughed and hopped to his feet. "Right away, Master!" he said. "Never fear, Gundara is near!"

Then, to Nerisa, "The only reason I said anything at all, my dear, is that you were nice to me. Gave poor Gundara a sugar treat to snack on, you did. If those men outside were coming for my sour-humored Master, I wouldn't have said anything at all.

"But they're coming for you, Nerisa. And if you're the cunning little dear I think you are, you'll get out of here quick!"

With that there was a sharp *pop!* and Gundara vanished.

Instinct jolted Nerisa to her feet and without a word she threw herself at the window. She disappeared through it just as the door slammed open and four very large, very pale men rushed inside. Safar scooped up the idol, hiding it in his robes as he scrambled to his feet to confront the invaders.

"What's the meaning of this?" he demanded.

The tallest and palest of the men answered, "Any meaning I like, Acolyte Timura! Now, tell me where the thief Nerisa is! And tell me quick if you value your hide!"

Safar's heart climbed into his throat.

The man confronting him was Lord Kalasariz—Walaria's notorious spymaster.

## 11

## KALASARIZ

Tall as Safar was, the spy master was taller and so thin and pale in his black robes and skull cap that he looked like a specter.

Safar should have abased himself—should have fallen to his knees and knocked his head against the floor, begging his Lord's forbearance. But he had to give Nerisa time to escape so instead he brazened it out, rudely yawning and stretching his arms as if he'd been awakened from a deep sleep.

"Forgive me, my friend," he said, "but I've been studying late. Exams coming up, you know."

"How dare you call me Friend!" Kalasariz roared.

Safar peered at him in mock surprise, then shrugged. "My mistake," he said. "I can see from your attitude that few, if any, would care to make that claim."

"Don't you know who I am?" Kalasariz thundered.

"Apparently not," Safar lied. "Or I'd know how to properly beg you to please lower your voice. I'm of nervous disposition. Loud sounds make me ill and I find it difficult to concentrate."

"I am Lord Kalasariz," the spy master hissed. "Do you know that name, bumpkin?"

Safar scratched his head, then pretended to jolt and gape. "Forgive me, Lord," he said, bobbing his head. "I had no idea that—"

"Silence!" Kalasariz commanded. "I asked you a question when I entered. Answer it now—where is the thief, Nerisa?"

Safar put on his best look of puzzlement. "Nerisa? Now, where do I know that name? Nerisa? Is she the wife of the baker on Didima Street? No, that can't be..." He snapped his fingers. "I've got it! You mean that child that hangs around the *Foolsmire*? Is that who you seek?"

"You know very well who I mean, Acolyte Timura," Kalasariz said.

Safar nodded. "I do now, Lord," he said. "But I don't know where she is. Except...have you checked at the *Foolsmire*? She sleeps there sometimes."

"I *know* that," Kalasariz gritted out.

"I suppose you would," Safar said. "Being chief sp—I mean Guardian of Walaria and all."

"Do you deny you were in her company today?" Kalasariz demanded.

"No, I...uh...suppose I don't deny it," Safar said. "But I can't confirm it either." He gave a sheepish grin. "I was taken drunk most of the day, you see. I don't remember much about it. Maybe I saw Nerisa. Maybe I didn't. Sorry I can't be of more help."

"I dislike your manner, Safar Timura," Kalasariz said. "Perhaps you think you're safe from me because you are under the protection of Lord Umurhan. That I have no sway over University affairs."

"Forgive my rough mountain manners, Lord," Safar said. "Sometimes I unintentionally give city people offense. I know quite well that you are charged with seeing the law is kept in Walaria. Quite naturally those duties would include the temple and university."

Kalasariz ignored him, peering about Safar's room, long nose twitching like a hunting ferret's.

To draw away suspicion, Safar plunged onward. "Pardon my foolishness, Lord," he said, "but why would someone of your eminence be looking for a common thief? And a child thief, at that?"

Kalasariz' eyes swept and Safar suddenly felt very cold as he was confronted by the spymaster's glittering eyes. "I was told you were the brightest student at the university," the spymaster said. "Too bright for your own good, perhaps. And disdainful of rules and authority."

He paused, waiting to see if Safar would be foolish enough to answer. At last he nodded in satisfaction. "At least you're bright enough to know when to keep your tongue still," he said. "I'll answer your question two ways, Acolyte Timura. If you're so intelligent you'll know which one to choose for a correct answer.

"The first is this: I'm looking for the girl because an informant has reported that she is a vital messenger for a group of traitorous students."

Safar needed no acting help to make his eyes widen. "*Nerisa?*" he said, amazed.

Kalasariz' eyes gleamed with renewed suspicion. "Are you claiming you know nothing of these students?"

Safar knew better than to lie about something that was common knowledge in Walaria. "I've heard, Lord," he said, "that there are certain students at the University who are misguided enough to question the policies of the good King Didima." Then seeing that this bit of truth had been swallowed without difficulty he chanced a lie. "I have no personal experience or knowledge about those foolish ones," he said. "Just as I had no idea who you were when you came into my room. I have no interest in politics, My Lord. Nor have I ever displayed any."

Kalasariz looked Safar up and down, studying every crease in his costume, every twitch in his face. Then he said, "The second answer is that the girl, Nerisa, is only an excuse. And that I'm here for an entirely different reason."

Kalasariz paused, fixing Safar with a stare. Then he said, "I understand you are a close friend of Iraj Protarus."

Safar was too startled to hide his surprise. "Why, yes, I am," he said. "Or I was some time ago. I haven't seen him or heard from him in years."

"What if I told you I had different reports, Acolyte Timura?" Kalasariz said. "What if I told you that I have a reliable informant will to testify that you are communication with Protarus regularly?"

"I'd say your informant was a liar, My Lord, " Safar replied, quite firmly. "And I'd also say, who cares? Iraj Protarus has nothing to do with Walaria."

Kalasariz curled a lip. "Are you claiming ignorance of Protarus' activities?" he asked. "Are you saying you know nothing of his many conquests?"

Safar shrugged. "I've heard the market gossip, Lord," he said. "Some of it might even be true. When I knew Iraj he was determined to become leader of his clan. And I understand he's achieved this. That he's undisputed ruler of the Southern Plains."

"Oh, his claims are disputed, all right," Kalasariz said.

"You mean by his uncle, Lord Fulain," Safar said. "And his uncle's ally—Koralia Kan. Iraj told me about them years ago. He hated them with good reason, it seemed to me. The last bit of market gossip I heard was that Fulain and Kan were routed and have fled to Lord Kan's kingdom. "

"You know much," Kalasariz said, "for one who pretends no interest in politics."

"Iraj was my friend, Lord," Safar said. "It's only natural I'd take an interest in any news I heard."

"Then how did you miss the news, Acolyte Timura," Kalasariz said with a sneer, "that Iraj Protarus has been proclaimed an enemy of Walaria?"

Safar reacted, shocked. "When?" he said. "I've heard nothing of this."

Kalasariz smiled. "Actually," he said, "it hasn't been announced yet. The king has entered into an alliance with the Lords Fulain and Kan. He suspects Iraj will not be satisfied with his southern holdings and will soon seek to extend his borders. This alliance will be announced tomorrow."

Safar had every reason believe everything Kalasariz said was true. He remembered quite clearly Iraj's dreams of grand conquest—as clearly as he recalled his own vision of Iraj leading a great army.

Kalasariz' harsh voice broke through his thoughts. "Do you still claim, Acolyte Timura, that you have had no communication with the barbarian who now claims a royal title?" He spit on the floor. "King Protarus," he sneered. "Such savage pretensions."

Safar took a deep breath. "I have not spoken with him, or corresponded with him, My Lord," he said, quite truthfully, "since I left my home in the mountains. I doubt if Iraj even remembers me. Why should he? I'm no one of importance. We were just boys thrown together by circumstance."

Kalasariz gave him another long, probing look. Then he nodded, as if satisfied. "You will send word to me, Acolyte," he said, "if you hear from your old friend."

Safar bobbed his head, relieved. "Certainly, Lord," he said. "Without fail."

It was a lie, but one Safar thought was unlikely to be tested. What reason would Iraj have to seek him out after all this time? Like he told Kalasariz, it had been a boyhood friendship—long forgotten.

Then the spy master suddenly turned on his heel, signaling his men he was ready to depart. Safar sagged as Kalasariz stepped through the door. But any relief he felt was short-lived. Just as Kalasariz reached the door he swung back.

"You may or may not be the fool you claim, Acolyte Timura," he said. "Be advised that I will make it my personal business to find out."

And he was gone.

Safar heard a dry chuckle coming from the inside pocket of his robe. It was Gundara.

He heard him say: "Nice friends you have, Master. And good fortune for me. When they kill you I'll be in much better company."

Then, to his twin, "Shut up, brother! Save it for the demons. You'll have your turn soon enough."

Safar swatted the bulge in his pocket and heard Gundara give a satisfying "Ouch!"

"Don't trifle with me," Safar warned. "I may only be a student, but the handling of Favorites is a first year course. And the number one rule, according to my master, the Lord Umurhan, is never to trust a Favorite. The second is to use a heavy hand. I don't agree with Umurhan about a lot of things, but from your behavior so far I intend to take his teaching to heart."

He swatted the bulge again. "Do I make myself clear?"

"Okay, okay," Gundara said from his pocket. "What ever you say, Master."

Then to his twin: "Shut up, Gundaree! Shut up! Shut up! Shut up!"

The letter, although written on expensive paper, was smudged from camp smoke and battered from being passed through many hands.

Kalasariz smoothed it out on the table and moved an oil lamp closer so the two other men could see.

This is what the letter said:

*My Dear Safar*

*All you predicted has been coming true and at a faster pace than even I expected. Even as I write my whole camp is drunk with wine and joy at yet another grand victory. Once again our losses were few, while our enemy suffered greatly. My army grows larger and more able each day. But I'll tell you this, my friend. I've learned that success can be more dangerous than failure. Every city I capture, every border I cross, increases the pressure to achieve more. For if I stop my enemies will have time to join forces against me. The greatest problem I face, however, is that I'm surrounded by self-serving advisors whose words and loyalty I'd be a fool to trust.*

*But you, my friend, I know I can trust. We proved our mettle together in that fight against the fiends. You know my mind, my private thoughts, more than any other. Just as I know yours.*

*I beg you, Safar—come to me at once. To help speed you to my side I have deposited ample funds in your name with the Merchants' Guild in Walaria.*

*I have great need of you, friend and oath brother.*

*May the gods look with favor on you and your dear family in Kyrania.*

When the men had finished reading the letter Kalasariz said, "I have verified the signature. Without question it's that of Iraj Protarus."

"This is most disturbing news, gentlemen," King Didima replied. "Most disturbing indeed."

"Damned embarrassing for me," Umurhan said. "Can you imagine how *I* feel? To think I've been nursing a viper at my bosom all this time."

"There, there, Umurhan," Didima said. "No one's blaming you. How were you supposed to know? After all, the young man came so highly recommended."

The three men were gathered in the king's private study. They'd ruled together for so long—equally dividing power and wealth—that they were at ease in each other's company. They were accustomed to compromise and once a goal was set they worked smoothly towards its end. Didima was a stumpy man, with thick limbs and a barrel-like trunk. His face was round like a melon and shadowed by a dark thick beard streaked with gray. Umurhan was every inch a wizard, silver eyes glowing under a sorcerer's peaked hat. He had heavy, bat-winged brows and a beard of flowing white. And Kalasariz was the dark presence who made this unholy trinity complete.

"Thank you for your confidence in me, Majesty," Umurhan said. "Although I must say I *have* become suspicious of young

Timura lately. I wanted to dismiss him from the school, but I didn't want to offend his sponsor, Lord Muzine. Instead I was going to make sure Timura failed the upcoming exams. Then I'd be rid of him without controversy."

"I'll speak to Muzine," Didima offered. "He'll be grateful we gave him a chance to distance himself from the little traitor."

"Let's not mention this to anyone just yet," Kalasariz cautioned. "I want to see where this leads us."

"That's good advice," Didima said. "Why seize one troublemaker when we might have a chance to sweep them all in." He absently combed his beard with thick, blunt fingers. "These are dangerous times, gentlemen, as I've said many times before. Two years of poor harvests. Plague outbreaks among our cattle and sheep. More bandits stalking the caravans than we've seen in years. Which has done nothing to help trade. And this increasing reluctance, which I lay to poor upbringing, of our citizens to pay the increased taxes we require just to keep the kingdom whole and on the right course.

"Now this upstart, Iraj Protarus, comes along with his army of barbarians invading the realms of innocent, peace-loving kings. Why just last month my old friend, King Leeman of Shareed, had his head cut off by this Protarus fellow. After he'd sacked the city, of course, and burned it to the ground."

Didima touched his throat and shivered. "It isn't right," he said, "cutting off royal heads. It injures the dignity of thrones everywhere."

"I couldn't agree more, Majesty," Umurhan said. "And I think we made a wise decision to ally ourselves with Protarus' enemies, Koralia Kan and Lord Fulain."

"We'll have to raise taxes again," Didima warned, "to pay for the mercenaries and arms we promised our new friends."

"It will be worth every copper," Umurhan said, "if it stops Protarus once and for all. Someday our citizens will thank for saving them from that madman."

"Thank us, or curse us," Kalasariz said, "they'll pay just the same. But that's old business and as much I'd like to talk politics with you two all night I want to set a proper course concerning Safar Timura. How shall we proceed?"

Umurhan indicated the intercepted letter. "How did this fall into your hands?"

"I have an informant at the *Foolsmire*," Kalasariz said, "which as you all know is a favorite meeting spot for the students. Safar is a close friend of the owner and has all his messages and post directed there."

"I know of this place," Umurhan said. "The owner is a cranky but harmless old fellow who distrusts authority. Katal, I think his name is. I can't imagine him having a sudden change of heart and turning informer for the crown."

Kalasariz smiled thinly, making him look even more like a skeleton. "It's the owner's grandson who is in my pay," he said. "Zeman's his name. He's as dim-witted as he is ambitious. Full of cunning and all of it low. Zeman is anxious to inherit, but unfortunately for him his grandfather gives every sign of living on for many years. My emissaries have led young Zeman to believe that if he helps us we might hasten his grandfather's journey to the grave."

"Excellent, excellent," King Didima said. "The blacker the soul the more willing the flesh."

Kalasariz chuckled. The sound was like a broken bone grating against itself. "That's certainly true in Zeman's case," he said. "He seems to particularly hate Safar Timura. I don't know why—to my knowledge Timura has never done anything against him. I think he's jealous because his grandfather holds Timura in such high affection. There's also a child at the *Foolsmire*, a thief named Nerisa, whom he appears to hate nearly as much as Timura. Once again, I can't say why. Nor do I care. Suffice it to say Zeman has been looking on his own for evidence against Timura for some time. We had no reason to suspect him, the gods know. And then this letter came along and Zeman contacted us immediately."

Kalasariz made another death mask smile. "He managed to construct the accusations so they involved the child as well."

"My, my," Didima said. "Two enemies at one blow. Zeman must be a very happy fellow."

"Not as happy as he's going to be if this works out right," Kalasariz said. "I believe in keeping my best informants rich enough to dream large, but poor enough to keep those dreams just beyond their reach."

"What did Timura say when you confronted him with the letter?" Didima asked.

"I didn't mention it," Kalasariz said. "I let him lie. He claimed he'd heard nothing from Protarus since they were boys. He also said he doubted his old friend even remembered him."

Umurhan snorted. "A likely story," he said. "That letter is clearly one of several urging Timura to join Protarus in his evil adventure. And look here..." he jabbed his finger at one phrase in the letter..."Protarus says he's deposited funds for Timura at the Merchants' Guild."

Kalasariz snorted. "I've seized them, of course," he said. "One hundred gold coins."

Umurhan's bat-winged brows flared up in surprise. "So much?" he said. Then, "That's more proof, as if we needed it. No one would give away such an amount casually."

Didima leaned forward. "Why do you think Timura has resisted Protarus' pleas?"

"That's simple enough, Majesty," Kalasariz said. "He's holding out for a greater share of the spoils."

Umurhan looked thoughtful. Then he said, "I'm sure that's part of his game. However, I'm also certain he wants to steal my most important magical secrets to take along with him. I caught him in my private library the other day. That is why I nearly dismissed him. The books and scrolls there are forbidden to anyone but a few of my most trusted priests and scholars."

A long silence greeted this revelation. Then, from Didima, "What of this battle Protarus refers to? The bit about the fiends? What do you make of that?"

"Some boyhood adventure, I suspect," Kalasariz answered. "Exaggerated, of course."

Didima nodded. "Yes, yes. What else could it be?"

He thought a moment, then asked, "What shall we do about Acolyte Timura?"

"Nothing just now," Kalasariz said. "Let him have his head. At the right time we'll make certain he pays a very public visit to our executioner to have it removed." He slipped a scroll from his sleeve and rolled out it out on Didima's desk, saying, "And to that end, Majesty, I'll need your signature authorizing his execution and the execution of his fellow conspirators when the time comes to sweep them up. We don't want any messy trials or other delays that might give their supporters time to whip up public support."

The king chuckled, picking up his quill pen and charging it with ink. "I see you have only Timura's name listed now," he said.

"Oh, there'll be more, Majesty," Kalasariz said. "You'll notice I left a great deal of room on the page."

The king nodded approvingly. "Tulaz *is* anxious to improve his record," he said. "We'll make a day of it, eh? A public holiday. Free food and drink. A bit of carnival to mark the moment." He scratched his name on the document, saying, "There's nothing like a mass execution to calm the citizenry."

Kalasariz smiled thinly, blew on the wet signature and passed the document to Umurhan. "I'll need you to witness this," he said. "Just a formality."

Without hesitation, Umurhan signed. "It's a pity," he said, "I had such hopes for the lad."

Some hours later Kalasariz made himself ready for sleep. While his pretty maids drew the blankets and plumped up the bed he drank his favorite hot sweet potion, laced with brandy and mild sleeping powders.

He was a not a man who slept well. It wasn't all the blood he'd spilled that disturbed his dark hours, but the constant worry that he'd overlooked something. His tricks and betrayals were legion and he had so many enemies he didn't dare let down his guard. He was a master of the great lie and was therefor continually occupied with keeping track of his untruths and half-truths. During the day he never had a weak moment, but at night his dreams were bedeviled with plans that went awry because of a stupid mistake or oversight. Without his nightly ritual he'd awaken so exhausted from nightmares that he'd be stricken with doubts. And so, despite the lateness of the hour, he let his maids pleasure him after he'd had his potion. Then they'd bathed him and dressed him in a nightshirt of black silk.

He dismissed them, reaching for the black silk mask he wore to shut out any stray light. Just before he put it on he remembered the document of execution, still sitting on his dressing table.

Despite the sleeping potion and the attention of his maids he knew he wouldn't sleep well as long as it sat there unattended. Never mind that no one would dare creep into the home of Walaria's spymaster, much less rob his sleeping chamber. His unguarded mind was so active that as he tossed and turned through the night he would come up with countless scenarios in which such an unlikely deed would suddenly become real.

Close as he was to sleep, he got up to attend to it. He'd taken much care to collect the signatures of his brother rulers on Safar's death warrant. His name did not go on it—a remarkable absence in its own right. Kalasariz rolled it up with another document which *did* bear his name. It was an official protest of the decision, praising Timura as a young man of many notable qualities and virtues. He locked them away in his special hiding place behind the third panel from the entrance of the bedchamber.

Kalasariz had no ambitions besides survival in his current position as co-ruler of Walaria. He certainly had no more desire to see Didima dethroned than he did to see himself king. But as Didima had said, these were dangerous times. If by some distant chance the young upstart, Iraj Protarus, should someday be in the position to seek revenge for the death of his friend, Kalasariz preferred to be viewed as one of Timura's champions. The spymaster had little doubt he was right to support the decision for Walaria to ally itself against Protarus. But there was a slight chance the alliance would fail and Protarus and his army might someday show up at the gates. Didima and Umurhan would pay for their crime with their heads. Tulaz would most likely perform the honors, since good executioners are difficult to find and he'd be instantly welcomed into the new king's service. Armed with the documents proving his innocence, Kalasariz would also be welcomed. Protarus would need a spymaster, and who could be a better man for the job than Kalasariz himself?

Timura had presented Kalasariz with a unique opportunity. One the one hand, as a friend of Iraj Protarus it was necessary to remove whatever danger he might represent. On the other, as an outsider great blame could be heaped upon him. He would be declared the ringleader of all the young hotheads who opposed Walaria's rulers. A dozen or more of his "lieutenants"—in reality the real leaders of the opposition—would also earn the ultimate punishment. This would not only quell their followers and sympathizers, but outside and unnamed influences would get the ultimate blame.

There was a saying about "getting your sweet and eating it too."

Kalasariz wasn't fond of sweets. But he did enjoy the sentiment.

The spymaster slept well that night. But just before First Prayer he had a dream about a strange little creature with a man's body and a demon's face. It was gobbling up a sweet roll, scattering crumbs, left and right.

When it was done it brushed itself off and looked him square in the eye.

"Shut up!" it said. "Shut up, shut up, shut up!"

He didn't know what to make of the creature or its antics. But for some reason it frightened him.

## 12

## THE GRAND TEMPLE OF WALARIA

Unlike Kalasariz, Safar slept little that night. Every straw in his mattress and lump in his pillow made itself known. A few days before the only major worry he'd had was a vague and somewhat academic fear that the world faced some great threat. At the age of twenty summers he was incapable of taking it personally. The spy master's visit, coupled with his recent difficulties with Umurhan, made him feel less immortal. He was in trouble and that trouble had grown from the granite hills of Umurhan's displeasure to the bleak peaks of Kalasariz' suspicions.

In short, he was besieged from all sides and was in a confusion about what he ought to do. Adding to that morass was the confusion created by Nerisa's gift plus his fears about Nerisa herself. Someone, for whatever reason, had marked her.

Everyone on the streets knew Nerisa ran personal errands for anyone at the *Foolsmire* with a copper or two to pay. Most certainly some of the young men who hired her held controversial views. That didn't make Nerisa a conspirator. This was also a fact all knew—including any of Kalasariz' minions who made the *Foolsmire* their territory. So why had the informer lied? Why had he singled Nerisa out?

Then it occurred to Safar that he was the target. Someone might be striking at him through Nerisa. But once again came that most important of all questions: Why? Then he realized that answer or not, his fate might be racing toward an unpleasant conclusion. The only intelligent thing to do was to flee Walaria as quickly as he could. Such an act would certainly turn Kalasariz' suspicions into an outright admission of guilt. Safar thought, however, it would be even more dangerous to remain in Walaria at the mercy of the spymaster.

He decided to run. He'd flee home to Kyrania as fast as he could. But what about Nerisa? He'd have to come up with some plan to protect her from any reprisals his flight might cause.

Safar was relieved as soon as he made the decision. He'd learned much in Walaria, but it had been a mostly unpleasant stay in an unpleasant city. He missed his family and friends. He missed the clean mountain air and blue skies and molten clouds and snowy slopes.

Only one thing stood in his way—a lack of money. To make a successful escape he'd require a hefty sum. He'd need a swift mount and supplies for the long journey home and money for Nerisa as well. Where could he lay hands on it? There was no sense asking his sponsor, Lord Muzine. Not only would the money be denied, Safar thought it likely the request would be immediately reported to Kalasariz.

There was only one person he could think of who could help.

But once that approach was made, there'd be no turning back.

Safar rose before first light. He washed and dressed and made a quick trip to a nearby bakery and bought a sticky roll filled with plump currants. He rushed home, brewed a pot of strong tea and while he drank it he summoned Gundara.

The little Favorite popped out of a cloud of magical smoke, coughing and rubbing sleepy eyes.

"Don't tell me you get up early *too*!" Gundara whined. "The gods must hate me. Why else would they allow me to fall into the hands of such a cruel master?"

Instead of answering, Safar held up the sticky roll. The Favorite's eyes widened. "Is that for me, O Wise and Kind Master?"

"None other," Safar said.

He extended the roll and the Favorite grabbed it from his hand and gobbled it up, moaning in pleasure and scattering crumbs and currants all over the floor.

When he was done he sucked each taloned finger clean, smacked his lips, then said, "If you gave me another, I'd *kill* for you, Master." From his tone Safar knew it was no jest.

"You'd kill for a piece of pastry?" Safar asked.

Gundara shrugged. "Money is no good to me. Or jewels or treasures. I live in a stone turtle, remember? But a bit of something sweet...mmmm...Oh, yes, Master. Lead me to your victims this instant. I can help you conjure a decent poison guaranteed to reduce an entire city to a hamlet."

"I don't kill people," Safar said.

"More's the pity," Gundara answered. "Killing's much easier than most tasks." He stretched his arms, yawning. "If it isn't killing, Master, exactly what is it you want me to do?"

"Make yourself as small you can," Safar said, "and hop up on my shoulder."

"How boring," Gundara complained, but he clicked his talons together and instantly shrunk to the size of a large flea. Safar had to look very hard to see him. Gundara called out, voice just as loud as when he was full size, "You'll have to help me with the shoulder part, Master. It's too far to hop."

Safar held out his hand and the black dot that was Gundara ran up it, scrambling over the rough cloth of his sleeve until he reached his shoulder.

"I have some important business to conduct this morning,"

Safar said. "I want you to keep a close watch for any danger or suspicious people."

"Do I get another roll when I'm done, Master?" came Gundara's voice.

"If you do a good job," Safar promised.

"And one for Gundaree too?" the Favorite pressed.

Safar sighed. "Yes," he said. "Gundaree can have one too."

"Make it with berries, next time," the little Favorite requested. "Currants give me gas."

The city was stirring to life when Safar set out. Traffic was light but a few shops were opening and workmen were gathering in the front of others, munching olives and black bread while they waited for their employers' arrival. Safar passed the wheelwrights' shop, which always started early to repair wagons that'd broken down on the way to market. A hard-eyed man leaned against the wall near the entrance. He stared at Safar when he went by.

Safar bent his head closer to shoulder. "Any trouble there?" he asked.

"Just a cutpurse," the flea speck that was Gundara answered. "Don't worry. You're too poor for his taste."

Safar went on, but kept his pace slow so his Favorite could sniff for spies. He was certain Kalasariz would order his informers to trail him. Although Safar was only a mountain lad, unwise in the ways of the city, he had much experience with nature to rely on. Animal or human, hunters always behaved the same way. Wolves on the stalk, for instance, might post a sentry near their intended victim. When the flock moved about the sentry would keep close watch on the sick sheep that had been chosen for dinner. As the flock moved from place to place the wolf would follow only so far, passing on his duties to another sentry so as not to arouse suspicion. And so on throughout the day until the intended victim fell behind the flock, or strayed too far from the rams. Then the sentry would howl the news and the pack would strike.

This is how Safar imagined Kalasariz' informers would work. They'd post a spy on the street near his home, who would alert the others when he emerged. Then he'd be passed along from spy to spy until he returned home for the night.

As he neared the end of his street an old woman with rags for clothes and a torn horse blanket for a shawl rose up from beside her push cart. There were pigeons cooing in a wooden cage on one side push cart, hot meat pies steaming from a basket in the other.

"Fresh pigeon pies?" she called out to Safar. "Two coppers a pie, sir."

"No thank you, Granny," Safar said, moving by.

The old woman gripped his sleeve. "That's my usual price, sir. Two coppers a pie. And fresh and hot they is, sir. Fresh killed this morning. But you're such a handsome lad, sir, if you don't mind me saying so. You make this poor granny's heart sing like she was a maid. For you sir, for bringing back my girlhood, I'll charge only a copper for two."

The spy saw Safar hesitate, then nod and hand over a copper in exchange for two pies which he tucked into his purse. He said thank you to the granny, polite as you please, and passed on—turning the corner and heading down a broad street. The old woman waited until he'd disappeared from sight then quickly opened the door to the pigeon cage. She grabbed the only white bird, which was also much larger and fatter than the others. She petted it, whispered soothing words and threw it high into the air, moving with a surprising agility for someone who appeared so old and bent.

The pigeon flew up and up—circling the street as it oriented itself. Then it shot for the high tower that marked the entrance to the Central Market. The spy smiled, knowing what would happen next. The pigeon was trained to circle the tower three times. This would alert all the informers planted about the city that Safar was on the move. Then the pigeon would return to the pushcart for a nice treat and whispered praise that it was such a smart and pretty bird.

The old woman, who was the spy, was quite fond of the pigeon. She'd raised it from the egg and spoiled it more than any other bird she'd had. She watched proudly as her little darling flew toward the tower. Then she gasped as a deadly black figure winged its way over the rooftops and headed for the pigeon. The hawk hurled itself at her prize bird, talons stretching out. The pigeon sensed its peril and tried to dodge but the hawk was quicker and there was an explosion of blood and feathers. The hunter flew away, the remains of the pigeon clutched in its claws.

The spy groaned in dismay. She'd not only lost her favorite pet, but Safar as well. Quickly she grabbed a passing boy by the ear and gave him a coin to mind her cart, promising more if all was safe when she returned. Then she hurried off to warn her superiors that a hawk had spoiled their plans.

Two streets away Safar cut around a corner at top speed, then slowed to a fast walk. It was a tenement neighborhood with high, crooked buildings. There was no one about except housewives illegally emptying chamber pots into the street, instead of paying the slopwagon men to carry away the filth. Shutters would bang open, slop would stream into the street, then they'd bang shut before anyone in authority could see. And woe betide the passerby who didn't jump in the correct direction when he first heard the shutters open.

Safar slipped smoothly to the side as a murky stream poured down the heavens, avoiding getting even a spatter of filth on his robes. He whistled and the hawk darted down from a roof. It landed on his shoulder, beak and chest feathers clotted with blood. Safar made a face at the mess, then gestured and the hawk transformed into Gundara who became a flea spot on his shoulder.

"Look at me! I'm covered with pigeon blood," the Favorite complained. "The gods know I hate the taste of blood, especially pigeon blood. You don't know where the filthy things have been. They're worse than chickens."

"I'm sorry," Safar said. "Still, you did a good job."

"I have a ninny for a master," Gundara said. "Of course I did a good job. What did you think, that I'd just been spellhatched? I've been doing this for more centuries than I care to mention because it depresses me so much.

"Yech! There's blood in my mouth, too. And feathers. You have no idea what it does to you when you bite down on a feather."

Safar felt sorry for him and soothed him as best he could. A few streets later he bought a dish of pudding, floating in sugared rose water. He ate half the pudding, then pushed the remainder aside with his wooden spoon so Gundara could jump in and bathe.

He continued on, Gundara a fat wet black spot on the shoulder of his robe.

The Favorite burped. "Maybe you're not such a bad master after all," he allowed. "Do you eat rose pudding every day?"

"I will from now on," Safar promised.

"You hear that, Gundaree?" the Favorite said to his invisible twin. "I'm absolutely soaked with sugar water! Existence is wonderful. And I have the best master in all the world. So go sod yourself, see if I care!"

Safar grimaced at the one-way conversation. He was glad he only had to deal with one Favorite at a time. Together they'd drive him mad.

He was moving under a large awning shading the entrance to a rug shop, when he heard someone hiss from overhead—"Safar!"

It was Nerisa. He covered his surprise, looking around to make sure no one was near. Then he chanced a look upward and saw a dark eye gleaming through a hole in the awning.

"Don't look!" the girl commanded.

"I'm sorry," Safar whispered back. He toyed with a pile of rugs near the entrance, pretending to examine them for quality. "Are you all right?" he asked under his breath.

Nerisa snorted. "Scared half to death, is all. What'd I do to get Kalasariz after me?"

"You saw him?"

"I hid outside until he left. I thought I was seeing things at first. Or maybe I was in the middle of a nightmare and couldn't wake up. Then he went by my hiding place and I got a good look and knew it was no nightmare. Who could miss that face of his? Looks like somebody who doesn't see the sun much. Or a ghost."

Safar nodded, fingering another rug. "Listen," he said. "I don't have time to explain what's happening. They're just using you as an excuse to get to me. I don't know why. But I'm going to do something about it now. Just keep low. Stay away from the *Foolsmire*. And meet me tonight."

"Okay, Safar," Nerisa said. "Tonight then. Say three hours after last prayer?"

"Where? My place isn't safe."

"Don't worry," Nerisa said. "No one will see me. Just be there. I'll come to you."

He started to argue, but there was a slight rustling noise above and when he looked up at the rent in the awning the eye was gone.

Safar was troubled as continued on his way. Nerisa took too many chances for his liking. But there was nothing he could do about it now and so he pushed away the worry as best he could to concentrate on his mission. Before long he reached his destination. He smiled to himself as he approached, thinking all the spies who'd been set on his trail would be scurrying all over the city looking for him. But he'd be hiding in plain sight in a place they'd never think to look—the Grand Temple of Walaria.

It was an ugly edifice—a series of massive buildings and onion-domed towers enclosed by high, fortress-like walls. The temple had begun as a simple stone structure. It had been built centuries before by the first high priest in the days when Walaria—which meant the place of the waters—was little more than a few ramshackle buildings encircled by immense corrals to hold the great cattle herds that enriched the original settlers. Legend had it Walaria was founded by a wandering wizard. It had been nothing more than a dry thorny plain then. According to the myth, the wizard had thrust his staff into the ground. The staff instantly grew into a tall tree and a spring had burst out from under its roots. Over time a great market city had been born from that spring, with a king to rule it and a high priest to build and tend that first temple.

Afterwards each high priest constructed another holy structure—more to glorify *his* name then those of the gods. Temples were hurled up willy nilly, with each high priest competing with the bad taste of the man he'd replaced. Most of the buildings were dedicated to the many gods worshipped by the people of Esmir. It was Walaria's boast there were idols to as many gods as there were stars in the heavens.

Safar went through the main gate, passing by scores of shops and stalls catering to the business of worship. There was incense of every variety and price, holy oils, special candles and thousands upon thousands of idols of the different gods—large ones for the household altar, small ones to make talismans to hang from a chain. On both sides of the thoroughfare were hutches and small corrals containing animals and birds that could be purchased for sacrifice. Blessings and magical potions were also on sale and if you were a pilgrim with foreign coin, or letters of credit, there were half-a-dozen money changers eager to service you from first prayer to last.

A crowd was already gathering when Safar arrived and he had to elbow his way through the throngs. He turned right when he reached the end of the main boulevard and here the street was empty except for a few students like himself hurrying to the university—a low-slung building two stories high and three deep.

The top level was where Umurhan and the other priests lived—although Umurhan's quarters took up almost half that space. The ground level was for offices and classrooms—and the great meeting hall where they all gathered for special ceremonies and announcements. Two of the below-ground levels were given over to dormitories for students too poor to come up with the price of a private hovel or garret such as Safar's.

Leering gargoyles decorated the portals leading into the university. Safar shivered as he passed under them.

"There's no danger," Gundara said from his shoulder. "It's only stone."

Safar didn't need the reassurance. He knew quite well the gargoyles were nothing more than lifeless symbols to ward off evil spirits. Still, even after being confronted with those leering stone faces every day for nearly two years, he couldn't help the reaction.

Just beyond the portal was a large courtyard with stone steps leading to an altar. It was here the students practiced making blood sacrifices to the gods. An animal would be driven out from barred cages to the left of the altar. The animals were always drugged so they rarely gave any trouble. A priest would direct a youth in the grisly task of slicing the creature's throat. Others would dash in to catch the flowing blood before the animal fell. Then prayers would be said as the animal was butchered out and the meat and blood burned in sacrificial urns to glorify the gods. Safar had always been uneasy about blood sacrifices and the more he learned the less he thought they were necessary. He'd also noticed that the best cuts of meat were set aside for Umurhan and his priests—hardly an act that would please a deity.

As he went by the altar he saw five acolytes cleaning up after a recent sacrifice. Their shabby robes were hiked up and they were on their hands and knees scrubbing the steps and platform with worn brushes.

Safar remembered a time when that grisly task was his sole and constant duty.

As he passed by the laboring youths he recalled the moment when he'd first met Umurhan.

It was a dreary winter day and the skies were as ashen as the altar stone. Safar had lost count of the weeks he'd spent on scabby knees washing the steps and platform. It was so cold that every time he plunged his brush into the scrub bucket a film of ice formed moments after he withdrew it.

He'd reported to the repetitious priest each morning, asking when he'd be allowed to attend classes. The answer had always been the same—"You came late in the year. Late in year. Keep working. Working. Soon as there's an opening…an opening…I'll let you know. Let you know."

And Safar would say, "Yes, Holy One," as contritely as he could—just as Gubadan had instructed him before he'd left Kyrania. As each day blended into miserable day he became more impatient. He'd come Walaria to learn, not to scrub floors. Moreover, Coralean was paying a high price to fund his studies. Safar was supposed to be a student, not a slave.

On that particular day he'd reached the sheerest edge of his patience and was thinking mightily of packing his kit and setting off for home—and to the Hells with Walaria. He was actually in the act of rising from his knees when there came a sudden hubbub of activity.

The repetitious priest rushed into the courtyard, surrounded by other priests and a great crowd of acolytes from the Walaria school of wizardry. It was an elite group of less than a hundred. These were the students deemed to have talent enough for intense instruction in the magical arts. Safar's own sights were not raised that high. At that time all he wanted was a chance to join the main student body and get a thorough grounding in general knowledge. But when he studied the group, saw their look of immense superiority, noted the weak buzz of their magic, he experienced a momentary flash of jealousy. He brushed it aside and as the excited group crowded into the courtyard he grabbed up his bucket and moved to a far corner where he could watch without being noticed.

From the murmuring of the acolytes he gathered that an important man had approached Umurhan for a great favor. It seemed the man had committed some wrong the group was evenly divided between betrayal of a relative, and the murder of a slave and wanted to make sacrifice to the gods beseeching their forgiveness. But he wanted to do it as privately as possible, so he'd made a large donation to the temple to pay for a non-public ceremony. After the cleansing, Safar heard the acolytes say, rich gifts would be passed out among the students to buy their silence.

When he heard this he made himself even less obtrusive, ducking behind a column overgrown with thick vines.

A moment later cymbals crashed and two men strode into the courtyard, boys scampering before them tossing petals onto the path and waving smoking incense pots to sweeten the air they breathed. There was no mistaking that one of the men dressed in the flowing robes of a master wizard, was Umurhan. Even if he were blind, Safar would have sensed the man's presence, for the air was suddenly heavy with the stink of sorcery. Then Safar was rocked by another surprise. For the richly dressed, heavily bejeweled man striding beside Umurhan was none other than Lord Muzine. Although he'd never been personally introduced to Muzine, the merchant prince had been pointed out to him one day when he passed in his luxurious carriage, drawn by four perfectly matched black horses. Muzine had a face like a double-headed hammer turned handle up. It was long and narrow until it reached the chin which bulged out on both sides.

The courtyard was hushed as the two men mounted the platform and approached the altar of Rybian, the king of the gods and the deity who created all living things from holy clay. Umurhan and two brawny lads in robes of pristine white solicitously helped Muzine kneel before the stone idol of that kindly visaged god.

Umurhan turned to face the acolytes, his eyes fierce under his bat-winged brows.

"Brothers," he said, "we are here today to assist a good man, a kindly man, who by unfortunate circumstance has stumbled off the path of purity he has tenaciously traveled his whole life. We are not here to judge him, for who among us could judge a man known far and wide for his sweet disposition and generous charity? This man has come to me, his heart bared, his soul in torment. He has sinned, but who among us has not? So we will not judge him. Instead we will beseech the great and merciful Rybian, father of us all, to take pity on this poor mortal and forgive him for any transgressions the Fates forced him to commit.

"And so I ask you today, my brothers of the spirit, to join me willingly and wholeheartedly in this mission of mercy. The man you see humbled before you is one who deserves no less and it is an honor for our university and temple to help him in this most delicate of matters."

While Umurhan spoke the lads in white gently removed Muzine's tunic, leaving him bare to the waist, the soft pink flesh of his heavy richman's torso revealed to all. Then they uncoiled small whips, belted about their waists.

"Are there any objections?" Umurhan asked. "Is there anyone present who cannot find it in his heart to help this man? If so, I kindly ask you to withdraw from our company. You will be thought no less of for making such a decision. Your conscience, we all know, must be your guide."

Umurhan swept the crowd with his fierce eyes, but no one stirred.

He nodded and said, "More to your credit, brothers. The gods will bless you for this."

Safar heard someone nearby mutter under his breath, "So will my tavern bill, Master."

There were a few chuckles at this, covered by Umurhan's signal for all to kneel. The acolytes dropped to the ground as one, bowing their heads low and beating their breasts.

Umurhan announced, "Let the blessing ceremony begin."

From somewhere came the sound of lutes and bells and drums. Priests led the acolytes in song after song, begging Rybian's attention.

The first song was Umurhan's famous Last Prayer that everyone heard every evening at the close of day.

*"We are men of Walaria, good men and pious.*
*Blessed be, blessed be.*
*Our women are chaste, our children respectful.*
*Blessed be, blessed be..."*

While the assembly sang, the white-robed lads gently touched their lashes against Muzine's flesh in the motions of whipping. Muzine wailed as if he were being severely tormented, believing, as all did, that the louder his cries, the more painful-sounding his shrieks, the more the God Rybian would be fooled into thinking Muzine was being sorely punished.

Finally, Muzine gave a scream more terrible than the others and collapsed on the floor. His minders quickly anointed his back—which was unmarked—with soothing oils, kissing him and whispering words of sympathy in his ear. When Muzine deemed sufficient time had passed for him to make a recovery, he rose up with much pretended difficulty and pain. Tears streamed down his long face, which was split by the beatific smile of one who has found the Light again. The lads helped him with his tunic and gave him a tumbler of spirits. Muzine drank deeply, wiped his eyes and then joined in the songs.

Safar became bored with the farce and looked about to see if there was a way he could creep off without being noticed. Just then the iron gates of the animal cage clanged open and his head swiveled back to see what poor creature Muzine had chosen to bribe Rybian's forgiveness.

To his surprise, he saw an old lioness being led out on a slender silver chain. Muzine must have done something really awful, Safar thought. He'd been at the temple long enough to know that a lion was the most expensive and therefor rarest single animal to be sacrificed. Safar decided the sin must have been murder, and probably not that of a slave.

He looked closer at the huge lioness—which stood nearly as high as the white-robed boy who led her. Her movements were slow, paws dragging as she took each step toward the altar. Her eyes were so heavy from the drugs she'd been fed that they were mere slits on either side of her broad face. Despite the size of the lioness, Safar's heart gave a wrench, for she reminded him of his family cat in Kyrania who patrolled the goat stalls for greedy rodents. It had sat on his lap for many an hour, cleaning itself and consoling him when he told it his boyhood miseries.

Then he noticed the lionesses' large, swinging pouch and heavy teats and knew she'd recently given birth. Even drugged, he thought, she must be in a torment wondering what had happened to her cubs.

Umurhan signaled and the singing stopped. He turned to the altar, saying, "O Rybian, Merciful Master of us all, take pity on this poor mortal before you. Forgive him his sins. Accept this humble gift he presents you. And let him sleep once again in all innocence."

Umurhan motioned and one of the boys led Muzine to the lioness. He handed the merchant a large sacrificial knife. The other boys crowded close, holding elaborately decorated jars to catch the blood. Muzine gingerly gripped the lioness by her scruff. She made no motion or sign that she understood what was happening. The Muzine drew the knife across her throat. Blood dribbled from the cut, but the flow was so slight that Safar knew Muzine's nerve had failed and he hadn't been able to cut deeply enough to end the lioness' suffering.

Muzine tried again and this time a boy gripped his hand, pushing hard and making sure the deed was properly done. The lioness moaned and blood gushed into the bowls.

She sagged to the floor.

Everyone cheered and jumped up, praising Rybian and welcoming the sinner Muzine's return to the fold. Muzine came forward, Umurhan at his side, to accept the acolytes' congratulations. Behind them the three white-robed lads got busy butchering the lioness out to prepare for the next stage of the ceremony.

Then the din was shattered by a spine-freezing roar and everyone's heart stopped and everyone's head jerked toward the half-skinned corpse.

The air above the dead beast turned an angry red and then all gasped as the lioness' ghost emerged, crouching on the body, tail lashing, lips peeled back over long yellow fangs, screaming her hatred.

The ghost lioness leaped and the frozen tableaux became

unstuck. There were screams and the crowd ran for cover, tangling and jamming the exits with their bodies.

Safar stayed in his hiding place and saw that despite the hysteria a dozen priests and acolytes quickly surrounded Umurhan and Muzine and got them to safety through a small door at the edge of the altar.

Meanwhile, the ghost cat sailed into the mass of fleeing figures. She struck out with her translucent claws. Blood sprayed in every direction and there were screams of pain from the wounded. Then she caught someone in her jaws and held him down while the others scrambled away—jamming the exits and hugging the walls.

The ghost lion crouched over her victim, gripping him by the shoulder and shaking him furiously back and forth. The young man she'd caught was still alive and wailed most piteously.

Suddenly what felt like an unseen hand pushed Safar out of hiding. He walked slowly toward the raging lioness, one part of him gibbering in fear, the other intent only on the soul of the poor Ghostmother, alone and agonizing over her newborn cubs the only way she knew how.

The ghost saw him and dropped the screaming acolyte. She snarled and paced toward him, extended claws clicking on the stone. But Safar kept on, his pace slow and measured. He held out his right hand—two fingers and a thumb spreading wide in the universal gesture of a wizard forming a spell.

He spoke, his voice low and soothing. "I'm sorry to see you here, Ghostmother," he said. "This is a terrible place for a ghost. So much blood. So little pity. It will spoil your milk and your cubs will go hungry."

The lioness ghost kept coming, eyes boiling, jaws open and slavering. Safar went on, closing the distance between them, talking all the while.

"Evil men did this to you Ghostmother," he said. "They trapped you and slew your cubs. They brought you to this place to die. But the guilty ones aren't in this courtyard, Ghostmother. There are only human cubs, here. Male cubs, Ghostmother. And it your duty to see that no harm comes to male cubs."

The stalking ghost growled, but her fury seemed lessened. A few more steps and then the two met—and stopped.

Safar steeled his nerves as the lioness, instead of killing him on the spot, sniffed his body, growling all the while. When she was done she looked him in the face, cat's eyes searching deep into his own for any lie that might be hidden there. Then she roared and it was so loud he was nearly lifted out of his sandals. But he held steady, and then the ghostly form of the lioness sat back her heels—face level with his own.

"You see how it is, Ghostmother," he said. "I had nothing to do with your sadness, although I mourn the loss." He gestured at the cowering acolytes. "And these male cubs are as innocent as I. Please don't harm them, Ghostmother."

The lion ghost yawned its anxiety, but sank down at Safar's feet.

"It's time you thought of yourself, Ghostmother," Safar said. "Your cubs are dead and their little ghosts are hungry. You should go to them quickly so they don't suffer. Think of them, Ghostmother. They have no experience in this world, much less the next. Haven't you heard them crying for you?

"Why, listen—they're crying now."

Safar made a gesture and there came the faint sound of mewing from far away. The ghost's ears shot up and she cocked her head, eyes wide with concern. Safar gestured again and the mewing grew louder and more frantic. The lioness whined.

"Go to them, Ghostmother," Safar said. "Leave this place and find peace with your cubs."

The lioness bolted up. Safar forced to himself not to react in alarm. Then she roared a final time and vanished.

For a moment the only sound was the echo of the lioness' roar. Then all became confusion as everyone shouted in relief and ran to Safar to thank him. Then, in the midst of this chaos, the crowd suddenly went silent and parted. Safar, still dazed and weary from his effort, saw Umurhan approach as if in a haze.

"Who is he?" he heard the wizard ask.

"Safar Timura, Master. Safar Timura. A new acolyte. He's new."

Umurhan's eyes swiveled to Safar. They looked him up and down, measuring. Then he asked, "Why didn't tell anyone you had the talent, Acolyte Timura?"

"It's nothing, Master," Safar said. "My talent is very small."

"I'll be the judge of that, acolyte," Umurhan answered. He turned to the repetitious priest. "Begin Acolyte Timura's education tomorrow," he ordered.

Then, without another word or look at Safar, he stalked away.

All became confusion again as Safar's fellow students crowded around to clap his back and congratulate him for being admitted to the ranks of the university's elite.

Safar hurried down the long main corridor of the first floor. There was no one to be seen—most of the students and priests would be gathered in prayer in the main assembly hall at this hour. The classrooms and offices he went by were empty and he could smell the stale stink of old magic from the practice spells his fellow students had cast the day before.

At the end of the corridor he came to the vast stairwell that joined the various levels. One group of stairs led downward, into the bowels of the university. The other climbed to the second floor where Umurhan and the priests lived. Safar hesitated, torn between his original purpose and the sudden thought the knowledge he sought in Umurhan's library would most likely be unguarded. He'd have about half an hour before the daily assembly ended and Umurhan and the other priests returned to the top floor.

"You can go either way," Gundara whispered from his shoulder. "Both are safe."

"Maybe later," Safar muttered, and then he ran down the stairs before the new idea could delay him from his most important task.

Although Safar met with Umurhan many times after the incident with the lioness, the wizard never thanked him or even raised the subject again. As Safar's education progressed and it soon became clear to all that he was a remarkable student of sorcery, Umurhan not only kept his distance but seemed to become colder—and Safar would look up suddenly from his studies and find the wizard watching him. Gubadan had warned Safar about Umurhan before he'd left Kyrania. Although he'd never told the old priest about his abilities, Safar got the impression during that last conversation somehow Gubadan had guessed something was up—and that there was magic behind it.

"Lord Umurhan has the reputation of being a jealous man," Gubadan had told him. "He doesn't like students or priests who show off their intelligence or powers. So beware, my lad. Every teacher doesn't receive his reward from guiding a young man to heights they could never achieve themselves. Go carefully in Lord Umurhan's presence, is my best advice to you. And never, never show him up."

Safar took Gubadan's advice to heart. As he progressed through his classes and spell-casting sessions he was always careful not to outshine Umurhan—although it soon became apparent to him that he could, especially as he learned more and delved on his own into the arcane arts of sorcery. He occasionally made purposeful mistakes when he thought Umurhan was becoming suspicious. Umurhan always took particular pleasure when Safar pretended to bumble, chastising him loudly, calling him a mountain bumpkin and other names intended to humiliate.

Umurhan loved to lord his mastery over the acolytes. He also held back his knowledge. When the classes became more advanced and the students were closing the ground on Umurhan, he protected his self esteem by teaching only so much and no more. When a spell was particularly powerful Umurhan tended to make his explanations so obscure no one could follow them, much less duplicate the spell. He also had a way of excusing himself when a thorny question was asked. He'd nervously plead other business, disappear for a short time, then return and answer the question with a confidence his previous demeanor hadn't shown.

Where he went during that time was no mystery to any of the students. They were at a cynical age, an age when details older people might overlook were easily apparent to them. It was an open secret Umurhan retired to his private library during those moments, cribbing from ancient masters to shore up his own facade. No one but Umurhan was allowed to peruse the books in that library. The excuse given was that there were forbidden books and scrolls on the black arts stored there that were so deadly, so evil, that no one but the High Priest of Walaria should read them—and then only in an emergency and only to ward off black spells cast against the city.

Safar's intense curiosity had led him to investigate the library.

The library *did* contain material on black magic. But it was mainly a massive and confused collection of knowledge gathered by Umurhan's predecessors—rare scrolls, books by forgotten masters, volumes in strange languages and hand-written dictionaries of those languages, with magical symbols added by later men as marginalia. Using the books at *Foolsmire*, Safar had gradually deciphered the languages. His late night studies and secret visits put him on the trail of Asper, the ancient master of all master wizards, who also happened—Safar suspected—to have been a demon. One of the bits of marginalia even gave him strong reason to believe Asper's work was hidden somewhere in the chaos that was Umurhan's private library.

He'd been searching for it when he was discovered.

Safar crouched in the darkest of the library, a candle stub his only aid, as he hurriedly combed through cob-webbed scrolls and books with cracked binding—searching for the strange, four-headed snake symbol he knew to be Asper's seal.

Then an oil lamp had flared into life behind him and he whirled to find Umurhan hovering over him—eyes blazing like spear points fresh from the forge.

"What are you doing here, acolyte?" he thundered.

Safar fumbled excuses—"Forgive me, Master. I was worried about the exam and, I, uh...uh...I thought I, uh..."

"Are you claiming to be a cheat, Safar Timura?" Umurhan roared. "Is that your puny reason for violating my privacy?"

"Ye-es, Mas-ttter, ye-ye-yes," Safar stuttered.

"Then why are you among the forbidden books, acolyte?" Umurhan shouted. He pointed down the narrow aisle to the front of the library. "Why didn't I find your filthy, cheating personage up there? Why weren't you stealing your answers from writings that have not been condemned?"

Safar wanted to shout that no knowledge should be forbidden. And that, as a matter of fact, even the supposed innocent works in this library were denied to all but Umurhan. Instead, Safar pretended to panic—with Umurhan looming over him it wasn't hard—babbling that he was only trying to hide from the light and had come here by accident. He streamed forth such a mad babble of half-confessions and false apologies and pleas for mercy that Umurhan's suspicions were quieted.

"Silence," Umurhan shouted, cutting Safar off in mid babble. "You do understand I could have you seized this moment and charged with heresy?"

"Yes, Master," Safar answered, humble as he could.

"The only reason I'm not going to do so is that I believe you are nothing more than a low cheat."

"Yes, Master. Thank you, Master. I'm sorry, Master. It won't happen again, Master."

"Oh, I know you won't do it again, Acolyte Timura. I will see to that. I will withhold my punishment just now. I want you to contemplate your sins while I consider your fate."

"Yes, Master. Thank you, Master."

"The only reason I'm not immediately expelling you...or worse, by the gods, because I could do much worse! You understand that, don't you acolyte."

"Yes, Master. I understand."

"The sole reason I don't condemn you on the spot is because of the respect I have for your mentor, Lord Muzine. For some reason I shall never fathom he has a certain regard for your future and well being."

"Yes, Master," Safar mumbled, knocking his head on the ground. But he knew that what Umurhan was really remembering was the lioness and her ghost.

Although Safar had never been called into Muzine's company, his allowance had been increased after the incident. It had been coldly announced by Muzine's major domo, who harshly cautioned him about ever mentioning the ceremony or the event. It was plain to him now Umurhan feared the incident would get out if Safar's crime became a public matter. Questions would be raised about the sin Muzine wanted expunged. And even greater questions would be asked about the quality of Umurhan's magic. How could such a great wizard allow something like that to happen? And worst of all—perhaps Umurhan wasn't as powerful as he claimed.

Safar had been granted a reprieve, but he knew now it was a short reprieve—and getting shorter every moment.

***

"Hsst!" came Gundara's warning. "Danger ahead!"

Safar stopped. Below him was the final bend in the stairwell. It spilled out into the deepest and least glamorous level of the university. It was a place of boiling kitchen pots, foul garbage bins and huge clay pipes running overhead that carried water in and sewage out. Safar listened closely and after a moment made out the sound of a cleaning brush being rubbed against stone.

He resumed his journey, but at a slower pace. When he rounded the bend he saw a young acolyte kneeling on the steps. There was a bucket of water beside him and a brush in his hands. He was making lazy, half-hearted swipes at the steps with the brush—doing little more than dribbling water on the begrimed stone. But soon as he sensed Safar's presence the lazy swipes were replaced with vigorous scrubbing. The young man looked up, brow furrowed deeply as if the job required great concentration. But when he saw Safar he relaxed. He sat back on his heels, a wide, insolent grin splitting his face.

"Oh, it's only you, Timura. Gave me a start there for a minute. Thought you might be that whoreson, Hunker. Sneaking down here to catch me taking a little break."

Hunker was the priest in charge of punishment details. Any student in trouble learned to hate him on sight. He assigned the filthiest jobs and drove the workers like the spavined ox of the meanest miller.

Safar snorted. "That's me, Hunker, in the flesh. And I'm down here to set all you sinful bastards a good example. That's why I'm going to spend my entire day crouched over a shithole and setting it on fire. Love the smell of that stuff burning. Love to show all you lazy swine how a real wizard works."

The acolyte, whose name was Ersen, had the reputation of being the most indolent troublemaker in the university. Ersen was a constant, unruly presence on the punishment details. It was well know that the only reason he hadn't been expelled was because his father was an elder on King Didima's court. Despite his noble background, Ersen was popular with everyone. He took his punishment in good humor and always presented a sympathetic ear to his fellow miscreants. A sympathy many hoped would translate into protection for that miscreant through his influential father.

Ersen burst into laughter—a loud donkey braying Haw-Haw-Haw that endeared him to every student, but was hated by the priests—since they were usually the object of his uncontrollable laughter.

"I would love to see that, Timura," he said after he'd recovered. "Why, I'd trade my father's fortune—and throw in his flabby old balls as a bonus—to see old Hunker down here burning the shitters."

Safar chortled. "What about your own equipment?" he said. "Would you throw them in, as well?"

Ersen acted shocked. "What, and disappoint all the whores in Walaria? Why, the whole city would be filled with females weeping if their little Ersen was denied them. Besides, my father doesn't have much use for his anymore. He already made me. And there's no way he can improve on that historic feat."

Safar rewarded the reply with more laughter. But the whole time he kept thinking of Gundara's warning. Was Ersen the source of the danger? On the surface it seemed ridiculous. He was the class jester, the instigator of the best practical jokes aimed at authority. It there was mischief, everyone knew instantly that Ersen would be at the bottom of it. How could he be an informer? Then he recalled the comet streaking across the House of the Jester and it dawned on Safar just how good a cover Ersen's behavior would be if he were a spy. Everyone spoke freely in his company because what was there to fear from someone who was always in trouble himself for mocking authority?

Cold realization knotted in Safar's gut. This was exactly the sort of subtle game Kalasariz would play. He looked at Ersen with new eyes and saw the twitch in his cheek, the nervous, preoccupied drumming of his fingers on the steps—small leaks through his genial facade.

Safar sighed and stretched his arms. "Well, it's nice to dream about Hunker taking my place on the punishment detail," he said. "But that's not getting the shitters burned."

"What did you do to deserve that, Timura?" Ersen asked. "Set fire to Umurhan's beard, I hope."

Safar scratched his head. "I don't think so," he said. "The last thing I remember was getting drunk at the *Foolsmire*. Hunker jumped me when I showed up this morning. He screamed a lot, called me the usual names, and ordered me to report for shitter burning. But now that I think of it, he never did say what for."

"It must have been something pretty bad, Timura," Ersen said. "It'll probably be all over the University before the day is over."

Safar grimaced. "Let me know when you find out," he said. "And I pray to the gods that whatever I did was worth it."

With that he strolled away, Ersen's bray echoing after him—"Haw Haw Haw."

When it was safe Safar whispered to Gundara, "Was he the one?"

"How could anyone miss it?" the Favorite replied. "I swear, when the gods made humans they must have run short of intellect to stuff into your skulls."

Safar had no grounds to disagree at the moment, so he continued on in silence, taking a corridor that led away from the kitchens and stank of sewers. The tunnel finally spilled into an immense room pocked with great pits. The sewer pipes emptied into those pits and Safar thought the odor was rich enough to give a starving pig convulsions.

As he entered the room he saw a group of acolytes tending to a pit on the far side. They dumped big jars of oil into it, someone threw in a flaming brand and then they all jumped back as red and yellow flames towered up with a whoosh. Clouds of sewer smoke followed the flames, billowing out over the acolytes who cursed and choked on the filthy air.

The smoke was thinning as Safar came close and one of the acolytes saw him. He shouted something at the others, then ambled forward to meet Safar.

"That's Olari," Safar whispered to Gundara. "The one I have business with."

"I can't say if he's *entirely* safe," Gundara answered. "Only you can judge that. But I can say this—he isn't a spy."

Safar whispered thanks to a few gods for this answer, hedged though it was, and made a hurried prayer to a few others to help him with his plan.

Olari was the second son of the richest man in Walaria. As such he would not inherit command of the family fortunes and so some other worthy occupation had to be found for him. His magical talent was as small as Ersen's—so small that if he had been an ordinary youth he would never have been permitted into the school of wizardry. Everyone knew this, including Olari's father. It was assumed Olari would enter the administrative side of the business of magic, where canniness and family contacts were much more important than sorcerous ability. Safar did not underestimate him because of this. He knew that was the same road Umurhan had taken to power. Olari's reputation was as controversial as Ersen's. Except where Ersen presented himself as a jester and the laziest of all the lazy students, Olari was a rebel.

He was one of the student ringleaders who constantly and loudly challenged the status quo in Walaria. Safar had spent many an evening at the *Foolsmire* listening to Olari and his band of committed brothers debate the great issues of the day, fueled by copious quantities of strong spirits. They deplored the oppression of the *common man*, which Safar thought humorous since the only common men Olari and his rich friends knew were the slaves who waited on them and the tradesmen who catered to their exclusive tastes. Olari and the others roundly denounced the heavy taxes Didima demanded and the corruption of a system where bribery was the rule, not the exception. They condemned the city's leaders as old men, cowardly men, greedy men, who lacked all capacity to understand the new ideas and grand reforms offered by their farseeing children.

Olari and his companions had tried to recruit Safar into their company. He was popular with all the other acolytes and if he joined them it would do much to strengthen their appeal with the university's intellectuals. Safar had always diplomatically refused, saying he wasn't a citizen of Walaria, nor did he intend to remain here when his studies were completed. He had no stake in Walaria, he said, and it would be wrong of him to take sides. Actually Safar considered the young rebels' ideals empty. Except for Olari, he thought their protests and petty conspiracies nothing more than spoiled children defying their parents. He excepted Olari because he thought it entirely possible the young nobleman was mapping out a shortcut to power. But the main reason he refused was that Olari and the other ringleaders were protected by their noble births. They were coddled by their families, who correctly said they'd soon grow out of this hot-headed stage. So it took no courage at all for them to express their views at the top of their lungs. Someone like Safar, however, would quickly find himself being hauled before Kalasariz as a traitor. In the past that fate had been only a strong probability. But now that Safar had actually met Kalasariz he knew it as a fact.

Another blast of fire and smoke thundered from a sewer pit, adding an odd drum beat of drama to the moment when Safar and Olari took the last few steps that closed the gap between them.

"I won't offer you a glad cry of welcome, Timura," he said, "because you'd curse me for it."

"And no one would blame me if I beat you about the head and shoulders as well," Safar laughed.

"Soon as I saw you," Olari said, "I thought—I'll be poached in shit sauce, if it isn't Safar Timura! The only time he's put on a work detail is when the whole class is being punished."

Safar shrugged. "It's my country upbringing that saves me," he said. "I'm good at ducking for cover and not getting caught."

"And did you?" Ersen asked. "Get caught, I mean. And what in the hells for?"

"Ersen asked the same thing," Safar said. "He seemed as surprised as you to see me here."

"And what did you tell him?" Olari asked.

"I lied," Safar answered, "and said I was here to help you burn the shitters. And that whatever it was I did to deserve it I'd forgotten because I was drunk."

Olari cocked his head, a small smile playing on his lips, considering what Safar's statement meant. Tall and darkly handsome, with deep brooding eyes offset by a dazzling white smile that charmed all who knew him, he was every inch a patrician, even in work robes and daubed with smoke and filth.

After a moment he nodded in satisfaction, smile spreading wider. "Come into my office, and we'll talk."

He gave Safar a follow me gesture and led him to a rubbish heap that hid a small cavelike opening in the wall. Olari dropped to his knees and crawled into it, Safar close behind. After a few feet the hole broadened into a small room. Olari lit a candle, revealing that the room was decorated with old mattresses and blankets. There were makeshift shelves bolted to the wall filled with sealed jars of food.

Olari lit a few more candles and a little smoke pot of incense to cover the sewer smell. Then he sank onto one of the mattresses and laid back, hands behind his head.

"What do you think of my office?" he asked.

"Considering the place it's in," Safar said, "I'm impressed."

"We take turns hiding out here," Olari said. "One group keeps watch while the other sleeps, or eats and even..." he reached to a low shelf, grabbed a stoppered jar and tossed it to Safar..."drinks."

"This is starting to take on the air of a palace," Safar said as he uncorked the jar. He took a long drink of what turned out to be a fine wine, then passed the jar to Olari.

The youth sat up and raised the jar, saying, "Here's to lies." And he drank.

As he passed the jar back to Safar he said, "I'm guessing that you're here because you've reconsidered my offer."

"That I have," Safar said. "I've decided to take you up on it."

"And why is that, my friend?" Olari asked. "What has suddenly made you see the light and decide to join our cause?"

"To be absolutely honest," Safar said, "I have no intention of joining anyone's cause. Although I'm risking the loss of your good opinion of me, I'll tell you straight out, Olari—I have a sudden need for a large sum of money. Call it a family emergency, if you will."

"There's no shame in that," Olari said. "Although I'd prefer it was your heart that guided you to me, not your purse."

"Oh, my heart's always been with you," Safar said. "You know I agree with most of what you say. I just don't feel involved because this is your home, not mine. If we were in Kyrania you'd feel the same."

"Perhaps I would," Olari said. "Perhaps I would."

"When we last spoke," Safar said, "you asked me to do a bit of creative sorcery for you."

Olari became as excited as his patrician mask would allow. Which meant his brooding eyes lit up and he crossed his legs. "Are you sure you can still do it?" he asked. "There isn't much time, you know. The Founder's Day festival is only two days off."

"There's time," Safar said.

"Are you certain? We need something really big. Something that will knock them out of their boots. Something that will show everyone what kind of fools we are ruled by."

"I think everyone in Walaria already knows that, Olari," Safar said. "They just don't talk about it much. Especially in public."

"Well, they'll talk after Founder's Day," Olari said. "If your magical event is big enough and public enough. The timing is crucial."

"I've thought of that," Safar said. "The spellcast I have in mind would work best if it came off at the Last Prayer ceremony. Right after the bells and the song when Umurhan does his annual magic trick to impress the masses."

"Where would you do it?" Olari asked.

"In the stadium, where else?" Safar answered. "Right in front of altar where Umurhan and Didima and Kalasariz will be holding court."

Olari whistled. "Right under their noses," he said. "I like that. And I can follow it up with spontaneous demonstrations and protest parades all over the city." He slapped his thigh. "That'll make them sit up and take notice."

Absently, Olari took another drink from the jar. "What exactly do you intend to do?" he asked.

"If you don't mind," Safar replied, "I'd really rather not say. It's a very complicated spell and very very delicate. Just speaking about it could disturb one of its parts and have a disastrous effect on the whole." He was lying. He hadn't had time to come up with the kind of magical disturbance Olari wanted. "But I promise you," he continued, "that it will be beyond your wildest wishes." This was only a partial lie. Safar *did* intend to deliver the spellcast, he just didn't know what it would be.

"The word of Safar Timura," Olari said, pricking Safar's conscience, "is good enough for me."

Safar hesitated, then took the plunge. "About the money," he said.

Olari gave a dismissive wave. "Don't worry," he said. "I've not forgotten. I promised you fifty gold coins. But I can see now I was being tight-fisted. Make it a hundred."

Safar's heart jumped—*so much*? "That's very generous of you," he said. "My, uh, family, will be more than thankful. But there's, uh, one other thing I'd like to ask."

"What's that?"

"Can I get it in advance?"

Olari stared at him long and hard.

"Just so you have all the facts you need to make up your mind, I'll tell you this," he said. "I intend to leave Walaria right after I do the casting. I know I'm putting a very large burden of trust on your shoulders, but I assure you I wouldn't ask if it wasn't necessary."

As Safar had hoped, the negative bit of information about his leaving helped sway Olari's decision.

"I think I can manage that load easily enough," the young nobleman said. "I'll do as you asked. Meet me at the *Foolsmire* tonight."

Safar thanked him and they shared a few drinks from the jar.

"I wish I could persuade you to stay," Olari said. "Things really will be different when we get rid of this lot."

"I'm sure it will be," Safar said. "But I worry about you. You've caused them no end of grief of late. Big demonstrations that have nearly turned into riots. Broadsides condemning them spread all over the city. What if they tire of it? Or worse, what if they suddenly think you are a great danger to them?"

"I want them to," Olari said. "That's my intent. How else can we achieve change?"

"I understand that," Safar said. "But you know, times really have been troublesome the past two years. And you can't blame it all on the Unholy Trio, as you call them. The weather has become increasingly unpredictable. As have the harvests. And there's been locust swarms and outbreaks of flux and plague. Not just in Walaria, either. It's happening all over Esmir."

Olari shrugged. "The gods are in charge of those things," he said. "And since it's their responsibility, what can I do? Besides, times will get better. They always do. History tells us that. And things aren't really so bad as you say. Deaths have been few. There's no mass starvation. Actually, many people live in relative plenty. And there's good news in the land as well. What of Iraj Protarus? He's our age. And look at all he's doing to change Esmir for the better."

"I don't call wars and raids on other people's kingdoms change for the better," Safar said.

Olari gave him a puzzled look. "I thought you two were friends?"

"We are," Safar said. "Or were, anyway. But that doesn't mean I agree with him."

Olari chuckled. "It seems Protarus and I have both had the same experience with you," he said. "You give us your friendship but not your company in our cause."

"I suppose you're right," Safar said. "But I've never been enamored of causes. Politics don't interest me. Only the science and history of magic."

"I suppose you'd like to put that interest to real use someday," Olari said. "To help people, for instance. To better their lot, their condition, with your skills."

"I'll admit I've thought of such things," Safar said.

"That's a cause isn't it?" Olari said. "Your cause, of course. But a cause just the same."

"I suppose it is," Safar said.

"So why do you shun my cause, and the cause of your friend Protarus. We're all the same age. We all have similar ideals. It's time for a change, dammit. A massive change. We've lived under the heels of old men for too long."

Safar couldn't say he theorized change might already be occurring. But it was a change on a scale much greater than two young men who wanted to be king.

Instead he said, "Allow me my delusions, Olari. I'm sure you and Iraj will soon prove me to be a blind fool. And I hope you forgive me when that time comes."

"You're forgiven already, my friend," Olari said. "Just make sure that when the time comes you know which way to jump."

"That's wise advice," Safar said. "I'll remember it. But I hope you'll also remember mine. Be careful of Kalasariz. I have a feeling he's becoming anxious."

"What if he does?" Olari said. "What can he do to me? The brutal truth of the matter is that there are two kinds of people in Walaria. Those who have reason to fear Tulaz' blade. And those who do not. And I, my bookish friend, belong in the first category by reason of my birth and my father's fortune."

Just then Gundara whispered in Safar's ear. "The spy approaches!"

Safar held up a hand to silence Olari. A heartbeat later they heard Ersen's sarcastic voice. "Do I hear sounds of merrymaking within?"

Ersen ducked into the room and saw the wine jar in Olari's hand. "What a greedy lot of beggars," he said. "Keeping the wine for yourself when your poor friend Ersen is nearly dying of thirst."

Olari laughed and handed the jar over. Ersen took a long drink, then sat on a mattress. "What are you fellows up to?" he asked. "Plotting the overthrow of the world as we know it, is my guess."

Ersen was not a member of Olari's group. He was too much of a jester to be welcomed. Still, Safar was worried that Olari would say too much. He made a hidden gesture of warning, then said to Ersen:

"You found us out, you canny devil. We've been sitting here for hours planning our revolt. We're thinking of starting with Didima. I've got a recipe we can slip into his food that'll make him limp as a wet rag."

"That's a good start," Ersen said. "What about Kalasariz? I've heard he doesn't have a tool at all."

"Exactly what I've been telling Timura," Olari said. "We have to come up with something different for him."

"Well, I'm just your man," Ersen said. "See if you can find another jar of wine in there, Timura. There's a good fellow. Conspiracy makes thirsty work."

# 13

# ZEMAN'S REVENGE

It was just after Last Prayer and the *Foolsmire* was filling up with thirsty students. Inside the shop Zeman kept an eye on the alley entrance while he handed out books and collected rental fees. The word had come down from Kalasariz that Safar was expected to visit tonight in order to meet with Olari and his group of malcontents. Zeman's orders were to learn the purpose of that meeting and to report back what he found.

Zeman was vastly pleased with himself. His grandfather had been away when the letter from Iraj Protarus had arrived for Safar. Soon as he saw it Zeman thought his fortune was made. As anxious as he'd been to pass it on to the spymaster, he'd first taken time to examine the opportunity from every angle.

He'd been in Kalasariz' employ for over a year. He had a small copper chest under his bed filled with money earned from all the information he'd passed on to the spymaster. The *Foolsmire* was an ideal place to pick up gossip from wine-soaked students and learn of their crimes; past, present, and planned. It was a task Zeman found himself ideally suited for. His awkward ways, bad manners, and sly, short-changing habits had made him an object of derision among the young customers. He'd suffered their mocking remarks for years. Like most insensitive people Zeman's own feelings were extremely delicate and the remarks wounded him deeply. His reaction had been to become more abrasive and to cheat them every chance he had. Once he became a paid informer, however, the jibes no longer injured him. As an informer he was a man of power who secretly repaid every insult with a report that put a black mark next to their names. Also, except for the jibes, no one paid any attention to Zeman when he came near. The students thought so poorly of him they spoke freely in his presence, unaware all they said was being passed on to Kalasariz.

Safar was one of the few regulars who never joined the others in the game of Zeman-baiting. Zeman hated him for it. He saw condescension, not kindness, in Timura. He also strongly believed Safar had designs of his own on the *Foolsmire*. Look at how he toadied up to Katal, pretending he actually liked the old man and cared what he thought. Zeman saw his grandfather as a crazy, irresponsible old man who lived in a dreamworld where food for thought was more important than food for the table. Katal had the audacity to tell him some months ago that when he died he'd made arrangements for two small bequests—one for Timura and the other for that little thiefbitch, Nerisa.

Zeman had been scandalized by the news. The old man was giving away what rightfully belonged to his grandson. He became convinced the bequests had been Timura's goal all along. Safar was stealing Katal's affection and if Zeman didn't put a stop to it soon the old man would end up handing over all his worldly goods to Safar, leaving Zeman with nothing. As for Nerisa, why it was as plain as a full moon on a cold night that she was in league with Timura. Look at how she played on the old man's weaknesses—pretending to be a helpless orphan but all the while cozening up to Katal so she could win a place in his home and at his table. Zeman also believed her relationship with Timura was scandalous. He was certain they were sleeping together, which made Nerisa a child whore and Timura a whoremaster who probably traded her around to other decadent men who savored the flesh of children.

Zeman considered it his holy duty to put a stop to it. He'd plotted long and hard to find the rock that would crush them both. The letter, combined with Nerisa's robbery of the stall-master, had given him that opportunity. When he'd finally delivered the letter he'd added a report linking the two together as conspirators against Walaria.

Now his plan was about to bear fruit. Other evidence had been found against Timura. At least that's what he surmised when the urgent message came that he was to watch Safar carefully tonight and report back all that he'd found. Zeman sensed a crisis coming—a crisis for Safar and Nerisa, at least. When it arrived the only thing that would make Zeman's world even more perfect would be if he could rid himself of his grandfather as well. He didn't know how he could accomplish that feat just yet. But he was confident if he were especially watchful the idea would come.

A voice broke into his thoughts: "What's the matter with you, Zeman? Got dirt stuffed in your ears?"

He looked up and saw the sarcastic amusement in a young customer's face. "I've told you twice, now," the student said, "that you've given me too much change."

Zeman glanced at the rental book in the student's hand and the coins on the desk. He'd been so lost in thought that he'd forgotten his original intent—which was to shortchange the student. He made a quick count of coins and saw that instead he'd returned too much.

"I don't mind cheating *you*," the student said. "The gods know you've robbed me often enough. But that was for your own pocket. This is for old man Katal."

"No one's forcing you to come here," Zeman snarled as he pulled in the excess change. "If you don't like I how do business, go someplace else. You won't be missed by me."

Instead of getting angry the student laughed at him. "No one cares what you think, Zeman," he said. "You don't own this place. Your grandfather does. We only put up with you because of old man Katal."

He grabbed his change and walked into the patio, laughing and telling the others about the encounter. Zeman was about to shout an insult when he saw Timura coming down the alley. Quickly he put out a coin basket and little sign telling the other bookstore patrons to wait on themselves. It was an honor system Katal had instituted long ago for the busiest hours. Zeman disliked the practice and had argued against it many times. He planned to end it soon as Katal gave up his stubborn hold on life and died. But just now it served his purpose.

As he headed for the patio and the crowded tables of wine drinkers someone tried to stop him and hand him money for a book.

"What are you—blind?" Zeman retorted, pointing at the basket. "Put your money there. I've got other things to do."

He rushed out, not hearing the response. His grandfather was at the well, drawing up buckets of cold wine jugs and stacking them on trays. Zeman saw Timura head for a large table in the far corner where Olari was holding court. Zeman was thrilled—the intelligence he'd received about the predicted meeting was evidently correct.

He snatched a tray from Katal's hands. "Here, let me help you with that, grandfather," he said to the startled old man.

Zeman ignored the pleased expression on his grandfather's face. He balanced the tray above his head and moved slowly through the crowd. People shouted for service as he passed, but he paid them no mind, concentrating instead on Safar and Olari. Timura's arrival was met with shouted welcomes and Olari rose to greet him, slapping him on the back and then leaning close to whisper something in his ear. Safar laughed as if he'd just been told a grand joke, but Zeman saw Olari pass him a small object, which he tucked into his robe.

Instead of going directly to Olari's table Zeman delivered his tray to the one closest to it. Moving at a snail's pace, he put a jug in front of each person; his focus was entirely on the discussion swirling around Timura.

He could pick up only snatches of the excited babble: "...history in the making...teach them a lesson they'll never forget...Umurhan will just shit...it's gonna be the best Founder's Day ever!"

When the tray was empty he stepped over to Olari's table; as usual, no one paid him the slightest attention, other than to order a drink or to berate him for being lazy and slow. Zeman smiled blandly at the insults, gradually working his way toward Timura. He was just at Olari's elbow, bending his head close as he could to hear the whispered conversation between the two, when Safar suddenly looked up and saw him. His eyes were wide as if someone had just said something surprising. Then they narrowed in what seemed to be sudden understanding.

Zeman couldn't bring himself to tear his gaze away from Safar's stare.

He *knows*, Zeman thought. Timura knows I'm an informer. But that's not possible! How could he?

Then Timura broke his gaze and touched Olari's hand in warning. The young noble snipped off whatever it was he was saying and leaned closer so Timura could whisper something in his ear. Zeman saw him jolt and start to turn to look in his direction, but another warning touch from Timura stopped him.

Zeman calmed himself. His imagination was running wild, he thought. There was no way Timura could know he was a spy. Safar's behavior was the result of guilt, not knowledge. He and Olari were obviously planning something and Timura was smart enough to make sure that not even someone he held in such contempt as Zeman would overhear. But he still felt uncomfortable, so he hurried away from the table on the pretense of fetching the orders for wine.

***

Safar watched Zeman dodge through the crowd, the empty tray clutched tightly to his side.

"How do you know he's an informer?" Olari asked. "He's so stupid and lazy, it's hard to believe Kalasariz would ever want him."

"Trust me," Safar said. "Or at least, humor me. My information comes from an impeccable source."

Gundara's hissed warning had come just as Olari was discussing the disturbances he intended to stage after Safar's spellcast disrupted the Founder's Day ceremony. Safar had been nearly bowled over when he realized the little Favorite had fingered Zeman. After his initial surprise he had felt pity for poor Katal. His next thought was the realization that it was none other than Zeman who had put Kalasariz on his trail with trumped up charges. Anger boiled over in his belly, rising to sear the back of his throat. It was Zeman's fault that his life and Nerisa's were in danger. Under the circumstances anger was futile, as were any thoughts of revenge that would delay his flight from Walaria.

"You probably think I've suddenly gone mad," Safar said. "Insane or not, you can't be harmed by following my advice and being careful around him."

"I don't think you're mad," Olari said. "But I do wonder how you got your information."

"I can't say," Safar said.

"Anyone else we should be wary of?" Olari asked.

Safar knew if mentioned Ersen, Olari really would think he'd gone crazy. So he said, "Look at it this way—if someone like Zeman can be a spy, then who *can* you trust? The most unlikely person could be a direct pipeline into Kalasariz. Why, even Ersen—jester that he is—could be with the enemy."

"Ersen?" Olari said. "What brought his name into this?"

Safar shook his head. "Please, just be careful. Question everything. Everyone."

"Actually," Olari said, "Ersen makes more sense than Zeman. His father ran into some trouble with Kalasariz a few years ago. He seemed doomed for awhile, but then suddenly everything was fine again. And he's done nothing but rise in the ranks of the Walarian Council since Ersen started at the University."

Safar didn't respond and after a bit Olari realized he wasn't going to say anything more.

"For a man who doesn't like politics," Olari said, "you sure have a talent for wading into it up to your neck."

An hour later Safar lit the oil lamps in his rooms above the old city wall and got out his chest of magical implements. He had an idea for the spellcast he'd promised Olari and he thought he'd work on it while waiting for Nerisa.

The spell links came to him quickly and he jotted them down for reference and then got out a clean casting scroll and his brushes and magical paints. Gundara was busy devouring the sweet rolls he'd been promised and was quiet for a time. As he nibbled on the last of his treats, the little Favorite noticed what Safar was doing and watched with some amusement—picking dried berries and crumbs off his tunic and popping them in his mouth.

Safar used a narrow brush to paint sorcerous symbols on the rough white surface of the scroll, building up the spellcast's foundation.

"You can tell you're a student," Gundara criticized. "Too complicated. And do you really want to put the water sign in the center? Most wizards I know shove it in a corner out of the way."

"I'm not other wizards," Safar said. "And in this particular spell water goes in the center."

"O-kay," Gundara said. "If that's what you *really* want. But I think it's pretty stupid." He'd finished the rolls and with no other tasties in sight he didn't see any reason for continued politeness.

"You'd better pray I'm right," Safar said, "because you're the one who's going to carry it out."

"Oh, that's just wonderful," Gundara complained. "Here I am, the product of history's greatest wizardly minds, reduced to student pranks."

"This happens to be a prank," Safar pointed out, "that may save your master's life."

"Oh, in that case," Gundara said, "leave the water sign in the center. I'll get a new master quicker."

Safar, mind buzzing with the spell cast he was forming, started to get irritated. But when he saw the Favorite licking the sugary remains off his ugly little face he had to laugh.

"You win," he said. He dabbed white magical paint over the blue water sign. "Will the right hand corner do, O Wise One?"

Gundara shrugged. "Put it where you like. Makes no never mind to me. The Master knows best, that's my motto from now on."

"Fine, I'll put it there," Safar said. "Now, what symbol would you suggest for the center?"

Gundara got interested in spite of himself. "How about Fire?" he said. "That's a good symbol."

"Fire it is, then," Safar said, loading his brush with new paint and making red flame-like flares in the center."

"Of course, Lord Asper would've used his serpent symbol," Gundara said. "But I suppose he's out of favor with the younger wizards these days."

The name caught Safar by surprise. "Asper?" he goggled. "You know of Asper?"

Gundara sniffed, superior. "Certainly I do. You don't spend a couple of thousands years knocking around wizards' laboratories and not run into Lord Asper. Of course, his stuff was always more popular with demons. Since he was one. And I don't do demons. That's Gundaree's job. But I've picked up enough about him over the millennia to get by."

Safar pushed the scroll in front of him. "Show me," he said, holding out the brush.

Gundara hopped closer and grabbed the brush. Small as it was, it looked like a large spear in the little Favorite's taloned paws. He washed off the red in a water dish and loaded it with green paint.

Gundara lectured as he drew. "The serpent had four heads so it could see in every direction. Each head had four poison fangs to help guard the center." He daubed in the long body. "And there was a poison stinger on the tail in case the serpent was attacked from overhead. And then up here, right below where the heads join, you need to give the serpent wings so he can escape into the air if he needs to."

When he was done, Gundara stepped back to examine his work. "Not bad," he said, "even if I do say so myself."

His twin must have uttered an insult, for he suddenly turned toward the turtle idol, which was sitting next to the brazier. "Oh, shut up, Gundaree!" he snarled. "Shut up, shut up!" He turned back to Safar. "He's so *rude*," the Favorite said. "You can't believe the things he says to me!"

Safar, who was getting used to the one-way exchange between the twins, paid no attention. He examined the scroll and when he was satisfied he made a magical gesture, stirring the air with a forefinger. A miniature tornado—about the size of Safar's little finger—sprang up over the paper, quickly drying the paint. When it was done Safar blew on it and the tornado vanished.

Then he rolled the scroll into a tight tube and gave it to Gundara.

"Keep it," he commanded. "When you hear me chant the words to the spell you are to activate it. Do you understand?"

"What's to understand?" Gundara said. "You humans make such work out of magic. Demon wizards know it all comes from the gut, not the head. They just do it, while you're still thinking about it."

Despite the retort the Favorite did as he was told, collapsing the paper tube into an object the size of an infant's finger and tucking it into his sleeve for safe keeping. For a change, however, Safar was stung by Gundara's comments.

He'd learned much in Walaria. He had a mental storehouse of spells to confront almost any possibility. And he had the sound intellectual knowledge to create new spells to meet eventualities rote learning didn't cover. Compared to the other students and, yes, even compared to Umurhan, he had much greater power. He could feel it surging forward when he cast a spell—so strong he had to hold back so he didn't betray his true abilities. Still, the force was nothing like he'd experienced when he'd bested the demons in the snowy pass years before. He'd tried in private many times but he'd never been able to equal the river-like surge he'd felt during that life-and-death moment. The failure frustrated him. At first he tried to tell himself it didn't matter. That magic really wasn't his true purpose—which was to find the answer to the puzzle of Hadin. But the more he'd studied, the more he'd realized the solution would only come through sorcery.

"When I have time," Safar said, "which probably won't be until I'm safely on my way home, you and I need to sit down and have a long talk about Hadin."

"Best place in the world," Gundara said. "Smartest mortals around. They made me, which ought to be proof enough. Although, somebody sure made a big mistake when they made Gundaree. Probably a human assistant. You know how there are. Of course, anything I have to say will be pretty old news. The gods were still in swaddling clothes last time we were there."

"Anything will help," Safar said. "Also I want to hear about Asper."

Gundara yawned. "That'll be a pretty short conversation," he said. "All I know is what I've heard from other wizards."

"I understand he wrote a book about his theories," Safar said. "Have you ever seen it?"

"No. And I don't know anyone who has."

"I think there's a copy in Umurhan's library," Safar said. "Among his forbidden books."

"Then why didn't you steal it today?" Gundara asked. "You could have gone upstairs. I told you it was safe. And once you were inside I could have sniffed it out for you easy. You wouldn't have even had to give me another sweet roll."

"There's wasn't time," Safar said. "Now I'm afraid there never will be. I don't dare go back to the University. And after Founder's Day I'll be running as fast as I can. With a lot of angry Walarians chasing me."

Nerisa's voice came from behind them—"I can get it for you."

Safar and Gundara turned to see her perched on the window sill.

"I was starting to worry about you," Safar said.

Gundara snickered. "Stick with worrying about yourself, Master," he said. "She does just fine. I sensed her climbing the watchtower fifteen minutes ago. But you didn't notice a thing until she was inside and announced herself."

Nerisa giggled. She jumped off the sill, dug a sweet out of her pocket and walked over to give it to the Favorite.

"I knew it was my lucky century," Gundara said, "soon as you stole me from that stall." He popped the sweet into his mouth, closing his eyes and chewing with great gusto.

"Why don't you go rest for awhile?" Safar told him. He gestured and the Favorite disappeared in a cloud of smoke. The turtle idol rocked on its legs as the smoke funneled into the stone. Then all was silent.

"His lip smacking gets to you after awhile," he told Nerisa.

"Never mind that, Safar," Nerisa said. "I really meant it. About the book. I can get in and out of Umurhan's place in no time. Especially with Gundara to help me."

"It's too dangerous," Safar said.

Nerisa put a hand on her hip. "Nobody's ever gotten close to me yet," she said. "What could be so hard about an old library? Let me have Gundara and I'll be back before First Prayer."

Safar shook his head. "You don't know what you're saying, Nerisa," he said. "Things are a lot worse since last night."

He made her sit down, brewed her a pot of mint tea, and told her an edited version of what he'd learned. He left out the bargain he'd made with Olari, figuring quite correctly that she'd want to get involved.

Tears welled up when he said he was leaving Walaria.

"It isn't safe for either of us," he said. He dug into the heavy purse Olari had given him and pulled out a handful of gold coins. "Here. This is for you."

Nerisa struck them away. Coins scattered across the floor.

"I don't want money," she said. "I can get money anytime."

Safar gathered them up again. "I'm not abandoning you, Nerisa," he said. "This is *just in case* money. If I'm caught, or...there's some other emergency. If all goes well, you can go with me if you want."

Nerisa grinned through her tears. "You'd really take me with you?" she cried.

"It won't be very safe," Safar warned her. "There'll be a lot people after me."

Nerisa threw her arms around him. "I don't care," she said. "Let them come. I know all kinds of tricks. They'll never catch us."

Safar unstuck her, gently pushing her back into her seat amongst the pillows. "You don't have to go all the way to Kyrania," he said. "It's a pretty boring place for someone who grew up in Walaria."

"Well, it won't be boring to *me*," Nerisa said, thinking that for all she cared Kyrania could be the dullest place in all Esmir. It didn't matter as long as she was near Safar.

Safar patted her hand. "We'll see," he said. "Once we're clear of Walaria we can talk about this again."

"Anything you say, Safar," Nerisa said, dreamy.

Then she yawned and stretched. "I'm so tired," she said. "Can I sleep here for awhile? I've been ducking and hiding all day."

Safar hesitated. "They know to look for you here," he said.

Nerisa yawned again. "That's okay," she said. "Gundara will warn us if anybody comes."

Safar started to say it was still too big a chance to take. Then heard her breathing deepen and looked over and saw that she'd fallen asleep. In repose she seemed even younger and more vulnerable. Her lashes were delicate fans on her soft cheeks. He could see the fine bones of her face and thought that someday she'd be a great beauty. If she lived long enough to reach womanhood. He didn't have the heart to awaken her. So he banked the coals in the brazier and pinched out the wicks in the oil lamps. He found an extra blanket and covered her. She sighed, clutching the blanket tight and murmuring his name. Safar found a comfortable place a few feet away. So much had happened he doubted he'd be able to do much more than rest. But he'd barely closed his eyes when sleep rose up to carry him away.

It was a dreamless sleep, although once he thought he heard the rustle of fabric and felt soft lips brush his.

The next thing he knew the door crashed open and four burly men rushed inside.

He rolled out of his blankets but before he could come to his feet the men were on him. They clubbed him down and pinned him to the floor.

Then a heavy boot crashed into his head and stars of pain flared. He lost consciousness for a moment, then he heard steel strike flint and he opened his eyes to see Kalasariz standing over him, an oil lamp in his hand.

"Acolyte Timura," the spymaster intoned, "you are charged with conspiracy against the crown. What do you have to say for yourself?"

Safar was dazed by the beating. He tried to speak, but his

tongue was thick and refused to work. Then he remembered Nerisa. His heart jumped and he turned his head to see where she was. But she was nowhere in sight. Relief flooded in—thank the gods, somehow she'd managed to escape. Then another thought pierced the haze. Why hadn't Gundara warned him about Kalasariz' approach?

The spymaster held a heavy purse over Safar's head. It was the purse of gold Olari had given him, minus the coins he'd shared out with Nerisa. Kalasariz shook the purse. "What's this?" he said. Then he opened it and spilled coins into his palm. "This is a great deal of money for a poor student to have in his possession," he gloated.

Safar said nothing.

"Where did you get so much gold, Acolyte?" the spymaster demanded. "And what did you swear to do to earn it?"

Safar still said nothing. What was the point?

Kalasariz kicked him again. "It will do you no good to hide in silence, Acolyte Timura," he said. "Your fellow conspirators have already confessed."

Safar regained enough wit to say, "Then you don't need to hear from me, do you, My Lord?"

The reply won him another kick, this time in the ribs. They hauled him to his feet, gasping for breath.

But he still had presence of mind to look over at the brazier where he'd last seen the stone idol.

It was gone.

The only thing he could think was, Nerisa must have it.

Then Kalasariz roared, "Take him away! The sight of this heretic offends me!"

And they dragged him out the door.

"Hsst! Someone's coming!"

A dim light appeared and Nerisa dropped to the ground. She hugged the stone as a dark figure shuffled out of a corridor and headed her way. She was on the top floor of the University—no more than a hundred feet, Gundara had informed her, from Umurhan's library. The Favorite was a flea speck on her sleeve—he'd told her about Safar's method of carrying him about and she'd adopted it.

The shuffling figure was an old priest. He mumbled to himself, cursing the cold stone on his bare feet and muttering deprecations against the devils who had conspired to hide his sandals. He was carrying a small oil lamp with a nearly burned out wick that gave off just enough light to make her nervous. She flattened herself as he walked right up to her, then veered to the side to fumble at a door. He broke wind loudly and Nerisa guessed the door led to a privy. The priest went inside and shut the door.

Nerisa came up like a cat and ghosted down the corridor until Gundara told her to stop because she'd found the library. It was locked, but that only delayed her for a few seconds. She fished a narrow bar from her pocket, slipped it into the keyhole and forced the big tumbler back. In an instant she was inside, quietly closing the door behind her.

The library was a sealed room and so dark she couldn't make out even the largest objects. But she could smell the dusty odor of old books, just like the ones at the *Foolsmire*, except there was heavy sulfur smell of magic that made her throat feel raw.

"I can't see," she whispered to Gundara.

There was a sudden glow and the Favorite appeared before her full size—which meant he came up to about her knee. His body gave off a dim green light and she could see the hulking shadows of furniture and book shelves.

Gundara made a slow circle, sniffing the air. In her pocket she felt the stone idol become warm as the Favorite drew on its magical power.

Then he said, "This way," and scampered off into the darkness.

Nerisa followed and they moved along the twisting aisles until they came to the far side of the room where tall bookcases lined the blank wall. Gundara hopped from shelf to shelf until he was eye-level with Nerisa.

"There it is," he said, pointing a glowing talon. "Asper in the flesh." Gundara snickered. "The book's bound in leather," he said. "Get it—flesh! Ha ha. I'm pretty funny tonight."

"It must be the sugar," Nerisa said through gritted teeth.

At first she'd thought the Favorite was a cute little thing. She felt sorry for him because he had to live in a hunk of stone. But after several hours in Gundara's company she just wanted to get the job over with and hand him back to Safar. Honestly, he asked such personal questions. Statements, actually. Like accusing her of being in love with Safar. Which was true, but it was none of his fiendish business.

Gundara gripped the edge of a slender book and heaved mightily. It came out so fast he lost his balance. He squealed as he fell, scaring Nerisa half to death. She caught him in midair, but the book slammed to the floor, echoing loudly.

"Be careful," she whispered. "You'll wake them up!"

"Oh, piddle pooh," the Favorite said—although he *did* whisper. "You could shout at the top of your voice and those old gas bags would never wake up."

"Just the same," Nerisa said, "I wish you'd be more quiet. I'm used to working alone and loud sounds bother me."

"You're a pretty good little thief, dearie," Gundara said. "But I bet you wish you had me around *all* the time. You'd be rich! We'd steal everything that wasn't nailed down."

"Riiight," Nerisa said, bending down to pick up the book.

It was thin and seemed to contain so few pages Nerisa feared Safar would be disappointed. The leather was cracked and old, but from the light Gundara gave off she could see the worn image of a four-headed serpent.

"That's Asper's book all right," Gundara said. "There's probably not more than five or six in the whole world." He preened, proud of his work.

She started to fish a treat from her pocket to reward him, when he suddenly said—quite loud—"You shut up, Gundaree. You couldn't of found it if it were on fire. So there. Don't you call me that! Shut up, you hear me? Shut up! Shut up! Shu—"

Nerisa clamped a hand over his mouth, cutting off the rest.

"Stop that," she said. "Or I'll wring your neck. I swear I will."

When she took her hand away Gundara hung his head. He kicked at the floor with his elegant little foot. "I'm sorry," he said. "He just gets me soooo mad, sometimes."

"Just don't do it anymore," Nerisa said. Then she gave him the treat.

Gundara grinned and gobbled it down. "I like you, dearie," he said. "I hope Safar gives you a nice little diddle after he gets the book."

"Don't talk like that," Nerisa said. "It isn't nice."

"But it's what you want, isn't it?" the Favorite teased. "A big old sloppy kiss and then get diddled all night."

Nerisa tucked the book away with the stone idol. "That's enough," she said. "And if you say one word like that to Safar, I'll, I'll...never speak to you again. See if I don't."

Apparently this was a greater threat than a neck-wringing, for Gundara instantly apologized and said he'd never, ever do such a thing. Then he led the way back to the library door, shrunk down to flea size again and they slipped out into the corridor. After an hour of creeping about in the dark, Nerisa sprinted through the big main gate and headed down the broad avenue—leap frogging from shadow to shadow as she made her way back to Safar's place.

She arrived just as Kalasariz and his men were dragging Safar down the stairs.

It was a night of terror in Walaria. Kalasariz' men swept through the city, breaking down doors and hauling frightened young men into the streets where they were beaten and questioned under the shuttered windows of their families' homes. Then they were taken to the spymaster's torture rooms where they were questioned further and forced to sign confessions. There were about fifty in all, although less than half were acquainted with Olari. The others were innocent, but had been marked for seizure by Kalasariz' informers who did a record business that night collecting bribes from enemies of the young men and their families.

Justice was swift. There was no trial, nor were any of the condemned present when a High Judge sentenced them to death. The mass execution was set for the following day—which happened to be Founder's Day. Town criers went through the city, shouting the news of the executions and posting notices listing the names of the condemned and their crimes.

At the top of the list was the name of the ringleader—one Safar Timura, foreigner.

At the bottom of the list was the name of one of his dupes—Olari, citizen.

"Apparently I misjudged my family's influence," Olari said.

Safar wrung out the rag, freshened it from the pail of cold water and wiped the blood from Olari's face. He had been beaten so badly his head was swollen to half again its size.

"You always were a master of understatement," Safar said.

Other than the bruises he'd suffered when he was captured, Safar was unscathed. For some reason he hadn't been tortured and his "confession"—an unsigned document with Kalasariz' seal—had been good enough for the High Judge.

"The real pity of it is," Olari said, "I'm not even getting any credit. I'm to go down in Walarian history as a mere minion."

"And I the minion in chief," Safar said. "On the whole I'd rather pass on the honor. But Kalasariz was quite insistent. You know how persuasive he is."

"My father most likely paid a handsome sum to have me listed as a dupe of your devilish tongue," Olari said. "Protecting the family honor and all that. Stupid, I guess, is better than king of the traitors."

The two young men were in the company of six other youths, all suffering from the ghastly work of the torturer. They were slumped in the center of the cell, barely able to chase away inquisitive insects and rats. All eight of them were to be beheaded by Tulaz, the master executioner. The others, crowded in nearby cells, would be parceled out in lots five or less to ten other executioners.

"There is *one* consolation," Olari said.

"What's that?" Safar asked. "I could use a bit of cheering up."

"I'm to go last," Olari said. "Which means whether Tulaz succeeds or fails, I'll be remembered. If he strikes off my head with one blow, I'll be helping him break his record. If not, why I'll go down in the wagering books as the one who ended Tulaz' remarkable streak."

Safar laughed. It was a bitter sound. "I wish I could be there to see how it turns out," he said. "Unfortunately, I go first."

Olari tried to laugh. A sharp pain in his ribs turned it to a low groan. When he'd recovered, he shook his head, saying, "I always was—"

His words were cut off by a coughing fit. Safar held him until it stopped. Then his companion spit blood into the pail. There was a plop as one of his teeth fell into the water.

He looked up at Safar, grinning a bloody grin.

"What I was trying to get out before nature so rudely interrupted me," Olari said, "was that I've always been a lucky dog.

"And it looks like that luck is going to stick with me until the very end."

# 14
# DEATH SPEAKS

"You're too tense," the trainer complained as he kneaded the massive body stretched out before him. "Can't get the kinks out 'less you relax."

"Slept like shit," Tulaz said. "Don't know what's wrong with me. I al'ays sleep like a babe. 'Specially afore a work day. But it weren't like that last night. Kept dreamin' about this little fiendish thing. Body like a man, face like a toad. Kept on sayin'—'Shut up, shut up, shut up!"

The trainer's brow knotted in worry. The executions—moved to the main arena to handle the Founder's Day crowds—were less than an hour away. All his savings had been risked on the outcome.

"Bad luck, a dream like that," Tulaz went on. "Got me all out of sorts, it did. Can't figure out what I done to bring it on."

"You purged yourself like I tole you?" the trainer asked, pummeling Tulaz' thick body.

The Master Executioner of Walaria snorted. "'Course. Filled five buckets, didn't I?"

"And you've been stickin' to your diet?"

"Gruel and water'd wine, nothin' more," Tulaz said. "It's this big rush that's botherin' me. I usually get some notice, you know? Couple of days at least to get into shape. 'Sides, I just broke me own record couple a days ago.

"Seven heads takes a lot out of a man, which most people don't appreciate. They just come and see me lop 'em off. Miss all the fine points. Don't know how hard I works to keep a good form. I ain't recovered from the seven, yet. Now I gotta go for eight, afore I'm even ready."

"Don't think about it," the trainer advised. "It's just one more day like any other. Keep that in your noggin' and it'll work out fine."

"Sure," Tulaz said. "That's the trick. Just another day. Nothin' special about it."

The trainer poured scented oil on Tulaz and started working it in. "And each head, too," he said. "Look at 'em the same way. Don't count how many you gots to go. One or eight, what's the difference? They all gotta come off one at a time. Nothin' special about that."

"Yeah," Tulaz said. "That's the only way they go—one at a time. Thanks. I'm feelin' much better already."

The trainer chuckled and said thanks weren't necessary. He finished his task, covered Tulaz with heavy towels and advised him to take a nap.

"I'll call you in plenty of time," he said.

He crept out of the training room, but just before he exited he looked back at Tulaz. The giant executioner was lying face up, a brawny arm shielding his eyes.

And he was muttering to himself: "Shut up, shut up, shut up. Wonder what he meant?"

For the first time in Tulaz' long and illustrious career he was obviously distracted and suffering from a decided lack of confidence. The trainer left the room, wondering where he could get some money quick to lay off his bets.

The crowd roared. Safar was led out first, followed by Olari and six others, all manacled and chained together. Forty-two heads had already been severed and the crowd was bored by the spotty performances of the executioners. But this was the main event: Tulaz, the Master Executioner of Walaria, was going for an eighth and record head.

Safar was nearly blinded by the bright morning sun. He tried to shield his face, but his arms were brought up short by a chain linked to a thick iron waist band. A guard cursed and prodded him along with a spear butt.

When his vision cleared Safar could see that he was being taken to a large, hastily erected execution platform in the center of the arena. It had been thrown up next to the dignitaries' stand, where King Didima, Umurhan, and Kalasariz sat in pillowed and canopied comfort.

When Kalasariz announced the results of the roundup, Didima had decided to make the mass executions part of the Founder's Day ceremonies. The king prided himself on making quick, tough decisions, even if others believed them too daring or tradition-breaking. He thought the executions would whet the appetites of his citizens for the festivities that would follow.

"It will bring us all together at a special time," he told Umurhan and Kalasariz. "Heal the discord among our citizens."

Umurhan, a usually cautious man, had agreed without argument. Although he didn't state his reasons, the High Priest of Walaria had been troubled of late that his annual display of sorcery wasn't being greeted with the sort of respectful enthusiasm and awe it deserved. Fifty severed heads would go long way to warming up the crowd.

Kalasariz also thought it was an excellent idea, although he too chose not to mention them to his two comrades. For his purposes it was always better to get political executions out of the way as fast as possible—before families and friends and loved ones had time to work up a good, lasting grievance. Swift executions put the fear of the gods in them, quelling vengeful thoughts.

The crowd gathered to witness the event was the largest in Walaria's history. It spilled out of the stands onto the floor of the arena. Hundreds were packed within twenty feet of the execution platform itself and more were squeezing in every minute, crowing over their good fortune and clutching prized tickets Didima's soldiers were selling at premium prices.

Safar's guards had to push people out of the way as he and his companions in misery shambled toward the platform. People shouted at him, snaking hands past the guards to try to touch him. For luck, he supposed. If so, it was a sorry sort of fortune.

Some cursed him. Some cheered him. Some cried "courage, my lad."

Hawkers mingled with the crowd, selling food and souvenirs. One enterprising young man had fistfuls of candied figs mounted on pointed sticks. The figs were painted with food dye to make them look like human heads. Blood-colored food dye streaked sticks to mimic the sharpened stakes Safar and the others would soon have their heads mounted upon.

Safar was too numb to know fear. He concentrated on putting one foot in front of the other. If he had any feeling at all it was to wish it would be over quick.

All eight were led onto the platform, slipping on the bloody planks. Men with buckets and mops were cleaning up the gore from the previous executions. Others sprinkled sand around the cutting block to give Tulaz decent footing. The condemned were lined up at the edge of the platform, where guards doused them with cold water and gave them wine-soaked sponges to suck so they wouldn't faint and spoil the show.

Then Tulaz himself mounted the platform and the crowd thundered its approval. The Master Executioner was dressed in his finest white silk pantaloons. His immense torso glistened with expensive oil allowing the bright sun to pick out the definition of his mighty muscles picked out by the bright sun. His white silk hood was spotless, without a crease or stray thread to spoil its symmetry. Thick bands of gold encircled his wrists and biceps.

Tulaz went right to work, paying no attention to the crowd. First he checked the steps where the condemned would kneel, then the hollowed-out chopping block where each man would stretch his neck to receive the blade. When he was satisfied he shouted for his sword case. While he waited he drew on special gloves created just for him by the best glove-maker in Walaria. The palm surface was pebbled and the fingers were cut out to improve his grip. The crowd was hushed as an assistant presented the open case and Tulaz bowed before it, muttering a short prayer of greeting. The hush turned to a deafening roar when he removed the gleaming scimitar and held it up high for the gods to see.

Tulaz lowered the blade, caressing it and whispering endearments as if it were his child. Then he removed his favorite whetstone from a slot in his wide, leather belt and he began to hone the edge. Each slow practiced movement drew cries of admiration from the crowd, but Tulaz kept his eyes averted, his attention fully on the sword.

After a few moments Tulaz walked over to the condemned, still stropping his blade. He paused in front of Safar, who looked up and found himself peering into the darkest, saddest eyes he'd ever seen.

"It'll be over soon, lad," Tulaz said, his voice remarkably soothing. "There's nothin' personal, you know. Law says what it says and I just do me job. So don't fight it, son. And don't jerk about. I'm your friend. Last friend you'll ever know. And I promise I'll make her nice and clean and send you to your rest quick as I can."

Safar didn't answer—what was there to say? Nonetheless, Tulaz seemed satisfied and he turned away, stone whisk-whisking along the steel edge.

The executioner had mounted the platform still feeling edgy, unsettled. But after talking to Safar he found his nerves steadying. He thought, That's good. Al'ays nice to talk to your first head. Let's the gods know you're serious about your work.

He turned to the soldiers guarding the condemned. "Get those chains off'n my heads," he said. "And rub 'em down good afore the bodies stiffen up."

Safar suddenly felt lighter as the chains fell away. Strong hands massaged him, bringing life back to his numb limbs. Then he was guided forward and he heard Olari call to him, but the words were lost in the crowd noises.

"Steady, lad," he heard Tulaz say as he was pushed into a kneeling position before the block.

Safar raised up to take one last look at the world. He saw a sea of faces screaming for his death. Some snapped out at him with remarkable clarity. There was an old man, howling through toothless gums. There was a matron, babe at breast, watching the proceedings with a look of remarkable serenity. Then, just below him, he saw a young face—a girl's face.

It was Nerisa!

She charged out of the crowd and rushed the platform. Soldiers grabbed at her, but she ducked under their outstretched hands. The nails of those grasping hands raked blood streaks on her arms. Fingers tightened on her tunic, but she pulled away with such force that all they captured was torn cloth.

"Here Safar!" she shouted. "Here!"

She threw something at the platform. It sailed through the air and landed next to the cutting block with a heavy thud. Safar didn't look to see what it was. Instead, he watched in horror as the soldiers reached Nerisa.

A mace crashed down on her head—blood spraying everywhere.

Then she was buried under a dozen soldiers.

The crowd roar diminished to puzzled shouts and then a low buzz as people asked each other what had happened.

Tulaz' voice rose above the buzz—"That's it! I can't work like this. The whole thing's off!"

Safar heard another man speak most urgently—"You can't quit now, Tulaz! Think of all the money riding on this, man! They'll skin you alive!" It was the trainer, who'd evidently found enough coin to copper his bet.

Then a great voice thundered, "Citizens! Friends!"

It was King Didima, who'd come to his feet to address the crowd, his voice magically amplified by Umurhan.

"Today is a great day in Walaria's history," Didima said. "It would be wrong of us and an insult to the gods who favor our fair city to allow a malcontent to spoil these holy ceremonies. We have all had a marvelous time this morning. And we owe a debt of gratitude to Lord Kalasariz for his thoughtful efforts to present us with such marvelous entertainment, while at the same time striking a blow for all law-abiding citizens.

"Now, let us resume our entertainment, my good friends and fellow Walarians. Our great executioner, Tulaz, was about to astound us with a feat never before attempted."

The king turned toward Tulaz, shouting, "Let the executions resume!"

Someone grabbed Safar by the hair and forced his head on the block. Under royal command Tulaz stepped forward, slashing the air with his sword to warm up.

"Hold him steady," he shouted.

The hand tightened its grip in Safar's hair.

Just then a small, familiar voice hissed from beside him, "Shut up, Gundaree! I don't need your help."

Tulaz froze, his nightmare coming back to haunt him. "Who said that? Who said shut up?"

And Gundara said, "Shut up! I'm not listening, Gundaree. Uh, uh. No, no. Don't care what you say. Shut up, shut up, shut up!"

The fingers loosened and Safar jerked free. He glanced down and saw the object Nerisa had thrown—it was the turtle idol. He looked up and saw Tulaz towering over him, scimitar raised high to strike. But the executioner was motionless, stricken with fear.

"The dream!" he said. "It's coming true!"

"Forget the dream," the trainer cried, pushing at the brawny executioner. "Quick! Cut off his head!"

Safar grabbed up the idol. "Appear, Favorite!" he commanded.

There was a boil of smoke and Gundara leaped out onto the platform.

Tulaz goggled at the little figure. "No!" he shouted. "Get away from me!"

"What's he all excited about?" Gundara asked Safar.

"Never mind that," Safar snapped. "Do something about the sword before he changes his mind."

"Okay. If you insist. But it looks like a pretty nice sword."

"Just do it," Safar said.

Gundara made a lazy gesture, there was a loud *crack!* and the sword shattered like glass.

Tulaz screamed in horror and leaped off the platform.

Gundara brushed his claws together, as if knocking away dirt. "Anything else, Master?"

"The spell," Safar said. "Help me cast it now!"

Gundara plucked a tube of paper from his sleeve and tossed it to Safar. It grew to full size as it sailed the short distance and Safar snatched it out of the air.

As he readied himself chaos erupted all around him. The crowd roared in fury at the interruption. Gamblers attacked odds makers and odds makers shouted for their bully boys' who waded in. The fights spread like a plainsfire and the stands and arena floor became a swarming mass of struggling bodies. Didima thundered orders and soldiers rushed toward Safar and Gundara.

Safar chanted:

*Here are the hypocrites of Walaria,*
*Cursed be. Cursed be.*
*King Didima and Umurhan and Kalasariz,*
*The unholy three. Unholy three.*
*Devils and felons are welcome in Walaria,*
*Say the three. Say the three.*

The scroll burst into flames and Safar flung it into the faces of the charging soldiers. The fiery bits exploded into a white-hot mass flinging the soldiers back, screaming and twisting in pain.

Safar snatched up the stone idol and Gundara hopped onto his shoulder, crying, "Run, Master! Run!"

He leaped off the platform into the madness of the crowd. A soldier slashed with a sword, but Safar dodged the blow and cracked his head with the idol.

Behind him Olari had shouted the other condemned youths into life and they all swarmed off the platform and raced for cover.

Didima's amplified voice thundered, "Seize the traitors! Don't let them escape!"

Safar rushed toward the place where he'd last seen Nerisa. Gundara conjured a flaming brand that shot off spears of magical lightning. Holding tight to his master's collar, he waved the brand about, scattering the crowd. Safar came to the spot where Nerisa had been attacked.

There was nothing there but a drying pool of blood.

"She's dead, Master," Gundara shouted. "I saw her die!"

Rage gripped Safar and he whirled around to face the royal stage. He saw Didima and Umurhan being rushed away to safety by Kalasariz and his men.

He was helpless in his fury. He could feel great pools of power gathering near him. He only had to reach out and take it and then strike. But his enemies disappeared before he could form the killing spell and then a mass of armed men was charging toward him.

He gestured and a white cloud formed overhead. A deadly hailstorm erupted from that cloud, ripping through the soldiers' ranks. Men cried out, falling to the ground, moaning from broken heads and limbs.

Gundara kicked at him with small sharp heels. "Run, you fool!" he shouted. "Quick, before they send more!"

Safar ran.

He bounded up the emptying stands like a mountain goat until he came to the highest wall. On the other side was a broad street leading to the main gate—not more than a hundred yards away. Just beyond was freedom. Safar jumped, tucked and rolled when he hit, and raced for the unguarded gate.

And then he was gone.

Despite the chaos Safar left in his wake, Kalasariz regained order by day's end. He shut down the city at Last Prayer, imposing a dusk-to-dawn curfew. All violators were killed on the spot. Then he sent his men out to seize anyone who might threaten the throne before Didima had a chance to recover the dignity of his office. Only one of Safar's seven companions was recaptured. The rest, including Olari, seemed to have vanished. Kalasariz wasn't concerned about the missing youths. He'd always seen them as more of a symbol to be exploited than a real danger.

He'd once viewed Safar Timura as such a symbol. Now he wasn't so certain. Umurhan certainly viewed Timura as a threat, demanding that men be sent out immediately to capture Safar, and babbling for nearly an hour about the tortures the young man would suffer for his crimes. Kalasariz saw naked fear in the High Priest's ravings—a fear that could only be caused by the magical powers Timura had displayed in the arena. The spy master was no expert on such things, but when he added Umurhan's fear and Timura's friendship with Iraj Protarus, he thought it best to take extra precautions.

The first hedge involved the group of hunters he'd sent after Timura, who were hand-picked for their loyalty. He'd given them secret orders to kill Safar on sight. They were also told if Timura managed to elude them for any length of time they were to give up the chase and return home. By no means was he to be captured and returned to the city as King Didima had demanded.

The incident in the arena prompted Kalasariz to take one other major precaution. Umurhan had unintentionally revealed that as a wizard he was all bluff. Otherwise he would've used his magic to destroy Safar—or least block his spell. It was plain to Kalasariz that if Walaria were ever attacked there'd be little help from the High Priest. This was a huge hole in the city's defenses, a gap that couldn't be filled.

So the spy master penned a careful message to Iraj Protarus. In it, he deplored the actions of Didima and Umurhan. He also subtly hinted if the day ever came when Protarus might wish his assistance, Kalasariz was his humble servant and would be pleased to comply. With the message he included the documents he had hidden away: Safar's death warrant and Kalasariz' letter of protest.

The message was sent the day his hunters returned with the sad news that Safar Timura was nowhere to be found.

Nerisa crouched in the corner of her cell, a blood-crusted bandage wrapped around her forehead. She was weak from hunger and loss of blood. She had no idea how long she'd been in the cell or how long she'd remain before they came to take her.

Despite her weakness, she remained stubbornly unafraid. She held firm to a prisoner's ultimate defiance—they can kill you, but they can't eat you.

She'd rescued Safar. This was satisfaction enough. No one could take that back. If she were to be sacrificed for her love, so be it. Safar would go on living and he'd have the magical idol and Asper's book—which she'd given to Gundara—to remember her by. She was certain he would make a great future for himself and no matter what happened to Nerisa, she would always be a major part of that future.

Nerisa had one real hope. When she'd been captured her unconscious body had been dumped in a holding cell with others caught up in the arena riots. When she'd regained consciousness she'd had the presence of mind to swallow the gold coins Safar had given her. If she ever had the opportunity she intended to use those coins to win her freedom. At the very worst she could bribe the executioner to make her death swift and painless.

It was a slender hope but it was hope just the same.

A rattle of keys and heavy footsteps brought her up. She saw the warder unlocking her cell door. There was another man behind him.

"Oh, it's you, Zeman," she rasped. "What are you doing here? Run out of flies to torture?"

Zeman stretched his lips into a nasty grin. "You should be more polite to me," he said, waving an official looking document at her. "I'm your new owner."

Nerisa spit. "No one owns me," she said.

Zeman stepped into the cell. "They do now," he said. "You have no idea how far-thinking and kind the law is in Walaria when an underage child is involved. I've just paid out a small sum to rescue you from this cell.

"In return for my generosity you have been given to me as a slave."

Nerisa was shocked. The fear she'd fought against since her capture rose up to grip her heart in icy fingers.

She clutched at hope "Your grandfather will never allow it," she said. "Katal doesn't believe in slavery."

Zeman snickered. "Don't look to my grandfather for help," he said. Then he made a mournful face. "Poor old dear. He's dead you know. Something he ate didn't agree with him."

Nerisa became numb. She had no doubt Zeman had poisoned the old man. Tears welled. She shook her injured head violently, using pain to quell the tears. She'd be damned if she'd give Zeman the satisfaction.

"You are looking at the sole proprietor of the *Foolsmire*," he said. "And the sole owner of *you*, as well."

"What do you want with me?" Nerisa snarled. "You know I'll run the first chance I get. Either that, or kill you in your sleep."

"Oh, I don't intend to own you very long," Zeman replied. "I've already approached a buyer who's willing to take you off my hands. I'm making a handsome profit, if you must know. Although not as much as your buyer is going to make. Apparently there are certain men—rich men, I'm told—who have an appetite for little whores like yourself."

Zeman pasted on another of his ugly smiles. "And after you've grown breasts and are no longer any good to your new owner, I'm sure he'll make other arrangements for your future."

Zeman snickered. "He gave me his word on that."

Nerisa screamed in fury and launched herself at Zeman—nails coming out like a cat's to rake his eyes from his head.

The warder stepped in and clubbed her down. She fell to the floor, unconscious.

The warder raised his heavy stick to strike again.

Zeman stopped him, saying, "Let's not damage the merchandise."

Safar huddled in the slender shade of a desert succulent. His robe was hitched up over his head to protect himself from the merciless sun. A hot wind blew over the desolate landscape, intent on wringing every drop of moisture from his body. His tongue was a thick raw muscle, his lips cracked and drawn back over his teeth. He scraped at the hard ground with a jagged piece of rock, trying to dig a deep enough hole to expose the moisture held by the succulent's roots. He'd been working at it for hours but was so weak he'd barely managed a slight depression.

The sun had only just reached its zenith. The hottest and longest hours were still ahead. It was unlikely that he'd last until nightfall. But he kept at it, knowing neither hope or despair. He was like an animal with no thought in its head except survival.

A few days before he'd had life enough left to know joy when he saw his pursuers turn back. The hunters from Walaria had tracked him doggedly for a week, forcing him to flee deeper into the desert. With Gundara's help he'd cast spells of confusion to shake them off. Although he'd managed to elude them several times, the hunters kept reappearing on his trail. Gundara said it could only mean they had magic of their own to assist them.

The hunters gave up when they ran out of water. Safar, who didn't have that luxury, had run out long before. Divining spells proved to be useless—he never had a chance to stop and resupply himself. Finally he was even denied Gundara's company and help, the intense desert causing the little Favorite to grow weak and retreat into the stone idol. After that, Safar had paused when he could to kill a lizard or snake and suck out its moisture. It was a losing battle, with the sun and wind draining his life as quickly as he'd drained those poor creatures.

Safar made one more swipe at the dry depression. Then all his strength fled and the rock fell from his grasp. He sagged back on the ground, gasping for breath.

Then even breathing seemed to require too much effort and he thought, Well, I'll just stop. But to his disgust his chest insisted on heaving in and out, drawing in air filled with sharp bits of grit. Then he thought, it has to end sooner or later. I'll lie here until it does. He sighed and shut his eyes.

Then Safar heard music—distant pipes and bells. He thought, this must be what it's like to die.

The sound grew louder and he was overcome with a vague curiosity to look this strange, music-playing Death in the face.

He opened his eyes and wasn't disappointed. A huge low-flying creature swept across the desert towards him. It looked like an immense head, swirling with all sorts of marvelous colors. There were no wings or body attached to the head, but in Safar's daze this seemed quite natural. The creature flew closer and now he could make out its face.

He had strength enough to feel surprise. He thought, I didn't know Death was a woman. And such a beautiful woman—a giantess with sensuous features painted in glorious colors like a savage tattooed queen.

The music seemed to be coming from her lush mouth as if she had a voice composed of wondrous pipes and bells and harp strings.

The woman's head was hovering over him now. Safar smiled, thinking Death was finally going to take him. He closed his eyes and waited.

Then the music stopped and he heard someone speak. It was a woman's voice, but smaller than he thought a giantess would possess.

"Merciful Felakia," the woman said, "spare me this sight. He's only a lad. And a handsome lad at that."

"Handsome or plain, makes no difference to the buzzards," came another voice—a deep baritone—"He's dead, Methydia. Come on! The Deming fair's only two weeks off and we gots a long ways to go."

Safar was disappointed. This wasn't how Death was supposed

to behave. Was she going to leave his body here? Abandon his ghost to this wasteland?

He stretched his lips and tried to speak, but only managed a croak.

"Wait!" said the woman. "Sweet, merciful Felakia—he's alive."

No I'm not, Safar tried to say. I'm dead, dammit! Don't leave me here!

Then from above he heard a loud whoosh of escaping air and he felt a huge presence drifting down to him.

Safar smiled. Death was on her way. He ached for her embrace.

# Part Three
# Wizard of the Winds

## 15

# THE DEMON KING

Do you see anything, Luka?"

"No, Majesty. I see nothing."

King Manacia frowned, his royal brow a deeply plowed field of displeasure.

"Are you certain, Luka?" he asked his oldest son and heir. He jabbed a long talon at a point on the horizon. "Isn't that something, or someone, moving over there?"

Prince Luka shielded his yellow eyes with a claw—peering out over the Forbidden Desert. Manacia and his court were camped on the edge of the blackened wasteland. The King sat on his traveling throne, placed on thick carpets and shaded by a white canopy, billowing in the desert wind. Behind him was the main camp—a city of gaudy tents that housed his court.

After looking long and hard the prince sighed and shook his bony head—a dozen heavy golden chains of office rattling against his armor.

"I don't believe so, Majesty," he said. Then, soothing, "But it's early, yet. Perhaps Your Highness is hungry, or thirsty. Why don't you retire to your tent and I'll send for the stewards. Possibly you'd enjoy a little nap. You look so weary, Sire, that it nearly breaks my heart.

"I'll alert Your Majesty the instant Lord Fari returns."

Manacia exposed his fangs—a wide, multi-rowed smile of fatherly pride. "You're a good and loyal son, Luka," he said. "No king could ask for a better prince. But it wouldn't be seemly. A king must not fear to suffer the same trials and tribulations as his subjects."

Prince Luka laid a claw of sincerity across his mailed heart. "You are an inspiration to us all, Majesty," he said. "I worship and study at your feet, praying I will have half Your Highness' courage and wisdom on that most regretful day when the gods decree that I must succeed you to the throne."

The whole time the Crown Prince spoke he was thinking, I hope you choke on a bone, you horrid old fiend. I hope the sun fries your brains and the hyenas feast on your liver.

Manacia chuckled fondly. "To think I nearly wrung your neck at birth," he said. "I thought you'd grow to be a conspiring little savage like your mother. Instead, you've matured into the most civilized and considerate subject in my kingdom. It's a pity I couldn't let your mother live to see what a fine son you've turned out to be."

Prince Luka bowed low, humbly thanking his father for his kind words. But he thought, You old fool. You wouldn't look so smug if you knew Mother made me swear on her death bed that I'd avenge her.

Manacia gestured and a slave crawled over on his belly with a cup of cold wine. The king sipped, reminiscing.

"Looking at you, my son," he said, "no one would ever guess your mother was a barbarian. You are my strong and serene right claw. And to think when I bedded her the first time she tried to stab me with a knife she'd hidden in her girdle."

He smiled at the memory. "Your mother was understandably overwrought," he said, "because I'd just killed her father and brothers. I had to have her tied to the bed before I could mount her."

"Your Majesty has regaled me many times with the tale of that illustrious moment," Prince Luka said. "I never tire of hearing it."

The king laughed and slapped his knee. "Did I ever tell you what your mother said after I'd had my pleasures?"

"Yes, Majesty," the prince said. "But it was such a delicious incident I'd be pleased if you told me again."

"She said I'd raped her!" the king chortled. "Can you imagine that? *Me*, rape *her*?"

"She should have thanked you for honoring her with your royal seed, Majesty," the prince said. "But she was young and of a savage tribe. Mother didn't know what she was saying."

The king was impatient to complete his story. "Yes, yes," he said. "But that's not the point. We already know she was a savage. I said so, didn't I?

"The point is she accused me of raping her. And do you know what I replied?"

"No, Majesty. What did you say?"

"I replied—'that wasn't rape.' 'That was'—now get this—'assault with a friendly weapon.'"

Manacia howled with laughter at his joke. The prince forced sounds of immense amusement.

Then the prince said, "One thing you've never told me, Sire...what was Mother's answer?"

The king's laughter cut off in mid-snort. "What was that?" he growled, green skin mottling with building anger.

"I said, what did Mother reply after you made that marvelous jest about rape being nothing but assault with a friendly weapon?"

"It doesn't matter what she replied," the king snapped. "That wasn't the joke. The joke was the friendly weapon part. Not what she said after. Who cares what that fiendbitch thought? It's what the king has to say that's important. Whole histories are devoted solely to the remarks of kings. In my case, I'm also noted for my sense of humor. The anecdote concerning your mother is only one especially revealing example."

"Absolutely, Sire," the prince said. "How foolish of me not to see it right off."

The king's mood turned from fair to foul. Muttering oaths, he resumed his watch— searching the bleak horizon for some sign of his Grand Wazier.

In the king's opinion—which, as he often said, was the only one that mattered—few truly appreciated how hard he'd labored these past few years. Nothing had come easily and every platter of victory he'd been served up always seemed to hide a nasty little insect under the tastiest morsels.

All of the demon lands had been brought completely under his control. His kingdom now bore the name Ghazban, after the ancient emperor who'd first welded all the demon lands together. Zanzair was now the seat of the mightiest kingdom since the time of Alisarrian, the human conqueror who had cut short Ghazban's long and honorable dynasty.

No sooner had the naming festival ended when trouble began to gnaw at Manacia's accomplishments. First there was the drought, which still held the kingdom in its grip—turning the harvests to ashen husks. Then there were the locust swarms—great clouds that first blackened the sky and then the earth as the insects descended to devour whatever had managed to defy the drought.

Plagues mysteriously erupted across the land, ravaging the populace—turning cities to towns and towns to desolate villages. There were reports of ghastly phantoms rising from graveyards, giants suddenly appearing to threaten distant crossroads, Jinns crouching in ambush to devour unsuspecting travelers.

Manacia and his wizards had worked at a dervish's pace to halt these outbreaks. Huge spell machines were constructed and hauled out to the troubled regions. Whole forests of cinnamon trees had been felled to make the incense that was burned in those machines. Day and night the furnaces churned out immense clouds of fragrant healing smoke. The expense sometimes made the king nostalgic for simpler times when his realm was smaller and less expensive to maintain.

Despite Manacia's efforts, trouble continued to dog Ghazban. His subjects were becoming increasing restless and unruly. It was whispered that the gods were punishing all demonkind for allowing such a greedy pontiff to rule them. Word leaked out about his experiments with the curse of the Forbidden Desert, fueling further religious fears and discontent.

In the past Manacia had dealt with such things by immediately invading a neighboring kingdom. It not only released domestic pressure but gave him a brother monarch to blame and then bring to task for his sins. This was no longer possible in the brave new world that was Ghazban, where the subjects had only Manacia as a target for their suspicions.

In the beginning Manacia's dream of ruling all Esmir as King of Kings was only that—a private dream. Now it had become a necessity. He needed to challenge his subjects, to fix their minds on a great peril; an historic enemy—godless humans—to bear the blame for their ills.

To achieve this he had to solve the riddle of the curse that kept demonkind and humankind apart. Once he thought he had the answer and sent the bandit chieftain, Sarn, across the Forbidden Desert to spy out an invasion route. But Sarn had never returned.

The king falsely blamed the curse and spent every free moment searching for the solution to its riddle. He had ripped apart his original spell and then reformed it many times.

None of his efforts worked. It was as if he had gone back to the original days of failure when hundreds of slaves and felons were forced out into the Forbidden Desert to die horribly before the eyes of the soldiers who had prodded them there. Distracted as he was by domestic toil, it took Manacia a long time to return to the spell he'd used to shield Sarn and his outlaws. He added a few improvements and tried again.

The very first effort met with success. The villain used for the experiment not only survived, but was able to walk to the most distant hill, the soldiers playing out rope and tying on additional lines until he was nearly out of sight and had to be dragged back so he wouldn't escape.

After his experience with Sarn, Manacia was wary of this success. He called for his Grand Wazier, Lord Fari, and asked his advice.

"We require a volunteer, Majesty," Fari said. "Someone loyal, above reproach."

"Exactly my thinking," Manacia said.

The old demon built on this success. "Perhaps Prince Luka," he said. "It would be a mighty accomplishment he could add to his deeds, thus assuring the admiration of your subjects when he assumes the throne some day."

The Grand Wazier hated the Crown Prince and this seemed an excellent time to be rid of him—if the king's spell failed, that is.

Menacia, who kept a firm talon on the pulse of his court, knew what Fari was up to.

"What an excellent thought," he said brightly. Then he frowned, "Unfortunately, that can't be. At this particular time I need him by my side."

He clicked his claws against the arm of his throne, pretending to ponder further. Then he smiled. "I've got it!" he said. "And I have you to thank for the idea, Fari. For it made me focus on who my most loyal subjects were. And the answer was there in an instant. For other than my own son, who could be more loyal than you, my dear fiend?"

The Grand Wazier was aghast. "*Me*, Your Highness? You want *me* to cross Forbidden Desert?" His voice quavered. "As much as I'd love to have the honor to serve in you this, I fear I am too old, Majesty."

"In this case," Menacia said, "advanced age makes you even an even better choice. To begin with you have many years of wizardly experience to draw upon. And if by some distant chance the experiment meets with failure, why you can't be that far away from your natural death.

"It would be tragic, of course. But not as tragic as if a younger wizard were cheated out of a long life."

Fari realized it was hopeless to argue with the king. It was obvious the choice had been made before Menacia summoned him. The advice seeking had only been for appearance's sake.

The Grand Wazier acceded to the king's command with as much grace as he could muster. Preparations were made, detailed instructions were given, and in less than a month Fari and a small expedition set out across the Forbidden Desert. Their orders were much simpler than Sarn's. Once they reached the humanlands they were to turn back immediately and report their success to the king.

Demon scholars estimated the crossing and return journey should take no more than eight weeks. When the time drew near for Fari's return King Manacia became so anxious he ordered his whole court transported from Zanzair to the edge of the Forbidden Desert.

There he sat, day after talon-biting day, waiting for his Grand Wazier. Eight weeks became nine. Nine became ten. The king was so restive he rose before dawn and paced before his traveling throne until late at night.

He'd all but given up hope when Lord Fari finally appeared.

It was at dusk and the sun was just disappearing beneath the horizon. The western-most rim of the desert was a thick red smear that drew the king's eyes like an insect drawn to flame.

His whole being flew out to the rim. He whispered prayers and curses to gods and devils alike. Then his heart bumped hard against his chest. Shadowy figures formed at the horizon. They seemed to be moving, growing larger as they approached. Fearing to spoil his luck the king said nothing, waiting for his lookouts to shout the news.

The cry came and still the king said nothing. He remained motionless, giving no sign of the chaos raging inside.

Then night fell and far out in the desert a score of torches flared into life, bobbing in the darkness like fireflies.

There was no doubt now that it was Fari.

The riddle of the curse of the Forbidden Desert had been solved.

Prince Luka shouted his congratulations, pounding his father on the back—wishing his hand held a knife. Officers and courtiers crowded around the king to praise his wisdom and perseverance.

Manacia was not moved. His excitement had died quickly—he'd waited too long for joy to find a resting place.

When the weary, bedraggled expedition bearing Lord Fari arrived the king was already huddled with his generals in the command tent.

Prince Luka had the great pleasure of seeing the aged demon's shock of disappointment at his poor reception. The journey had taken a heavy toll on Lord Fari.

Slumped in the saddle, every bone aching, he peered first at Luka and then the lights of the tent city.

"Where's the king?" he asked, voice quavering from age and weariness. He despised himself for letting the weakness show in front of Luka, but he couldn't help it.

"My father asked me to relay his apologies," the prince answered. "He said you'd understand that he couldn't actually be present to congratulate you.

"He's busy right now, you see, planning the invasion of the humanlands."

# 16
# THE CLOUDSHIP

For a long time Safar floated on a balmy sea. Below were mysterious depths where nightmares were sea dragons pursuing his dreams.

He dreamed of Kyrania and its fruited fields. He dreamed of clouds melting in the Sun God's forge, dripping colors on the land. He dreamed of clay that leaped into fantastic shapes the moment he touched it. He dreamed of maids bathing in the lake and they were blessed with figures as beguiling as Astarias' and faces with winsome smiles and starry eyes like Nerisa.

But each time a dream popped into being it was devoured by the swift-moving nightmares. He saw the volcano overwhelm the people of Hadin. He saw the demon cavalry charging the caravan. He saw Tulaz lift his sword, saw Kalasariz peeping through a dungeon grate, saw Katal die at Zeman's hands—and Didima's soldiers slay Nerisa.

He dreamed of Alisarrian's cave where he crouched beside Iraj, watching smoke form into a woman's seductive lips and he saw them move and he heard the Omen speak:

*"Two will take the road that two traveled before. Brothers of the spirit, but not the womb. Separate in body and mind, but twins in destiny. But beware what you seek, O brothers. Beware the path you choose. For this tale cannot end until you reach the Land of Fires."*

Eventually the intensity of this sleeplife lessened and Safar became aware of the world around him. It seemed as mysterious as the ocean of dreams.

He still felt buoyant as if he were floating on that sea, except now he seemed to be lying on a cushioned raft. Instead of hissing surf he heard the flutter-drum of the winds and the whistle and ping of it singing through taut lines. He heard the rhythmic pumping of bellows and the low roar of a furnace.

Strong, gentle hands lifted his head. A spoon touched his lips, which parted and he lapped up a meaty broth. The spoon dipped up more and he ate until he heard the hollow scrape of wood, signaling the bowl was empty and he drifted away again.

The next time he became aware he heard odd voices saying even odder things, like, "Tighten that carabiner." Or, "Work the mouth, dammit! Work the mouth!" And, "Who's minding the burner? It's almost out!"

Once he heard the woman whom he'd thought was Death cast an incomprehensible spell.

*"Come to us Mother Wind.*
*Lift us in hands blessed*
*By the warm sun.*
*We have flown high.*
*We have flown well.*
*Take us in your arms, Mother Wind.*
*And when you are done,*
*Set us gently on the ground."*

Safar wondered at the purpose of the spell. While he was puzzling he fell asleep.

Time passed. A time of dreamless drifting. Then a current of cold air washed over him and he opened his eyes.

There was the shock of sudden sunlight and then vision cleared.

He seemed to be lying on a firm surface at the bottom of a fantastic canyon with dazzling walls of many colors. The walls curved inward until they seemed only a few feet apart. Through that hollow he could see skies as blue as the high vaults above the Bride and Six Maids.

Then hazy reason formed and he thought—That's no cliff. It's too smooth. Also—I've never seen slate with all those colors. And so bright! Like they were painted. Then he realized the canyon walls were moving as if they were made of living skin.

Maybe a giant swallowed me, Safar thought, and I'm looking up into his guts. But that conclusion made little sense—it didn't allow for the sky.

I must still be dreaming, he thought. Then a leg muscle threatened to cramp and he stretched the limb until the pain eased.

And he thought—There is pain, which proves I'm awake. But exactly where am I awake? He considered. Then it came to him that he was flying—or, lying upon something that was flying, at any rate. Perhaps he was awake, but in the middle of a vision and in that vision he was perched on a mighty eagle flying to wherever the vision commanded.

No good. Where were the wings? If he were riding an eagle, there'd be wings.

He tried to sit up and reconnoiter his surroundings.

Someone shouted. Weakness overcame him and he fell back. Dizzy, he closed his eyes.

Slippered feet approached.

A whiff of perfume as someone knelt beside him.

He opened his eyes and found a beautiful woman bending over him. She had almond eyes and long silvery hair streaked with black. It was the face of the woman he'd seen floating across the desert; the woman he'd believed was Death herself come to take him away. But this face was of normal size and it wasn't painted with all sorts of savage colors. Her skin was white and smooth as the most expensive parchment, with a fine, barely visible net of age etched on the surface.

"I did this once before," Safar told her. "Awaken from the dead, I mean. With a beautiful woman hovering over me." He was thinking of Astarias.

The woman laughed. It was a rich, earthy laugh. A laugh with appetite.

Instead of answering she turned her head and called to someone, "The lad wakes up pretty as he sleeps, Biner. He has the *loveliest* blue eyes. And you should hear the compliments. First time I've blushed in thirty years."

"That's enough hot air to lift us another thousand feet, Methydia, " Biner replied. His voice was a familiar baritone.

Heavy feet thudded forward. "Last time you blushed," Biner said, "the Goddess Felakia was a virgin."

Safar craned to look. From the deepness of the voice and the obvious weight the feet were carrying, Safar expected to see a huge fellow come into view.

Biner was immense all right. He had the girth of a giant, the mighty arms and hams of a giant, but all that size had been squashed by an enemy giant's hand into a body that stood less than four feet high. He had a huge bearded face with an overly wide mouth filled with broad teeth.

Biner saw Safar staring at him. He displayed his teeth in what was meant to be a comforting smile. "Bet you're glad I wasn't the one to wake you up, lad," he said. "I got a face that'll peel the reflection right off a mirror."

Safar struggled to answer. He didn't want to be rude by appearing to agree with an all-too-obvious truth.

Methydia patted him. "Don't worry about Biner's feelings,"

she said, guessing what was on his mind. "Ugly as it is, he's proud of that face. People pay good money to see it. Almost as much as they pay to see him lift a wagon of pig iron. Or smash a pile of bricks with his fist."

Biner toed the floor, embarrassed. "Aw, that stuff isn't much," he said. "Just tricks to wow the fair crowds. Besides, Methydia does some of her witchy business first to soften them up."

Methydia gave Safar a look of immense sincerity. "Biner is a fine actor," she said, a dramatic hand going to her flowing bosom. "The best male lead in all Esmir, in my judgment."

Safar's head was swimming. He was very confused. "Excuse me, dear lady," he said. "But would I be wrong in guessing that I've been rescued by, uh...*entertainers*?"

Biner and Methydia laughed. Biner stood as tall as he could, shouting: "Come one, come all! Lads and maids of Alllll ag-es! I now to present to you—Methydia's Flying Circus of Miracles!

"The Greatest Show In Esmir!"

Methydia applauded, crying "Bravo! Bravo!"

Safar became alarmed. He propped himself up on an elbow. "Excuse me again," he said. "I know it isn't polite to question one's rescuers too closely, but...What was that thing you said about flying?"

Biner seemed surprised. "Of course we're flying, lad," he said. "We're about two miles up, is my estimate."

Safar coughed. "Two miles up? In what?"

"Why, a Cloudship, boy. A Cloudship!"

Fear overcame weakness and Safar stumbled to his feet.

He went to a rail and looked down. Far beneath him was the floor of a wide, fertile valley. He could see a great double-humped shadow moving swiftly across the fields. His veins turned to ice as it came to him that he was probably part of that fast-moving shadow.

He called back to his rescuers, "How far up did you say we were?"

Biner replied, "Two miles, lad...Give or take a thousand feet."

First Safar threw up.

Then he passed out.

***

When he regained awareness a small crowd was gathered around him.

Methydia was beside him, trying to coax brandy between his lips. One look at the crowd and Safar opened his mouth wide and choked down a flood.

Biner was in the center. To his left was a tall, skeletal fellow wearing nothing but a breech cloth and a turban. He had a huge snake draped about his neck—a snake with the face of a man. Just behind him was a stocky man with the hard muscles of an acrobat. He had a too-small head that was detachable, holding it up by the hair to see over the others, a long tube-like neck trailing down to his shoulders. Towering over the group was what had to be a dragon. A white dragon, with a long snout and a spiked tail, which curled up as Safar looked to scratch a place behind its ear. Then someone moved and Safar saw the creature wasn't *entirely* a dragon. The long torso was that of a well-endowed woman, complete with breast plates and a triangular modesty patch tied about the hips with a thong.

There was much to goggle at. But the dragon noticed Safar had fixed upon her.

"I altho' juggle," she lisped. "Thix globth and theven thwords. We thoak them in oil and I thet'm on fire with my breath."

She raised a claw to her snout and burped. Smoke and flames shot around her fist.

"Excuthe me," she said. "Mutht have been thomething I ate."

Safar nodded. What a polite dragon, he thought. Then he passed out again.

The last thing he heard was:

"Really, Arlain!" Methydia said. "Can't you control yourself? You've scared another guest half to death!"

"I'm thorry," the dragon wailed. "Wath'n my fault. The thquath we had for thupper mutht of been thpoiled."

Several days of dreamless sleep passed, interspersed with half-conscious feedings. Then the sudden moment came when he awoke and felt very strong and very alert. He smelled perfume and immediately he felt very *very*...

He opened his eyes. A dim, flickering light illuminated his surroundings. There was a cabin roof above his head, shadows dancing on the dark ceiling. Safar looked down and saw a certain part had made itself embarrassingly apparent beneath the blankets.

Safar heard a familiar, throaty laugh. Methydia's face leaned over him, lips parted in a smile, almond eyes dancing with humor. She glanced down, then back at him again.

"It's good to see you among the living," she said.

Safar flushed. He started to apologize, but Methydia put a finger to his lips, silencing him.

"Don't be embarrassed on my account," she said. "Consider your little upstart welcome. Any friend of yours, and all that."

Safar opened his mouth to speak, but once again a long, slender finger touched his lips.

"You're a young man," Methydia said. "Youth has its advantages and its disadvantages. The advantages are apparent." She glanced at the blanket. To Safar's relief his problem had subsided. "The disadvantages are—what to do with your advantages."

"Oh," was all Safar could say.

"Now, I suppose you have some questions," Methydia said. "Assuming your uninvited guest isn't so consumed with himself that he'll allow you to think."

"First off," Safar said, "I should tell you about myself before I have the right to ask any questions."

"Go on," Methydia said.

"My name is Safar Timura," he said in a rush. "I've just escaped execution in Walaria. I could swear on my mother's soul I didn't deserve such a fate. That I am no criminal. That I am only a student—a seeker of truth who has never done anyone harm. But none of that should matter to you.

"What should matter is that I am wanted by very powerful men who would most certainly do you harm if they learned you had aided me."

Methydia clapped her hands. "What a delicious speech," she said. "And so well spoken. My compliments to your mother and father for raising such an honest lad."

Once again Safar felt the discomfort of a blush. "I was only trying to warn you about what you might be in for," he said, a bit sullen.

Methydia kissed him and patted his cheek. "Don't mind me,

dear," she said. "I have an old woman's blathering tongue."

Safar's eyes strayed to her lush figure, swathed in a many-layered, translucent gown.

"You're not so old," he mumbled—and tore his eyes away.

"If you keep talking like that, my pretty lad," Methydia said, "we're going to get ourselves in trouble.

"Now. Allow me to compose myself."

Methydia, ever the actress as Safar eventually learned, fanned her cheek with a delicate hand, saying, "You have a way of troubling a woman's concentration, dear."

Safar had learned better than to automatically blurt an apology. He said, "Do you mind if I ask *you* a few questions?"

"Ask away," Methydia replied.

"First I want to ask about the Cloudship," he said. "Then I want to ask about the circus."

The answers consumed many days and many miles. In fact, during the months Safar spent with Methydia and her troupe, he never did hear the entire tale—although everyone from Biner, the muscular dwarf, to Arlain, the human dragon who preferred vegetables over meat, was more than willing to enlighten him.

The Cloudship had no life of its own and although complicated in design, it was an object and therefore easier to explain.

Essentially, it *was* a ship—a ship with its nose bobbed off and its masts and sails removed. It had a long ship's deck, a high ship's bridge and a ship's galleys and cabins. The timbers it was made of, however, were light as parchment and strong as steel.

Methydia said the rare planks were the gift of a woodsman—a long ago lover—who stole the trees from a sacred grove to prove he'd make a worthy husband. The woodsman's most ardent rival—a magical toy maker of great renown—turned the planks into a marvelous vessel, hoping to upstage his opponent.

"I was very young, then," Methydia said. "But although I was dumb enough to attract men I didn't want, I was bright enough to not only keep my gifts, but to avoid marrying my lovers without giving insult."

The body of the Cloudship dangled beneath two balloons, each ninety feet high and made of a strong, light cloth that was not only moisture proof but offered a marvelous surface for all the colorful paints the troupe used for decoration. Methydia's face graced the front, or forward, balloon. The legend, "Methydia's Flying Circus," the aft.

The quantities of hot air required to lift the vessel were provided by two big furnaces, called "burners," with magically operated bellows to fan the fuel—a mixture of crumbled animal dung, dried herbs and witch's powders that gave off a faint odor of ammonia. Ballast was ordinary sand in ordinary bags that could be spilled out to gain greater heights. To descend, you "worked the mouth"—pulling on ropes that widened the balloons' bottom openings so that gas could escape. One thing needing constant attention were the big clamps—or carabiners—that were attached the cables holding the Cloudship's body to the balloons. They tended to loosen in a rough wind and had to be tightened constantly.

Beyond that, the vessel seemed simple enough to operate. Although sometimes there were periods of intense—and to Safar, bewildering—activity, mostly the Cloudship seemed to run itself. Besides the main members of the troupe, there was a crew of half-a-dozen men and women called "roustabouts." They were usually busy attending to the equipment and props that went into making a circus, leaving the routine operation of the Cloudship to the performers.

Part of that routine was steering. The task was performed on the bridge, where a large ship's wheel was mounted. The spoked wheel was linked to an elaborate system of scoops, sails and rudders that provided steerage.

"How fast does she go?" Safar asked Biner one day. It was Biner's turn at the wheel, while Safar had the task of keeping an eye on the compass.

"Depends on the wind," Biner said, "and the temperature. We've made as much as three hundred miles in a day. Other times we've been becalmed and made less than thirty in a week."

Safar watched Biner work the wheel. Despite the elaborate steering system it seemed to him direction was mainly determined by the wind.

"What happens in a storm?" he asked.

Biner chortled. "We pray a lot. And Methydia casts her spells.

But mostly we pray. If there aren't any mountains about it's best just to let the storm be the boss. If there are, we tie up to something and hang on. Worst thing you can do is put her on the ground. That's if the storm doesn't give you any notice and you can't find a barn big enough to hold her. Wind can rip her up before you get the balloons collapsed and stowed away."

Safar could see straight off that, storm or not, the best place to be was sailing high above the earth where no one—king or outlaw—could reach you.

He thought of his recent troubles in Walaria and said, "It's too bad you ever have to come down."

Biner nodded understanding. Safar had told the crew an abbreviated version of his tale of woe.

"Gotta eat," he said. "Food may grow in trees, but not in the air." His massive shoulders rolled in a shrug. "Ground's not all bad. Wait'll you work your first show. Nothing like an audience's applause to restore your good feelings about folks. Especially the tikes, way their eyes light up warms you from the inside out."

It had already been agreed that Safar could travel with the troupe for awhile. To earn his keep he was being trained to handle the hundreds of small details that went into—in circus parlance—"wowing the rubes."

"How did you become a circus performer?" Safar asked. "Or were you born to it?"

Biner shook his massive head. "My parents were actors," he said. "Came from a long line of board trodders, as a matter of fact. Made my first appearance while I was still suckling my mother's breast. Played all kinds of child parts. Kept on playing them way past my time. I'm kind of short, in case you didn't notice. My mother and father were normal-sized and never did figure out what to make of me. Then I started growing out, instead of up. And I couldn't play tikes anymore."

Biner's face darkened at some painful memory. Then he shook it off, displaying his wide teeth in a grin.

"Swept theater floors and other drudge work for a time. Then one day this Cloudship sailed right over the town, music playing, folks way up in the sky waving at us like they were gods and goddesses. They shouted for everybody to follow. So I followed. And I was bitten by the circus bug the very first show. I begged Methydia for a tryout. She gave me one and I've been with her ever since. Going on fifteen years, now. Even gave me a new name after awhile—Biner, from the carabiners that hold us up. She said it's because she depends on me so much."

Although Biner's story was entirely different in its details from the background of the others, Safar soon learned the members of the troupe all had one thing in common—their appearances had made them outcasts from regular society so they'd formed their own. It was Methydia who'd given them that chance, coming along at just the right time, it seemed, to rescue them from unpleasant circumstances.

"Weren't fer Methyida," Kairo said one day, "I'd still be back at me village, gettin' conked wi' rocks." Kairo was the acrobat with the detachable head. "Uster hide in me house," he said, "so's I wouldn't get conked. So th' lads'd stone me house, breakin' windows and stovin' holes in th' roof. So me muvver threw me out. Rather I got conked th'n the house, I s'pose."

Rabix and Elgy—the snake charmer and the snake—had been seasoned circus performers when Methydia found them. But they'd had a disagreement with their employer over unpaid wages and had been left at a roadside in the middle of nowhere.

"We had not even a copper to buy a slender mouse for my weekly dinner," Elgy said in his oddly lilted tones.

Elgy was the snake with a man's face. He was also the "brains in the act." Rabix, he of the turban and breech cloth, was a mindless soul who sat or stood placidly wherever he was put. Elgy alone could communicate with him and cause him to act.

"He plays an excellent tune on the pipes," Elgy said. "As witless as the poor fellow is, he is a much better musician than the last man I had."

Arlain, the dragon woman, was being hunted by a mob set on vengeance when Methydia rescued her.

"I wath hiding in a thed and thort of thet it on fire. And then it thpread and thet fire to the whole thity." Arlain wiped her eyes, overcome by the memory. "It wath an acthident," she said. "I thaid I wath thorry, but they wouldn't lithen."

Arlain had no idea where she came from. "I thuppoth my

father dropped me when he wath changing netht," she said. "A farmer'th wife found me and raithed me ath a pet. But then I got older and tharted having acthidenth and her huthband chathed me off the farm. And that'th why I wath hiding in the thed."

Methydia was not so forthcoming as the others. Although she never refused to answer any of Safar's questions, her answers tended just to tease the edges of the central question. Details of her background came only in veiled hints or casually dropped remarks.

Much later, after she took Safar as a lover, he complained about her habit of never revealing anything personal.

Methydia was amused. "I was born to be a woman of mystery, my sweet," she said. "It is a role I have cherished all my life. And with each passing year the mystery deepens, does it not? For then there is more for me *not* to tell."

She shifted in his arms. "Besides," she said, "I fear you would be disappointed if you knew all there was to know. What if I was merely a milk maid who ran away with her first lover? Or a young town wife who fled a fat old husband?"

Safar thought for a moment, then said, "I can't imagine you as either one. You were never ordinary, Methydia. *That* I know for certain."

"Are you, now, my sweet?" she murmured. Then she nibbled her way up his neck. "Are...you...really...really...*entirely*...certain...?" She found his lips, shutting off any reply.

They made love and afterwards Safar thought she was an even greater mystery than before. A delicious mystery, he thought. Then he realized perhaps that was her point.

All he ever really knew about her was that she was a strong-willed woman, a kind-hearted leader others felt comfortable to follow.

She was also a witch.

Safar sensed it the first time he became fully conscious. The atmosphere had been charged with more than her seductive presence. Little whorls of energy swirled about her, making the hair rise on the backs of his hands. And deep in those almond eyes he could see flecks of magic that sparkled when the light struck just so.

He said nothing of his own powers, partly because he didn't know how she'd react. Would she be jealous, like Umurhan? But mainly it was because he was so shaken by his experience in

Walaria he was loathe to visit his magical side until he'd had time to recover.

Evidently Gundara felt the same way. The little Favorite was silent for a long time. For awhile Safar worried that the desert ordeal might have been too much for Gundara and his twin. He would take the stone turtle out of his purse from time to time to check. The idol was cold to the touch, but he could still feel a faint shimmer of magic. He thought of summoning Gundara to see if he needed anything, but then he wondered if the spell commanding the Favorite's presence might do more harm than any good he could offer. He thought, Let him rest and heal himself. And so that is what he did.

Early one morning, a few weeks after his recovery, Safar was awakened by loud music and excited voices. He crept out of the little storage room that was his bachelor's cabin, rubbing his eyes and wondering what was up.

The Cloudship was abuzz with activity. The crew was hauling chests of equipment and props out of the lockers. The members of the troupe were all doing stretching exercises or practicing their specialties.

The music came from Rabix, who was sitting—legs crossed—in the center of the deck, playing his pipes. It was a strange instrument, consisting of bound-together tubes of varying lengths. They were valved and Rabix played by blowing through the tubes while his fingers flowed gracefully over the valves. A marvelous stream of music issued from the instrument, sounding like an entire orchestra of drums and strings and trumpets and flutes. Elgy, anchored by a few coils wrapped loosely about his neck, rose nearly three feet above Rabix' turbaned head, weaving in time to the music.

Kairo practiced his high wire act, strolling along a suspended cable, then pretending to fall. He'd steady himself, then let his head drop from his shoulders. He'd catch it, squeaking in fear, then put it on again.

Arlain, who was so excited she'd forgotten her clothes, bounded naked about the deck, shouting joyfully, "Thowtime folkth! Thowtime folkth!"

There was a roar from Biner, "Here now, Arlain! Put something on! This is a family show!"

Arlain skidded to a stop, tail lashing furiously. She looked down, saw what she'd done, then turned from pale white to the deepest red.

A claw went to her mouth. "Oh, my goodneth grathiouth," she said.

Then she scuttled off, wailing, "I'm thorry. I'm thorry."

As she rushed into the wardrobe room, her tail hooking out to slam the door behind her, Biner shouted, "And watch out for the—"

Fire and smoke blasted out of the wardrobe room's window, cutting Biner off in midbellow. Arlain wailed something incomprehensible and a few crew members came running with buckets of water and sand to douse the fire.

"If only she wouldn't get so excited," Biner said. Then he shrugged. "Oh, well. She's a grand crowd pleaser. So what if she starts a few fires?" He grinned at Safar. "Temperament, my lad," he said. "All the best talent's got it. If you can't take the temperament then you might as well get out of the circus business."

"That's good advice, I'm sure," Safar said. "But would you mind slowing down for a minute, please, and tell me what in the hells is going on?"

"You mean nobody told you?" Biner was aghast.

Safar said, no, he'd not been informed of anything, thank you very much.

"Why, the Deming Fair's only two hours away. First show at dusk, second at eight bells. We'll be there a week. Two performances every night, plus two and a matinee on Godsday."

He clapped Safar on the back, nearly bowling him over.

"So it's just like Arlain said, lad—'It's Showtime, Folks!'"

The town of Deming was the center of a rich farming area, fed by a long snaking river. The fairgrounds sat just outside the town's main gates and it was already packed with people, strolling past tents blazing with color or crowding around exhibits and hucksters of every variety.

Methydia's Flying Circus made a dramatic entrance, swooping low over the town and fairgrounds, Rabix's music blaring through an amplifying trumpet. The troupe had changed into glittering costumes and lined the edges of the Cloudship, waving and shouting invitations to the crowd.

Arlain, wearing spangled breastplates and modesty patch, stood on a rail, breathing long spears of fire and waving her tail. Methydia had donned a red witch's robe, scooped low in front and slit on one side to the hip. She was provocatively posed beside Arlain, the wind whipping the gossamer robe aside to reveal her long shapely legs.

Biner, voice magically enhanced by one of Methydia's spells, bellowed: "See the fire breathing dragon! Gasp at the feats of Kairo, the Headless Marvel. Test the strength of the mightiest man alive! See the Snake Charmer dare the deadly Serpent of Sunyan! Wonder at the Miracles of the Mysterious Methydia.

"Come one! Come all! Lads and maids of all ages. Welcome to Methydia's Flying Circus of Miracles.

"The Greatest Show On Esmir!"

Once a big enough crowd had been gathered the Cloudship sailed slowly and majestically away, leading them to a wide field next to the fairgrounds. Then it descended, stopping about twenty feet above the earth. Biner and a few roustabouts, bags of tools slung over their shoulders, swung down on lines, then quickly hammered iron stakes into the ground and secured the Cloudship to the stakes.

One by one, the members of the troupe slid down the lines. Each pausing midway to show off some acrobatic feat to wild applause from the gathering crowd.

On the other side of the Cloudship Safar and the remaining roustabouts had the more mundane task of lowering chests and crates of equipment. But Safar soon learned even this job had its admirers. Wide-eyed boys were transfixed by the work, oohing and ahhing as each item was swayed to the ground. The roustabouts took immediate advantage of their interest. They handed out free tickets to the biggest lads in return for their help. Soon a score of muscular young men had stripped to the waist and were helping to set up the circus.

Dazed by the excitement of his first circus, Safar was jolted from job to job by barked orders. Before he knew it a huge tent had been erected, stands hurled up, and he was being pushed into a ticket booth at the entrance of the tent. Someone shoved tickets into his hand and he found himself shouting the seller's speech Biner had drummed into him during the journey:

"Five copper's our price, folks. Now that's not much."

He slapped coins down, counting, "One, two, three, four and five!"

Then he swept one away.

"Bring a friend, we'll make it four!"

He palmed a coin.

"If she's pretty, it's only three."

Then another.

"Two for your granny!"

And another.

"One for your babe."

Then he held up the remaining coin for all to see.

"Catch the lucky copper and the ticket's free."

He tossed the coin into the crowd. Children scrambled for it. Safar saw one little girl knocked down in the rush. She sat in the dirt weeping. His heart went out to her and for the first time since he'd joined the troupe he felt the tingle of magic in his veins. He whispered a spell, gestured, and the child suddenly shouted in glee.

She tottered to her feet, crying, "I got it! I got it!" She raised a hand, displaying the lucky copper. "See!"

The other children groaned in disappointment, but the adults were delighted. They lifted the little girl up and passed her over their heads until she was standing in front of Safar.

With a flourish, he presented her with a ticket. She stared at it, eyes huge with wonder.

Safar was really caught up in the spirit now. Words flowed smoothly from brain to tongue.

"We've got ourselves a lucky lady to start the day, folks!" he shouted. "Now, where's her mother and we'll make it two?" A young matron in a patched dress announced her presence and was pushed forward. Safar presented her with a ticket. "Step right in ladies," he cried. "Step right in and we will reveal to you the greatest wonders of Esmir."

As the grateful mother and her child stepped through the

entrance the crowd boiled around Safar, practically throwing coins at him in their fever to get their tickets.

He sold out in half an hour. Then he collected the coin box, closed the booth and slipped inside the tent.

The show had already begun. The audience was roaring laughter as Arlain, wearing a gaudy dress, pursued Biner—costumed as a lumpish clown soldier—around the ring. At appropriate moments she'd let loose a blast of fire at Biner's padded rear. He'd jump, hands grabbing his bottom, and let out a falsetto shriek of pretended pain. Then he'd run on, crying for help, Arlain at his heels.

Safar found a seat in a darkened corner and watched the show unfold, intent as any member of the paying audience.

The performance lasted three hours. During the whole time the troupe never stopped and there were so many costume changes it seemed as if there were fifty entertainers with fifty different acts to amaze the crowd.

Rabix and Elgy provided all the music. They were hidden beneath a small bandstand with stuffed dummies for musicians. Besides playing the clown, Biner costumed himself as a dozen different fearsome animals. Each would threaten the audience in some way, only to be foiled by Methydia, who played a mighty huntress dressed in outfits that seemed to get skimpier and gaudier with each change. Biner also displayed many feats of great strength, each more amazing than the last.

Arlain was every bit as good as Biner had said. She not only juggled fiery objects, she proved to be a fantastic acrobat who could swing from her tail wrapped around a trapeze while tossing flaming swords.

Besides his high wire act Kairo played catcher to Arlain, hurling her high into the air to another trapeze. When she swung back he'd pretend to drop his head, fumble getting it back on—then suddenly remember Arlain and catch her just in time.

Talented as everyone was, however, Methydia was clearly the star attraction. She appeared in her role as Methydia The Magnificent four times during the show. Dressed in her filmy red witch's robes, she made each entrance a treat in itself to the growing delight of the crowd. Multi-colored smoke would suddenly erupt, or there'd be a crash of forked-lighting, or a great wall of fire. Then she'd swing through the fire on a flaming rope. Or float above the boiling smoke. Or seem to dive out of the lightning, to be caught in Biner's powerful arms.

She bade objects both large and small to appear and disappear, always accompanied by some kind of dramatic pyrotechnics. She called volunteers from the audience and caused them to float above the ground. With Biner to aid her she put on magical skits, all with romantic themes that didn't leave a dry eye in the house. She sawed Arlain in half, then put her back together again.

To Safar the most amazing thing about Methydia's performance was that although he could feel a faint of buzz of real magic emanating from her, there didn't appear to be any sorcery behind the feats themselves. Some were so difficult he should have been hit by the sear of a powerful spellcast. Instead, he felt nothing but that faint buzz. A few of her feats, like the sawing in half business, were just plain impossible. No wizard could do that! The more Safar watched, the more mystified he became. How did she make magic without using magic?

Then there was a great fanfare announcing the show's end. As the lights came up Safar found himself whistling and cheering along with the rest of the audience.

As the people filed out, chatting excitedly about their experiences and carrying sleeping children over their shoulders, The crew started cleaning the stands and getting ready for the evening performance. Safar went to work with a will, sweeping where he was told to sweep, lifting what he was told to lift.

He was whistling a merry tune when Biner strolled up, wiping the last vestiges of clown makeup from his face.

"So, what did you think, lad?" Biner asked.

"I've never seen anything like it in my life," Safar said. "Especially Methydia. Oh, don't get me wrong. You were grand! Everyone was grand!"

Biner laughed. "But Methydia was just a little grander than the rest of us, right?"

"A *lot* grander," Safar said. "No offense."

"None taken, lad," Biner said. "It isn't just because she owns the circus that she gets top billing. She's the *real* star."

He gave Safar a hand with the heavy trunk, lifting his end with remarkable ease. "Suppose you might elect to stay on awhile, then, lad?" he asked casually. "Pay's not much, but we eat regular."

Safar laughed. "As long as you don't charge me admission," he joked. Then, seriously, "I'd just as soon take a rest from the outside world for awhile. Not much in it is all that worthwhile, from what I've seen."

"That's the spirit, lad!" Biner cried. "To the Hells with them all!

"And damn everything but the Circus."

That night after the final show, the troupe ate and retired to tents set up on the ground. The Cloudship, Safar discovered, couldn't be used for that purpose when a show was going on. He'd been so overwhelmed by all the new experiences he hadn't noticed a good portion of the Cloudship's body was disassembled and turned into parts for the circus, such as the stands the audiences sat in.

He was heading off to sleep in the roustabout's tent when Methydia emerged from a small, gaily-decorated pavilion and beckoned him.

"I think we need to have a little talk, my sweet," she said, gesturing for him to enter.

The pavilion, lit by oil lamps, was spread with thick carpets. Pillows were piled onto trunks to make comfortable chairs. A curtained hammock was strung at the back for a bed.

Methydia bade Safar to sit and poured him a little wine. She raised her glass in a toast, intoning, "May the winds be gentle, the stars be bright. May the crew be skilled, the landing light." And they drank.

After a moment, Methydia said, "I heard about your little trick with the lucky coin. Apparently you made a little girl and her mother very happy."

Safar became uneasy. Although Methydia was smiling and her words were gentle, he could see from the look in her eye the purpose of this visit had nothing to do with compliments. It was time to bare his soul.

"I haven't told you everything about me," Safar confessed.

"If you mean that you left out the small part about being a

wizard," Methydia said with exaggerated mildness, "I expect you're right."

"Only a student wizard," Safar hastened to add.

Methydia curled a lip. "I see. *Only* a student. Well, *that* certainly makes me feel much better."

"I'm sorry," Safar said, feeling as socially clumsy as Arlain. "I didn't mean to deceive you."

"Oh, you didn't deceive me," Methydia said. "I sensed you had certain powers right off. And after your little confession about being hunted by powerful men, I just wanted to see how long it would take for you to tell me the rest. But I've never been known for my patience. So I'm asking you to tell me now."

"I was really deceiving myself, more than anything," Safar said. "Magic has brought me nothing but grief. And after what happened in Walaria—I suppose I just wanted a rest. To live normally for a while."

"There was a girl," Methydia said. "Nerisa, I believe?" She saw Safar's look of surprise and explained, "You babbled quite a bit while you were unconscious. Her name was mentioned more than most. A young lover, I presume?"

Safar shook his head. "No, she was just a child. A street urchin who became my friend. She died saving my life."

Methydia drank a little of her wine, eyeing him across the rim. Then, "From the way you railed in your sleep, I *thought* something tragic had happened to her."

"I only wish it could have been Nerisa instead of me you found in the desert," Safar said.

"Some would say you ought to take comfort in the gods," Methydia said. "Pray that they had their reasons for choosing one over the other. Personally, I've never found that sort of thing much help. But *you* might."

Safar shook his head. "No."

Methydia drew a small vial out of her sleeve. "Give me your wine," she said.

Puzzled, he complied. She poured the contents of the vial into his glass and stirred it with a long, graceful finger.

She handed him the glass. "Drink it," she commanded.

"What is it?" Safar asked.

"Oh, just a little potion my old granny taught me how to make," she said. "It will help heal the wounds caused by your friend's death."

Safar hesitated. Methydia pushed the glass to his lips. "It won't make you forget Nerisa, my sweet," she said softly. "It will just make everything seem long ago. And therefore easier to bear."

Safar drank. The potion was tasteless, but when it hit his belly it frothed up into heady fumes that seemed to rise along the back of his spine. He felt his muscles relax, then his tight-strung nerves.

He closed his eyes and saw Nerisa's face with its twisted little grin.

The face filled his mind's eye for a moment, then receded—floating away, deep into darkness, until it was a small image.

Then he put her away in a special chest of memories where the sweet mingled with the bitter.

# 17
# THE WORM OF KYSHAAT

An unseasonable cold snap ended their stay at Deming and they sailed south to warmer climes, storms and blustery winds at their back.

Safar knew from first-hand experience the storms were from out of the seas beyond Caspan. They came regularly—although usually not this early—racing across the northern lands, bursting over the Gods' Divide, then rolling down the southern slopes of the Bride's gown to sweep across the wide plains to the mountains beyond Jaspar.

Although the Cloudship was untroubled by the storms—always staying just ahead of the frontal winds—it was moving much faster than before, covering as much as two hundred miles in a day.

With every mile Safar was flung farther from Kyrania and

soon, like Nerisa's image, all thoughts of home receded into the background. He was overcome by a marvelous feeling of freedom. They sailed across seas of crystal air, over great fluffy fields of clouds, through flocks of bright-feathered birds and under starry skies where the moon was so close it seemed you only had to turn the ship's wheel and you could fly to it.

They sailed on a loose schedule Methydia kept in her head. Day would blend into delightful day, then she'd suddenly issue orders and they'd prepare to land at a town or village where there was always a crowd to fill the ship's larder and the troupe's purses.

After that first night in Deming Methydia evidently came to some sort of decision and began to teach him her own brand of magic. Her training mocked all the forms and conventions of Umurhan's School of Sorcery. In Methydia's view presentation was more important than the spell itself.

"I suppose it's true that magic is a science," she told Safar one day. "There are rules and the scholars tell us there are reasons for those rules."

As she spoke Methydia was sorting through a large wardrobe chest looking for a suitable costume for Safar.

"Personally," she said, "the whys and wherefores never interested me. I'm an artist. I don't care *why* something happens. Only the effect it has on my art."

Methydia held up a dark blue shirt with a plunging neckline and floppy sleeves. It was decorated like a starry night, silvery constellations swirling in the dim light of her cabin's oil lamps.

"This is perfect," she murmured. "It'll bring out the blue of your eyes." Methydia set the shirt aside and continued rummaging.

She said, "I created a circus to display my art. I didn't have the idea until my lovers made the Cloudship possible. I was an actress, then. Billed as a woman of beauty and mystery. I kept my witchery locked in a box, like my makeup. I only used it to cure a blemish, trouble a rival or heighten my performance by wresting a sob from the audience.

"But soon as I saw the Cloudship the idea came to me—'Methydia's Flying Circus of Miracles.' My life as an actress—and hidden witch—suddenly seemed tawdry. Meaningless. Unfulfilling."

Methydia paused, holding up a pair of breeches that were a

near match to the shirt. She studied it, then wrinkled her nose. "Too *too* much," she muttered, tossing the breeches back into the chest and continuing her search.

"Where was I?" she asked, then—"Oh, yes. My life as unfulfilled actress." Her face turned serious, gestures dramatic. "I wanted more," she said, "and yes, I admit it, the 'more' was applause. I'm a self-centered bitch, but then what true artist isn't? The circus gave my art purpose. And in that purpose I found my heart. That is the gift I give to my audience now..." She laid a light hand on her breast. "My heart."

She held the dramatic moment, then went on. "I like to please people," she said, "to lift away their troubles, to thrill them with danger that is always happening to another, but in the end they know is safe. I like to help them remember how it was to be young, how it was to love, and if they're young—how what *might* be, *may* be."

Suddenly Methydia solemn expression dissolved into one of delight. She clapped her hands, making Safar jump with surprise.

"Here's just the thing!" she cried, hauling a pair of snowy white breeches from the trunk.

Methydia held them up, looking critical and turning them this way and that.

She tugged at the seat. "We'll have take them in here," she said. Then she grinned, "So the ladies can see your assets better."

Safar blushed, mumbling something about it not being seemly.

"Nonsense," Methydia replied. "If Arlain and I can jiggle about for the lads, the least you can do is give the maids a thrill. That's what makes a show. A little sex, a little comedy, a clown chase. All frosting on the cake."

She placed the breeches next to the shirt. "Now all we need is a wide belt and tight boots and you'll have the rubes eating out of your hand."

Then Methydia gave him his first lesson. To his surprise, she started by having him show her the coin spell he'd used on the little girl in Deming.

"That's easy," Safar said, "I did that when I was a babe—moving bright things around to amuse myself."

"Just show me, my sweet," she said, passing him a coin.

Safar threw the coin into the corner. While it was still rolling he gestured, made it vanish, gestured again, and it fell into Methydia's still-open hand.

"What's this?" Methydia said, but in disdain, not amazement. "You call *that* magic?"

She flipped the coin high into the air. Quickly she jabbed a dramatic finger at the deck. Safar's eyes followed. There was the sharp *crack!* of an explosion. A stream of green smoke bloomed up—drawing Safar's eyes with it—and the coin appeared to vanish in the cloud. Methydia leaned forward, her face coming so close Safar thought she was about to kiss him. Her lips grazed his, then she drew back, grinning.

She took his nose between finger and thumb, twisting it gently, once, twice, three times. And each time she twisted a coin dropped to his chest and rolled to the floor. She swept them up, threw them into the air, another crack! a stream of smoke and the three coins became one, which she snatched out of the air.

"Now, *that's* magic!" she said, holding the coin in one hand and rolling it up and down from finger to finger in one continuous, fluid motion.

"But you didn't *use* sorcery at all!" Safar protested. "I would have felt it if you had."

Methydia laughed. "Then how did I do it?"

"I don't know," Safar admitted. "It must be some kind of trick."

"But it's a trick that will get a lot more applause than your magic," Methydia said.

Safar thought he understood. "It's the smoke," he said. "I can make smoke."

He gestured at the cabin deck. A thin stream of smoke boiled out of a spot on the plank. He raised his finger slowly and the smoke became a long stream. Then he snapped his fingers and the smoke vanished. "Like that?" he asked.

"No, no," Methydia said. "It wasn't *what* I did, but *how* I did it. You used magic to make the smoke. I used this—"

She opened her hand, displaying a small green pellet. She made a fleshy fold with her thumb, gripping and hiding the pellet in the fold. Then she rolled her hand over, made a graceful gesture with her forefinger and once again there was crack! and green smoke rose up.

"I used a device," she said, "to cause an effect that looked like magic. You used real magic, but so clumsily it looked more like a device. The audience would have guessed—wrongly, as it may be—that you had something hidden in your hand. The point is, you would have spoiled it for them."

"What about the coin part?" Safar asked.

"Same thing," Methydia said. "You threw it in a corner. People will think you did that to divert their attention away from the real trick. Whereas I threw it up into the air, where it appeared to remain in plain sight while I worked my other diversions."

He remembered the jabbing finger that drew his eyes and the near kiss that clouded his view. "I think I see what you mean," he said. "But you *could* have used real magic, not fakery, to accomplish the same thing."

"Not for two shows a day, I couldn't," Methydia said. "*Plus* two and a matinee on Godsday. You have to pace yourself in this business. You need as much energy for the last act of the last show as you did when you started out. In entertainment, my sweet, that's what separates the green from the ripe."

But Safar was young and stubborn. "It seems to me," he said, "I did well enough with real magic when I conjured the coin into that little girl's hand. The crowd certainly *acted* impressed. And they bought out every seat in the tent to prove it."

"They thought she was a plant," Methydia said. "A part of the show. I overheard some of them talking afterwards."

"Oh."

"It was the spirit of the trick that impressed them," she said. "The poor little waif and her young mother." She smiled at Safar and patted his knee, saying, "Even so, I have to give you credit for the idea. It was a certain crowd pleaser and I think we should make it a permanent part of our act."

Safar was as thrilled as if the praise had come from a master wizard instead of a circus witch.

"You have good instincts, my sweet," she said. "And if you pay close attention to what your Auntie Methydia says, you'll make a marvelous showman."

***

The days that followed were among the most joyful in Safar's life. His heart was as serene as the skies they sailed through. His troubles seemed far off—like the dark storm clouds edging the horizon behind them.

As a mountain lad he'd spent many a hour perched on high peaks pondering the mysteries of the skies. He'd watched birds wing overhead and dreamed he was flying with them. In Methydia's Cloudship those dreams came true. Although his fellow passengers of the air could be a boisterous lot at time, especially during rehearsals when there was much joking and leg-pulling, at other times they seemed to treasure silence as much as he did. Hours would pass without a sound.

Each member of the troupe and crew had favorite solitary spots where they could watch the world pass by. Only the occasional hiss of the furnace and pumping of bellows intruded. After a time these faint sounds blended into the song of the winds that carried them above the lands where poor earth-bound creatures dwelled.

Safar was exhilarated by his new life. He threw all his efforts into soaking up everything Methydia and her troupe could teach him. He learned about trick boxes and trapdoors, smoke and mirrors, and wires so thin they couldn't be seen against a dark background, yet could hold hundreds of pounds suspended above the arena. Methydia helped him work up a mind reading act and he amazed the crowds during intermissions with details of their lives that seemed to be snatched from their thoughts. He used two sharp-eyed and big-eared roustabouts to gather the information before he staged his act.

Along with the illusions Methydia also added to his store of real magic. He learned subtle spells that enhanced his performance. Some caused a grumpy crowd to feel humor. Others heightened wonder, increased tension or stirred romance in cold hearts. She taught him how to make the magical charms and potions they sold after every performance. Safar added his potter's skills to this job, pinching out marvelous little vials to hold the potions and creating charms made of colorful potsherd necklaces and jewelry.

He learned how to read a fortune in a palm, instead of casting bones. Methydia said this kind of foretelling was more personal and therefore more accurate than "dead bones rattling around and scaring people half to death." Besides palmistry, he was taught how to cast a simple starchart in five minutes, rather than the hours and even days it took Umurhan and his priests.

"Those scholarly castings are so complicated, so ugly with all their mathematical squiggles, only a rich man would want one," Methydia said. "To show he was wealthy enough to hire such a wise dream catcher.

"But ordinary people—real people—want to know now, not days from now. And they want to be able to read the chart for themselves so they can hang it over the mantle and show it off to their friends by pointing out the highlights."

The other members of the troupe also pitched in with his showcraft education. The brawny dwarf, Biner, taught him the delicate art of applying makeup and altering his features so he could play many different kinds of characters. Arlain and Kairo showed him how to do simple acrobatics. They ran him through heart-stopping exercises and plied him with strengthening powders until his muscles vibrated with power. Elgy coached him on timing, getting Rabix to play rhythmic music as Safar performed his acts over and over again until his delivery was as natural as the mental beat Rabix drummed into his head.

To Methydia's amazement—and his own—Safar's magical powers increased with each passing day. It wasn't a gradual strengthening, like his muscles, but leap after leap from one pinnacle to the next. For the first time since he was a boy he actually enjoyed doing magic. The roar of the audiences swept away the shame his father had accidentally instilled in him. He delighted in their amazement. Especially—as Biner had said it would—the wonderment of the children.

As he became stronger and more skilled he even started dispensing with some of Methydia's tricks. His illusions became almost entirely magical, although he still used showmanship to "sell it," as Methydia would say. True, the performances drained him, just as Methydia predicted. Yet never so much he couldn't deliver as many encores as the crowd desired.

For a time Methydia kept herself at a slight distance from him.

She still teased him and made suggestive jokes that made him blush. But that was her nature. Mainly she behaved like a kindly teacher or mentor, correcting him when he needed it and praising him when he deserved it. Although Safar was powerfully attracted to her, it never occurred to him that she might feel the same. Why, she was old enough to be his mother. Perhaps even older. He ought to be ashamed of himself for thinking of such disrespectful thoughts.

During that time Safar noticed a small tension building among the troupe and crew, as if they were waiting for something long overdue. Occasionally when he and Methydia were out on the deck together—running through a new twist in the act—he'd noticed people glancing at the two of them. Then there'd be little smiles, whispered asides and shakes of the head.

Once he overheard the roustabouts wondering aloud if "maybe Methydia's lost her sweet tooth." Safar didn't know what that meant. He was doubly mystified when the men saw him and turned away, shamefaced.

The dreamlike days ended when they reached Kyshaat.

It was a regular stop in the troupe's circuit. Over the centuries the people of Kyshaat had turned the vast plains surrounding their walled town into wide fields of fat grain. The circus folk expected a large profit from their visit to the region and were dismayed when they saw the desolation of the usually lush fields. It was as if an enormous ravenous beast had swept through, devouring the grain—stalks and all—nearly to the ground.

Hungry and pitiful eyes stared up at the Cloudship as it sailed overhead. To Safar the usually joyful circus music had an eerie edge to it as they serenaded the crowds and Biner's big booming call of "Come one, Come all," seemed to be flattened and swallowed up by a thick miasma.

"Don't know what's happened here," Biner muttered to Methydia. "But maybe it'd be best if we moved on."

Methydia pressed her lips together and shook her head. "We were eager enough for their company when there was a profit to be made," she said. "I'll not turn away now because fortune no longer favors them."

Biner nodded and turned back to his duties, but Safar could see he was worried. On the ground hundreds of people followed the Cloudship's shadow, but they were so silent Safar could hear the wails of small children carried in their parents' arms.

A few minutes later the Cloudship was tied up over a barren patch and the roustabouts were swaying down the equipment.

When Safar's feet touched ground he turned to face the onrushing crowd. To his amazement they all stopped at the edge of the field. It was as if an invisible barrier had been thrown up. They remained there for two hours while the roustabouts put the circus together. Methydia had them dispense with the tents—the stands were set up in the open.

When she thought all was ready she beckoned to Safar and the two of them advanced on the crowd. About twenty paces away a shout brought them up short:

"Beware, Methydia! Come no closer!"

Methydia's pose was unbroken. Her eyes swept the crowd.

"Who spoke?" she demanded.

There were mutters in the crowd, but no one answered.

"Come on," Methydia insisted. "We've traveled many miles to entertain our friends in Kyshaat. What kind of greeting is this? Speak up!"

There were more mutterings, then the crowd parted and an old man, bent nearly double, hobbled out, supported by a heavy cane.

"It was I, Methydia," he said. "I was the one who cried the warning."

Bent over and aged as the old man was, Safar could see the skeletal outline of once broad shoulders. The fingers gripping the cane were thick, the wrists broad-bladed.

"I know you," Methydia said. "You're Neetan. The one with the seven grandchildren I always let in free."

Neetan's wrinkled face drooped like an old beaten dog's. "There's only two, now, Methydia," he said. "All the rest have been called to the realm of the gods."

Methydia's eyes widened. She took a step forward.

The crowd stirred uneasily and once again Neetan shouted, "Come no closer!"

Methydia stopped. "What happened here?" she asked.

"We are becursed, Methydia," Neetan said. "All of Kyshaat is becursed. Flee while you can, or the curse will afflict you."

Safar saw momentary fear register on Methydia's face. Then her chin came up, stubborn. "I'm not leaving," she said, "until I've heard what it is that has brought you to this state."

Neetan stamped his cane. "It wasn't one catastrophe," he said, "but many. First we were visited by King Protarus."

Safar was startled. "Iraj was here?" he asked.

"Beware how you address him, my son," the old man said. "Do not be so familiar with his royal name."

Safar ignored this. He pointed at the barren fields. "Iraj Protarus did that?" he demanded.

"Only some of it," Neetan said. "And it was one of his generals, not the king, who came. The general arrived with a small troop and demanded our fealty to King Protarus and food for his armies."

"And you granted this?" Safar asked, "Without at least asking payment?" It was inconceivable to him that his former friend would not at least offer to pay these people.

"What choice did we have?" Neetan said. "It is well known that King Protarus is not so kind to any who oppose him. Why, several cities have been sacked and burned for defying him. Then the men and old ones were killed and the rest sold into slavery."

Safar was furious. Methydia laid a hand on his arm, steadying him.

"You said this was but the first of many catastrophes," she said to Neetan. "What else has befallen you, my friend?"

"At least King Protarus left us enough to live," Neetan said. "But then we were visited by plague to ravage our homes, birds and locusts to denude our fields and beasts to devour our flocks."

While the old man enumerated the evils that afflicted Kyshaat, Safar caught a glimpse of a shadowy figure at the edge of the crowd. But when he looked directly at the spot the figure was gone. He suddenly caught a whiff of a foul odor. Then the scent vanished.

Meanwhile, Neetan was saying, "We are the most miserable of people, Methydia. The gods have forsaken us. Because we love you, because of all the joy you have brought us over the years, please leave this place. Leave us to our curse. Before you too fall under its thrall."

"Nonsense!" Methydia said. "I fear no curse. The circus will begin in one hour. All who want to come are welcome—free of charge. This is my gift to old friends. So do not insult me by staying away."

Then she turned and marched back to the others, leaving Neetan and the frightened people gaping.

Safar lengthened his stride and caught up to her. "There really *is* something here," he said." "It's…some kind of…" and then words failed him.

He gestured, wanting to convey the feeling he had of a cold, greasy breath at the back of his neck. "A presence, is the only thing I can think of.

"It's watching us."

Methydia suddenly quickened her pace. "Yes, yes," she whispered. "Now I can feel it too.

"I think I made a mistake coming here. We'd better get away."

Safar heard a sound like boulders grating against one another and then the ground heaved up beneath his feet.

"Run!" he shouted, grabbing Methydia by the hand and sprinting for the Cloudship.

Behind him he heard the screams of the crowd and the long tearing rip of the earth itself. Ahead he saw Biner and the others scrabbling for hammers and axes and anything that would make a weapon. Soon as he reached them, Safar released Methydia and whirled around to confront the threat.

He saw the ground coming up, the roots of bushes and small trees ripping away, gravel and earth and stones showering down a gathering hill. Before his eyes the hill became a towering earthen figure with arms and a head and a torso supported by two mighty legs. A hole opened in the place where a mouth ought to be.

The creature spoke, rocks and gravel tumbling from its lips:

"Mine!" it said, voice grating and grumbling like it was formed in a deep cavern.

It waved a huge arm, showering Safar and others with gravel and clods of earth.

"Mine!" it said again, gesturing at the crowd of people.

Then an immense arm came forward, a gnarly finger as long as a man shooting out—pointing at Safar and his group.

"Now, you mine!" the creature said.

It took a slow step forward and the ground shuddered. Small

bushes and trees crashed down. Instantly they took life, brushy limbs and hairy roots clawing up dirt, which formed around their woody skeletons to make bodies.

"Mine!" the earth creature howled and its spawn moved toward Safar and his friends, thorny hands reaching out to grasp.

The creatures fanned out into a half-circle which they tightened around the troupe, their earthen creator urging them on with bellows of "Mine!"

Biner lifted up a huge crate and hurled it at the oncoming horror. The crate crashed into the center of the line, bursting apart three of the monsters. But the others moved on, dragging themselves toward the troupe.

Arlain reared back, drawing in her breath and bracing herself with her tail. Then she jerked forward—long flames shooting from her mouth. There was a series of meaty *pops!* like termites exploding in a forest fire. One whole side of the advancing line burst into flames.

Then the whole circus charged—Biner in the lead—flailing away with axes and hammers and spars.

Safar gripped Methydia's hand, holding her back. He was concentrating on the earthen giant.

"Mine!" it roared, sending off more showers of rock and dirt and brush that quickly formed into new monstrosities to replace the fallen.

"Help me, Methydia!" Safar shouted, squeezing her hand tighter.

He grabbed for her power, felt her resist and shrink back. Then the shield lifted and he had it—a strong, slender fist of energy he added to his own.

Safar turned toward the earthen giant. It was almost on them. He saw it reach out to grab for Biner, black maw gaping to expose the rocky millstones that were its teeth.

"No!" he heard Methydia cry.

Safar drew on a cloak of calmness. Everything became exceptionally slow, like the day he'd fought the demons. Even as the earthen giant's rocky palm was closing over Biner, Safar took his time.

He made a sharp probe of his senses and shot it forward. He felt it slip through the creature's rubble body, find the path of least resistance and drive the probe upward.

Deep inside he found the husk of an insect's body. A locust that had been drained of all its juices. And in that locust he found something small and mean. It wriggled when his probe found it, rising up and bursting out of the locust's corpse.

It was a worm, no more than a finger long. It was maggoty white, with a large black spot on its head that Safar thought was an eye. It was a thing that fed on misery and pain. As Safar probed around, he realized the creature was the infant form of something even more deadly. He could see half-formed legs kicking beneath the worm's skin and an arced tail tipped by a budding stinger.

The little creature blasted him with voracious thoughts. "Mine!" it shrieked. "I want...Mine!"

Safar heard Methydia shout, "Hurry, Safar!"

But he took his time. He made the probe into two thick fingers. He reached for the worm, dodging small sharp knives of hunger and hate.

Then he caught it between the two fingers. The worm struggled, fighting back, searing his senses with blasts of sorcery.

He ignored the pain and crushed the worm.

Immediately he was assaulted by the foul stench of death. He staggered back, drawing his spirit self with him.

Safar heard a rumbling sound. Dazed, he looked up and saw the earthen giant crumbling into huge pieces of rock and dirt clods. As it came crashing down Biner leaped away just in time. A thick cloud of dust exploded as it hit, pebbles and debris showering everywhere.

Then the dust settled and there was nothing to be seen but a large mound of rubble.

Safar felt suddenly weak and confused. He turned to Methydia and recognized the look of awe in her eyes. It was the same look Iraj had given him when he'd brought the avalanche down on the demons.

"It was just a worm," he tried to say, but it came out as a mumble. "A stupid little—"

And he pitched forward on the ground.

The people of Kyshaat got their circus. Many said Methydia and her troupe staged the best performance of their careers. Children would grow old and regale their own disbelieving grandchildren about that fateful day when the creature that had caused so much misery had been defeated. And of the wild celebration that followed.

Safar, the hero of the hour, saw none of it. He lapsed into a coma for nearly a week. When he regained consciousness he was aboard the Cloudship and they were sailing through a storm.

Once again he was lying on a pallet in Methydia's cabin. It was dark and outside he could hear the winds moan through the lines and rain lash the deck.

He was thirsty and fumbled around with a blind hand until he brushed against a tumbler. He drank. It was warm wine and honey.

There was a blast of cold air as the door slammed open. He looked up. Methydia was standing there, a hooded parka covering her from head to ankle. Lightning crash followed lightning crash, illuminating her. She glowed in it, an aura forming around her slender body. Her eyes were glittering wells, drinking him in. A gust of wind hurled the parka aside. She was dressed in a thin white gown, nearly transparent from the rain.

Another gust of wind blasted past her, but the cold seemed to light a fire in him.

"Close the door," he said.

At least he thought he said it. His lips formed the words, but he heard nothing come out.

Just the same, Methydia closed the door.

Then he held out his arms and whispered, "Please!"

Methydia floated across the room into his embrace.

He burrowed into the warm heart of her. Found the storm and let it loose. For a long time all he knew was the sensation of their love making and the sound of her voice calling his name.

# 18

# THE WINDS OF FATE

King Manacia—Lion of the gods, Future Lord of Esmir, Courageous Protector of Ghazban, Perfect of Zanzair, His Merciful Majesty—suffered from nightmares.

In his dreams he was pursued by naked human devils, with their scale-crawling ghoulish skins, talonless claws and thick red tongues that looked like eels grown fat from eating carrion.

He would no sooner slake his royal lust on a concubine and close his eyes to drift off to sleep, when the human hordes would come charging out, screaming blood-curdling cries and gnashing their flat, flesh-grinding teeth. The king would try to run but his limbs wouldn't obey him. He'd stand frozen as the ugly creatures surged forward, howling their hate.

Two tall humans always led the ravenous crowd. One was fair-skinned, with a golden beard and golden locks encircled by a crown. The other was dark and beardless, with long black hair that streamed behind him. The dark one had huge blue eyes that bored into his soul, ferreting out all Manacia held sacred and secret.

The dreams left him shaken and weak. For a long time he tried to ignore them, telling himself they were caused by nothing more than stress from his royal duties. His plans for invading the humanlands had him overwrought, that's all.

The planning was not going well, which added to his agitation. His generals were driving him mad with their overly cautious counsel. They wanted to gather an army so large, with supply lines so deep, that no human force could stand in their way.

At first King Manacia had nothing against this strategy. Overwhelming force was the common sense answer to any military difficulty. But what the generals considered overwhelming, the king soon learned, was always double whatever figure he proposed.

Manacia understood the careers and very lives of his generals and their staff depended on the outcome. The king made no apologies for his feelings regarding failure. He had no use for the weak or the unlucky, purging any and all who were associated with less than total victory. Yet his generals' caution disappointed him. Where was their patriotism? Where was their sense of duty to king and Ghazban? You had to take a chance in this life, Manacia thought, or nothing great would ever be accomplished.

When the invasion came it was true the king intended to sorely punish any failure. But in his view the rewards he was offering for success should more than overcome his generals' fears.

For some reason they hadn't. The plan was simple enough.

Manacia intended to first conquer the regions north of the Gods' Divide. The mountain range was a natural barrier that would allow him to work his will, then gather his strength for the final assault over the mountains. True, the ancient maps gave no hint on what route should be taken to cross the Divide. But Manacia was confident—given time and absolute rule over the northern humanlands—that passage would be found. He would find Kyrania, by the gods! Or there were certain lazy, talon-dragging generals who would experience his royal wrath.

To accomplish the first part of his plan—the subjugation of the north—his forces would cross the Forbidden Desert and set up a base camp just beyond the edge. Supply trains and reinforcement columns would pour into that camp, while the main force leaped forward to wipe out the humans.

It was Manacia's opinion that surprise would carry the day. Yes, he wanted a large force to mount the invasion. But it needn't be as large as his generals said, or attached to such unwieldy supply lines. No one in the humanlands had even a glimmer that their demon enemies were gathering for an assault. Manacia had made certain of this by refusing any request to send vulnerable scouting parties to investigate the humanlands. He'd already taken too great a chance by sending Sarn and didn't intend to dare the fates by repeating that error.

His generals, however, had seized on this secrecy, saying the blade cut both ways. Yes, they said, the wise course was to keep the humans in ignorance. But that meant the demons would know nothing of what transpired in the humanlands. When the king struck, he'd be cutting at the dark. There was no way of knowing who might return the blow and with what force.

The only safe thing, prudent thing, to do, his generals said, was to attack with a well-supplied army of such size that anyone who opposed them would be doomed.

Manacia's generals were a backbiting lot, always maneuvering behind the scenes to attack their brother officers, but on this issue they were united. In a rare alliance, Lord Fari and Prince Luka also joined together to back the generals.

Fari, kept from probing the humanlands with intelligence-gathering spells, had similar concerns as the military. So did the prince, who as heir to the throne was expected to lead the vanguard of the invasion.

"If I am to have the high honor of carrying your banner into glorious battle, Majesty," the prince said, "I want to make certain there is no chance it is sullied or befouled in any way.

"I would fight to the death to prevent that from happening."

"Quite right, too," King Manacia said. "My father expected the same from me when I was Crown Prince. And I risked my life many a time for his standard."

Prince Luka placed talon to breast and bowed low, honoring his father's youthful bravery. As he did so, he thought, You cunning old fraud. You cut your father's throat in his sleep and seized his standard. And if I only have the chance, I'll do the same to you.

"You are a constant inspiration to me, Majesty," the prince said, smoothly. "And I'll need ten thousand fiends for my vanguard."

The king gave them to him.

After much discussion with his generals, he also agreed that a five hundred thousand demon army would be raised—the largest force in the history of Esmir. Backing them with war magic would be two thousand wizards, led by Lord Fari.

The preparations were massive and seemed to move on as slowly as the Turtle Gods carried the continents across the seas.

Making the task even more difficult were countless emergencies calling for his armies' attentions. Within a single month troops had to be rushed to trouble spots a half-a-dozen times.

Manacia felt as if his whole kingdom was bulging at the seams, ready to erupt.

The feeling was intensified by the nightmares. As troubled night bled into troubled night, the king began to fix on the two human devils who always led the rush—the golden haired one and his blue-eyed companion. They became very real to him and he began to wonder who they might be.

When he could bear it no longer he called on Lord Fari and his wizards for an answer. He tried to make light of the dreams, but he knew he was fooling no one and Fari would mark it down as a weakness.

Starcharts were cast, but proved useless since no chart agreed with the next. With the gods at sleep, the heavens held no answers, although the dreamcatchers were ignorant of the reason for their failure.

Bone cups were rattled, the king had his palm read scores of times. All to no avail.

Finally Lord Fari had a human slave brought forth. He was tortured so his cries would please the gods, then while he was still alive—his belly was slit so the king's wizards could read the entrails.

Manacia watched with much interest as Fari leaned over the moaning victim, sniffing at the gaping wound.

"A healthy odor, Majesty," the old wizard reported. "That's a lucky sign."

He scooped up a coil of entrails with a claw.

"Mercy, have mercy," the victim groaned.

Fari peered closely at the rope of tissue. "Better still, Majesty," he said after a moment. "This is a good strong bowel, symbolizing the soundness of Your Majesty's policies."

The human made a weak cry as Fari pulled up more of his innards. "Please," the man whimpered, "please."

"Aha!" the old demon said. "Here's our trouble, Majesty."

He held out a glistening coil. A thick rope of internal muscle jutted off of it, dividing into two blunt-ended tubes about an inch out.

"It's a cancer, Majesty," Fari said. "Attached to the main branch. You see how it divides into two?"

Manacia nodded, he did indeed. Fari extended a talon and sliced each tube. Black blood gushed out.

"Mother of mercy!" the victim screamed. And then he sagged, unconscious.

Satisfied that he had enough information, Fari let the entrails fall. Two slaves slithered over on their bellies to offer him perfumed water and towels to clean his claws.

Fari paced back and forth, wiping his claws and thinking. While he thought two other slaves approached and dragged the human away.

Fari noticed and his snout came up. "The king will want the heart for his dinner," he ordered the slaves. Then he went back to his pacing.

Finally, when Manacia thought he no longer bear the suspense, Fari began to speak.

"Here is how I read it, Majesty," he said. "The cancer, I fear, does represent a threat. The twin ropes drawing off energy from the main bowel are the two humans who bedevil Your Majesty's dreams. One is a king. The other a wizard."

"So *what* if one's a wizard?" Manacia growled. "Human magic is too weak to be a threat to us."

"Most certainly, Majesty," Fari said. "But perhaps when joined with the king he makes a more imposing adversary. I cannot say. The entrails gave no clue to such things.

"But they did tell me that right now these two forces—king and wizard—are apart. They began together, but then separated for some reason. At the moment each is independent of the other."

"When will they come together?" the king asked.

Fari sighed, wiping the last of the gore from his claws. "That was not revealed to me, Majesty," he said. He let the towel fall and a slave scrabbled over to pick it up.

"But what of my invasion?" the king pressed. "How long dare I wait? It seems to me the longer the delay, the more chance there is these two forces will come together."

"Quite true, Majesty," Fari said.

"Advise me," the king demanded. "When do I invade?"

Fari didn't hesitate. The old demon felt quite sure of himself. The entrails had been that plain.

"In the spring, Majesty," he said. "Soon as the first snow melts."

"And what of this king and this wizard?" Manacia asked. "They won't be together by then?"

"I don't believe so, Majesty," Fari said. "They're too far away from one another. And unless some great wind sweeps one up and delivers him to the feet of the other, we have nothing to fear."

The storm that hastened the Cloudship over the Plains of Jaspar lasted for more than a week. The winds that drove it were as fierce as the love-making in Methydia's cabin.

For Safar it was a wondrous journey to the heart of a woman. In many ways Safar had always preferred the company of women.

He'd been raised in a household of generous and intelligent females. As a child he'd sat in their company, so quiet they soon forgot he was about, and he'd listened intently to their troubles and dreams. Safar thought women dreamed better than men. They saw nuances and dimensions where men only saw flat featureless plains. Safar had been unfortunate in his first adult experience with women. Astarias had wounded him. Although he'd been careful not to judge all women by that experience, he couldn't help all the small doubts and fears that remained.

Methydia wiped them away in a stroke.

For Methydia the affair was altogether different. It shook her sensibilities. It rocked her mortality. She'd had many affairs; some for gain, some for lust, perhaps one or two for love—although as she grew older she'd started to think all three were the same and equaled love of self. But with Safar there was something extra—a tantalizing mystery just beyond her grasp.

What Methydia always liked about young men was that they *appreciated* you so much. A woman merely had to be a *woman* and take the upper hand. Young men—well brought up young men—were so accustomed to obeying their mothers they were invariably relieved when responsibility was taken from them. She could beguile them with a look. Arouse them with a touch. Hold them at bay with a frown. Methydia was a consummate actress and could be all things to all men, but with the young it took less effort. There was more time to *enjoy*. As Biner often said, "The boss likes her toys, she does. She likes 'em young with a key to wind 'em up."

Safar could have been such a toy, although she'd plucked him from the desert only out of kindness. When he became well and she'd noted his personality was as pleasing as his appearance, she'd considered him for her bed.

But what truly captivated Methydia was Safar's magical self. It was a beautiful essence, powerful and passionate. It was potent—never in her witchy days had she sensed such strength—but there was good at the heart of it. Safar's spirit self wanted to call you friend before it called you foe. It was young, but graceful rather than clumsy. It had known death—was miserable for being the cause of it—and was reluctant to come out into the light again. For a time Methydia was intimidated by Safar's magical self. She didn't fear it, but she did worry if she wasn't careful she'd injure it so badly all the kindness would vanish. As a villain, a black wizard, a fully mature Safar Timura would be a terrible gift to the world.

Attractive as Safar was, she'd held herself back for a long time. In fact, Methydia had all but decided it'd be best to deny herself an affair.

The incident at Kyshaat had ripped her from that mooring.

In her long life Methydia thought she'd encountered just about everything. She'd visited many realms, entertained many people. She'd dealt with danger and evil aplenty; but in her heart she believed good more than outweighed evil, there were more blessings than ill fortune and she'd made it her life's work to remind people of these qualities.

As a witch she was well aware the sorcerous landscape was riddled with magicians and entities whose sole purpose was to cause harm. She'd always managed to evade such things. To Methydia magic came from the earth itself. She believed she drew her powers directly from nature, which to her was a loving, grandmotherly presence.

The creature she encountered at Kyshaat had badly cracked that image. When it rose out of the ground it was as if the earth itself were attacking her. That nature had suddenly revealed its true self and it had a jackal's face. In that awful moment when the earth beast had towered over her she'd thought she'd lost both her life and her soul.

Safar had saved them both.

She'd fled into his arms for comfort and safety and sheer joy at being alive. For a week she hid there from all the terrors the creature had aroused. Yet they gnawed at the edges. Deep in the night, while the storms howled outside and Safar slept, Methydia let them come out one by one. Examining them in turn. In the end she concluded the beast at Kyshaat was the harbinger of doom. That it was only the first of many evils that lay ahead.

Her instincts told her only Safar could fight the dark tide.

As soon as she thought this she knew she'd lost him. It wasn't possible for Safar to remain with the circus. It would be a much happier life for him, but it was Safar's tragedy that all such happiness would be denied him. And one day it would be Methydia's sad duty to point him down the bleak road of his fate.

She said nothing of this to Safar. When she thought the time was right she gently quizzed him about further details of his past. Everything he said confirmed her view. He told her about the vision of Hadin and its destruction, his fears of future disasters, his search for knowledge in Walaria, his discovery of the demon Asper and how in the end the master wizard's works had been denied him. He showed her the stone turtle Nerisa had given him and she mourned with him the faint pulse of nearly dying life inside.

"I was a fool for even trying to find the answer," Safar said bitterly. "What would it matter if I did? There's nothing a potter's boy from Kyrania could do about it."

Then he swore he'd always love her, always stay with her and he'd never return to the dull, heavy existence of earthbound mortals who stared up at the sky in wonder as the Cloudship sailed overhead.

Methydia kept her silence. It would do him no good to tell him what she thought. But she had to be certain Safar was prepared for whatever was in store for him.

She determined that in the time remaining to them she'd teach him everything she knew about magical guile and peoples' artifice. She'd give him all the love she had in her—emotions she'd kept locked away to better arm herself against the world. She'd bolster his confidence, free him as best she could from his own self-imposed restraints.

And when the time came she'd steel herself and make him confront his destiny.

The storms continued with barely a day between each new blow. The winds drove them onward—across the plains of Jaspar.

They saw much misery in the land the Cloudship passed over. Ruined villages, stripped fields where great armies had passed. Even in the heaviest rains they saw thousands of refugees slogging along the roads, making their way to the gods knew where. They saw the aftermath of fighting; huge muddy fields littered with corpses of men and animals.

The sight made them all moody. Only the most necessary words were exchanged. Safar was moodiest of all, staring out over the bleak landscape before them. Then one day they crossed a low mountain range. And when they broke through the clouds the skies were sunny, the air brisk.

They were floating over a large, peaceful valley. The valley floor was a patchwork of bright green orchards interspersed with blue creeks, gaily-painted villages, bordered by shaded gardens. All looked healthy and prosperous and there was no sign of the troubles they'd encountered before.

A fresh wind pushed the Cloudship forward. At the far edge of the valley was a small city with pearly walls and graceful buildings rising up from behind them.

Safar leaned out over the rails to get a closer look. The sight brought a smile to his face.

"What is this place?" he asked.

"The city of Sampitay," Methydia said. "We've never played there before. But I've heard good things about it. An entertainer's paradise, I'm told."

Safar mused, dimly recalling Gubadan's geography lessons. Then he recognized the orchards—white mulberry trees. Sampitay was well known for its fine silks and the royal yellow dye taken from the roots of the trees.

"Sampitay," Biner said. "That's a lucky place. Now I'm sorry I cursed the gods so harshly for all that bad weather."

Safar turned and looked back at the mountains. Big banks of clouds, driven by a far off storm, were scudding across the sky after them. It was about time, he thought, that the winds of fate took a gentler turn.

## 19

## THE RETURN OF PROTARUS

Safar knew there was something wrong before the first performance.

The crowds greeting them were enthusiastic enough, as were the soldiers who directed them to the field outside the city gates. The roustabouts set the circus up in record time and the seats for the first show were sold out before the ticket booth was in place.

The good citizens of Sampitay were so hungry for entertainment they lined up, begging to be relieved of the price of admission, while the Cloudship was still unloading. Methydia's troupe was forced to give a hasty first performance, cutting the encores short so an impatient second audience could be admitted.

No art was required to please them. They roared laughter at the slightest clown antic, gasped in terror at the merest slip of an acrobat, moaned in suspense at Methydia's and Safar's slightest magical gesture.

Oddly enough the troupe was discontented.

"I could fart and get a laugh," Biner complained.

"I could whistle through my fangs and they'd be thrilled," Elgy said.

"They're tho eathy I want to thpit," Arlain said. "And the godth *know* what happenth when I thpit!"

Green as he was, Safar felt a wrongness in the overly-wild applause he received when he cast the first purple-colored smoke pellet that began his performance. He sensed an hysterical edge to the crowd's huzzahs.

During his mind reading act he announced a maid named Syntha was to be wed soon and her love would always be true. The young woman in question shrieked such joy at this news—which Safar had received courtesy of a big-eared roustabout—the entire audience was reduced to tears.

"What's wrong with them?" he asked Methydia between performances.

Methydia smiled thinly. She seemed distracted, applying her makeup with a heavy hand. "Are you so accustomed to applause," she asked, "that you've already begun to question it?"

"Come on," Safar said. "I'm not the only one. Elgy said the last time he played before an audience like this it turned out his troupe had wandered into the middle of a plague."

"The fear of death," Methydia said, "*does* have a way of exciting people's interest in life."

"Do you know something the rest of us don't?" Safar asked, growing irritated.

"Only this," Methydia said, passing him a large ornate card with a distinctive seal of gold wax. "We are to give a command performance tonight for Queen Arma and her royal consort."

Safar looked at the card, an honor at any other time, and said, "Why is this bad news?"

"Because it was accompanied by a chest of silk," Methydia said. "And that silk, according to the messenger who delivered it, is an advance payment on a week's worth of free performances for the queen's subjects."

"A morale booster?" Safar asked.

"I'm talking about a dozen bolts of the *finest* Sampitayan silk," Methydia said.

Safar, who'd spent his life on a caravan route, had a good idea what *that* was worth. "How much morale-boosting do they *need*?" he said. "And why?"

"I don't know," Methydia answered. "The messenger was quite polite, but he worked hard to avoid answering my questions. It was as if he expected us to pack up and leave at the slightest hint of trouble. He went on for an hour about what a wonderful ruler Arma was, the excellent health of her children, the esteem all her subjects hold her in. And the soundness of her kingdom."

Safar winced. In Walaria he'd learned to read fear on the face of royal posture. "Maybe we'd better go," he said.

"I've arrived at the same conclusion," Methydia said. "I told the messenger we had pressing business elsewhere. And we couldn't stay longer than the week purchased by Her Majesty."

Safar, remembering the incident at Kyshaat, said, "What if we slipped off tonight?"

"I've also considered that course," Methydia said. "Much can happen in a week. But I don't think we dare cut our visit too short. We might bring down the wrath of Queen Arma by making a hasty exit. I think it'd be best if we gave the queen the command performance she asked for, then quietly loaded the circus back on the Cloudship. We can do without some of the sets. And make it look like we're unloading things while we're actually putting them aboard. Three nights, no more, and we'll be on our way."

"But the queen paid in advance," Safar pointed out. "What about all that silk?"

"I'll leave it behind," Methydia said. "It's bad money and I don't want any part of it."

As it turned out three days was too long. The circus overshot its luck the night of the command performance.

Knowing she was going to abandon Sampitay as soon as possible, Methydia roused the troupe to put on its best show ever.

Safar, drawing on his years of schooling in Walaria, had created a new kind of magical lighting. The circus tried out his ideas for the first time the night Queen Arma held court in the main tent.

A blazing full moon greeted the royal visitors as they entered the tent. Safar made the moon a spotlight, picking out the grand moment of each performance, then dimmed it with onrushing clouds during costume changes. Flares burst up in the arena during the featured performances, turning all into a mystical herky-jerky of amazing motion.

To close the first half Safar and Arlain debuted a new act they'd been working on for some time.

From the time of its inception—which had merely been to improve on the old "saw the maid in half" gag—the trick had grown into a full-blown tale. Safar cast himself as the villain of the piece—an evil wizard. Arlain and Biner were the odd lovers—the ugly dwarf and the beautiful creature who was part woman, part dragon.

In the story Safar hunts the lovers in bleak otherworlds full of swirling lights, fountaining smoke and spurting flames. Eventually he corners them, appears to slay Biner, then captures Arlain. She fights off his attempts to ravish her but is punished by being put into a deadly trance. In that trance Safar levitates her, then proceeds to slice her in two with his sword. Defiant to the last, Arlain breathes fire. Then the fire is gone. Suddenly Biner is aroused. He heals Arlain. A fight commences. And in the end the two lovers defeat Safar and embrace. Then a lovely note piped by Elgy and Rabix brings the lights down.

Tears and cheers greeted the three performers when they took their bows.

Despite his worries, Safar was feeling mightily pleased with himself as he rushed off to get ready for the second act. The high wail of a herald's horn brought him up short. He turned, alarmed at this sudden interruption of circus routine.

In the royal box Queen Arma was on her feet. In front of her was a boy dressed in the elaborate livery of a court herald. At a signal from the queen he raised his horn and blew again—commanding all present to be silent and attend to the queen.

Arma was a middle-aged woman, running to fat. She had a round pleasant face made to seem rounder still by the tall fore-peaked crown she wore. Sitting beside her was her consort, Prince Crol, a handsome, silver-haired man in the glittering dress uniform of a general. The queen drew in her breath to speak and just before the first words issued from her lips Safar saw the soldier gesture and felt the sting of magic. He knew immediately the man was a wizard and the gesture was a magical spell to amplify the queen's words so all could hear.

"Citizens of Sampitay," Queen Arma said, high-pitched voice filling the main tent. "I am sure we are all having a lovely time tonight, are we not?"

The richly dressed crowd answered with loud applause. Arma turned her head, nodding at Methydia who stood near the performers' exit—regal-looking in her own right in a dazzling red gown and slender tiara, decorated with a tasteful spattering of gems.

"We have the good Lady Methydia and her talented troupe of entertainers to thank for bringing a bit a joy to Sampitay during its crisis," the queen said.

Methydia bowed low, but from the stiffness of her bow Safar could see she was as surprised as he at the queen's remarks. And what was that Arma said about a "crisis?"

"As you all well know," Arma continued, "your queen and her representatives have been in almost constant communication with King Protarus and his emissaries for over a month now."

The crowd murmured, troubled—as was Safar at the mention of his old friend's name.

"We have kept you all well informed regarding the nature of those communications," Arma said. "The first message was a demand that this kingdom end its long and historic policy of neutrality. Protarus *commanded* it—and it would be wrong of us to use a weaker word to pretty up his barbaric diplomacy. Our answer to that outrage was a firm although courteous reply that this queen is not his to command!"

A thunderclap of applause greeted this statement. Safar thought of Iraj and knew it would have been unlikely for him to take the queen's refusal well.

"Shortly afterward," Arma went on, "Protarus' emissaries arrived with new demands. He was no longer asking us to ally ourselves with him against his enemies. Instead, he commanded our immediate surrender. He even gave us this..." and Safar saw her raise up a familiar banner, bearing the red demon moon and silver comet that was the sign of Alisarrian "...to hoist over the palace, marking our subjugation."

The crowd reacted angrily, shouting words of defiance.

Queen Arma waited until the shouts died down, then said loudly, "We refused!"

More shouts and thunderous applause. The queen waited, then at a key moment she signaled for silence.

"It would dishonest of me, my loyal subjects," Arma said, "if we didn't admit our nights were long and sleepless with worry after we made that reply. King Protarus, whose armies now range at will across the Plains of Jaspar, is not known to brook any defiance from any kingdom or monarch whom he deems to stand in his way. Fearing reprisals, we put our own troops in a state of readiness. We were prepared to die to the last defending the sanctity of our realm."

Pandemonium reigned for many long minutes as the crowd roared its approval.

When they had quieted, Arma said, "Tonight it is our supreme pleasure to announce to you the gods have stood firm with the good and righteous people of Sampitay."

She'd dropped the banner and was now holding up a long slender parchment roll.

"This is the latest communication from Protarus," she said. "I received it only this morning.

"Apparently the young King Protarus has seen the error of his ways. He now understands the value and rightness of our neutrality. He has taken back all his demands and now only asks—

quite politely, I might add—that we sell his army badly needed supplies at a fair price."

The queen's news charged the crowd into an even greater fever. They shouted joy until they were hoarse, applauded until their fingers were numb.

Then Arma said, "What say you, my loyal subjects? Shall we be magnanimous in our victory? Shall we show King Protarus what civilized people are like?"

Shouts of agreement sealed the bargain. People wept and clutched one another, praising the gods for coming to their aid in this time of need.

In the middle of the chaos, Safar crept over to Methydia. "This isn't good," he said. "I know Iraj. He'd never back down so easily."

Methydia nodded. Safar had told her about his boyhood friendship with Protarus and the vision he'd had of Iraj's conquering army. He'd left out only the fight with the demons.

"We'll finish this show and make ready to leave," she said, not bothering to lower her voice in the din of all those tearful, joyous people. "We'll depart at dawn," she continued. "The whole city will be so sick with from celebrating no one will notice."

They completed the show, although the whole troupe—sensing the wrongness in the air—was much subdued. The queen thanked them when it was over and rewarded Methydia with more bolts of rich Sampitayan silk.

It wasn't easy to make preparations to slip away. There were so many well-wishers and celebrants about the troupe could do little more than pack their things and place them as close to the Cloudship as possible. The roustabouts were given strict orders to rouse everyone an hour before dawn so they could board the Cloudship and flee.

They slept in the tents that night, their most important belongings close at hand so they could make a hasty exit.

"I wish I could send a message to Iraj," Safar said as he and Methydia settled down for a few hours sleep.

"What would you say?" Methydia asked, wiping away the last vestiges of her makeup with a damp sponge. "Spare the city? Or just spare us?" She gave him a cynical look. "I'd like to know the proper way to appeal to a blood-thirsty barbarian."

Safar shook his head. "Iraj is no barbarian," he said.

"You saw the burned cities," Methydia said, "the refugees by the thousands. If that isn't barbaric, I'd like to know what is."

"The whole world is barbaric as far as I'm concerned," Safar said, growing angry. "Iraj is no more a savage than those who confront him. Walaria is supposed to be the civilized center of Esmir. There's nothing but self-serving cutthroats in command there. Look at Sampitay. It's not much better. Queen Arma and her court have their silk trade, their riches. But what of the common folk? They are as poor and put upon as the people of Walaria."

"Perhaps King Protarus is merely ill-advised," Methydia said coolly. "Perhaps he didn't notice all the misery we saw in our journey. Misery caused by his armies."

Safar was silent for a moment, thinking about what she'd said; trying to sort out his boyhood from his adulthood.

"I haven't seen Iraj for a long time," he finally said, "but I don't think he could have changed so much. There was good at the heart of him."

"Maybe *you* were that good," Methydia said. "Maybe your presence brought out whatever finer feelings he had."

"Iraj is his own man," Safar insisted. "The good I saw was his own. It needed nothing from me. He's also a warrior born and although I disagree with his methods, in the end Iraj is seeking a better place than we have now.

"Iraj didn't make the droughts, the plagues or the horrors like the worm at Kyshaat. He didn't make the old kings and nobles who are as great a plague on Esmir as the ones nature sends us."

"Still," Methydia said, "you're as anxious to get out of the way of his wrath as I am."

"Armies have no heart," Safar said. "And it's Iraj's army we'll see first. Queen Arma was fool enough to defy him. His soldiers will have their orders to make an example of Sampitay. And I don't want us to be in their way."

"Are you really so unfeeling about the plight of these people, Safar," Methydia asked. "Am I seeing a side of you I never noticed before because I was so smitten?"

Safar took her hand. She let him, but her manner was wary. "What can I do?" he asked, and there was so much pain in his voice her wariness vanished. "Tell me and I'll do it at once."

"Speak to Iraj," she said. "Reason with him."

Safar thought about her request for a time. He felt he was at the edge of a cliff. At the bottom was a world he wanted to escape. A world of petty kings and wizards. A world where girls like Nerisa died for no good reason. And then he thought of all the maids and lads in Sampitay who would suffer Nerisa's fate, or worse, when Iraj's soldiers came. Methydia squeezed his hand. He took strength from it and made his decision.

"We'll go find Iraj in the morning," he said. He grinned, but it was such a sad grin that Methydia ached for him. "He shouldn't be hard to find. We'll just look for the largest army."

Methydia held back tears and embraced him. They made love, clinging to one another as if they were the last people in the world.

Then they fell asleep.

Safar dreamed of Hadin. He danced with the beautiful people, all cares wiped away by the rhythm of their drums.

Then the volcano exploded with such violence that he was hurled far out to sea. He was suddenly without the ability to swim. He pawed madly at the water, trying to stay afloat—burning embers raining down on him.

And then a familiar voice urged, "Wake up, Master! Wake up!"

Safar's eyes snapped open. Gundara was perched on his chest, sharp little teeth chattering in fear. Safar blinked, thinking he was still dreaming. The last time he'd checked the stone idol—which he always kept near him—it'd seemed like there was barely any magical life inside.

Then he felt the Favorite's weight on his chest and although it was slight, it was very real.

"Where did you come from?" Safar asked.

Gundara ignored the question. "They're coming, Master!" he said, hopping onto the floor. "Hurry! Before it's too late!"

Safar heard sounds of fighting outside and came fully awake. He scrabbled for the knife he kept under his pillow and rolled to his feet. Realizing he was naked, he hastily pulled on clothes. The turtle fell out of his tunic pocket and bounced on the earthen floor. Gundara instantly disappeared into it. Then he heard Methydia cry out from the bed and he shouted for her to stay down. He scooped up the turtle and thrust it into his pocket just as the soldiers burst through the tent opening.

Safar didn't give them a chance to get set, but charged directly into them. He dodged a blow and sank his blade into softness. He heard a gasp, tried to pull his knife free, but it stuck. Behind him Methydia screamed a warning and he let the knife go, ripping the sword out of his victim's dying grasp.

He whirled, striking out blindly. He didn't have time or room to turn the blade so only the flat of it struck his attacker. But the force of his blow was so great it sent the soldier reeling back, exposing his belly. Once again Safar felt soft flesh give under his weapon. He didn't wait to see the man fall, but turned again as other soldiers crowded through the tent opening.

He attacked with such fury they fell over each other to escape his wrath. Then he jumped back, heaved up a chest he'd normally have needed help to lift, and hurled it through the opening. Satisfying yelps of pain told him that he'd hit his target.

Methydia was out of the bed now, hastily drawing on a robe.

"This way," he shouted, slashing at the rear of the tent. The cloth parted and they pushed through the opening.

The night was a mad thing of screams and clashing armor and weapons. Fire raged whichever way they turned.

Methydia clutched him, pointing. Safar turned to see her glorious Cloudship going up in flames.

There was an explosion and the Cloudship became a shatter of burning wood splinters and smoldering cloth. Methydia sagged and he caught her in his arms.

Mailed horsemen charged out of the boiling smoke, flailing about with curved blades that cut anyone down who got in their way.

A banner, carried by the lead horseman, fluttered over them. It bore the ancient symbol of the demon moon and silver comet.

The warriors were shouting, "For Protarus!"

Six horsemen split off from the group and rushed toward Safar. He let Methydia drop to his feet, and grasped his sword in both hands.

He made a spell of strength and power surged through his body until he felt like a giant. He made a spell of sharpness and sliced the air with his blade. It shimmered with the force of his blow.

Then the horsemen were on him. He cut the legs out from under the first steed, slew its rider, then leaped on the horse's body to confront the rest.

A spear floated toward him and he ducked it easily, coming up to deal a death blow to the one who'd hurled it. A huge man with a black beard struck at him with a scimitar. Safar parried and the man's bearded mouth became a wide "O" as Safar's sword pierced his throat. Then there was a horseman behind him and he whirled just as the soldier's mount trampled on Methydia's prone body.

Safar howled in fury and leaped at the man, his weight carrying horse, soldier and himself to the ground. The quarters were too close to swing his blade, so he hammered at the soldier with the haft of his sword, crushing the helmet.

Then he was up again, parrying the next blow, killing the next man.

He fought for what seemed like an eternity. But no matter how many he struck down, there were always others crowding in to take him.

Then there was a sudden respite and he was swinging at empty air. Cutting back and forth, meeting nothing, but still slashing, still fighting, as if there were invisible devils all around him.

He stopped, finally realizing no enemy was within reach.

Safar looked up and all was a haze in his battle-lust view. Then he saw a grizzled old veteran mounted on a warhorse about ten paces away. Safar's head swiveled. He was surrounded, but now instead of swords there were raised bows confronting him, arrows drawn back—waiting for the order to fire.

"You've done yourself proud, lad," the old veteran said. "Now put your sword down and we'll spare you."

Safar grinned. He was covered with the gore of other men and made an awful sight.

Then, instead of tossing his sword down, he pushed it point first into the ground and leaned on it.

"Tell Iraj Protarus," he said loudly, "that a friend awaits him. And begs the pleasure of his company."

The veteran reacted, surprised. "And who might that friend be, lad?"

"Safar Timura of Kyrania," he replied. "The man he once called his blood oath brother.

"The man who once saved his life."

## 20
## ALL HAIL THE KING

It was well past dawn when Iraj finally came.

The smoke and soot from the burning city was so thick it made the day more like night. The air was filled with the stench of death and the loud weeping of Sampitay's survivors as they were led out to meet their fates.

Safar was pacing within the same circle of bowmen. Although they'd lowered their weapons, he noted they were ready to lift them again and fire if he made a wrong move. They were all fierce plainsmen, small in stature, muscular in build, with misshapen legs from so many years on horseback. They wore flowing robes, cinched by wide leather belts bearing scimitars on one side, long daggers on the other. Their boots were felt, with sharp spurs strapped to them. They had turbans for head coverings, with steel caps beneath and most sported long, drooping mustaches, giving their dark faces a grim, determined look.

A small part of Safar—the child that weeps for its mother even at a great age—quaked at the sight of them. The rest was armed with a cold, tightly-gripped rage he was ready to release at the slightest pretense.

The soldiers didn't know what to make of Safar. He was either the mightiest of liars or truly the king's blood oath brother. The only thing certain was Safar had more than proven himself as a warrior. It was for this reason, almost more than his claim of friendship with the king, that had stayed their hands. Safar had leaned heavily on their respect to rescue most of the members of the troupe and he'd bullied the old sergeant into letting them join him.

He used the circle like a shield, pacing the perimeter to keep it intact, pointing the tip of his sword accusingly at any soldier who dared stray closer. In the center the troupe was silently tending the unconscious Methydia. Safar feared for her—she'd been badly trampled by the warhorse—but he didn't dare show his concern in front of the bowmen. He knew it would be taken as a sign of weakness.

Then he heard a great horn blare and war drums beat a tattoo. Orders were shouted and the ring of bowmen suddenly parted.

A tall warrior mounted on a fiery black steed cantered down the path they made. He wore the pure white robes of a plains fighter. His head was wrapped in a white turban, with the tail pulled about his face like a mask.

The warrior pulled the horse up a few paces away. He studied Safar for a long moment, taking in the gore stained costume, bloody sword and soot-streaked face. Safar stared back, making as insolent a grin as he could manage. Finally the warrior's gaze came to Safar's eyes and there was a sudden jolt of recognition.

"Safar Timura, you blue-eyed devil," Iraj cried, sweeping away the mask, "it *is* you!"

"In the flesh," Safar said, "although as you can see that flesh is a little worse for wear and definitely in need of a bath."

Safar, remembering the first time he and Iraj had met, pointed at the soldiers and said, "I think I could use a little help here. It seems I'm completely surrounded by the Ubekian brothers."

Iraj roared laughter. "The Ubekian brothers!" he shouted. "What a sorry lot they were!"

Then, to the amazement of his soldiers, the king leaped off his horse and threw his arms around Safar, gore and all.

"By the gods I have missed you, Safar Timura," he shouted, pounding his old friend on the back. "By the gods I have missed you!"

Iraj called for a mount and personally escorted Safar back to his command tent—set on a hill overlooking Sampitay. When Safar indicated the unconscious Methydia and the others members of the troupe Iraj asked no questions about Safar's odd company, or even acted surprised. He immediately issued orders all were to be well cared for and the best healers summoned to tend to Methydia.

"And I want hourly reports on her progress," Iraj demanded. "I don't want my good friend, Lord Timura, to worry unnecessarily."

Lord? Safar thought. How did a potter's son suddenly become a lord? He glanced at Iraj, saw the look of warning in his eyes and realized it wouldn't do for a king to have a blood oath brother who less than noble born.

During the ride back to his command post Iraj kept the conversation light, loudly regaling his aides and guard with exaggerated tales of his youthful adventures with "Lord Timura."

"Why, if it weren't for Safar," he said, "I wouldn't be here today. And you'd all be serving some other king, a weak-kneed, inbred bastard, no doubt. Someday I'll tell you the story of how he saved my life. You've already witnessed how bravely he fought here, so you can all rest assured it is a stirring tale that will take a long winter's evening to give it proper justice.

"But I will tell you this. After the battle the people of Kyrania were so grateful to us for saving them from that gang of bandits that they trotted out fifteen of their prettiest virgins for us to deflower."

He laughed. "I gave up after five."

He turned to Safar. "Or was it six?"

"Actually, it was seven," Safar answered.

Iraj's grin told him that he'd lied correctly.

"Seven it was," Iraj said. "But that was nothing compared to my friend here. He deflowered the remaining eight, then strolled out of his tent, easy as you please, and announced he was still feeling peckish and wouldn't mind a few more."

The aides and guardsmen roared laughter and crowded in close to slap Safar on the back and praise his prowess as a fighter and lover.

"Mind you," Iraj said, "he wasn't playing fair. Even as a boy Lord Timura was a mighty wizard. He confessed to me later that he had a secret potion for such occasions."

Again, Iraj turned to Safar—a frown of mock accusation on his face. "If I recall, my friend," he said, "you promised to supply me with some. A promise you never kept."

Safar held out a hand, palm up. "I was hoping you had forgotten that, Your Highness," he said, adding the royal honorific for the first time and pleasing Iraj immensely. "You see, there were only five virgins left in all Kyrania. And I didn't want us to quarrel over them."

More bawdy laughter—led by the king—greeted his clever reply. The royal party continued on and there were many manly jests and many manly boasts to mark the journey.

They wended their jocular way past scenes of incredible brutality. Sampitay's dead and wounded littered the battlefield. Captives, working under the stern direction of Iraj's fierce soldiers, piled the dead in mounds. Oil was poured on the corpses and they were set on fire; greasy black fumes, smelling like sacrificial sheep, rose to mix with the smoke of the burning city. Other soldiers moved across the field, slitting the throats of the groaning wounded. Thousands of civilians were being separated into groups of young and old, men and women. Construction crews were hammering together execution blocks for the aged and infirm. Sharp-eyed slavers were moving through the rest, drawing up estimates of the price each would bring and whether it would be worth the care and feeding they'd require.

Safar felt as if he were trapped in the worst kind of nightmare—one that required him to wear a mask of light-hearted unconcern amid all that horror. And soaring above that was the dark raven of his fear for Methydia.

Although Iraj had greeted him warmly—as if only a few months rather than years had separated them—Safar didn't let down his guard. His old friend had the same easy, open manner. Other than the beard he looked much the same as before. His manner was casually royal, but it had always been so. He'd also matured. With the beard, which Safar suspected Iraj had grown to look older, he appeared to be in his thirtieth summer, rather than in his early twenties like Safar. He still had that cunning look in his eyes, a cunning he'd had develop at an early age to survive family wars. But Safar could see there was no malice, no cruelty.

Somehow Iraj had drawn on the mantle of a conqueror, had been the cause of much bloodshed, yet seemed untouched by it.

It made Safar, who was wary and secretive at heart, warier still.

Iraj still had the look of a great dreamer. There was an innocence about him—the innocence of all dreamers. That was what confounded Safar the most. How could Iraj appear so innocent, yet move through scenes of such awful cruelty—which he'd ordered—with his innocence intact?

He glanced at Iraj, once again noting his remarkable resemblance to Alisarrian.

For the first time Safar truly understood the enigma Gubadan had unknowingly posed when he'd asked his favorite rhetorical question: "Who was this man, Alisarrian? A monster as his enemies claimed? Or a blessing from the gods?"

Safar wondered if he'd ever learn the answer.

He put confusion aside. His first duty was to Methydia and his friends. After that he'd try his best to keep his promise to Methydia and see what he could do to ease the suffering of the people of Sampitay.

Beyond those two immediate goals was a chasm, deep and wide. Fate seemed to be driving him toward the brink of that chasm.

And there was nothing he could do about it.

After Safar had bathed, changed into fresh clothes and heard a promising first report regarding Methydia's health, he was summoned to Iraj's private quarters.

Other than its size and placement, there was nothing to mark Iraj's tent as the dwelling place of a king. It sat in the center of scores of similar tents, all made of a plain, sturdy material. The hillside encampment was a bustle of uniformed officers and clerks and scribes in drab civilian garb. Safar later learned Iraj conducted all of his business from tents like these—a kind of traveling court, moving from one battlefield to the next. Iraj ruled a vast new kingdom—ranging from The God's Divide to the most distant wilderness—while on the road.

The furnishings in Iraj's tent palace were spare and utilitarian. Chests were used as tables, saddles were mounted on posts to make chairs. A plain portable throne—with Iraj's banner hanging over it—sat on a raised platform against the far wall. When Safar entered the throne was empty. The two aides assigned to him ushered him past officers and sergeants who were bent over maps, or absorbed in reports.

Heavy curtains blocked off one large section of the tent and as Safar approached he caught the scent of perfume. Surprised as he was by this oddity in a place of such military bearing, he was even more amazed when the curtain parted and two young women dressed like soldiers stepped out. Although they were both remarkably beautiful, they had eyes as fierce as the weapons belted about their slender waists.

Without a word they searched him for weapons. It was an odd sensation being handled so intimately by such beauteous, deadly women.

When they were satisfied they escorted him into the room. In the center, wine cup in hand and lolling on soft pillows, was Iraj—surrounded by a dozen other women warriors.

"Safar," he called out, "come join me. It's been a long time since we've had a drink together."

He clapped his hands and women rushed about to fetch food and drink while others plumped up pillows to make Safar comfortable.

It was all very bizarre being waited on by these mailed, perfumed handmaids and Iraj chortled at Safar's bewildered expression.

"What do you think of my royal guard?" he asked.

Safar shook his head. "I'm not sure whether I'm supposed to fight them or make love to them," he joked.

"I've often wondered that myself, " Iraj said, smiling. "Sometimes we do both just to keep the nights interesting."

The women laughed at the king's jest and their eyes and actions were so adoring there was no mistaking their pleasure was genuine.

"You of all people know my weakness for women," Iraj said.

Safar grinned. "Very well."

"Then you will admire my military solution to that weakness," Iraj said. "Instead of a baggage train of courtesans and their belongings to slow me down, I've hand-picked a platoon of beautiful women to make up my royal guard. They are all highly-skilled fighters—I saw to their training myself, and let me tell you there is not an assassin in existence who could get by them. And they are marvelous bedmates as well—also due to my personal training."

Safar laughed. "It's a hard job being king," he said. "But I suppose someone has to do it." He toasted Iraj with the goblet that had been thrust into his hand. "Here's to royal sacrifice."

Iraj roared enjoyment at this. He banged his goblet against Safar's—wine sloshing over the brim—then drained what remained in the cup.

He pulled one of the women onto his lap, nuzzling her. "Tell me, Leiria," he said to the woman, "what do you think of my friend, Safar? Isn't he all that I described?"

Leiria gave Safar a sloe-eyed look, guaranteed to light a fire in any man—any man but Safar, that is, whose complete attention was fixed on the situation.

"And more, Majesty," Leiria answered, smoldering gaze still fixed on Safar. "Except you didn't say he was so handsome. And his eyes! I've never seen a man with blue eyes before. It's like looking into the sky."

Iraj slapped her well-rounded haunch. "What?" he shouted, but it was a shout of pleasure, not anger. "You lust for another?"

Leiria tangled her hand in king's golden beard. "Maybe just a little bit, Majesty," she pouted. "But only so I can learn more and return to you with greater pleasures."

Iraj kissed her, long and deep, then pulled away and looked at Safar, eyes filled with amusement.

"You see how it is, my brother?" he said. "It will always be a problem between us. The same women want us. What shall we do about it?"

Safar instantly felt he was walking on dangerous ground. "Thankful as I am at the flattery, Majesty," he said, "Leiria was only being kind, I'm sure."

"Nonsense," Iraj said. "She wants you. Very well, you shall have her."

He untangled himself from Leiria and pushed her into Safar's lap. Leiria went willingly, cooing and snuggling and tracing patterns on his chest with her fingers. Safar shifted his position—her dagger was digging into his side.

"I only ask that you be kind to her," Iraj said. "And send her back in good condition. She's known no man but me." He waved at the others. "None of them have. I am not in the habit of making my women a gift to other men."

He smiled. "In fact, it has only happened one time before. Do you remember when that was, Safar?'

Safar remembered very well indeed. "Astarias," he said. "How could I possibly forget?"

"And what was the oath we swore then?" Iraj asked.

"That all I had was yours," Safar answered, "and all that was yours was mine."

"Freely given and with no ill will, correct?" Iraj pressed.

"Yes, Majesty," Safar said. "Freely given. And with no ill will."

"Good," Iraj said. "I'm glad you remember."

For reasons Safar couldn't determine, what had just occurred had been very important to Iraj.

"Another thing, Safar," Iraj said. "When we're in private, don't call me majesty or your highness or other such silliness."

"That's certainly a relief," Safar laughed. "The first time I said it—when we were with your officers—I kept thinking, this is the same fellow my mother scolded for tromping over her clean floors with muddy boots."

Iraj grinned, remembering. "I thought she'd kill me," he said. "She made me get down on my hands and knees and clean the mess up. A humbling experience for a future king, that's for certain."

He turned suddenly serious, eyes taking on a far-away cast. "But here I am, a king," he said, "just as you predicted in Alisarrian's cave."

Safar nodded, remembering.

"And you predicted other things, greater things," Iraj went on.

"Yes," Safar said.

"Tell me, brother," Iraj went on, "do you still see those things? Do you still see me as King of Kings, monarch of all Esmir?"

The answer leaped up unbidden—a vision of Iraj sitting a golden throne. "I do," Safar said softly.

Iraj was quiet for a moment, toying with his cup. Then suddenly he clapped his hands. "Leave us!" he ordered the women. "I want to be alone with my friend."

Leiria scrambled out of Safar's lap and exited the room with her sister warriors. After they'd gone, Iraj remained silent for a time, thinking.

When he finally spoke, there was an edge to his voice—"Why

didn't you come when I sent for you? I practically begged, which is something I'm not in the habit of doing."

Safar was confused. "You sent for me? When?"

"When you were in Walaria," Iraj said. "I sent a letter. And a large purse of gold, as well, to pay for your expenses."

"I received neither," Safar said. "And if I had, I certainly would have come." He grimaced. "Things didn't go well in Walaria."

Iraj searched his face, then relaxed, satisfied Safar had spoken the truth.

"I heard something of your difficulties," he said.

"That's how you came to find me with the circus," Safar said. "There are some very dangerous men in Walaria who want my head."

"You needn't concern yourself with them any longer," Iraj said. "Walaria paid most dearly for troubling you."

Safar's heart trip-hammered against his chest. "What do you mean?" he asked.

"Walaria is no more," Iraj answered. "I turned it back into a cattle station." He casually refilled his goblet with wine, then poured some into Safar's cup. "It wasn't entirely for you," he said. "They were fools. They defied me, like these people here in Sampitay. It was necessary to make an example of them.

"Although in Walaria's case, I took some pleasure in dispensing justice. I thought you were dead and I was avenging you."

Safar was horrified that such a thing had been done in his name.

Iraj noted the expression on his face. His face became mournful. "I'm normally a soft-hearted fellow who doesn't like to cause pain," he said. "It's my father's weakness in me and I have to guard against it. You have to be stern to rule. And much blood must be shed to make a kingdom."

Safar saw moisture well in Iraj's eyes and was surprised at the depth of the emotion.

"But I never knew I'd have to shed so much of it," Iraj said, voice thick.

Then he shook himself and wiped his eyes. He forced a smile on his face.

"You saw that too when we were in the cave, didn't you, Safar?" he said. "When you foretold my future you seemed sad for me."

"Yes," Safar said—almost a whisper.

"But it's my fate, so there's nothing to be done about it," Iraj said. "This is a terrible world we live in. And I am the only one who make it right. If only people could see into my heart and know my true intent they wouldn't resist me. I *will* bring peace to this land. I *will* bring greatness.

"I only wish so many didn't have to suffer first."

Passion burned in Iraj's eyes and for a moment Safar could see his boyhood friend staring out at him through those eyes.

"Will you help me, Safar?" Iraj pleaded. "I'm not sure I can do this on my own."

Safar hesitated, a thousand thoughts crowding into his mind, competing with one another to be heard. Then, in the middle of his mental chaos, there came a scratching at the door.

Iraj looked up, irritated. "In!" he commanded.

Two of his guardswomen entered, an old frightened man in healer's garb between them.

"What is it!" Iraj barked.

"Forgive me O Gracious Majesty," the healer burbled, "this poor worm of a healer trembles in Your Highness' presence. He abases himself for daring to—"

Iraj waved, cutting him off. "Stop driveling, man," he said. "What is it?"

The healer bobbed his head, saying, "I've come about the woman who was placed in my care."

"Methydia!" Safar cried, leaping to his feet. "What's wrong with her?"

"I fear she is dying, my lord," he said to Safar, so frightened his legs were about to give way. "She calls for you, my lord. You must come quickly before it is too late!"

Iraj saw the torment in Safar's face. "Go to her," he said. "We'll talk later."

Safar bolted away like an arrow loosed from its bow, the healer tottering behind him as fast as he could.

When he saw her lying on the camp bed, eyes closed, face pale as bleached parchment, the troupe gathered about her weeping silent tears, he thought he was too late. And she looked old, so old he almost didn't recognize her. But as he approached her eyes came open and she was once again his beautiful Methydia.

"Safar," she said, voice faint as a specter's.

He knelt by her side and took her hand, fighting back tears.

"I must look a sight," she said, voice a bit firmer. "What an awful way for a woman to greet her young swain."

"You're as beautiful as ever, my love," Safar murmured. "Only a little weak from your ordeal."

"You always did lie so sweetly, Safar," Methydia said. "But it isn't the time for sugary words. There's no getting around it—I'm dying."

Safar clutched her hand tighter. "I won't let you!" he cried. But as he said it he could feel her slipping away. "Stay with me, Methydia!" he begged. "I'll send for all the healers. I'll make a spell with them, a spell so strong not even the gods themselves could thwart me."

She smiled and he felt her rally, but faint, so faint.

"Let me tell you a secret, my sweet Safar," she said. "The gods aren't listening. They aren't listening now. And they haven't been listening for a long time. I know this because I'm so close to death I can see into the Otherworlds.

"And do you know what I see?"

"What?" Safar asked, voice quivering.

"The gods are asleep! So deep in their slumber that not even a thousand times a thousand voices lifted at once could raise them."

Safar thought she was raving and he kissed her, murmuring, "Nonsense, Methydia. It's only a fever dream you see, not the Otherworlds."

"I wish it were," Methydia said. "I wish it were."

Suddenly her eyes grew wider and she struggled to sit up. Safar gently pressed her down, begging her to be still.

"Listen to me, Safar!" she cried.

"I'm listening, Methydia," Safar answered.

"Only you can wake the gods, Safar," she said. "Only you!"

"Certainly, my love," Safar said. "I'll do it as soon as you're well again. We'll wake them together."

"I'm not mad," she said, suddenly stern and with such strength it surprised him. "I'm only dying. So don't argue with a dead woman. It isn't polite. Now listen to me! Are you listening?"

"Yes, Methydia," Safar said.

"You mustn't hate Protarus for what was done to me," she said. "It was an accident of war, nothing more. Promise me you won't hate him!"

"I promise," Safar said.

"Good. Now I want another promise from you."

"Anything, my love. Anything at all."

"Go with him. Go with Protarus. Help him. It's the only way!"

"Don't ask that of me, Methydia," Safar begged. "Please! Too many people are suffering."

"Ease their suffering if you can," she said. "But help Protarus get his throne. The throne isn't important. It's only the first step. Protarus isn't important. He's only on the road you must follow. I don't know what's at the end of that road. But you'll know what to do when you get there.

"You'll know, my sweet Safar. You'll know."

"Please, Methydia," Safar said.

"Do you promise me, Safar Timura? Do you promise?"

"I can't," Safar said.

Methydia gripped his hand, squeezing as tight as she could. Putting her all her will and remaining strength in that grip.

"*Promise me*!" she insisted.

"Very well," Safar cried, "I promise! Just don't leave me!"

Her hand went limp. Safar looked at her, tears blurring his vision.

There was a smile on her face.

An awful wailing filled the tent as the shock sank in and the other entertainers shouted their grief.

Methydia was dead.

Safar remembered Biner's words long ago when they'd first met:

"Damn everything but the circus!"

And now that circus was no more.

Safar hurried through the encampment, roughly pushing aside anyone who got in his way. Iraj wasn't at his tent headquarters. Safar snarled at a general for directions and his manner was so fierce the scarred veteran of many wars blurted the answer as if he were green stripling.

Safar found Iraj sitting on his traveling throne, which had been moved to a point about halfway down the hillside overlooking Sampitay. On either side of the throne two tall sharpened stakes had been driven into the ground.

Queen Arma's head was mounted on one stake, Prince Crol's on the other.

At the bottom of the hill long lines of the condemned were being herded to the execution blocks. Posts had been erected just beyond and naked men were tied to those posts, screeching in agony while gleeful soldiers tormented them with spears.

Iraj was surrounded by his royal guard and when some of the women saw Safar's manner they drew their swords and stepped in his way.

"Let him through," Iraj commanded.

Reluctantly they parted but they held their swords at ready.

Iraj was grim, face as pale and bloodless as Methydia's had been. He signaled his women to move farther away.

"Give us some privacy," he barked.

The women pulled back, but they weren't happy about it.

"Why did you come here, Safar?" he asked. "This isn't something that's necessary for you to see."

"I want to ask a favor of you, Iraj," Safar said.

Iraj stirred, irritated. "Can't it wait? This is hardly the time or place."

Then he, too, took note of Safar's expression. "What is it, my friend? What has happened?"

Safar shook his head, too overcome to answer.

Then sad understanding dawned in Iraj's eyes. "Ah, I see. Your woman died, is that it?"

"Yes."

"And you loved her?"

"Yes."

"I'm sorry for that. I hope you don't hate me for it."

"No."

"It was an accident of war."

"Methydia said the same thing before she died."

"A wise woman."

"She was that."

Iraj searched Safar's face, then asked, "What is it you want from me? What can I do to ease your pain?"

Safar pointed at the awful scene below. "Spare them," he said.

Iraj gave him a strange look.

"Let me explain why this would be good for you," Safar said.

Iraj shook his head. "You don't need to explain your reasons to me. You asked a boon. You shall have it. Freely given and without hesitation.

"After all, that is our agreement. Our blood oath pledge to each other."

Iraj shouted for his aides and they came running up to him. "Release these people," he commanded. "Return them to their homes."

"But, Majesty," one of the aides protested. "What of their defiance? We must make an example of people like this."

Iraj glowered at the man, who visibly shrank under the glare. "If you ever dare question me again, sir," the king said, "it'll be your head on one of those blocks. Do as I commanded! At once!"

The aides rushed off to his bidding. A few moments later horns blared, orders were shouted, and the chains were stricken from the limbs of the people of Sampitay. They fell to their knees, weeping and shouting praises to the heavens, thanking the gods and Protarus for sparing them.

Safar watched, thinking it was Methydia they should be thanking, not Protarus.

"To be frank, my friend," Iraj said, "I am relieved to grant you this favor. Viewing mass executions, much less ordering them, is one of my least favorite duties."

"Don't order them, then," Safar said.

Iraj's brow rose in surprise. His cheeks flushed. It was clear he was not used to be spoken to this way. Then he made a rueful smile.

"You speak honestly," he said. "No one in my court dares do that. Which is what I lack most of all. A friend who dares to tell me what he truly believes."

"Not an hour ago," Safar said, "you asked me to join you. Do you still want my service?"

"Indeed I do," Iraj answered. "But I don't want your answer

now. I granted you a favor. It wouldn't be right to ask one in return. It would be a stain on our friendship."

"You'll have my answer just the same," Safar said. "And it won't be a favor I'm granting you. I will join you, freely and gladly. All I ask is that you listen to my advice, which I will give you as honestly as I can."

"Done!" Iraj said, face lighting up.

He thrust out his hand. "Take it, my brother," he said. "And I will lift you as high as it is in my powers to do."

Safar clasped his hand.

Iraj said, "Safar Timura, son of a potter, wizard of the High Caravans, I, King Iraj Protarus, proclaim you Grand Wazier. From this moment on you are the highest of the high in my realm.

"And you may command all but myself."

Safar felt the world turn about. It was as if a great circus master had spun the Great Wheel of the Fates. Safar was strapped to it, his head the arrow point, spinning, spinning, spinning. And he heard the circus master's cry, "Around and around he goes...and where he stops...the gods only know!"

Safar gripped Iraj's hand tighter, partly to steady himself, but mostly to keep himself from snatching his own hand away. He wanted nothing of this. His greatest desire was to climb aboard the Cloudship with Biner and Arlain and the others and flee this place, this fate.

But the Cloudship was no more.

And he had made a promise to Methydia.

Safar steeled his nerve and said as firmly as he could: "I accept."

That night Iraj called his court into session. There was a small ceremony to proclaim Safar Grand Wazier.

The faces of the king's officers and courtiers were all a blur to Safar. He could pick out only a few. Some were friendly. Some were not. Mostly, there were only looks of curiosity and awe.

Who was this man who had been lifted so high, so quickly?

Did his presence bode ill, or fair?

Late in the night Safar dreamed that Methydia came to him.

In his dream he felt soft hands caressing him. He opened his eyes and saw Methydia's face and Methydia's slender body poised over him. He cried out her name and crushed to her to him. They made love, a floaty love like they were aboard the Cloudship once again. Then the Cloudship burst into flames, plunging for the earth and they clasped one another, riding the fire in an endless fall.

When he awoke in the morning Safar found Leiria snuggled in the crook of his arm, smiling in her sleep.

Feeling like a traitor, he gently tried to extract his arm. But Leiria came awake, purring and sloe-eyed and clutching him closer.

He untangled her politely, but firmly. "I have duties to attend to," he said.

At first Leiria pouted, then she giggled and got up, saying, "I mustn't be selfish and take all your strength, my lord."

Safar managed a faint smile for an answer.

She starting pulling on clothes. "You called out another woman's name in the night," she said. Her tones were light, but Safar could sense hurt in them. "Was she the one who died?"

"Yes," Safar answered softly.

Leiria shrugged. "I don't mind," she said. "It's good that your heart is faithful." She had her head down, concentrating hard on buckling on her weapons. "The king has ordered me to comfort you and guard you with my life."

She raised her head and Safar saw tears in her eyes. "The king orders," she said, "but I do it gladly. I will guard you and I will be this other woman for you for as long as you like.

"And perhaps someday it will be my name you speak instead of...hers."

Safar didn't know what to say. From the look on her face a word either way might cause a flood of tears. She would despise him for humiliating her.

So all he said was, "You honor me, Leiria."

Weak as that reply was, she seemed to find satisfaction in it. She nodded, finished her dressing, then kissed him—a quick peck on the cheek—and left.

Safar looked after her wondering how much was artifice and how much was truly meant.

And how much would she tell Iraj?

***

It wasn't long before Safar had a chance to test those questions. He'd barely had time to snatch a quick meal and don his clothes before Iraj summoned him.

Leiria was his guide and guard as he made his hasty way into the king's presence. She gave no hint of the night they'd had together. Her bearing was professional and military, her manner courteous and respectful.

When they came to the king's rooms he didn't have to undergo the usual search for weapons and was instantly swept inside. Iraj was seated in a simple camp chair, maps and charts spread out on a small table in front of him.

When he saw Safar he said, "It seems my little gift to you has caused all sorts of trouble, my friend."

Safar forced himself not to look at Leiria. "What ever do you mean, Iraj?" he asked.

Iraj tapped one of the maps. "I'm planning our next campaign," he said, to Safar's immense relief. "Winter is coming on and there isn't much time."

"What's the problem?" Safar asked. "And how was I the cause of it?"

"Sampitay is the problem," Iraj answered. "Now that I've given it back to its people, as you requested, I'll have those same people at my back when we march again."

"What makes you think they'll be a danger to you?" Safar asked.

"What makes you think they won't?" was Iraj's reply, eyes narrowing.

"Aren't you going to garrison the city," Safar asked "and put one of your own men in charge?"

"Garrisons are trebly expensive," Iraj said. "They cost money, soldiers, and good officers to run them."

"Yesterday," Safar said, "I offered reasons for my request. You kindly chose not to hear. I'd like to offer them again."

Iraj nodded. "Go ahead," he said.

"Sampitay is one of the richest cities in Esmir," Safar pointed out. "The source of its wealth, as you know, is silk. But it takes highly skilled people to produce that silk—skills few others in world possess outside Sampitay.

"So the people are worth more to you alive and free than dead or enslaved. Think of all the gold they'll pay in taxes. Gold you can use to wage your campaign.

"As for the soldiers necessary to garrison the city, why not enlist an equal number of Sampitay soldiers to take their place? You can them train in your ways easily enough.

"Finally, you must have many young officers who ache for more responsibility and promotion. They can replace the senior officers you leave behind to command the garrison to keep the peace and make certain your taxes are collected."

Iraj considered, then said, "I admit I'm in sore need of money. They don't tell you in the histories of warfare how much it costs to wage those wars.

"Thus far I've used plunder and the paltry taxes I'm able to collect from the cities now under my rule. Unfortunately, plunder tends to go more into the pockets of my soldiers than mine. They expect it and it is their right.

"As for the taxes, the rulers who have allied themselves to me are always whining they are hard pressed to pay what I ask. I don't have time to go back and give them a real reason for their moaning and so they've been cheating me without mercy."

"Then garrison them all in the manner I suggested for Sampitay," Safar said.

"What? And use their soldiers as well to replace my own?"

"What's wrong with that?" Safar asked.

"Up until now," Iraj said, "I've only used men from my native plains."

"That was certainly a wise policy when you started out," Safar said. "But if you are to be King of Kings, the true ruler of all Esmir, you must look for loyalty in the hearts of *all* your subjects, not just in the men of the plains.

"And that, my friend, is the best reason of all to end this policy of slaughter. Besides, you told me yourself you disliked all that bloodshed. Perhaps this reluctance really wasn't due to some weakness you inherited from your father. Perhaps it was in the back of your mind that a new way had to be found to rule the kind of kingdom that was once Alisarrian's.

"And all I've done was to put words to ideas that were there all along."

Iraj thought for a time, then said, "I'll do as you suggest," he said. "Starting with Sampitay."

He motioned to the maps. "It'll make this job much easier, that's for certain. Before winter sets in I'll have the whole south under my rule. And in the spring—" he traced a line across the God's Divide—"we'll take on the north, crossing at Kyrania just as Alisarrian did."

He sagged back in his chair, weary. "I'll have to fight my way all the way to the sea," he said. "I wonder how many years it will take? And if I'll live long enough to see it."

"You will," Safar said.

Iraj smiled, remembering. "That's right. We saw each other in that vision, didn't we? The demons under our boots as we marched on the gates of Zanzair."

"I remember," Safar said.

Iraj was silent for a moment, then he asked, "Do you think of the demons often? When we faced them together in the pass?"

"It's my least favorite nightmare," Safar said.

"Do you think Coralean was right? And they were just a group of bandits who strayed into the humanlands?"

"I've seen no evidence pointing either way," Safar said. "I combed the libraries in Walaria to find some historical precedence." He shook his head. "There wasn't any. However, many strange things have happened since that time. Droughts and plagues and wars."

Iraj made a rueful grin. "Well, we know where the wars came from," he said. He tapped his chest to indicate himself. "As for the other things, they could be naturally caused."

"I don't think so," Safar said. He told him of his investigations into Hadin. And he told him of the sorcerous worm he encountered in Kyshaat.

When he was done, Iraj said, "I've thought of that night on the mountain many times. And of your vision afterwards. I'm no seer like yourself, my friend. But I'll tell you what I think it was all about.

"Perhaps something did happen in far off Hadin. Personally, I think it was a sign from the heavens. A sign that fits perfectly into your other visions about me and Alisarrian.

"I truly believe the world is at a crossroads. In one direction lies disaster, although what that disaster entails I cannot say. In the other, hope and a bright future."

Again he tapped his chest. "And I am that hope and future. Once I succeed, all will be set right again."

"I pray you're right," Safar said. "I plan to do all in my powers to see you have the chance to prove it."

Iraj laughed. "Well said, my brother. Together we will conquer all. Nothing can stand in our way."

Safar's answer was a smile. But he was thinking, there's still the demons, Iraj. There's still the demons.

The following day Safar made his farewells to the circus. He plumped a bag of gold into Biner's hand. It was so heavy it caught the muscular dwarf by surprise and he nearly dropped it.

"What's this?" Biner asked.

"The price of a century's worth of tickets," Safar said, smiling. "I'm hoping you'll always save a place for me."

"We thirtainly will," Arlain said, dabbing at a tear with a kerchief.

"Won't be much of a circus," Biner said, "without Methydia and the Cloudship."

"I wish I could bring them back," Safar said. "The gold is all I can do."

"We'll make the best damn circus we can," Biner said. "We'll make you proud of us."

"I already am," Safar said. "And for the rest of my life I'll remember the months I was with you."

"You're a rich man, now," Biner said. "A powerful man. But if you should ever need us..." Emotion overcame him and he turned to honk his nose into a rag. When he'd recovered, he said, "Hells, you know what I mean!"

"Sure I do," Safar said, wiping at his own tears.

Then he embraced them all one by one.

When he was done he rushed off before he weakened and slipped away with them in the night.

The next time Leiria came to his bed he nearly refused her. In the end it seemed easier to accept her embrace than send her away. She was an ardent lover, a skilled lover. He never again called out Methydia's name, although it was Methydia he thought of. He didn't know what to make of Leiria. Was she truly smitten? Or was she Iraj's spy? She never gave a sign either way. At night she was fire in his arms, by day the cool professional, measuring any man who approached him for signs of ill intent.

Because of his doubts he waited several nights before he delved into a most important task. Then he gave her a difficult errand that would take much time to accomplish.

When she was gone he drew out the stone turtle and summoned Gundara.

The little Favorite was still extremely weak and couldn't take full form. Safar could see the tent walls through his wispy figure.

"I hope you don't have anything hard you want to do, master," Gundara whined. "I'm not feeling very well, you know."

"I have a treat for you," Safar said, offering Gundara a sweet he'd saved from the dinner table.

Listlessly, Gundara took it from his hand. He licked at the sugar, then sighed and let the sweet fall to the ground.

"Doesn't taste as good as it used to," he complained.

"I've never had a chance to thank you for the warning that night," Safar said.

Gundara made another deep sigh. "I almost couldn't get out of the stone," he said. "Gundaree pushed and pushed as hard as he could. It nearly killed us both."

"I'm sorry for that," Safar said. "Still, you saved my life."

Gundara shrugged. "I just hope I don't have to do it again real soon."

"So do I," Safar said. "But what about now? Am I in the presence of enemies?"

"Assuredly, master," Gundara said. "There are enemies all around you. So many I can't single anyone out in particular. Right now they seem afraid to do more than hate you. My advice, master, is to be as careful as you can."

"What about Iraj?" Safar asked. "What about the king? Is he my enemy?"

"No," the Favorite answered. "But he's a danger to you. All kings are. Beware of kings, master, is the best advice I can give you."

"And what of the woman Leiria?" Safar asked. "Does she mean well, or ill?"

"I'm too weak and her thoughts too confusing to say, master," Gundara answered. "When she's with you, she adores you. But when she's near the king, she adores *him*. All I can tell you is don't trust her...and keep her close."

Safar hid his disappointment. He'd hoped to get more from the little Favorite.

"Is there anything I can do for you?" he asked. "Anything at all to speed your recovery?"

"Rest, master," Gundara said. "That's all we need and that's all that can be done. We'll be better by and by."

Safar thought, "by and by" could mean a hundred years to a Favorite. He hoped that wasn't the case.

He started to make a motion to send Gundara back into the stone.

"Wait, master," Gundara said. "I almost forgot something."

The Favorite made a gesture and a small object appeared in his hand. He gestured again and the object plopped into Safar's palm, growing before his eyes.

It was a thin, battered old book bound in leather.

"Nerisa and I stole this from Umurhan's library," Gundara said. "She gave it to me to hold for you."

Safar looked closer. He caught his breath. On the cover, in worn gold leaf, was a familiar symbol.

"It's Lord Asper's book," Gundara said. "The one you were looking for." Then he vanished into the stone.

Fingers trembling, Safar opened the book. It took him a few moments to translate the scratchings. Then the words jumped out as if they were alive:

*"Long, long have I bewailed this world.*
*Long, long have I mourned our fates.*
*Swords unsheathed, banners unfurled,*
*Charge the ramparts fired with hate.*
*'Slay the humans!' we all cried.*
*'Drive the devils from our lands!'*
*I shouted the loudest, but I shouted a lie.*
*I feared to tell them all were damned!*

*Demon and human from a single womb,*
*Bound for Hadin where once I spied*
*A common death and a common tomb..."*

Safar grunted in frustration. Insects had destroyed the rest of the page.

He flipped the leaves. A few were damaged, most were not, but the rest of the book seemed to consist of magical formulas and scribbled notes, with other bits of poetry here and there. It would take much time to decipher the demon wizard's formulas and notes. But at least he'd finally found something—or someone—to point the way.

He thought of Nerisa. Actually, she'd never been far from his mind. Not a day passed when her face, with its huge sad eyes and crooked little grin, didn't rise up to haunt him. He smiled, thinking this book—Asper's book—was her final gift to him.

Outside his room he heard Leiria approach. He put the book away.

Poor Leiria, he thought. Two dead women for rivals, instead of one.

The army marched a week later, Iraj at its head and Safar at his side. Sampitay's citizens turned out for the march, lining the main road and shouting praises and well wishes to the Good King Protarus.

Not long after another city fell, adding to the jewels in his crown. Iraj dealt with this city like Sampitay, following Safar's advice on the treatment of its citizens and the manner of government. A month went by, a month filled with conquests. Some were bloody, some were not.

Then winter came and Iraj's army took up camp. There was plenty of fuel for fire and plenty of food and drink. Messengers came and went, caravans crept over the snow, carrying gold from the tax gatherers to fill Iraj's treasure house.

But the king was moody, pacing the grounds and staring out across the distance at the Gods' Divide, cursing all the cold days that remained until spring.

And he swore to his friend and Grand Wazier, Lord Safar Timura, that he would march for the mountains when the first green buds burst from the ground.

# PART FOUR
## The Demon Wars

## 21

# THE INVASION BEGINS

It was the largest military gathering in the history of Esmir.

A demon army—half-a-million strong—formed up along the edges of the Forbidden Desert, armor glowing in the pale spring sun. It looked like an enormous dragon with glittering scales and outstretched wings, poised to take flight to ravage the human lands. Whole forests of spears, pikes and archers formed its body. Huge baggage trains of arms and supplies made its tail. Trumpeting elephants and snarling cavalry mounts, mixed with the rattle of weapons and the shrieks of campfollowers gave it a voice.

Forming its head were ten thousand mounted troops, commanded by Crown Prince Luka.

It was an elite force, composed of the finest young demons in the land. All were of noble blood and all were anxious to shed that blood for Gods and King. They'd been whipped into a fighting frenzy and were impatient for the signal launching them across the desert. They grumbled loudly at any and all delays, gnashing their fangs and casting anxious yellow eyes at their adored Crown Prince, who was at the moment conferring with his father, King Manacia, and his Chief Wazier, Lord Fari.

The prince, pretending to be completely absorbed by his father's final words before the campaign began, heard their grumbling and hated them for it.

He couldn't imagine why they were so anxious to rush off to meet their Makers. The prince didn't care if they all died the most horrible of deaths. What he objected to strongly was he was expected to share their fates. He thought, they're all so inbred you could poke out both eyes with a single talon. They're all balls and no brains. They had thick necks with small heads, whose only purpose—as far as Luka could determine—was to carry a helmet. Why oh why, do the gods hate me so?

"The first part of the campaign rests squarely on you, my son," King Manacia was saying.

"Pardon, Majesty?" Luka said. "I'm sorry, but I'm finding it difficult to concentrate. I confess I was dreaming of the victories my troops and I will lay at your feet once we are in the humanlands."

Manacia exposed his fangs in a proud grin. "What a fighting prince I have for a son, Fari," the king said to his Chief Wazier. "He's so anxious to be off slaying humans he's barely heard a word I said."

Fari bobbed his head, old snout wrinkling into a smile. "Indeed, Your Highness," Fari said, putting claws to chest as he spoke and then adding one his favorite stock phrases: "Prince Luka is an example to us all."

Luka caught the gleam of amusement in the ancient demon's eyes. Fari could read his heart and was delighted at the prince's predicament. You old bastard, Luka thought. I swear I'll live just to spite you. No matter what it takes I'll survive to piss on your grave and shit on my father's.

"It's his mother's hot blood in him," Manacia said. Then, to Luka, "Did I ever tell you about the time your dear lamented mother accused me of raping her?"

"I don't believe you did, Majesty," the prince lied. "I'd be most anxious to hear that tale."

Manacia burst out laughing at the memory. "It was after she tried to stab me and I had to tie her down," he chortled. "She...She..."

The king broke off, calming himself. He wiped an eye and resettled his crown, which had been shaken over one ear from his laughter.

"Never mind," Manacia said. "We have more important business at claw. I'll save the tale for some night in the future when we're all gathered about a good campfire, sharing a roasted human haunch."

He jabbed at a map, drawing their attention back to the final planning session.

"I want you to cross the desert just as quickly as you can, Luka," the king said. "Ride like the winds. Don't stop for anything. And when you're on the other side I want you to secure a basecamp.

"Give the area a good scrub, mind you. If you see humans, kill them. In fact, it would be best if you scouted out a good fifty miles around the camp. Destroy any settlements you find and make sure no humans escape to spread the news of our invasion. We want to retain the element of surprise as long as we can.

"Once I have my army set and the supply lines secured, we'll roll over them like an eight-beast chariot run amok in the market place. Within six months I predict we'll be at the sea, enjoying a good fish dinner."

Luka bowed. "And it will be my great honor, Majesty," he said, "to cook your meal with my own claws." But he thought, If I have the chance I'll stuff it so full of poison it'll make your scales fall off, you filthy old coward, you.

Manacia rolled up the map and handed it to an obsequious aide, who dropped to his knees and knocked his bony forehead on the rocky ground before withdrawing in a backwards crawl.

"There's only the casting of the bones remaining, Fari," he said. "Then I'll give the signal for the march to begin. Assuming all bodes well, of course."

He glowered at the wizard when he said the last, making it quite obvious what would happen to Fari if the casting did not meet his liking.

"Never fear, Your Highness," Fari said, drawing his casting case from his sleeve. "I ordered special bones made up for this historic moment. That human we used for the last divining session proved so lucky I kept back the knuckles of his dexter hand when we disposed of his corpse."

Fari motioned and two slaves crawled over to unroll a small carpet at his feet. The carpet was night black, with the Star Houses picked out in silver.

He took an ivory cup from his casting case and a small drawstring bag made of silk. He untied the string and upended the sack. The knuckle bones made a dry rattling sound as they fell into the cup. He shook the cup and it was like the buzz of a desert viper as the bones swirled about.

And Fari intoned:

*"Unloosen thy secrets, let us behold*
*What tale the Gods will tell of us*
*When these blessed events unfold."*

He cast the bones on the carpet. King, prince and wizard leaned over to study the result.

"What's this?" Manacia said, delight in his eyes. "They've fallen in a pattern across the Demon Moon." He looked up at the wizard. "I believe the Demon Moon is due to rise soon, isn't it, Fari?"

"Indeed it is, Your Highness," Fari said, bobbing his head. "The Star Gazers tell us it appears but once every thousand years. And they predict that cycle is about to repeat itself.

"This casting brings us good news, Your Highness, as you can see for yourself."

He pointed a talon. "And look here, one knuckle has fallen on a comet. The Demon Moon and the Comet, as Your Highness well knows, is the sign of Alisarrian."

Manacia slapped his thigh in delight. "The Conqueror, himself!" he exclaimed. "Except this time it'll be a demon, not a devil human, who does the conquering!"

Fari gave a mental sigh of relief. He would have lied, if he'd dared, to make this casting come out as the king wanted. But Manacia was the most powerful wizard in the demonlands. He could read a casting as well, if not better, than any of his royal wizards. Such things bored him, however, and he left it up to his magical minions to study bones and entrails for some signpost of the future.

Overcome by emotion, Manacia rose and threw his arms around the Crown Prince. "The gods are with us, my son," he said, embracing Luka. "Let their will guide you on this holy mission."

Luka returned the embrace awkwardly, wishing mightily for a dagger to plunge into his father's back.

"I will do my best, Majesty," he said.

Manacia drew back. "Mount up, my son," he commanded, "and I will give the signal."

Luka bowed low, then strode over to his steed, a huge mailed beast with a long graceful neck, glistening fangs and polished claws. As the prince tried to mount, the beast took a swipe at him with one of those claws. Without breaking stride the prince dodged the claw and vaulted into the saddle, raking the beast with his spurs so hard he drew blood.

The beast shrieked and reared back, pawing the air.

"Good show!" Manacia shouted to his son. "Nothing like a spirited mount to carry one to victory."

Luka was struggling to keep his seat, but he covered this indignity by again raking the beast with his spurs.

"To victory!" he cried, drawing his sword and waving it in the air.

His warriors echoed the cry, roaring in unison. "TO VICTORY!"

Luka pressed the sword against his mount's neck, his next words covered by shouts pouring from ten thousand demon throats. "Get your claws on the ground, you louse-bitten piece of slime," he said, "or I'll cut your throat."

The beast understood and dropped back to earth as agilely as a house cat.

Luka booted his mount to the command point in front of his demon force.

Again he shouted, "To victory!"

"TO VICTORY!" they roared, drawing their own swords and waving them madly in the air.

"The prince is going too far," Manacia complained to Fari under his breath. "This is my moment, not his."

Fari shook his head, hiding his pleasure at this criticism of his enemy. "Just high spirits, I'm sure, Your Highness," he said. "I'm certain it wasn't intended."

"Maybe so, maybe so," Manacia grumbled. "But we'd better hurry it up just the same."

Fari signaled and demon slaves jabbed at the king's great white elephant. It lumbered forward, grand howdah lurching back and forth. More jabs brought it to its knees and the king was hoisted up, panting a little and wondering if perhaps he was letting himself become too fat.

Never mind that, he thought as took his place in the howdah. You'll be slim enough when this campaign is over.

He signaled. Trumpets blared, drums rolled and the whole army came to attention with a great rattling of armor and weapons. A slight pause followed, just a bit longer than good drama warranted.

"For the gods' sake, Fari," Manacia shouted down from the elephant, "cast the damned spell!"

Fari broke out of a delightful reverie in which Manacia and Luka were shrieking and turning on a spit over a slow fire.

"Immediately, Your Highness," he called back.

He threw a glass globe to the ground. It shattered, spilling a thick yellow liquid across the stone. The liquid began to bubble, then to smoke. A sulfurous cloud boiled up, rising high into the sky.

Then the cloud took on the shape of a gigantic King Manacia. Huge lips parted, baring fangs of tremendous length.

"ONWARD, MY FIENDS, ONWARD!" roared the gigantic Manacia. "FOR THE GODS AND THE KING!"

"FOR THE GODS AND THE KING!" a half a million voices shouted in reply.

The whole army lurched forward, shattering the air with war cries.

The elephant handlers had to give the king's animal several sharp jabs to get it moving fast enough so Manacia wasn't overrun. But in a few minutes all clumsiness was gone and the massive army clattered out onto the Forbidden Desert, an immense juggernaut aimed at the humanlands.

Far out in front Luka and his ten thousand elite were speeding over the badlands, battle cries ululating through the thin air. Within moments they'd reached the high dunes that marked the horizon's edge.

Then they vanished from view.

Despite his inner feelings, Luka was an able commander. Although he drove his fiends hard, he drove himself even harder and it wasn't long before the ten thousand thundered out of the Forbidden Desert and entered the humanlands.

All were weary from the mad dash, but Luka gave them no time for respite. He quickly found a likely campsite for his father's army. It was nestled among gentle hills and centered at what had once been Badawi's farm. There was nothing remaining of that farm, thanks to Sarn and his bandit horde, except a few charred timbers and a half-a-dozen caved-in roasting pits where Badawi's family and livestock had been cooked and eaten.

Luka sent out patrols to scout the region, but other than a few ragged families huddled in homes made of sun dried mud bricks, there were no human groups of any significance to be found. Partly this was because few dared to settle so close to the Forbidden Desert. Mostly it was because Sarn had gone about his duties enthusiastically, wiping out any of the small settlements he'd found. Luka didn't know this and so he concluded it was superstition alone that had done the work.

Several weeks passed and there was still no sign of Manacia and the main army. Luka pressed a few trusted human slaves into service, sending them deeper into the humanlands to spy out and map the region. Before they'd left he'd promised them rich rewards for success and reminded them he had their families back in Zanzair as hostages if they betrayed him.

"I'll flay every babe you call your own," he warned. "I'll rip off the limbs of your women and stake out their still-living bodies on ant mounds."

They took his words to heart and by the time the first elements of Manacia's gigantic army hove into view, Luka had maps and detailed intelligence covering hundreds of square miles.

"You certainly took a lot on yourself," Manacia grumbled when Luka showed him the fruits of his efforts.

The king was tired and dirty from his long ordeal. The slowness of the pace, the constant bawling of the animals and the absence of certain creature comforts vital to a king's well-being had made his anger swell like a boil. Luka was careful not to prick it.

Luka apologized profusely, saying, "I'm sorry, Majesty. There's no excuse for my behavior. I promise I won't let it happen again."

Manacia was soothed, although he complained the time would have been better spent making the royal camp more comfortable. When he'd grumbled himself out he took a closer look at the maps and reports his son had gathered.

"I suppose these will be of *some* use to us," he allowed. One of the maps he was studying was a rough eagle's view of all the major hamlets and towns from the Forbidden Desert clear to the great human city called Caspan. "I'll have the scribes make copies and pass them out to my generals. I doubt we can rely on them too greatly, but there's no sense wasting effort well-meant."

"Yes, Majesty. You are too kind, Majesty," Luka murmured.

Meanwhile, he was thinking, You misbegotten still-birth of a camel, I've just given you the keys to the whole damned thing. But you won't admit it, you old fraud. Getting praise from you is like pulling fangs. Well, keep your praise. It's your throne I want.

You'd better watch your back, you foul old fiend, because I fully intend to take that crown away from you and mount your head on the gates of Zanzair.

The demon juggernaut swept along the Gods' Divide, ravaging any force that dared stand in its way.

Mostly the humans were stricken with such terror at the sight of the demon hordes they surrendered on the spot. Believing the gods had abandoned them, they gave themselves up meekly, accepting any terms King Manacia demanded.

Some he slew, some he enslaved, but mostly he followed the practices that had won him a demon empire. If the humans threw down their arms without a fight he tended to be merciful. He let the rulers keep their posts and made them swear fealty to him, recognizing him as the one true monarch—the King of Kings—Master of Esmir; lord of all humans and demons alike.

He sealed them to their oath by requiring them to sign documents in their own blood, telling them the documents would always be by his side and if they betrayed him he would cast a spell that would let loose a voracious worm in their guts.

Manacia left only a small garrison force at each place he took, relying on fear and sorcery to keep his human subjects contrite.

First he sent his sniffers out to find and kill any human with magical talent.

Then he had small temples erected at the key cities and hamlets, with a demon wizard in charge of each edifice. Portable spell machines were installed in the temples, spewing out spells by the hour meant to keep the populace fearful and humble and strike terror in the hearts of any outside enemy who might attempt to retake the city.

Once he'd secured the spine of the humanlands—the great mountain range called the Gods' Divide—he struck toward Caspan.

That region proved more difficult. The cities were much larger as were the armies who defended them. He also no longer had the element of surprise. The human monarchs and generals he encountered swallowed their terror and fought grimly to halt the demon invasion.

The enemy generals conscripted everyone of fighting age, hurling the ragged, weeping hordes before Manacia's forces. Most of the humans died, but in dying they slowed Manacia's drive enough so the professionals could attack the weak points. True, ten humans might fall for every demon. But Manacia had no way of replacing his losses.

Manacia began losing fiends at an alarming rate. Of the half-a-million he started with, less than four hundred thousand remained when he approached the gates of Caspan.

Crown Prince Luka's shock troops had suffered the most. When the human hordes charged out to meet him he had only five thousand mounted fiends to meet that charge.

"This is it," Luka thought as he led his fiends into the battle. "This is when I die."

The humans were horrid things, ugly as the devils from the Hells. Flat faces, piggy little eyes and filthy little mouths that screamed hate and fury as they fought.

They had good armor, sturdy weapons and were mounted on huge mailed warhorses that reared up to fight the demon steeds with iron-tipped feet. It was hoof against claw, talon against hand, swords and axes flailing about at close quarters, blood spraying everywhere.

Archers and slingmen sent shower after shower of missiles into the melee, not caring who fell—friend or foe—so long as the demons were kept from the gates.

Two horsemen crowded Luka from either side. A pikeman reared up in front of him. His mount slashed at the pikeman, disemboweling him. But as he died he plunged forward, burying his pike into the beast's shoulder. The animal screamed in pain, but kept its feet. Luka swung left, sword biting through human mail and finding flesh. His opponent toppled from his horse, but before Luka could turn to meet the other he felt a sharp pain in his side.

The human had struck first.

Howling in agony, Luka slashed at the man with sword. In a haze he saw blood gout, feared it was his own, then he saw the human fall and felt relief rush in to dull his pain.

His mount staggered and Luka leaped off moments before it crashed to the ground. Now he was standing in the middle of plunging horses and demon beasts, dodging blows from every side. He saw one of his fiends topple from his mount and Luka vaulted into the saddle and grabbed the reins.

"Victory!" he bellowed. "For the gods and the king!"

His cry rallied his soldiers and they returned his shout—*"Victory! For the gods and the king!"*

They charged the humans with spirits renewed, smashing and slashing them down.

Finally, the humans broke, fleeing through the gates.

Luka and his fiends pursued them, hacking their way through the gates' defenders.

Suddenly there was no one to kill anymore. Luka and his soldiers found themselves in a large square, panting and heaving and bleeding from many wounds.

Behind him he heard trumpets sound.

His father's trumpets.

Then there was a great roar of demon voices and a sea of Manacia's soldiers poured through the gates.

Rising out their midst was his father's royal elephant. The huge animal moved smoothly across the square to Luka.

Manacia grinned down at him from the howdah, fangs displayed in full gleam.

"Thank the gods you are still with us, my son," he shouted. "I saw you fall and feared for the worst."

Luka bowed, fighting not to show pain.

"Caspan is yours, Majesty!" he cried. "It is my gift to you, and demon history!"

And he thought, this was for you, Mother, for you!

And Manacia thought, how dare he make a gift of what is already mine? Then he remembered the day when he'd said something similar to his own father.

The next time Luka falls, he thought, I must make certain he doesn't rise again.

Manacia was a dutiful king, a hard working king, and he had at least twenty other sons to take Luka's place.

I'd best choose the youngest to succeed him as heir to my

throne, Manacia thought. Princes grow up so quickly these days.

Why, I was nearly thirty winters old before I slew *my* father.

"Coralean is desolate," the caravan master said. "He is a coin clipped of its worth. A sway-backed camel with more fleas than spirit.

"It seems it is Coralean's fate that each time he greets you, my king, whom I dare call friend, that he drags demons, or news of demons, into your highness' august presence."

"Come now, Coralean," Iraj protested, "I'm not one of those city-bred despots who forgets his friends soon as he wins the throne. And I'm certainly not one to harm the messenger who brings ill tidings.

"Isn't that right, Safar?"

Safar stirred in his seat—a smaller version of Iraj's traveling throne.

"Actually," he deadpanned, "Iraj had his royal torturers put out the eyes and slit the tongue of the last fellow who was in here babbling about demons."

Iraj frowned. "What a thing to say, Safar," he protested, "I gave the man a purse of gold. Don't you re—" he broke off, laughing. "You're joking again," he said.

Then, to the caravan master, "You see how it is, Coralean? My friends are always making jests at my expense!"

"King Protarus speaks the truth," Safar said. "You'll notice I still have both my eyes and a whole tongue, and yet I bring him bad news daily."

He gestured at the empty main room of the command tent. "Why, our king is so grand a monarch he even permits his friends to use his common name in private.

"Isn't that so, Iraj?"

More laughter from the king. "Don't pay any attention to him, Coralean," he advised. "Safar is just punishing me for ignoring his advice."

He leaned out from his throne. "I had to let my men sack the last city we took," he said. "I was short of gold and they hadn't been paid all winter. Safar was opposed to the sacking. He said it was bad business."

Coralean's merchant smile lit the dim room. "An honest dispute among right-thinking men," he said. "One looks at future profits. The other at more immediate concerns. There is no right or wrong in such a disagreement."

He bowed his craggy head in Iraj's direction, saying, "The pity should go to the master, who must torment himself for being forced to ignore his advisors and act according to his best judgment."

The look of pleasure on Iraj's face made Safar fully appreciate why Coralean had been so successful in his long and dangerous career. Despite his common man pretense, Iraj had proven to be a prickly monarch. His dark moods had made the winter long. Then spring had brought the first news of the demon invasion and had plunged him deeper into depression. Iraj had allowed the first city he'd taken to be sacked not to please his men, but to vent his rage.

"What a lucky man I am to have two such loyal friends," Iraj said. "One uses wise and well-put phrases to guide me, the other amusing barbs—which also serve to remind me I am only human."

Don't forget money and magic, Safar thought. We bring you that as well.

Safar had created and cast his first battle spell to help Iraj take the city he later sacked. Coralean, that canny old merchant, had funded Iraj's ambitions from the start. He'd been handsomely rewarded with exclusive trading contracts.

You haven't done so badly either, Safar chided himself. In the short time he'd been at Iraj's side Safar had become a wealthy man by anyone's measurement. As Grand Wazier he had been given vast tracts of land and chests of rare gems and metals.

"So tell us your news, my friend," Iraj said to Coralean. "Don't spare my feelings. I'm braced for the worst."

"Caspan has fallen," Coralean said.

Coming from such a normally loquacious man, his brevity was a shock. Iraj flinched, then tried to cover his concern.

Fingers rapping on the arm of his throne gave him away. "I see. Well, we were expecting that. Weren't we Safar?"

Safar nodded. They'd heard rumors of Manacia's drive toward Caspan and he'd made a castings that did not bode well for the city's defenders.

"Coralean barely escaped with his life," the caravan master said. "I sent my wives into hiding and fled the city just in time."

He went on to describe the series of battles that led to the taking of Caspan. Trying to add a note of cheer he went into some detail on the great losses Manacia had suffered in the campaign.

But Iraj kept rapping his fingers against wood. "So few," he murmured. "I'd hoped he would have suffered more."

He looked up at Coralean. "I suppose it won't be long before he comes over the mountains," he said.

"I fear so," Coralean said. "The last I heard he was preparing his army and searching for the route to Kyrania."

The mention of Kyrania was a heavy spear aimed at Safar's heart. Intentional or not, Safar bent a closer ear to what Coralean had to say.

"A caravan master's life isn't worth a copper on that side of the Gods' Divide," Coralean said. "Many of my brother merchants have been seized and tortured for the information. Luckily the demons know so little of human affairs they keep seizing the wrong men.

"But they only need one success and Manacia's army will be on the march to Kyrania."

Iraj was silent for a time; fingers rap, rap, rapping. Then he said to Coralean, voice so low he could barely be heard, "Leave us for a time, my friend. I must speak with my brother."

The caravan master bowed, murmured a few kind words and departed.

Soon as he was gone Iraj turned to Safar, face full of anguish. "You said I would be king of kings!" he cried.

"And you will," Safar replied.

"Are you certain your talent isn't playing you false?" Iraj demanded. "Am I a fool, bound to a fool's vision?"

"Let me speak plainly," Safar said. "There's no question that you are a fool. Who else but a fool would want to be king of Esmir? But fool or not, that is your destiny."

"Beware!" Iraj snapped. "I'm in no mood for insults, friendly though they may be."

"If you don't want to hear the truth," Safar said, "then command my silence."

"I've given you power," Iraj said.

"Take it back," Safar replied. "It's more of a burden than I care to shoulder."

"I've made you rich," Iraj pointed out.

"In Kyrania," Safar said, "wealth is a bountiful harvest that all share.

Iraj grew angry. "Are you saying that in your view all I've given you is worthless?"

Taking a lesson from Coralean, Safar replied, "Not your friendship. I value that most highly, Iraj Protarus."

Iraj was mollified. His finger rapping ceased. "What should I do, brother?" he asked. "How do I achieve what your vision foretold?"

"Why don't we look at the problem a different way?" Safar said. "Why don't we turn it about and see if luck's barren goat will still give milk?"

"I'm listening," Iraj said.

"When you started out your greatest difficulty was a family feud," Safar said. "An uncle opposed your rightful claim to leadership. A few of your kin were greedy enough to support that uncle. But most—out of long family feelings and tradition—supported you."

"True enough," Iraj said. "Although it was more complicated than that."

"To counter that natural feeling," Safar continued, "your uncle went to an outsider. A man hated by all in your family."

"It gave him a temporary advantage," Iraj said, "but in the end it was a help to me. After a few successes, my family rallied to me."

"So your uncle's alliance with an enemy," Safar said, "was his downfall."

Iraj thought for a moment, then nodded. "Yes. That is so."

"There you have it," Safar said. "The presence of a hated outsider gave you power to rally your clan. Afterwards, you put clan together with clan to take to the road as a conqueror.

"But to those people *you* were the outsider. The barbarian from the Plains of Jaspar.

"They opposed you, fought you, dared to call you a greedy upstart, instead of as the savior of all Esmir. Which is how you see yourself."

"But I am," Iraj said. "You saw it in the vision."

Safar didn't say he'd never seen such a thing. In the vision Iraj had been a conquering king perched on a white elephant, leading his army toward Zanzair. Whether he was a savior or not was another matter.

"Good," Safar said. "I'm glad you believe that. Because that is how you will defeat Manacia."

Iraj's expression was puzzled. He didn't understand.

"The whole human world fears the demons," Safar said. "Use that fear against Manacia. Raise your standard, claim all humankind as your clan...and strike him down.

"Before winter set in you faced the prospect of many years of battle to claim Caspan as your realm. Manacia has done your work in less than a season.

"Defeat him and you have the north."

Iraj brightened. "And the demonlands," he pointed out. "I'll have them as well."

"First we have to cross the Forbidden Desert," Safar cautioned.

Iraj gave a cheery wave. "You mean the curse? Hells, I was never worried about that. You'll figure it out when we get there.

"Besides, if Manacia can do it, so can you."

"I'm glad you still have confidence in me," Safar said, again taking a lesson from Coralean and letting a measure of humility leak through.

"As I see it," Safar continued, "our greatest danger will be Manacia's magic. It's well know that demons are much more powerful sorcerers than humans."

"An overblown reputation, as far I'm concerned," Iraj scoffed, gaining confidence by the minute. "I saw you bring down an avalanche on a whole pack of them, remember?"

Safar had few delusions about himself. He'd spent the winter testing his powers and at first had been amazed at the newly possible. But in reading the Book of Asper, the demon wizard, he saw glimmerings of a power that might be beyond him.

"I caught them by surprise," Safar said. "Besides, it was only a score or more we were faced with. Not a whole demon army—with a legion of wizards to support them."

"You just worry about Manacia's wizards, Safar," Iraj replied. "I'll take care of his damned army."

***

Worry is not such an easy thing to limit. The mind may decree borders, but once erected those borders are immediately beset by fears both large and small. Nights become sleepless landscapes littered with innumerable difficulties and imagined pitfalls threatening the mightiest of beings. Large things may seem insurmountable mountains during those torturous hours when others sleep. Small things may suddenly erupt into fears rivaling those mountains.

In the north, King Manacia consolidated his army and searched for the route over the Gods' Divide. But his nights were haunted by imagined plots involving his son, Prince Luka. Then word filtered through of a mighty human king with flowing hair and beard of gold. This monarch—King Iraj Protarus—bore the standard of Alisarrian and was rousing the populace to oppose Manacia and destroy his long cherished dreams of empire.

Sitting at the right hand of that king, it was said, was a human wizard so powerful he was the equal of any demon lord of sorcery. The wizard, Safar Timura, had eyes as blue as the sunlit heavens.

When Manacia slept at all he was troubled by nightmares in which his son suddenly turned into a human with a golden beard and sky blue eyes. In this nightmare Manacia would be forced to embrace his son and heir before his court, knowing full well a dagger would be thrust into his back.

In the south, King Protarus massed his forces and toured his realm, spreading the news of the demon invasion. He gave thundering speeches, decrying the atrocities committed by the demons—some real, some created. He was a handsome young prince, a compelling speaker who quickly made his subjects forget the atrocities he had committed himself in winning his kingdom. People rushed to support him, swelling his armies, crying for revenge against the demon invaders.

But Iraj's nights were as sleepless as Manacia's.

What if Safar was wrong? What if he were not as great a seer as Iraj believed? And what if his friend was not truly his friend? If he were as powerful a wizard as Iraj believed, might he not seize the throne of Esmir as soon as Iraj had won it? And if not, why not? Which brought him back to the original worry that Safar was so weak Iraj was a fool to rely on him.

Safar was no king, which gave him ample reason to harbor fears equal to both monarchs combined.

If Iraj believed Safar was in the way he'd betray him with barely a thought. Safar wondered about the vision in which he'd seen Iraj's victorious march on Zanzair. What if that part were true, but in reality it was Safar's ghost who'd witnessed it? He'd certainly felt like a spirit during the vision. What if his dream-catcher self had slipped past the part where Safar was betrayed and slain by his blood brother? It troubled him he'd never been able to see past that moment when Iraj's armies marched on Zanzair. And what of the other vision—the vision of Hadin—in which all was for naught and the world was rushing toward its end?

Then there was the greatest fear of all.

For either king—Manacia or Protarus—the key was Kyrania.

What if the two monarchs met in battle in the High Caravans?

What if Safar's valley and everyone he loved—mother, father, sisters, friends—were destroyed in that confrontation?

After a time this worried Safar even more than the destruction of the world itself.

It was impossible to imagine the last.

But frighteningly easy to see the first.

In the end it was fear for Kyrania that drove Safar. He was willing to dare anything to save it.

# 22

# THE DEMON FEAST

Safar crouched in the flowered peaks above Kyrania. It was early summer, the rains had been sweet, the heavens kind, and his valley was a misty shimmer beneath the pale morning sun. The fields were emerald green, the lake was a great blue diamond fed by springs flowing down the mountains in a silvery pilgrimage to the Goddess Felakia.

"So this is your home," Leiria said in awe. "I've never seen anything so beautiful. It's like a dream."

Safar motioned for silence. His magical self had arrowed past Leiria's dream and found a nightmare. In his innermost pocket the stone idol blistered warning.

He signaled to the men—fifty of Iraj's finest mounted warriors. They dismounted, positioned feed bags to silence their horses and quickly shifted their gear to ready themselves for battle.

Leiria raised an eyebrow. "What's wrong?"

"Watch," Safar said.

He plucked a glass pellet from his pouch and hurled it to the ground. It shattered and pale green smoke whooshed up, swirling to the height of a knee. First a landscape, then figures toiling in that landscape, took form in the smoke. There were at least two score of them—miniature humans moving through the fields of Kyrania. They seemed agonized, smoke forms twisting and leaping in pain. Larger columns of smoke funneled up, hardening into the givers of that pain. They were creatures of snouted fangs and taloned claws.

Leiria caught her breath. "Demons!"

Safar didn't answer. He gestured and the smoke image vanished. He slumped onto the boulder, so mournful it was all Leiria could do not to console him—branding herself as a weakling in the eyes of her fellow soldiers.

"This changes everything," she said, colder than she'd intended. "We'd best return immediately and tell the king the demons have seized Kyrania."

Safar nodded absently. His thoughts were barely of this world. He was imagining the terrors his family and friends were suffering.

Safar had intended to warn his people of the coming peril, then set up shields to confuse the demons if and when they attacked through the pass. Iraj was even now gathering a force of shock troops to be rushed in to fill the gap until his main army had time to arrive. Safar had convinced Iraj even greater haste must be made—that he should go out in advance of the troops and prepare the way. Now it seemed his mission to Kyrania, which had required much cajolement to win Iraj's approval, was a failure before it started.

"You're right," he replied, mechanical as a clockwork toy. "We must inform the king."

Leiria winced at his pain. But she said nothing. She walked back to the men to order a withdrawal. It would be done quickly, but silently. Weapons and gear were strapped down so they wouldn't rattle. Rags stuffed with brush were tied onto the horses' hooves so all noise would be pillowed.

When all was ready Leiria returned to say it was time to go. She touched him and he suddenly came back to life.

"I must see for myself," he said.

"You can't," Leiria protested. "We might be discovered."

Safar insisted. He made it clear the only way he'd leave now was if he were bound and gagged and tied to the back of a horse.

Everyone was terrified of committing such an indignity to Lord Timura, the Grand Wazier. But they were equally as terrified of his plan.

"The king will have our heads if you're captured," Leiria protested.

"No he won't," Safar said. "Here. I'll make sure of it."

He scrawled a hasty message to Iraj. No one was to be held accountable for his actions. He added a brief report on what he'd seen so far and what should be done if he didn't return. The message was placed in the care of Rapton, the young lieutenant who commanded the warriors. Strict orders were given. If Safar and Leiria—who insisted on accompanying him—did not return by dusk Rapton and the troops were to make all speed to Sampitay—where Iraj and his court were currently ensconced—and deliver the news.

When he was done Safar called for silence. He prepared Leiria and himself, coating their clothes and skin with a smoky herb that would confound sensitive demon noses. He made a spell to shield their human auras from demon wizards. Last of all he hauled out the stone turtle and alerted Gundara to keep watch for danger.

The little Favorite and his twin, Gundaree, were back to normal again. Drawing inspiration from Lord Asper's book, Safar had devised a healing program to hasten their recovery—special powders mixed with warm honey and wine. For two weeks the stone idol had rested in that potion, which Safar refreshed daily.

At first nothing had changed. If anything the faint buzz of life had grown fainter.

Then one morning Safar awakened to a familiar—"Shut up, shut up, shuuut upp!" And he knew things were well again in the small world of the Favorites.

Safar turned to Leiria. "I know it's your habit to lead the way," he said.

"It's more than habit, my lord," she said. "It's my duty. I am your bodyguard. I must keep you safe."

"Yes, yes," he said, impatiently. "And you perform your duty well. But this time we have to change the order of things. I was raised here. I was once a boy roaming these hills. I know all the secret places boys know. I know all the secret paths boys favor.

"I want you to follow *me*. Keep close as you can. Walk in my tracks if possible. Do all I do. And nothing that I don't. Do you understand?"

Leiria swore she did and a few moments later they were hurrying down an old deer trail, so faint it might have been made by a population of mice.

They hadn't gone a hundred yards before Safar suddenly veered to the right and was gone.

Leiria nearly panicked, looking madly about for some sign of Safar. Then she saw where the leaves wavered and plunged after him. She heard him hiss before she saw him, jerking back just in time to avoid stepping on his heels. They traveled in silent tandem for a time, jumping onto to trails and jumping off again, veering left and then right and then straight ahead. But from the tension in her calves Leiria could tell the general direction was downward.

Down—to the broad lake and rich fields of Kyrania.

Khadji Timura slipped his trowel into the claybed. He felt the blade grate through sand and gravel and he pushed it in a little deeper. He lifted the load up, hiding his distaste at the poor quality of the clay and all the trash it contained, and dumped it into the waiting bucket.

"Hurry up, old man," the demon said. "I'm weary."

"Forgive me, master," Khadji said. "I am old, as you have repeatedly reminded me this entire day, and my joints give me pain. If I had help, which you have wisely informed me is not possible, I could work more quickly."

The demon, whose name was Trin, scowled at Safar's father, saying, "You think because you are human and demons can't read human expressions that I don't realize you're mocking me."

He swatted Khadji with his club. Khadji grunted and nearly fell. He steadied himself with a hand and blinked away tears that were more from humiliation than pain. Trin was experienced at such things. He knew how to rap a human skull with just enough force to gain their attention, but not so hard they'd be incapacitated.

"You are probably cursing me and your fate right now," Trin said. "This is good. It teaches you how you stand with me. I have better things to do than spend my days here in the damp and cold watching you dig up clay. If I had my way I'd empty your brains from your skull and join my mates in some spirited drinking."

"You're right, exalted one," Khadji said. He'd recovered and was rising, full bucket in hand. "And I thank you for the reminder of what a fortunate person I am.

"Why, what would become of me and family if your superiors weren't so wise? What clever fiends they are. I've often remarked on it to Myrna, my wife.

"Good Timura pottery equals much gold on the marketplace. Gold your king requires to fight his wars."

Trin snorted. "A pot's a pot, as far as I'm concerned," he said. "You put something in it. And you empty it out. I used to pinch them out by the dozen when I was young. Some broke when they were fired. Some didn't. Who cares? The clay costs nothing. And the fire only wants a little fuel."

"Who am I to quarrel with such an expert on pottery?" Khadji said.

"No one," Trin agreed. "I was a potter before I was a soldier. I know good work when I see it."

He looked at the bucket, then dug a tentative claw into its contents. "A little gritty, isn't it?" he said.

"All the beds are nearly worked out, master," the potter lied. The best clay was on the other side of Lake Felakia, snuggled in grit-free beds he had no intention of showing the demons. "This is the best we can do under the circumstances."

Khadji saw two figures steal out of the brush behind the demon. As if sensing their presence, the demon started to turn in that direction.

The potter lifted up the bucket to capture his attention.

"It only needs a little cleaning, exalted one," he said. "And if there are imperfections, why we'll cover them up with the glaze. Like you said, master, a pot's a pot. But when I put my name on it—Timura—there are plenty of fools at the marketplace who think the name is more important than actual quality."

"My father," Trin said, wiping a talon on Khadji's smock, "who was a potter of great renown, used to tell me the same thing."

"He sounds as wise a fiend as his son," Khadji said.

The demon glared at him. "Are you mocking me again, human?" He raised his club. "Are you?"

There was a thunk. The demon's yellow eyes suddenly widened and club fell from his hands. An arrow point protruded through his throat.

Trin pitched forward, quite dead.

Khadji upended the bucket on the corpse and spit.

"A pot's just a pot, is it?" he growled. Then he opened his arms to embrace Safar. "Welcome home, son," he said.

To Safar's immense embarrassment, Khadji started to weep.

"It's all right, father," he murmured, patting him uncomfortably. "It's all right."

"We'd heard about all the troubles in Esmir," his father said, sipping from the mug of trail wine. "Droughts and plagues and wars. But it's always been so in the outside world. And although we worried, especially for you, Safar, we never thought those troubles would arrive to take up residence before our very hearths."

Leiria and the soldiers were gathered about Safar and his father, listening closely to the old potter's tale. Less than an hour had passed since the demon had been killed, his body hidden in the brush. The group was gathered in a safe place high above Kyrania. Guards were posted to give warning if anyone came.

"Not long ago Lord Coralean came this way," Khadji said, "and we heard the news of the demon invasion and capture of Caspan." He looked at Safar, eyes red-streaked, skin sagging from his long ordeal. "We all remembered the demons you and Iraj encountered up in the passes of The Bride And Six Maids."

Khadji sighed. "Lord Coralean was wrong, wasn't he, when he said they were only rogues who'd strayed into the humanlands?"

It was a question that didn't need answering. Safar refilled his father's cup. The old man took another sip of the restorative.

"Anyway, that's when we started worrying," he said. "It seemed only logical the demons would have to come through Kyrania to attack the other side. We've always been blessed by peace in these mountains. But now it seemed that peace would be no more.

"The Elders met. There was much talk of this and that, but it was mostly nonsense, for who among us had ever faced such a situation before? Coralean had promised us he would plead with King Protarus for help, but we didn't know if the help would come at all, much less in time. So we decided to mount our own defenses."

Khadji made a bitter laugh. "The lads drilled and trained and we rebuilt the walls of the old fort. But it was clear that although Kyranians can fight well enough, none of us have the killing instincts of a soldier." He glanced at Leiria and the others. "I hope you don't take offense," he said. "I was only speaking of professional training, not doubting the human kindness I'm sure is natural to you all."

"No offense given, or taken, Father Timura," Leiria said. "We know what you meant."

Khadji looked up a Safar, anguished. "In the end," he said, "there was no time for resistance. They took us in our beds. And then they rounded us up and put us all in that fort we'd labored so hard to rebuild. They killed some of us to set an example. They were humiliating deaths.

"They made us watch."

Khadji brushed away a tear. "I learned what it was to be a weak and selfish mortal," he said. "Much as I mourned the deaths of my friends, I'm ashamed to say I knew joy because I still lived. *And* your mother *and* your sisters."

He drained the cup, covering the mouth when Safar offered more.

"And Gubadan?" Safar asked.

"Gone," his father answered. "He was among the first. The demons have witch sniffers, you know. Gubadan didn't have much magic. But it was enough for them to find him out."

He touched Safar's hand, tentatively, as if amazed his son wasn't a ghost. "It's a good thing you weren't here, son," he said. "We've all heard what a great wizard you've become. They would have found you out immediately."

"I'm surprised they let any of you live, Father Timura," Leiria said. "We have the gods to thank for that."

"Not the gods," Khadji said, "but a human traitor. And it isn't thanks we owe him, but all the curses we can manage."

Safar's eyes narrowed. "There was a human leading them?"

"Not leading, actually," his father answered. "Although they listen to his counsel with much respect. Apparently this human has powerful friends among the demons. Some even say he has the ear of Crown Prince Luka."

"Who is this man?" Safar demanded. "Do I know of him? Would I recognize his name."

"I believe so," Khadji answered. "He certainly knows you."

When he said the name Safar jumped as if he'd been stung.

Kalasariz strolled out of the Temple of Felakia into the warm sunlight. It was late afternoon and the atmosphere in the temple, which he'd turned into his quarters, had suddenly felt too close. So he'd left his scribe to complete the report to Prince Luka and ambled outside to refresh himself.

It was a day of sharp colors and deep shadows. The sun was spun gold, the clouds pure silver, the lake and sky startling blue. He filled his lungs with air, which was heavy with the scent of blossoms. He breathed out, savoring the air's fruity aftertaste. A few birds sang a melody from the small grove down near the lake. Their song made Kalasariz smile.

Another delightful day in Kyrania, he thought. So different from the bustling, smoky squalor of Walaria. Kalasariz, who had spent his entire career eliminating surprise, was amazed at how his life had turned out. Turned upside down, actually, he thought. The only thing unsurprising was that he'd managed to land on his feet when the great emptying had begun. Kalasariz was an agile master of balance. Even his enemies would say that. He grinned—Especially his enemies!

Another bird joined the songfest at the grove. The chorus was quite compelling.

Kalasariz let his feet carry him toward the lake so he could enjoy the concert close up.

He supposed things had gotten rather...stressful...when King Protarus had shown up at the gates of Walaria. Not surprising, though. Kalasariz refused to accept that description of his feelings those many long months ago when panic raged all about him. He'd kept calm. Kept his footing. Formed his plan. And taken action.

He'd been rather...alarmed? No, no. Too strong a word. Disappointed, perhaps. Yes, he'd been disappointed when his carefully laid plan to join Protarus had failed. His secret messages and doctored files claiming friendship with Safar Timura had not found a receptive audience in King Protarus. At first he'd been...irritated. Not angry, but irritated. Kalasariz admired suspicion. It was a tool no worthy monarch should be without. But in his view Protarus had taken suspicion beyond reason.

So what if there were a few lies in Kalasariz' messages? He'd honestly intended to fulfill his side of the bargain. Hadn't he seen to it that a certain gate was left unguarded at the appropriate time? Hadn't he delivered Didima and Umurhan just as he'd agreed? And hadn't he promised long and faithful service to his new king?

Kalasariz was sorely wounded Protarus hadn't seen what a valuable ally he would have been. Good spies are difficult to find. And Kalasariz, who wasted no time on things like false modesty, knew he was the best of all.

The best proof of that were the spies he had in Protarus' court. They'd warned him just in time the king meant to betray him and he'd barely escaped with his life.

Kalasariz found it amusing the king's betrayal had ended up being a blessing. Why, if he had joined the king he wouldn't be here in Kyrania so well placed on the winning side. So what if they were demons? They had what Kalasariz considered an enlightened attitude toward human abilities. Luka had immediately seen Kalasariz' potential. As had Lord Fari. Of course, the two would probably appreciate him less, but admire him more, if they knew he'd made separate arrangements with them both.

He stopped at the edge of the grove. The birds broke off their concert and flew deeper into the shadows. There they perched on an old nut tree, branches bursting with bounty, and took up their song again. The music was sweet, very sweet. I must see what sort of birds these are, Kalasariz thought. Then a sudden vision came to him of one of the birds leaping down on his finger. In the vision he carried the creature away and put it in a cage where it serenaded him all the night long.

Teased by the vision, he followed the birds into the woods.

Kalasariz hadn't deluded himself about his safety from Protarus anywhere on the Walarian side of the Gods' Divide. Even if he could have found a suitable place, he had no intention of spending his days as a man without influence, without power, ducking and dodging through alleyways. So he'd decided to cross the mountains and see what kind of life he could make in Caspan. He had well-placed spies in that city, which was an even better start than the fat pouch of gems he'd carried away with him when he'd escaped.

Those were exciting days, he thought with the fondness that distance and success give to anxious times. Disguised as a merchant, he'd hired a place in a caravan traveling to Caspan. He'd crossed the mountains at Kyrania with that caravan, noting with much interest the richness of the valley. He'd even purchased a fine set of wine cups from Khadji Timura, enjoying much private amusement as the old man and his wife smiled and chatted while they wrapped the cups in felt and packed them carefully away in a carved box for his journey. He'd nearly laughed aloud when the dear old couple had boasted of their son, Safar Timura, who was a great scholar and boyhood friend of Iraj Protarus.

He remembered the conversation as if it were yesterday.

"Perhaps you've heard of him?" Khadji asked.

"Safar Timura?" Kalasariz replied. "No, I'm sorry I haven't had that honor."

"No, Iraj Protarus, I mean," Khadji said.

"Certainly I have," Kalasariz said. "Who hasn't heard of the great King Protarus and his famous victories?"

Then Myrna shyly asked, "Some say he's cruel. Is this true?"

"Not at all, good mother," Kalasariz said. "Why, he's the kindest of kings. Oh, there have been deaths, of course. But when isn't there in a war? No, he's a grand king, this Protarus. And good for business as well."

Myrna acted much relieved. "I'm pleased to hear that," she said. "He lived here for a time, you know. He was a *good* lad. A little wild and strong-willed, of course. But a *good* lad. His mother would have been proud, may the gods bless her dear departed soul."

Kalasariz chuckled at the memory. He looked up and saw the birds had moved, but only to a lower branch. He wondered what kind of nut tree it was. Cinnamon, perhaps?

He'd barely settled in Caspan—reacquainting his spies with the solidness of good Kalasariz gold—when the demons struck.

Once again he found himself in a city under siege, hysteria raging all about him. But he'd kept his head low, ordered his spies to do the same, and once the demons had taken the city he'd poked it up again. The demons had engaged in the usual slaughter. But when they thought the lesson had been taught—and taught well—they set up an administration to run the city. Some of those administrators were from the previous government. They were all low level bureaucrats—the kind who do most of the real work and take little notice of who or what might be the current resident of the throne. Among them were Kalasariz' spies.

Once he knew the lay of the land, Kalasariz had approached Luka and Fari—separately, of course. He had many things to offer. The most valuable of all was Kyrania. The key that would unlock the gate to Protarus' kingdom.

He paused under the tree, the birds just above him, but silent now.

So here I am, he thought, enjoying my reward. The first of many and greater rewards to come.

The birds fluttered, catching his attention. He noticed one bird in particular. It was bright green, while the others were drab brown, and seemed to have a large red spot on its breast. It was a plump little fellow. Deliciously so.

Kalasariz recalled that song birds were supposed to be the best meat of all. The sweeter the song, it was said, the sweeter the flesh.

He looked closer at the tree. He was certain now it was a cinnamon. Ah, he thought, a song bird fed on cinnamon. What a meal I could make!

Kalasariz held out his finger. "Fly down, fly down my pretty little bird," he called. "Light upon me. I have nice things for you."

He was mildly surprised when the bird hopped from the branch and perched on his outstretched finger. He'd only been amusing himself—thinking of the vision. But now it seemed that vision was about to turn into dinner.

"Sing to me little bird," he cooed. "Sing to Kalasariz. Sing as sweetly as you can, my pretty. And then I'll wring your little neck and have you for supper."

To his delight the bird opened its beak as if to sing.

"Shut up, shut up, shuutt uuuup!" it said.

Kalasariz' jaw dropped. "What? What did you say?"

"I said shut up, Gundaree," the bird went on. "I saw him first. I don't care if he smells like a demon. He's a people. Look for yourself, you stupid thing!"

I'm dreaming, Kalasariz thought. I fell asleep in the temple and I dreamed I took a walk. And now I'm dreaming this bird is talking to me. He lifted his hand, examining the red spot on the bird's breast. How odd, he thought. It's in the shape of a turtle.

Suddenly the bird sank sharp claws into his finger.

Kalasariz shrieked and tried to fling the creature off.

"Get away, get away!" he cried.

But the bird only sank its claws deeper, grating against the bone.

Screaming, Kalasariz flung himself about, trying to shake the bird from his wounded hand.

"Stop that you stupid human!" the bird shouted at Kalasariz. "You're hurting me."

Then the bird transformed into a snarling little fiend with long sharp teeth. It leaped onto Kalasariz' face, clutching his cheeks with its talons. Then it bit him on the nose.

Kalasariz froze. He felt pain, felt the creature clinging to his face, felt blood flow into his mouth, but he couldn't move. Couldn't even twitch, much less make a sound.

He heard footsteps and saw a figure step from the tree.

And Kalasariz, a man who refused to recognize even mild surprise, much less stark terror, knew both.

"You'd better let go of him," Safar said. "You're getting blood all over your clothes. And you know how you hate that."

Gundara released Kalasariz, then hopped to the ground. The little Favorite examined his gore-stained costume.

"Now, look what you've done," he accused Kalasariz. "If you'd have stayed still like you were supposed to there'd have only been a little pinch. And almost no blood."

Kalasariz, stricken dumb as well as spellbound, could only manage a strangled gag. He saw Safar haul out a stone idol, shaped like a turtle.

"Why don't you go clean yourself up?" Safar said to Gundara. "You can have your treats later."

"What a good master," Gundara said. "What a kind master."

He hopped up on the stone, shrinking in size so he'd fit. He hesitated, clearly torn. "You won't forget, will you?" he said to Safar. "The sweets I mean."

"I won't forget," Safar reassured him.

"Promise?"

Safar sighed. "I promise," he said, as patiently as he could.

Gundara squealed delight. Then—"Look out, Gundaree! Here I come!"

And he vanished into the stone.

Safar put the idol away and approached Kalasariz. He looked him up and down. The spymaster felt another shock when he saw how blue Safar's eyes were—blue as that sky, blue as that cold lake he'd admired only minutes before.

"I suppose you're wondering why you are still alive?" Safar said, so mild it was frightening.

Kalasariz hadn't reached that point yet, but as soon as Safar mentioned it his mind made the leap. His reaction was so violent that a faint tremble of fear made its way through the numbness.

"Good," Safar said. "I can see it in your eyes. Now that you traveled that far you're a bright enough fellow to know the answer. Am I right?"

Kalasariz made a gagging sound.

Safar looked disgusted. He snapped his fingers and Kalasariz suddenly had the ability to speak. Although he was still as immobile as a statue.

"Thank the gods you've come, Safar!" Kalasariz blurted. "You're just in time to—"

Safar snapped his fingers again, returning him to dumbness.

"Don't bother with your lies," Safar said. "I've spoken to my father. I know what's going on here. And I know you're responsible."

He leaned closer, face inches away from Kalasariz. "For your sake, I hope I've made myself clear."

Kalasariz choked on an answer rising up in his frozen throat. Another snap of the fingers and it burst out.

"Yes! Very clear!"

"I'll decide whether to continue to let you live *after* you've helped us with the demons," Safar said. "How many pieces of you remain to enjoy that life is entirely up to you."

Some of Kalasariz' craft returned to him and with it, boldness.

Still, he stumbled on his first attempt. "I can do more than rid Kyrania of the demons, Aco—I mean, my friend."

Safar seemed amused. "You almost called me acolyte, didn't you?" he said. "Odd, isn't it, how things change? The grand become small." He gestured at Kalasariz. "The small become grand." He touched his breast.

Kalasariz recovered from his mistake. He smiled that old thin smile.

"Yes, it is odd, Lord Timura," he said. "But you see how easily I can change with the events? Your new title comes flows smoothly to my lips, sir. And I must say it fits very you very well."

Safar chuckled. "You're good, Kalasariz. I have to admit that."

The spymaster moved for that gap. "Good enough, Lord Timura, to be of immense value to your king. I know the demon court well. I know King Manacia, Prince Luka and their Grand Wazier, Lord Fari. I know their weaknesses, which are legion, and other important things as well.

"King Protarus might be very angry with you if something happened to me and he missed such a great opportunity."

"Oh, it's an absolute certainty that Protarus would want to hear all these things," Safar said. "Preferably from your living lips, rather than a dry report I made after I tortured the information from you.

"But understand this, Kalasariz. The king and I are friends. Close friends. If I killed you I would go to him and confess my error. Then I'd excuse myself, saying, 'But I couldn't help it, Iraj!'"

He paused, chilling Kalasariz with his easy grin. "I call him Iraj in private, you know. And he calls me Safar. Just like when we were boys playing together."

Then he went on, "Anyway, I'd say, 'I couldn't help it, Iraj! I had this sudden hate for him. I wanted his blood to answer for his crimes against me and my family.' Then I'd hang my head in shame and wonder aloud if my mistake was so grave that it might cost us many more lives to win the war.

"And you know what he'd say? He'd say," and Safar deepened his voice to sound like Protarus, "'Well it couldn't be helped, Safar. I'd have done the same thing in your place. When blood cries, it must be answered. Come, my friend. Let us send for the women and strong drink. We'll mourn your failings like men should. We'll get drunk together and pleasure ourselves until dawn!'"

Kalasariz' stomach burned as if lava had flowed into it.

Safar laughed at his discomfort.

"You see how it is for you?" he said to Kalasariz. "You understand your position."

"Yes, Lord Timura," Kalasariz said, barely controlling the quiver in his voice. "I understand quite well."

He heard a rustle in the woods and saw several soldiers step out behind Safar. They wore the uniforms of Protarus' men.

Then he noticed the soldier leading the group was remarkably handsome.

No...beautiful! And it was a woman, not a man.

She came up to Safar. "That was magnificently done, Lord Timura," she said.

But her voice was low and the way she spoke revealed that she called him by more loving names in private.

She gave Safar such a look of adoration it crept past Kalasariz' numbness and lit his cunning.

Adoring women, he thought, can be very dangerous.

Both to the enemy of the man who'd earned that devotion.
And to the man himself.

Kalasariz raised his cup in a toast. "My friends," he said, "this night is just one more proof—no matter how small—of King Manacia's grand vision of a united Esmir."

He glanced around the open air banquet area. Rough board tables were spread across a freshly mowed lawn. Immense mounds of food were heaped on the tables, with jugs of heady Kyranian wine running down the center. Demons, scores of demons, sat before the tables, fixing him with their yellow eyes. Cups lifted expectantly, waiting for him to end his toast.

"Even here in far Kyrania," he continued, "a human sits among his demon brethren, supping and drinking. An equal among equals. A mortal—"

"Oh, finish the damned toast, Kalasariz!" the big demon sitting beside him growled. "I'm thirsty!"

"Yes, well, uh," Kalasariz faltered, "Uh—Here's to King Manacia! Long may he reign."

The demons shouted approval, downed their drinks and turned back to their tables, refilling goblets and stuffing their maws with steaming food.

Nervously, Kalasariz slopped wine in his cup and downed it in one quick gulp. Hidden under his clothing—next to his skin—was the stone idol, so warm with anticipation it was almost hot. Once in awhile he even heard—quite faintly—Gundara's excited hiss of "Shut up, shut up," to his twin. Kalasariz had been warned that any suspicious action would bring the little Favorite boiling out to punish him.

Moving through the tables were human slaves, heads low, platters high, going from demon to demon to offer more delicacies. The demons ate greedily, as if all the free food supplied by Kalasariz in this spontaneous banquet had made them more ravenous than normal.

"Would the master wish more wine?" murmured a voice at his elbow. It was Safar, dressed as a slave and bearing a jug. The other humans in the banquet area were his soldiers posing as slaves, all waiting for the signal to strike.

"Yes, please," Kalasariz said, offering his cup. It was refilled and Safar bowed humbly and stepped back.

"Why are you so polite to him?" the demon—whose name was Quan—asked. "Are you drunk?"

"No, no, I'm not drunk," Kalasariz said.

"That's your problem, then," Quan said. "You're distracted by a low level of spirited fluids. That's why you're spoiling our slaves, instead of giving them good solid blows for asking, instead of anticipating.

"Your cup was empty. He should have filled it!"

Quan turned to Safar. "Do the same to me, you little human worm," he said, "and I'll bite off your head."

"Yes, exalted one," Safar said, bobbing his head. "Thank you, exalted one."

Quan turned back to Kalasariz. "You see? That's how it's done!"

"I'll remember that, Quan," Kalasariz said. "It's good advice."

A beautiful slave girl—Leiria in disguise—moved along his table, bearing a tray of roasted kabobs. They smelled so delicious Kalasariz almost forgot the danger he was in. As she approached, hot kabob grease sputtering and splattering, his mouth filled with water.

He reached out a hand to grab a spear as she went by. Safar stepped between them, raising the jug and then leaning over, pretending to top up the wine cup.

"Don't eat the kabobs," he whispered, then withdrew.

Kalasariz suddenly found his mouth had gone dry thinking about what he'd almost done.

Beside him Quan munched with much gusto. "This is delicious, Kalasariz," he said. "You should try it!"

He waved the spear of savory meat beneath Kalasariz' nose. The delicious odor, magically enhanced, was so powerful he nearly forgot himself again. He snatched his hand back just in time.

"I wish I could," he said, making a mournful face. "It does smell wonderful. But I'm forbidden to eat lamb this month. My religion, you know."

All over the banquet area the other demons were gobbling down the kabobs, smacking their lips, wiping their chins and shouting for the slaves to bring more.

"That's the trouble with religion," Quan said with some sympathy. "Always forbidding this and forbidding that. There's so many forbiddens that a poor fiend barely knows what to do."

He stripped the rest of the meat off the spear and popped it into his maw. He chewed mightily, then swallowed, a look of pure bliss on his face.

"You know the first thing I'd do," he said, "if I were king?"

"What's that?" Kalasariz asked.

"I'd banish religion. Toss it right out. Start my own religion. And the first thing I'd do after that is turn the forbiddens on their head. All that was forbidden would become compulsory. And everything that was compulsory would go the king's committee for a good long study."

He gave Kalasariz a friendly jab with his claw.

"I'll bet I'd be damned popular," he said. "The most popular king in his—"

And Quan broke off as his eyes suddenly glazed over and he pitched forward.

Kalasariz yanked his arm away and Quan's head struck the table with much force.

The banquet area was suddenly filled with similar sounds of demon heads slamming into wood. Then there was silence.

Kalasariz looked about and saw the demon guards had noticed something was amiss and were running forward.

Leiria shouted a war cry, ripping off her robe to show the mail beneath. She drew her sword and rushed the guards. Other cries rang out as Safar's soldiers revealed themselves and leaped into the fray.

It was quick, bloody work. Before Kalasariz knew it all the demons but three were dead. And Leiria, along with half a dozen human soldiers, was pressing in to end that annoyance.

Safar dumped Quan's corpse out of the chair and slid into it. He cleaned a winecup with his sleeve and filled it up.

"I won't ask you for a toast," he said to Kalasariz. "Your friend was right." He indicated the dead demon slumped on the ground. "You're much too long winded."

And Safar drank the wine down.

# 23
# PRELUDE TO BATTLE

Safar slipped the stone idol from his pouch. He patted it, long soothing strokes like a child caressing a cat.

He leaned close, whispering, "Behave yourself, now. We're in the company of the king."

Still stroking the idol, he walked over to Iraj, who was staring up at a painting, deep in thought.

They were in Alisarrian's cave, torch light reflecting off the luminous walls. The picture Iraj was musing over was the magical painting of the Conqueror in his heroic pose.

"I still feel like a boy," Iraj murmured to Safar.

Then he turned, a wry smile on his face. "When we were here before," he said, "I was hiding from my uncle and his friend. As it turned out, neither were more than petty chieftains. But at the time what I had to overcome seemed like the greatest problem in the world."

He gestured at the heroic figure of Alisarrian, who had Iraj's golden beard, but Safar's blue eyes. "When I saw that—somehow, for reasons I can't explain—it made my dream of ruling all Esmir seem not so difficult." He shrugged. "I mean, all I had to do is defeat my uncle, then Esmir would crack like an egg. It felt that easy.

"Now I see the picture differently. I see a man whose accomplishments I truly admire. I've stood in lesser boots and fought in lesser battles. It's difficult enough to hold on to what I've won, much less win more."

"I'm sure Alisarrian had similar doubts about himself," Safar said. "Maybe even more so. He didn't have a great Conqueror to emulate, after all. You *know* it's possible because it's been done before. He didn't have that advantage."

"And the demons," Iraj said, brightening a bit. "He also had to face the demons."

"Exactly," Safar said. "Not only that, but no human king had *ever* defeated a demon army. You know that can be done as well, thanks to Alisarrian."

Iraj frowned again. "Except Alisarrian was not only a great general, but a great wizard as well. I'm only good at war. I know nothing of magic."

"You've got me," Safar said.

"Sometimes that worries me," Iraj said. "What if I didn't have you?"

"That's nonsense," Safar said. "The Fates have apparently decided to put us together. Why worry yourself over something that couldn't have happened?"

"Yes," Iraj said, eyes gleaming, "but what if you decided to leave me?"

Safar snorted. "That's ridiculous," he said. "Why would I do that? For money? You've made me rich. To be richer? Money doesn't mean anything to me anyway. What's next?

"Power? As in power over others? You know I have no such desires."

Iraj's mood lightened. The dangerous gleam in his eyes vanished. "That's true," he said. "You don't even have any *respect* for power. As I am always reminding you, my friend, when you give a kingly fellow like myself such a difficult time."

Safar grinned. "I *know* you're human," he said. "I saw the Ubekian brothers beating on you like a temple drum."

Iraj made a face. "At the time I thought, 'wait'll I get to be king. I'll chop off your tiny heads.' Now that I am king it doesn't seem so important."

Safar guffawed. "Can you imagine their faces," he howled, "if you came walking up to them right now and..." the rest was lost in laughter.

Iraj joined him and the cave rang with the sound of the amusement of two old friends. But there was an edge to it and it went on too long. It was the kind of barely controlled laughter that grips people when they are facing a fearful task.

When it stopped, it ended abruptly. The two young men avoided each other's eyes, embarrassed.

"We'd better get started," Safar said, voice a little thin.

Iraj nodded. "Yes, we'd best."

"Sit over there," Safar ordered, pointing to a place at the edge of faded pentagram inscribed on the cave floor.

Iraj did as he was told and Safar sat across from him. Within the pentagram were a host of ancient magical symbols, the ones that had once so mystified him. Some still did, but he was learning more daily from the Book of Asper.

Safar placed the turtle on one of the symbols. The stone began to glow, but very faintly.

"That's the comet," he said.

Then he slid the idol onto another symbol. The idol glowed a little brighter.

"That's the demon moon."

He moved the turtle to a point between them.

"That's us," he said. "Approximately, that is. The real heavenly bodies are moving together right now. In fact, we should see the demon moon very soon."

Iraj shook his head in admiration. "That's something, Safar," he said, sounding like a boy watching a circus performance. "*Really* something."

Safar kept his features immobile. He couldn't help but play the stony-faced master performer. Besides, he'd noticed it didn't hurt to keep Iraj's awe of his magical abilities stoked to the fullest.

"When I cast the spell," he said, "you must sit absolutely still. Do or say nothing. You'll see me here beside you. But I won't be in my body."

He gestured toward the cave mouth. "My spirit will be out there someplace." He pointed at the stone idol. "Keep your eyes on that," he said, "and you'll see everything my spirit sees."

Iraj squirmed. "Remarkable," he breathed.

"Are you ready?" Safar asked.

Iraj licked his lips and nodded. Safar tossed a handful of glass pellets on the floor. Iraj gasped. Curling up were columns of thick smoke, all of a different color, all filled with glittering bits that floated up and down the columns.

This wasn't something that was really necessary, but Safar had learned from Methydia to put on a good show.

He drew in his breath. Deeper and deeper, drawing as if his lungs were a giant's. The columns of smoke, coiling around each other like ribbons, wreathed into his mouth, following the inrushing air.

Then he exhaled. It made a sound like a hard wind whistling through a narrow opening. The ribbon smoke, now tightly coiled into a hazy rope, shot out, bursting over the stone idol like a waterfall.

Safar's vision hazed and he saw things as if in a dream. He saw Iraj look startled, mouth gaping open. He saw Gundara, the object of the king's amazement, leap out of the stone and crouch there, chittering. He heard Gundara squeak one, "Shut up!" Then gleap and snap his jaws shut when he saw Iraj.

Suddenly wings burst from the little Favorite's back—large gossamer wings, pearly like the snow butterflies that come in early spring. Gundara reached out a claw. It stretched, then stretched more, reaching beyond belief—longer and longer, closing the distance between Favorite and master.

Safar raised his own hand. A spectral image of that hand emerged from his body.

His spirit self gripped Gundara's claw.

Then he was flying, flying through mountain stone, then erupting out of the mountain itself and taking to the air. He had no sense of Gundara's presence. It was as if Safar were doing the flying, soaring with the wind, moving his arms to correct his flight.

He flew north, over the topmost peaks of the Bride and Six Maids. Far below he saw a boy leading a flock of goats to pasture. He cleared the last peak, so close he was tempted to see if his spectral hand could disturb the snow.

He soared down the mountain slopes, caught a warm wind, then sailed out over the great northern desert.

Above him thick clouds skated under a blue sky. Below, the white desert sands glittered in the sunlight. Beyond, a limitless horizon.

Safar shifted his arms and flew up to the clouds. He caught a wind and skimmed beneath them, heading for the thin blue line marking the spot where sky and earth met.

He flew on for a time until he came to a place where two enormous rocks speared out of the stony ground. They were sheer on all sides and each seemed to be formed from a single piece a hundred feet high. They were so large they seemed close together, but when Safar came upon them he could see they were a less than half a mile apart.

He flew on toward the still empty horizon.

When he first saw the army he didn't know what he was looking at. It emerged as a long dirty line rising from the horizon's rim. Beneath the line he saw a streak of solid black. The closer he went the broader that streak became, but fading grayer, like charcoal on a sketch. Slowly the streak separated into figures. And then the figures became soldiers.

Demon soldiers.

Safar shot over them, spectral heart fluttering against spectral ribs.

The whole desert plain swarmed with demons, a colossal colony of monstrous ants streaming south toward the Gods' Divide. They flowed beneath him, wide columns of demon soldiers, led by thick spears of mounted cavalry. Hundreds of great baggage trains followed in their wake, winged by immense herds of animals to supply fresh food and mounts.

It took a frighteningly long time to come to the end of the demon army. When he did, he swung around and flew toward the front—looking for the heart of this great creature.

He found Manacia and his court just behind the main cavalry units. The demon king lolled in a rolling howdah perched on a glorious white elephant. Safar recognized the elephant immediately. It was the same one he'd seen Iraj ride in that long ago vision.

Steeling himself, he flew nearer. Manacia's huge head and massive jaws were just becoming clear when Safar felt the sting of magic. It was like running naked through a swarm of bees.

Safar shot upward, rising as fast as he could, then the stinging sensation was gone and he knew he was beyond Manacia's reach. When he'd recovered he realized it was some kind of shield, or warning net, or both. Safar tested for danger and was relieved when he became certain Manacia hadn't noticed his presence.

Then, gathering his nerve, he flew around the shield, testing its width and breadth. Soon not the only size became apparent, but also that he was safe as long he kept to the edges.

From far off he heard someone call his name. "Safar...Safar..."

A hole opened up and he fell into it, plunging down and down, through smoke and heat and then boom! he was back in the cave, crouched on his knees and spewing his guts onto the floor.

When he was done Iraj wet the edge of his cloak and gave it to him to wipe his face, then he handed him a cup brimming with strong brandy. Safar drank it down like water. One more and his nerves steadied.

"I thought I told you to keep silent," he said. "You could have killed me."

Iraj looked surprised, then sorrowful. "I'm sorry," he said. "I thought it was seeing all those demons that made you sick. I was almost ill myself."

"Sure, it scared the Hells out of me," Safar said. "But it was being snatched back so quickly that made me sick! I know you're my lord and master and all, but have a pity, Iraj! Go easy, next time."

While Iraj hung his head and muttered apologies, Safar braced himself with another cup of false courage. Then he picked up the stone idol, whispered a promise of rewards to come for good little Favorites and returned it to his pouch.

"When I saw Manacia's army," Iraj said, "I thought, this is hopeless! Unstoppable! I might as well go dig myself a deep hole and pull the dirt in after me."

"I had similar thoughts," Safar said, "but I couldn't see how I could dig a hole deep enough."

"In the entire history of Esmir," Iraj said, "there is no precedent for what we're facing. No army that size has ever been fielded. And if we closed with him, there's no comparison to any battle ever fought."

"Let's not close with him," Safar said. "That's my strong advice to you."

"Actually," Iraj said, "that's advice I'll immediately reject. The only way we can win is to meet him head-to-head on the field of battle."

"Come, Iraj!" Safar objected. "Put a little more brandy in your blood. And quickly. Senses must be regained."

"I'm not joking," Iraj answered.

"I know you're not," Safar said. "That's why *I* am! Otherwise I'd be frightened to death. You wouldn't say such a thing if you didn't mean it.

"Sometimes I wonder about your sanity, my friend, but never your ability."

"After I was done quaking," Iraj said, "it came to me that if an army that size had never been fielded before, it was also true no army that size has ever been *commanded* before."

Safar nodded. "I see what you mean. Manacia would be have to be not only the greatest general ever, but so far above all the others he'd be a giant among generals."

"He's able enough," Iraj said. "I'll give him that. I've gathered some very reliable intelligence on his battles. He's no fool. And he has that son of his, Luka, leading every attack. There's no fear in them—at least that they show—which is fairly impressive in itself.

"Luka's demons attack so fiercely, so professionally, it takes the heart right out of the enemy. Several times Manacia hasn't had to do much more than mop up."

"Then you have to eliminate Luka," Safar said.

"Perhaps," Iraj said. "I don't know. I'm thinking about the big army, right now. That's what I have to beat."

"Assuming we survive Luka," Safar said.

"I'm not saying it'll be easy with Luka," Iraj said. "But I have to jump past that. Return to it later. Otherwise I can't think of a way to solve the big problem."

"Do you have any ideas?" Safar asked.

"A few," Iraj said. "But very vague. Number one, I have to use his size against him. Number two, I have to make him smaller."

"Don't forget," Safar said, "it won't be just demon soldiers we'll encounter, but demon magic as well."

Iraj's contemplative look turned to concern. "What of it?" he asked. "What did you see...if that's the word for a wizard looking at another wizard."

"Close enough," Safar said. "As close as your problem as a general is to my problem as your Grand Wazier.

"Manacia is very strong. Stronger than me, perhaps. I can't say because I have no experience in such things. I've never fought a battle. Hells, I had more two-fisted fights as a boy than I've ever had magic against magic."

"I was there for your first sorcerous fight," Iraj reminded him. "And it so happens it was against demons."

Safar started to protest, but Iraj waved him down. "Don't tell me you were lucky," he said. "Of course, you were. I'm lucky. Not just good, but lucky. So are you. And lucky wins."

"I won't argue," Safar said. "We'll find out if you're right soon enough."

"But you do have some ideas about Manacia?" Iraj asked.

"Only one just now," Safar said. "And that's this—Manacia may be the wizard of all wizards, but he's no magician."

Iraj looked at him, puzzled. "What are you talking about?"

"Something I learned in the circus," Safar said. "Smoke and mirrors.

"The art of the Grand Illusion."

While the demon army marched, the humans prepared to meet them.

Manacia's progress was slow. The sheer size of his forces, as Iraj had predicted, made him unwieldy and kept the pace to that of a desert tortoise. He also had to maintain huge supply lines stretching all the way to Caspan.

The humans used that time well. Gear was repaired, horses shod, weapons honed. New training instituted in which speed and quick thinking were emphasized. Iraj wanted no brave death charges. Against Manacia's might, he couldn't afford the losses. Loads were lightened; they'd take only what they needed into the desert. Supplies would also be the minimum required to reach Manacia.

If they lost there'd be no return. If they won they could take what they wanted from Manacia.

As they prepared, Iraj's musings became full blown ideas. He introduced new tactics and had special equipment made.

Safar was similarly occupied. He had only a few wizards, but although their powers were weak they had battle experience. They told him what he could expect and he prepared remedies.

Safar made everything as simple as possible. He created small amulets and used some of the tricks he'd learned from the Book of Asper to make them very strong. The wizards mass produced these amulets and passed them out to the men.

He dispensed with the need for large quantities of magical supplies—instead he commandeered several heavy chariots, drawn by triple teams. In each he put several kegs of certain oils and powders he'd mixed—another idea he'd borrowed from Asper.

The most important thing Safar did, however, was meet with his father.

It was like old times in his father's shop, the kiln glowing merrily, his sister, Quetera, at the wheel, his mother mixing glaze.

Apparently Myrna thought the same thing, for she said, "This is like the old caravan season days, Khadji. I used to love those times. All of us together making pots and plates as fast we could to sell to the caravan masters."

Quetera groaned. "The last time we did that," she said, "I was pregnant." She held her hands out from her sides. "I was *this* big. I could barely get close to the spoke, and when I did it reminded me of that devil husband of mine who'd put me in that condition."

"As if you had no part in it," Myrna sniffed.

Quetera laughed. "Oh, I got my pleasure, true enough," she said. "But so did he. At the time it didn't seem fair I had to do the rest by myself. It still doesn't."

Leiria, who stayed close to Safar even when he visited his family, stirred in the corner.

"I'm glad I chose my path instead of yours, Quetera," she said. "Fighting always seemed like it was less painful than birthing."

"It is," Quetera said. "But it got me Dmitri."

She smiled at the little boy in the corner, making a messy business with his child's potting wheel.

"I was happy in the end."

Quetera suddenly laughed and covered her mouth. "What am I saying? My *end* was definitely not happy."

Everyone laughed, even Khadji who was embarrassed by discussions of that nature. But since it was Quetera who said it, and he loved her humorous nature, he allowed himself enjoyment.

Over in the corner little Dmitri had tired of the clay and was playing in his washing up bucket. He put a straw in the soapy water then held it up and puffed.

A bubble formed on the end of the straw. Delighted, Dmitri puffed more. The bubble became huge, then broke off and floated across the room.

"Look mother," he cried. "A balloon! I made a balloon!"

They all turned to look. The bubble, kiln light wobbling on its surface, sailed slowly into the other corner. It hovered over the glass-making equipment, then burst.

Everyone made automatic noises of sympathy.

"Don't worry, everybody," Dmitri crowed. "I can make more. Lots more!"

He happily dipped his straw in the bucket and started blowing streams of bubbles.

Safar's smile died. He turned to his father.

"I want you make something for me, father," he said.

Khadji frowned, wondering what was in his son's mind.

Safar pulled over some sheets of sketching paper and drew. "Make it like this," he said as he drew. "But make it thin. As light as you can. Don't worry about it being too fragile."

Khadji held up the sketch. "I'll do it, son," he said, "but whatever on Esmir for? What do you want with one of these?"

"Not one, father," Safar said. "It'll take a least a score."

"You're returning me to Manacia?" Kalasariz quavered. "But whatever for? What have I done, Your Majesty, to deserve such a fate?"

Kalasariz was standing before Protarus and Safar. He was blindfolded. He'd been blindfolded and kept out of the sight of the military preparations, since Iraj's arrival in Kyrania.

"Don't remind us about what you may or may not deserve," Safar said. "We probably have strong differences on that small matter."

"Don't worry, my friend," Iraj said. "Manacia won't kill you. We'll make it look good. You can claim you escaped. You have an agile mind. And I'm sure you can make it a very brave escape. What really happened will be our little secret.

"Make of it what you will. Gamble that I'll lose and join them.

Gamble that I'll win and keep your faith with me. You can do either, or both at the same time. Just choose well. Act well. And if you see me again in person you'll know what to expect."

"I have every faith in your eventual victory, Majesty," Kalasariz said. "I'll do anything you instruct me to."

"I have only one instruction," Iraj said. "I want you to deliver a message. And this is what I want you to say..."

The Demon Moon was rising when Kalasariz put spurs to horse and thundered across the desert.

It hovered just above the night plain, red as new death. The landscape had an orange tint to it and was pocked with inky shadows. Kalasariz steered his horse around the shadows, praying to the gods he was correct each time he changed course, digging in his heels to make the horse run faster still.

Low as it was, the Demon Moon captured the whole northern sky, wiping out any sign of the star houses that reigned there. Just above the Demon Moon was a comet so bright it was the only other light that bleared through.

It's the Sign of Alisarrian, Kalasariz thought.

Manacia claimed it was meant for him. Protarus believed the same. Kalasariz had no idea which way to jump.

In his madness he cursed the gods for not allowing him spies on the court of the Demon Moon.

Luka stared at Kalasariz in amazement.

"This is insane," the demon prince said. "How dare you approach me in such secrecy? If my father hears about it he'll have us killed!"

"If you'll forgive me for pointing this out, Highness," Fari said, "I think this human expected us to understand that...and therefore say nothing."

He looked at Kalasariz, yellow eyes glowing. His tones, however, were mild when he said, "Either by foolish design, or cleverness, it seems you have made us *all* conspirators."

Kalasariz kept his features blank. This was no time for arrogance to creep through. "I'm hoping it was by clever design, Exalted One," he said. "Clever for all of us, that is."

The Crown Prince was *not* mollified. "What angers me most," he said, "is for some reason this Protarus, this upstart king, believes I am such a traitorous son that I'd not immediately speak out."

"And me as well, Highness," Fari murmured. "I'm here beside you."

Again he glared at Kalasariz. But again his tones were mild. "I suppose you told him about the habits of our court," he said. "Filled him in on our personalities."

"I said as little as I could...under the circumstances," Kalasariz replied.

Fari's talon shot out. A burning light speared into Kalasariz who shrieked in pain.

"You really should learn to scream with less vigor," Fari said, letting the talon drop. "Someone might hear us and the conspiracy would be exposed."

"I told them everything," Kalasariz gritted. "Anything they asked."

Fari turned to Luka. "I think from here on he'll be more careful with the truth, Highness," he said.

Luka nodded. He'd become calm. More measuring. "I suppose Protarus knows that you and I are not the fondest of friends," he said to Fari.

"I expect so, Highness," Fari answered.

Luka looked at Kalasariz. "Why does Protarus believe we'd choose each other to help hatch a plot?" he asked.

"I don't know, Your Highness," Kalasariz said. "He simply gave me the message and ordered me to deliver it. In private."

"And that message is?"

Kalasariz took a deep breath, then plunged into it. "King Protarus sends his greetings, warm wishes for your health and said he hopes all will go well with you in the coming battle."

"He *does* intend to fight, then," Fari said.

"Never doubt that, Exalted One," Kalasariz said. "Protarus *will* fight."

"But the odds against him are impossible," Luka said.

"King Protarus guessed you would say that, Your Highness," Kalasariz said. "And he told me in reply that it was not unknown for the impossible to become possible during the Demon Moon."

Fari chuckled. "A lovely myth," he said. "I've heard it before, although it is very old."

"When the battle comes, Your Highness," Kalasariz continued, "he asked that you watch carefully. And if something should happen which gives you pause, to think on his offer.

"If you give him Manacia, he will give you his throne. He said he believed you would be an able administrator of the demonlands—under his direction, of course."

"I think we should just kill this worm," Luka said to Fari. "Kill him quick. And go about our business as if nothing happened."

"Don't be so hasty, Highness," Fari advised. "You will note the message is addressed to both of us. He requires agreement from two traitors, it seems, or his plan won't work. Curious, isn't it, that he also believes we both hate your father more than we dislike one another."

There was an uncomfortable silence.

"That's it?" Luka said to Kalasariz. "He only asks that we watch, and if the course of the battle goes badly—from our point of view—that we consider changing our alliance?"

"Yes, Highness," Kalasariz said.

Another long silence. Broken by a dry chuckle from Luka.

"Ridiculous," he laughed.

Fari also laughed. "Ridiculous in the extreme."

"One other thing, O Great Ones," Kalasariz said. "Safar Timura—his Grand Wazier— commanded me to give you this."

He handed Lord Fari a scroll. The old demon unrolled it and examined the contents. After a time he lifted his head, troubled.

"It's a formula for a spell, Highness," he said to Luka. "A formula that breaks the curse of the Forbidden Desert."

"Meaning the humans can cross as easily as we can," Luka said. "What of it?"

"It pains me to admit this, Highness," Fari said, "but I've never seen a spell so grand—a spell we worked years to perfect—done so simply. It's really quite elegant. And it has the feel of something that came through inspiration, rather than from years of tedious experiment."

"Quick or labored," Luka said. "Why should it matter?"

"Oh, it probably doesn't matter at all, Highness," Fari said.

"Although I'd be derelict in my duties if I didn't point out that only a master wizard could have done such a thing. A master wizard as great, or greater than your father."

Luka peered into the old demon's eyes. Then he turned away. There was another long and uncomfortable pause.

"We probably shouldn't bother the king with this," Luka said at last.

"I absolutely agree, Highness," Fari replied with barely disguised relief. "There's no need to burden him with such foolishness."

"What about me?" Kalasariz blurted, not certain which way things were going.

"Oh, I'd suggest you watch the battle," Fari said. He turned to Luka, "Isn't that right, Highness?"

"Yes, yes, that's what I'd do," the demon prince said. "Watch the battle. And see."

## 24

## BATTLE AND FLIGHT

King Protarus quick marched his army to the place of the Two Stones.

His scouts told him King Manacia's main force was two days away. Protarus had perhaps fifty thousand fighting men, nearly all mounted. With these he would oppose about three hundred thousand demons, some mounted, most afoot.

On the surface these odds seemed insurmountable. Protarus' generals told him so in daily meetings. They pointed out he had another seventy-five thousand men spread over his realm, keeping the peace. To this he could add two hundred thousand men who had recently volunteered to fight the hated demon enemy. If Protarus waited a month that number would easily reach five hundred thousand. So many hot-blooded young men were pouring in, begging to fight, Protarus' recruiters were nearly overwhelmed.

"I mean to fight now," Protarus told them. "Not a month from now. A month is too late. A month is certain defeat.

"And we don't have two days to prepare for Manacia, but a day and a half. I want him here faster. I want him here in time to settle into a comfortable camp. He'll want to feed his men, rest them and then surprise us with a dawn attack."

"How can get we get him here more quickly, Your Majesty?" one his aides asked. "We can't command Manacia to speed up."

"True, but we can entice him," Safar said.

Then king and grand wazier explained how this thing could be done.

•

The desert heat formed twin devils that attacked Manacia from above and below. The appalling discomfort made him angry and his slaves kept well out of kicking range. Manacia thought the gods were being unreasonable to the extreme. They'd determined his fate, hadn't they? They'd decreed he would be King of Kings. If this were the case—and Manacia had no reason to doubt it—it seemed unfair and undignified to make him suffer so.

Angry as Manacia was at the gods, his wrath knew no end when he considered the pretender, Iraj Protarus. Manacia had heard reports that Protarus shared his ambitions to rule Esmir. How dare he? Why, he was nothing more than a dirty plains savage.

Manacia's belly lurched uncomfortably with each roll of the elephant. The smells around him—beast smells, unwashed demon smells—were so thick it was difficult to breath without gagging. The sounds were so chaotic it was impossible to think—groaning life on the hard march, shrieking wheels in the heat, distant cries of demon kits and the babble of their complaining mothers.

And Manacia thought, Children? How did we end up carrying children with us?

He twisted around and although he couldn't see them, he knew there were thousands upon thousands of demon harlots straggling behind his army. He snorted, disgusted. Apparently he'd been in the field long enough for the harlots to breed.

Looking back, Manacia could see the Demon Moon, red glow smearing the northern horizon. Hovering above it was the light-spear of the comet. When the Demon Moon and comet had first appeared, the king had taken heart. He claimed it as his sign, the Sign of Manacia. A demon king for the Demon Moon.

But in the weariness of the long march to meet Protarus, King Manacia had begun to curse that moon. It was always present, day or night. He felt haunted by it, as if it were a heavenly force driving him on to who knows where?

Manacia felt a stony clatter against his magical shield. He jolted around to face the south—his enemy's lair.

His big demon head came up, yellow eyes drilling the far horizon.

The first thing Luka saw were his scouts racing back to his lines.

Next he spotted watery figures charging across the desert after the scouts. The figures firmed and became mailed horsemen—humans!

His first thought was, It's so hot! How can they keep up such a pace?

His second thought was, By the gods, he's coming! Protarus is coming!

Trumpets sounded the alarm all around him. Action only needed his signal.

He gave it.

His demon brothers howled their war cries and charged, carrying him along at their head.

Fari saw the twister snaking towards him. It was six feet high, which became twelve, and then double that and then it became a towering, screeching force of nature.

All about him he could hear the fearful cries of his colleagues as they leaped from their wagons to abandon Manacia's wizard caravan.

Fari ached to run with them, but he was too old to run and had to use his wits.

The twister struck the first wagons, lifting them up and hurling them in all directions. Fari calmed himself enough to see a human face staring out of that twister. It was many faces, actually, but the same face—a blur of sameness whirling with the twister. It was beardless, hawked nosed and Fari could swear he could see blue skies through eyeholes in the dust-and-debris-choked tornado.

And now it was coming for him, roaring his name, "Fa-ri! Fa-ri!"

Safar saw the old demon wizard and knew who he was. He called his name again, "Fa-ri! Fa-ri!"

He pointed his finger and Gundara hopped over to the twister and "pushed" it toward the demon wizard.

Tornado and demon were among many miniature ghostly figures spread out on the campaign table in Iraj's headquarters tent. At Safar's command, Gundara moved among them, towering over the living map like a giant.

Safar concentrated, barely noticing Iraj's presence next to him, much less the generals and aides crowding close to the table. His gaze swept over the field, taking note of the key figures.

Not far above the destroyed wizard caravan was Manacia, clinging to the howdah as his elephant mount stamped its feet and trumpeted in panic. Demon soldiers rushed all around him, adding to the confusion.

Some distance from Manacia he could see the diminutive figures of Prince Luka and his cavalry of monsters charging across the desert.

Safar turned his attention back to Fari and the twister. He nodded at Gundara, who gave the whirlwind another "push" and it leaped forward to close the distance.

Fari saw the trick just in time.

He felt the twister suck at him, saw the whirling faces, heard them shouting, "Fa-ri," and looked down the whirlwind's column until he saw its tail. It was a small, leaping serpent, no bigger than a demon kit's wrist.

Fari saw in an instant this was where its power resided. He marveled at how such a large force could come from so little energy. Then he made a slicing motion with his talon, cutting it in two.

The twister shattered, showering rocks and bits of debris everywhere. Fari suffered only a small cut on his left claw. But he was badly shaken.

He looked at the chaos raging around him and heaved a long sigh of relief.

Luka took his fear and made it his courage. His battle cry was drowned out by his brother warriors, but it took life from them at same time, wailing out in a long single ululation that resounded across the desert.

They were almost on the human cavalry, which was charging toward them unfazed by the sight and sound of so many demon killers.

Luka saw a tall horseman with a blonde beard and long golden locks flowing from under his helmet. Riding beside him was a dark-featured man, just as tall but beardless. Despite the blur of the charge Luka could see the man's burning blue eyes.

Those eyes were looking at him now.

The bearded man turned his head and caught sight of Luka.

Both humans changed course and charged toward the demon prince.

Luka waved his sword wildly and braced for the shock.

But no clash came.

Instead, he found himself shouting and slashing and jabbing at…nothingness. He whirled his beast about and saw his warriors fighting empty air.

The humans had vanished.

Luka blinked. But as it was fully sinking in that he'd faced and fought only his imagination, he saw a human—a real human, not a ghost—leap up from the sand.

The man cried out when he saw the prince. Luka heard similar cries all around. Then the human lifted up a long tube. Luka noted with dazed interest that the tube had probably allowed the man to breathe while he lay in wait buried in the said.

Then he saw the men load the tube with a dart, lift it to his lips…and blow.

The dart took Luka's mount in the eye. The beast howled in pain, then collapsed under him. Luka rolled off, taking shelter behind his mount's body. It had died so quickly that he knew the dart was poisoned.

He lifted his head and was amazed to see his human attacker

running away. He jumped up to follow, but had taken no more than a few steps when he stumbled over a mailed body. It was the corpse of one of his brother warriors.

Luka came to his feet. The ground was littered by many other demon corpses.

Then he came out of his shock and realized most were still mounted and uninjured. They were only confused, milling about wondering where their enemy had gone.

Luka saw the fleeing humans racing south toward a group of low dunes. They'd thrown down their dart tubes in their haste to escape an overwhelming demon force. From the dunes he saw a long line of horsemen dash out, each leading another animal.

The prince shouted for his fiends. He did not mean to let the humans escape.

Someone brought him a mount and Luka bounded into the saddle and led his warriors on yet another charge. But this time he had the enemy's back to him.

Snarling as wildly as his clawed-mount, Luka closed on the humans. He was so close he could hear their laboring breath.

He dropped his sword point low to take the first man in front of him.

"Now, Master?" Gundara asked.

"Yes, now!" Safar answered.

The little Favorite stomped on the table.

There was a deafening explosion and Luka's mount reared, shrieking in fear, claws pawing the air.

A cloud black as night and stinking of sulfur burst up between him and the fleeing humans.

Monstrous forms, all frighteningly ugly, all human, swirled out of the cloud, gnashing and grinding their flat teeth.

Luka heard his warriors howl in terror and knew they were experiencing the same thing. He tried to call out to them not to panic, to keep going until they reached the other side of the smoke curtain. But no one could make out his commands from the cries of hysteria.

Then it came to him that he was alone.

All his warriors had retreated and he was alone in the sulfurous darkness, filled with nightmare forms.

Luka wheeled his mount and retreated as calmly as he could.

When he'd cleared the smoky curtain he saw his father bearing down on him on his big white elephant.

"Why did you stop?" his father shouted. "Why didn't you go on?"

There was a thinly failed accusation of cowardice in his father's questions and Luka hated him for it.

"The humans caught us by surprise, Majesty," he said. "It seemed best to regroup. Besides, it was only a small force, and most of that was illusion."

Manacia jabbed a talon at the ebbing curtain of smoke. "Are you telling me Protarus isn't waiting out there?"

"I don't believe so, Majesty," Luka answered. "I think he waits where our scouts say he waits. Near the place of the Two Rocks. This was only a diversion. He was testing us."

"Well, you're a fool to think that!" Manacia snarled. "He's out there, all right. I can feel it." He rapped his golden mail. "In here I can feel it." He tapped his demon nose. "And I can smell him. I can smell the human wizard, too."

Lord Fari had come up in time to hear the last. "Are you certain, Your Majesty?" he asked. "I too sense a presence out there. But perhaps it is only another illusion."

Manacia snorted. "Bah! I'm surrounded by fools and cowards."

He shouted for an aide. "Sound the attack," he commanded.

A moment later the air was filled with the cacophony of trumpets and drums and booted feet and clanking mail as Manacia's vast army poured across the empty plain, seeking humans to kill.

To support them, Manacia gathered his best wizards together, including Fari, and they made a mighty spell.

Boiling clouds filled the skies. Lighting cracked Thunder rolled. Horrible beasts, dragons and winged lions, raged across the heavens.

Manacia worked himself to exhaustion, forming and casting war spell after war spell.

Several hours passed and the first scouts returned from the main force to report there were no signs of even a small band of humans to be found, much less a whole army.

By now Manacia had collapsed on his traveling bed, surrounded by his wizards. He'd just heard Fari report that the huge magical hammer they'd created had been for naught.

After Fari heard what the scouts had to say, he dared to approach his king. "I think it is clear, Your Majesty," he said, "that all our efforts are being wasted. There's no one out there."

"So I'm the fool, am I?" Manacia raged.

"Not at all, Majesty," Luka broke in. "Lord Fari meant nothing of the kind."

The old demon was surprised to see this unprecedented show of support from the Crown Prince.

"It is Protarus who is the fool, Majesty," Luka said. "How dare he toy with you? And such empty gestures. A few were hurt, even killed. But it's like a flea bite on a camel's ass. Nothing more."

Manacia was roused from his weariness. He slammed one taloned fist into the other. "I'll teach him to trifle with me," he said.

Again, the demon king shouted for his aides. "We march for the Two Rocks at dawn," he commanded. "We've seen Timura's magic. And it's nothing. Now let's see if Protarus can fight!"

Safar waved and the battlefield vanished. Gundara hopped onto his shoulder and quietly accepted his sugary reward. Safar turned to Iraj.

"Manacia should be good and angry now," he said.

"Good," Iraj said. He gave a hard jerk of his head. "Now, he'll get here quicker."

The night before the battle Safar and Leiria made love for the first time in a long time.

In the beginning Leiria was fierce, but later she wept.

Safar held her, letting her weep. Suddenly she raised her head, tears streaming down her cheeks.

"I would never betray you, Safar," she said, hoarse. "*Never*!"

Safar was surprised at this announcement. He wondered what could be its cause.

But all he did was hold her closer.

And all he said, was, "Of course not." Murmuring it over and over again. "Of course not."

Until she fell asleep.

***

On the second day—just as the sun reached its highest point—Manacia's scouts came to the place of the Two Stones. There they found Protarus waiting.

His forces were arranged strangely. The main group was focused in the center—but pulled well back from the rock columns as if they offered some sort of shield, rather than just two incredibly tall pillars springing out of an otherwise empty wasteland.

Out to the side were cavalry wings, all bristling with the small bows of the plains warriors. Behind them were ranks of slingmen, all on foot. The slingmen were thinly guarded by small cavalry detachments and a few well-armed foot-soldiers—muscular men with short heavy spears in each hand and axes in their belts.

The scouts roamed the edges, letting their witch sniffers loose to find the magical center. The creatures looked like squat dogs with hyena faces. They dashed about, scratching at the ground and sniffing the air.

In the end they returned to their demon masters, tails between their spavined legs to show failure.

Safar watched the scouts ride off—heading north toward the Demon Moon where Manacia's forces were slowly moving forward.

He was perched on the crown of the westernmost rock column and had an excellent view. With him were Leiria, and four wizard helpers. There was a similar number posted on the opposite column, commanded by Horvan, his most able mage.

The spells he'd cast to shield the rock columns from the witch sniffers had been child's play. What had not been child's play was getting on top of those rocks. The task had been so difficult—the rocks so sheer—Safar's plan had nearly been wrecked before he started.

Iraj's soldiers were all men of the plains. Mountains were unknown to them. The highest any had ever climbed was to the backs of their horses.

Safar had watched in awful suspense as the team Iraj had selected attacked the first rock column and failed time and again. They would get no higher than ten feet—fifteen at the most—

then come off the smooth rock all flailing arms and shrill cries, like clumsy chicks falling from their nest.

The only fortunate thing was no one got hurt, beyond skinned fingers, knees and pride.

Finally, there was nothing to be done but have Safar attempt it himself. Everyone protested, Iraj the loudest.

"I'll not have my Grand Wazier killed before the battle even starts," he said.

"I'm a child of the mountains," Safar pointed out. "And the only one with climbing experience. Besides, I'm eventually going to have make the climb anyway. The team was just supposed to set up ropes so they could hoist me and my mages into place."

He shrugged. "It seems silly to risk all our plans over something so easily solved."

Finally, Iraj assented and Safar found himself next to the western column, peering up at the crown. He made a few cautious experimental attempts, fingers and bare toes skittering on the smooth rock, searching for hairline cracks just deep enough to give purchase.

The whole army was watching—an army that feared heights—and each time he fumbled and slid gently to the ground they gasped in unison as if he were plummeting to his death.

It reminded Safar of the nail-biting crowds at Methydia's Circus when great acrobatic feats were being performed. The thought brought back the skills he'd learned from Arlain and Kairo, and so on his first true attempt he scampered up thirty feet without pause.

The fifty-thousand man army cheered and applauded like the greatest audience ever gathered under one tent. Safar became carried away with the moment. Although he had good purchase, he pretended otherwise and made as if he'd lost his grip and was falling.

The army moaned in horror. It was an awful sound, a frightening sound. Nothing like a circus audience, which know deep in their hearts the performer will ultimately prevail.

It came to Safar the warriors were putting all their hopes in him. Yes, they knew Protarus was a great king and a mighty general who had carried them through the worst circumstances. Iraj was not a monarch who believed in wasting his soldiers' lives. But they feared the demons, especially demon magic and they were looking to Lord Timura, the Grand Wazier, wizard above all wizards, to save them. Hadn't King Protarus himself attested to Lord Timura's abilities? And hadn't they already seen his early successes with the demons who'd held Kyrania, and in the shadow fight with Manacia?

To them, if Safar fell to his death it might very well portend their own. Safar took pity and ended his antics.

But he was showman enough to free a hand so he could wave while he nodded his head to show it was all in good fun.

A huge explosion of nervous laughter carried him the next ten feet.

He resumed the climb, but cautiously, soberly. It turned out to be much more difficult that way. Without the crowd-stirred energy of a performer to aid him he quickly became tired, his fingers and toes numb and a few times he really almost did lose his grip and come off the wall. When it happened he was at a height that would have crippled him, or spelled his doom.

He was exhausted when he finally reached the top. Although the cheers were thunderous, he felt nothing when he sent down the ropes to let the others up.

All he could think of was the other stone column. There was no getting around the fact it too had to be climbed—and by him and him alone.

The only true blessing the Old Gods granted living things, and this grudgingly, was that all ordeals, all pain, must eventually end—one way or the other. It was Safar's good fortune his ended well. And now he was perched on the first column he'd climbed, a little tired, but certainly ready for Manacia.

After awhile he saw the dust ridge rise up under the Demon Moon and knew the enemy was approaching. He flashed a palm mirror to signal Iraj. Orders were shouted from below, trumpets blared, and there was a shifting sea of warriors coming to life and moving into position.

The dust ridge grew larger by the hour, soon walling the entire horizon. Still it approached, until there came a point when Safar could almost make out the dark outlines of mounted demons.

Then all forward motion halted and the ridge became a huge dusty boil. It was like an old, weary dog who'd found a suitable place to rest and was turning round and round, to finally settle nose to tail.

Safar signaled again—Manacia was making camp.

The demon king scoffed at the battle map. It was clear to him what Protarus meant to do.

"He wants to use the stone columns to make us come to his center," he said to Luka. "That's where his main force is gathered."

He gestured at the wooden markers to the left and right of the main forces. "And he'll try to use his cavalry to pinch us in from the sides to make certain we stay on the course he prefers."

Manacia slammed his taloned fist onto the table, toppling the markers.

"Well, I don't intend to meekly follow this king's commands," he said. "I've fought this battle before. Hells, I've fought it four or five times at least."

He tapped his horned head. "It's all here," he said to his son. "A game of minds. I almost feel sorry for Protarus. It's clear he doesn't know who or what he is up against."

Fari cleared his throat for attention. "What of the wizard, Timura?" he asked. "He'll most certainly figure into Protarus' plans."

Manacia scowled. "It's true we haven't located him," he said. "Or any source of human magic for that matter. I suppose he's shielded himself. It's not an easy thing to do, so I mustn't underestimate him. Still, I've got similar shields in place, protecting a much larger wizardly force.

"We'll wait until he strikes and reveals himself. He won't stand a chance when we reply."

Luka and Fari exchanged quick looks. Each could tell the other was impressed with Manacia's reading of the situation.

The Crown Prince bitterly accepted his father's military expertise. He had no doubt when the battle commenced Manacia would prevail.

"We'll attack at dawn," Manacia said. "Just as the humans are stirring at the camp fires."

He gestured at the Demon Moon hanging over the northern horizon. "We'll have that at our backs to confound them," he said.

Manacia slapped his thigh in delight. "There's nothing I enjoy more than attacking an enemy with the light in his eyes."

Iraj surveyed his assembled troops. He let a broad grin play through his beard. "Here we are again, lads," he said. "Up to our callused behinds in hyenas and no way out!"

His voice, magically amplified by an amulet Safar had given him, rang with manly good cheer. The warriors roared laughter at their king's humor.

Iraj pointed a dramatic finger through the stone pillars, which perfectly framed the Demon Moon.

"Once again," he said, "we're facing a fellow who doesn't think we're fit to empty his piss pot."

The warriors rumbled their disapproval.

"But we've taught royal prigs like that a thing or two in the past, haven't we lads?"

The warriors shouted agreement.

Iraj waved them to silence. "It so happens that this time the prig we're facing is a demon."

There were low mutters, manly mutters, but forced.

Iraj thumped his chest. "I've fought demons before, lads," he said. "I fought them as a boy. And it was the demons who fell, not your king, boy though he was.

"You've never heard this story. It's a secret Lord Timura and I have kept for many years. But now I think it's time for all Esmir to know."

Iraj commenced to deliver an abbreviated, but highly dramatic account of the event.

"So you see, my lads," Iraj said when he was done, "demons bleed the same as all of us. They have magic, but so do we in Lord Timura. They have us outnumbered, but I've just told you a story of outnumbered boys so you know that's no problem to men like yourselves.

"But I won't lie to you. The demons are formidable foes. Yet, what would be the pleasure of fighting if all our foes were weak?"

This struck the men of Plains of Jaspar particularly well and they all thundered their approval.

"What do you say, lads?" Iraj shouted. "Shall we wait until Manacia brings the fight to us?"

This was met with a resounding "NO!"

"Shall we carry to the fight to him?"

This drew an overwhelming "YES!"

"Then let's go to him, lads!" Iraj thundered. "Let's catch him with his breeches down and buried to the hilt in some demon whore."

The skies shook with their roared approval.

As it so happened, Manacia *was* pleasuring himself with an enthusiastic demon maid when the news of the attack came. He wasn't "buried to the hilt," but he was definitely considering such an action when someone scratched at the entrance to gain his attention.

Manacia tumbled out of his harem tent, buttoning up his breeches. "Why do you disturb me?" he roared.

His aide gibbered, then pointed south. "Forgive mmm-mmm-me, Mmm-ajesty! But Pppp-protarus is attacking!"

Manacia's eyes shot south. It was dusk, but it was the eerie dusk of the Demon Moon, and the figures he saw—human warriors—were cast large and bloody red.

The demon king was no hysteric. He'd dealt with surprise attacks before. He calmed his fears and shouted for his generals to counter.

It was a Jaspar blood charge. No quarter given, none asked.

It was a screaming mass of horsemen, but not a man among them offered himself as a target. Each rode bareback, a thick leather harness girdling the horse's body, a slender rope lead to its mouth.

They whirled about the harness strap, sometimes to the left, sometimes to the right, sometimes hanging beneath the horse's belly. As they circled their mounts, they fired a constant stream of arrows from their small bows, so many that the sound was like a plague of biting flies descending in a black cloud on a cattle herd.

It was a mad charge, a charge where death was no consideration.

Arrow swarms disturbed the dusk with their black flight.

The screams of the demon wounded defied the desert calm.

And then they were among the demons, dropping their bows and drawing scimitars. Slashing this way and that.

They drove straight up the middle, nearly reaching Manacia himself, who was clambering aboard his elephant.

Iraj led that charge. He was a monster soldier, a soldier who could not be hit when the demon arrows swarmed back. His sword was a monster sword no blade could counter, no pike could match, no battle ax could confront.

He swept through the demon ranks. He was the arrow point, his men were its wounding flare, and the Demon Moon was his target.

He drove through the massed soldiers, aiming for the moon's blood spot, then he whirled and attacked the other way.

Iraj saw Manacia clambering on his elephant. A king-against-king fury took him and he struck toward his ultimate enemy.

But then Manacia's guard swarmed around him, spears tipped with deadly magic were hurled at him—countered by Safar's amulet which he wore about his neck—and Iraj wisely turned aside.

He led his warriors out of the demon horde, doing even more damage in his retreat than in the initial assault.

Gundara shouted, "Shut up, shut up, shuuuttt up!"

Safar broke in. "Quit arguing with your brother. I'm trying to concentrate."

"It's not my fault, Master," the little Favorite whined. "Gundaree won't stop bothering me."

Safar fought for calm. He'd learned from Methydia that Art and Temperament came in the same package. If you couldn't deal with the Temperament you had no business telling Art what to do.

He offered some treats.

"Here's two for you," he said, "and two for Gundaree. And if you behave yourselves, and aren't greedy little Favorites, there'll be two more for each of you when the job is done."

Leiria nudged him. "They're coming," she said.

Safar looked north. Night had fallen, but the Demon Moon was so bright all was clear. He saw Iraj and his men—about two hundred—streaming toward him. Behind them came Manacia's army. It was huge thing, a black plains' gobbling beast, gathering momentum as it came.

As Manacia had guessed, Iraj wanted the his enemy to come at him through the pillars where the main human force waited. If Iraj could squeeze the demons in from the sides, packing them so densely when they came through the pillars that they could barely move, the odds against the humans would be vastly reduced.

Although Manacia had fallen for Protarus' trap, the surprise attack and false retreat, he was no fool. The pursuit was orderly. Only one large group of demons, led by Crown Prince Luka, Safar guessed, was directly involved in chasing Iraj. The rest of the army was spread out across the plain, sweeping toward the humans in a broad wave so deep and strong they'd almost certainly be overwhelmed.

Safar motioned to his wizards. They touched brands to a heap of desert brush and dried dung. It burst into flames, flaring out so quickly the wizards had to jump back. Then it became steady, returning to a more comfortable size, and the wizards started tossing special powders on the fire. It hissed and boiled, sending up a shower of multi-colored sparks. Safar saw a similar glow on the eastern pillar and knew Horvan had joined him in the spell.

He let his mind slip down and down and then he was in a cold gray place with no top or bottom or sides. He called out, "Where are you, Ghostmother? It is I, your friend Safar Timura, come to find you."

There was no answer. Safar called again, "Come to me Ghostmother. Come to me please. I am in difficulty and have need of you."

Safar suddenly felt a presence. It was heavy and animal-like and smelled powerfully of cat. Then the grayness wavered and he could make out the faint of image of the old lioness.

"I am Safar Timura, Ghostmother," he said. "Do you remember how I helped you with your cubs?"

The lioness whined, the sound coming close to his ear.

"Will you help me, Ghostmother?" Safar asked. "As I helped you."

Another whine. And it came to him the old lioness had agreed.

"Thank you, Ghostmother," Safar said. "Wait here until I call, please."

Safar's head came up and he was suddenly back on the rock pillar again, the flames of the magical fire dancing and showering sparks only a few feet away.

He saw Iraj and his troops had almost reached the gap between the pillars.

"Get ready," he said to the wizards.

Manacia felt a warning buzz of enemy magic bloom into life. At the same time he saw the magical fires burning at the tops of the rock pillars.

The demon king gnashed his fangs in delight. "There you are, Timura!" he growled. "I've got you!"

He pulled back his claw, readying a soul-blasting spell.

Iraj and his cavalry swept through the gap.

"Go!" Safar shouted.

Four glass globes were hurled into the fire.

Out on the red-lit plain four white hot explosions erupted along the western edge of Manacia's oncoming army.

Then four more shattered the sky on the east as Horvan's wizards hurled their globes.

"Again!" Safar shouted.

Manacia was nearly hurled from the howdah by the force of the explosions. He was momentarily blinded, but when his vision cleared his first thought was that it'd returned too soon.

The explosions had punched big holes in his army's outermost wings. Other blasts followed and he heard screams of terror and pain. Then the wings started folding in on themselves as the soldiers on the edges scrambled toward the center to escape the blasts.

Manacia shouted orders to make them return to their positions, but in the chaos no one heard.

Furious, the Demon King's eyes swept up to westernmost tower of rock. He felt the presence of a powerful enemy wizard—Timura!

Manacia shrieked in fury and hurled his spell.

***

Safar was ready.

He sensed the pressure of the oncoming attack, and cried out, "Come, Ghostmother! Come!"

Manacia screamed an oath as he felt his spell blocked.

His attacking spell backblasted and he struggled for a shield and got it up just in time. A hot wave burst over his magical shield, spattering his spirit with hot drops of sorcery.

Before he could recover and strike again, he heard a mighty spine-cracking roar and a huge lion leaped out of nothingness and was on him.

Manacia grappled with it, and the lion's body was so cold it was like fighting death itself. He flung it away, and the lion tuck rolled and came to its feet.

It was then Manacia realized he was fighting a ghost. He could see right through the creature and when it opened its mouth and roared defiance, the sound had the ring of the unreal, the distant.

The lioness came for him again and Manacia dug as deep as he could into his bag of magical tricks.

Just before the massive jaws closed him he cast the spell.

The lioness vanished—returned to its ghost world.

Manacia sagged back, exhausted of all his powers.

Iraj whirled his horse about and prepared to meet the demon onslaught pouring toward the gap, Demon Moon at their backs.

They were packed tightly into a black river of warriors, but not as tightly as Iraj wanted. He signaled his flanks and the slingmen let loose, aiming at the edges of the demon column. At the same time the cavalry units charged in, backed by fast running ground troops.

A heavy swarm of missiles fell on the demons, killing and maiming many. Another swarm struck, dealing out more pain and death.

The human cavalry units slashed in, one from the east, the other from the west. They played a dancing game, darting in to savage the edges and darting out again before the demons could close on them. The ground troops struck immediately afterward, hurling their heavy spears, then grabbing axes from their belts and wading into the fight.

Gradually, the demon column narrowed more and when it finally struck through the portal between the two rock pillars the warriors were so densely packed they were easy pickings for the humans.

Iraj killed so many his sword arm grew tired, then his sword broke and he fought with a hand ax grabbed up from one of the fallen.

He saw Luka, separated from his guard, desperately fighting off three horsemen.

Iraj saw his three soldiers fall and Luka dash back into the demon ranks, a feat which drew Protarus' cold admiration.

Iraj fought on, raging against the demon tide.

Then slowly the battle changed. The sheer size of the demon army finally overcame all its flaws.

Iraj and his men found themselves being driven back as hammer blow followed hammer blow.

It wouldn't be long, he realized, before his lines cracked. And that would be the end of his army, his dreams and most certainly his life.

He chanced a look up at the western rock column.

And he thought, come on, Safar! Come on!

Safar readied his Grand Illusion.

It was the last weapon in his magical quiver.

He had no time to admire his father's artistry as he cast the spell that sent the fleet aloft.

Luka's fighting hopes were at their highest.

They were through the gap now and his army was spreading out, leaving themselves more room to use their weapons against the humans.

Luka could feel the enemy crumbling before him. One more hard effort, no more than two, and victory would be his.

Then, even above the noise of battle, he heard a murmur running through his troops, followed by collective gasps and cries of alarm. He saw several fiends pointing talons in wonder at the red-lit sky.

He looked up and it was all he could do not to gasp himself.

Sky borne warships were hurtling across the heavens to join the battle. They were the strangest vessels Luka had ever seen—fighting ships, suspended under big balloons, all crammed with warriors bearing spears with glowing tips. He couldn't tell what size they were. The ships seemed small and so he assumed they were at a great height. But certainly they were large enough to hold hundreds of warriors.

Then the ships were overhead and those warriors were hurling their spears into the demon masses. The spears grew before his eyes as they fell, each becoming easily as large as a tall demon.

They struck like lightning, glowing tips exploding, sending out great sheets of flame.

Another wave of spears hit. Then another. Blasting holes into the demon ranks. Filling the air with thunder and the smell of sulfur.

Then the demon army lost its nerve.

Luka could feel it, feel the fire go out of his warriors, smell the acrid stench of their fear.

They turned and ran. First a trickle, then a stream, then a full-sized river of shrieking demons, throwing down their weapons, shedding their armor and running over their own comrades to escape the horror from the skies.

Luka ran with them, spurring his mount to keep up. He wasn't running out of fear, although he was certainly frightened enough. He was racing to keep up, shouting for calm and order, doing his best to contain the rout.

Behind him he could hear the crack and thunder of the flying ships.

And the howls of Protarus' pursuing army.

Hours passed before Manacia restored order. But when he did the best he could manage was to wheel his forces about and set up a fortified camp.

In the distance Protarus paused and set up a camp of his own.

"The fight isn't over yet," Manacia railed, striding about his command tent, kicking and clubbing any slave who got in his way. "He can't stand up to me again. I'll hammer him into dust!"

***

Iraj paced his command tent, but his pace was measured, his manner calm.

"I hope we don't have to fight him again," he said to Safar. "If we do, it'll be out in the open on ground of his choosing. He won't fall for our tricks again."

"I suppose this where luck comes in," Safar said.

Iraj paused, considering, then nodded. "Yes," he said. "Now we get to see how lucky we really are."

"He's lucky, that's all," Manacia said, voice still shaking with fury. "Moreover, he was aided and abetted by cowards in my own court."

Luka, who'd been listening as patiently as possible, turned cold.

"What is it you are suggesting, Majesty?" he asked, not bothering to hide his anger.

Manacia turned on him. "I'm not suggesting anything," he said. "It's clear enough my son is a coward, who leads a band of cowardly fiends."

"Ah!" Luka said as if he'd suddenly made a great discovery. "You intend to blame me, is that it?"

"You've shamed me," Manacia said. "But I'll not hide that shame. Fault will be directed at its source, no matter if that source is my son and heir."

Luka came closer, as if to appeal for reason.

Instead he said, "Father, tell me about the time my mother accused you of rape. It's such a humorous incident it will give us all good cheer."

Manacia frowned. "What's wrong with you?" he snapped. "This is no time for humor."

"Oh, but it *is*, father," Luka insisted. "This is the very *kind* of situation that *does* call for humor."

Manacia drew himself up for another angry bellow.

But Luka quickly drew his sword and cut the bellow off at its source.

He watched his father's headless body flop to the floor.

Luka turned to the others, calmly wiping his blade.

"Any objections?" he demanded.

The generals and aides were frozen, gaping at this turn of events.

Fari was the first to speak. "Not at all, Your Majesty," he said.

Stiffly and with much joint cracking he lowered his aged bulk to its knees.

"Long live King Luka!" he cried.

The generals followed his lead, dropping to the ground and abasing themselves and shouting, "Long Live King Luka!"

Luka peered at his father's head, eyes open and staring.

"What's wrong, father?" he asked. "You're not laughing!"

Some weeks later Iraj crossed the Forbidden Desert, leading a grand victory procession down the road to Zanzair.

Kalasariz had carried Luka's surrender terms to Protarus and acted as a go-between in the ensuing discussions. The demon army was broken up into small groups and sent home. Luka offered himself as hostage, sending Fari back to Zanzair—Manacia's head stored in ice—to arrange for Iraj's arrival.

To Safar's displeasure Kalasariz was rewarded with much gold and a high position on Iraj's staff. Safar advised his king against it, but Iraj had brushed off his advice, saying there was always a desperate need for good spies.

At last the day arrived when the gates of Zanzair came into view.

They were marching along a misty highway, banners fluttering, drums rapping time.

Iraj rode Manacia's great war elephant, Safar at his side. A large flag made of fine Sampitay silk hung from the howdah. On it was the Crest of The Conqueror, the red Demon Moon and silver comet.

But it was no longer Alisarrian's flag. Iraj had claimed it as his own.

In a week an elaborate ceremony would be staged in Manacia's former palace. Dignitaries, both human and demon, would crowd the grand throneroom and humble themselves before Protarus.

There he would be declared King of Kings, supreme monarch of all Esmir.

The breeze stiffened and Safar saw the mist lift. Directly ahead were the gates of Zanzair.

"Look!" Iraj said, excited as a child. "We're almost there."

Hanging from a post above the gates was Manacia's gory head.

The gates swung open and an enormous crowd of demons poured out to hail their new king. Iraj waved a mailed hand in return.

The demon cries became wilder, chanting: "Protarus! Protarus! Protarus!"

Iraj turned to Safar, a broad smile on his face.

"My friend," he said. "I owe all this to you."

Then the smile became a loud laugh of surprise.

"I said that in the vision, didn't I?" he reminded Safar.

"Or something close enough to it," Safar answered.

Iraj clapped him on the back. "And it's all come true," he said. "Everything you predicted."

Safar smiled. "I suppose it has," he said.

But the smile hid gnawing worry. His vision had carried him to the gates of Zanzair, but no farther.

And now all he could think was...What happens next?

# Part Five
# Zanzair

# 25
# THIEF OF HEARTS

She was a rare woman. She had beauty, she had wealth, she had power.

She was also a woman of mystery, which in the time of the Demon Moon made her the rarest of women among men.

Her crest—the sign of the House of Fatinah—was a silver dagger and there was much talk of how it had come to be.

Some said it had been the crest of her late, unlamented husband, Lord Fatinah, a merchant among merchants so smitten by his young wife he'd left her his fortune. The Lady Fatinah, it was said, hastened her husband's departure from this world with his own dagger, which was made of silver. That the woman wore rich gowns all of mourning black and bearing the silver dagger crest added credence to this story.

Others speculated she'd once been the favorite courtesan of a king, perhaps even Protarus himself. In this version she'd come up the loser in a harem war and was driven out, but with many chests of gold and rare stones to speed her departure. Some said she'd slain her rival with a silver dagger, but the death caused such a scandal she was banished from the harem. Once again the tale of the aging Lord Fatinah came into play. Rumor mongers said the marriage was arranged to sidestep the scandal. They also said Lord Fatinah died before the marriage was consummated. Again, the dying nobleman had been so enamored of his beauteous wife that he'd bequeathed her all his worldly goods.

The curious throngs of Zanzair, with nearly as many humans as demons among them, babbled those tales and others when she passed by in her carriage, with the silver daggers emblazoned on each door.

The Lady Fatinah had demon outriders to push the throngs back and a human driver to hurry the matched black team of horses along. A burly demon guard sat next to the driver, sweeping the crowd with his ever watchful eyes.

Inside, Lady Fatinah's representative to Zanzair gushed on about all the arrangements he'd made in anticipation of her visit.

"You will see with your own eyes, My Lady," the man said, "that you chose wisely when you picked Abubensu to tend to your business in Zanzair."

He gestured out the window. They were traveling through the bazaar, an exotic scene of demons and humans haggling with stall keepers, or munching strange delights from the food carts; of families strolling along, purchases in hand, trailing human children and demon kits in their wake.

"Zanzair is surely the most marvelous city in the whole history of Esmir," Abubensu said. "Since our beloved king, Iraj Protarus, made it the center of his empire seven years ago, beings of every variety have flocked here, hoping against hope they can clutch the king's cloak and fly away with him to prosperity."

He raised a cautioning finger. "But Zanzair is also a most dangerous place, My Lady," he said. "Some who came were honest business folk, like myself. But many were thieves, both of the common and noble-born variety.

"And the intrigue!" He shuddered. "I can tell you stories about the intrigue and disgraceful goings on at the Royal Court that would set your teeth on edge."

"I'm sure you can," Lady Fatinah said smoothly. "And I'd be delighted to listen to your delicious tales at another time. But I hope you understand I have other things on my mind just now. Such as the living arrangements."

Abubensu beamed. What a genteel and soft-worded employer he had. Quite unlike a woman who'd supposedly killed her husband. And so beautiful! Abubensu had never been this close to such a woman. She filled her expensive black gown quite pleasingly. Her lips were full, dark eyes sparkling with what he dared dream was promise.

"You'll love the house I've found for you, My Lady," he said. "It sits on a hill, quite by itself. The night view of Zanzair is simply overwhelming. Especially the view of Protarus' palace. It's solid gold, you know, and when all the lights are turned on and the fountains are at play, why you would think it was the heavenly palace of a god."

"The view sounds most pleasant," Lady Fatinah said, wiping the chin of her child—a boy whose age was just past suckling and just short of speech. His name was Palimak, the Walarian word for promise.

"But to be frank," she continued, "it's more important to me that it have a good nursery."

"Remodeled to your exact specifications, My Lady," Abubensu said. "The grandest nursery ever created. No expense was spared."

"I hope it isn't too grand, Lady," the nurse broke in. She was a small woman, round and with a deep grandmotherly bosom. "Large spaces can be frightening to a child."

"There's a separate room for you right next to the young master's, Scani," Abubensu hastened to tell the nurse. "It's quite comfortable and you'll have no trouble keeping your eye on him."

Scani looked doubtful and started to speak, but Lady Fatinah silenced her with a warning look. The nurse took Palimak from Lady Fatinah's arms and fussed and cooed over him, making furiously whispered promises that no matter where he slept, Scani would always be nearby.

Abubensu went on. "Your neighbors," he said, "are all of wealth and breeding like yourself, My Lady. Their homes are close enough to give comfort, but distant enough to ensure privacy."

"I mentioned in my letter," Lady Fatinah said, "that I'd like to host a banquet as soon as possible to introduce myself to Zanzarian society."

"It has been done, My Lady!" Abubensu said with a pleased smile. "As a matter of fact I've taken the liberty of arranging an affair two nights from now. Invitations have been sent to a favored few—all beings of quality, mind you. And your staff, which I picked myself, is at this moment readying the banquet."

"There was one person in particular I asked you to invite," Lady Fatinah said. "Was that done?"

Abubensu bobbed his head. "Yes, My Lady. Lord Timura has been invited."

"And has he accepted?"

He hesitated. "Alas, My Lady, not as yet."

"But you expect him to?" Lady Fatinah pressed.

The little man shrugged. "I can't promise, My Lady," he said. "After all, he *is* the Grand Wazier, second only to King Protarus in importance."

Abubensu attempted a bit of gossip to steer conversation away from disappointment. "They were childhood friends, you know," he said. "They even call each other by their first names—Safar and Iraj—when in private."

He leaned closer, voice conspiratorial. "Although it is said that Lord Timura is not in such good grace with His Majesty these days. He has enemies who whisper ill things in the king's ear."

A dramatic shrug. "Who knows if these things are true, My Lady," he said. "Perhaps it is best after all if Lord Timura fails to attend. Why bring his political troubles to your esteemed doorstep?"

Lady Fatinah's eyes narrowed. "I *want* him at the banquet," she said, and there was no mistaking her firmness in the matter.

Abubensu struggled with his answer, clearly at a loss. "I will try, My Lady," he said, "but I can't swear that it's possible."

Lady Fatinah smiled, saying, "I have every faith in you, Abubensu."

She handed him a silk purse filled with coin. "Favor who you want with those," she said. Abubensu hefted the purse, brows rising as he noted the weight. "And you may keep whatever is left over for yourself.

"But make certain Lord Timura is there."

She turned to look out the window.

They'd come to a wide square and when she looked north she could see the blossoming trees that edged the Royal Gardens.

Beyond were the spires of the Grand Palace, glittering eerily under the ever-present Demon Moon.

Nerisa wondered if Safar would remember her after all these years.

"In the end," King Protarus said, "it all reduces itself to money."

He snorted in disgust, an action much noted by the members

of the assembled Royal Court. His snort would frame their discussions, dreams and nightmares for many days to come. Policy would be set because of that snort. Alliances threatened, reformed, or shattered. Thousands of miles away, men both small and large would tremble when news arrived of the king's sharply expelled breath.

"Every time I need to do something," Protarus said, "I'm told the cost is too dear. And when I—simple plainsman that I am—suggest the solution is to get more money, why I'm told there's no more to be had!"

The king's glare flowed down the several-leveled courtroom. First it took in Safar, his Grand Wazier and second in command, next the platform where King Luka—whose formal title was Prince of Zanzair—sat with Lord Fari and other important demons. Below were the Protarus' generals and top aides, a mixed lot that included demons and a few of his remaining rough plainsmen. Keeping himself slightly apart from this group was Kalasariz, who daily measured the distance and height between him and Safar. Beyond was the main floor of the courtroom, a vast area of hierarchical flatness where some courtiers were known to wear boosted up bootheels so they could stand taller and imagine they held greater favor with the king.

"Someone explain to me how this can be," Protarus demanded. "I am monarch of all Esmir. I number my subjects by the millions. All of whom seem to be going about making money and prospering, while their king lacks the basic means of running the kind of kingdom where they *can* prosper."

Protarus shook his head. "My problem is that I'm too generous," he said. "I made all my friends wealthy. Palaces, lands, money...Money! There's that word again!"

He looked at Safar. "You have money, Lord Timura," he said. "Why don't I?"

"You have only to ask, Majesty," Safar said, "and I will give it all back to you."

Frustrated, Protarus rapped the edge of his throne with bejeweled knuckles. "That's not the point, Lord Timura," he said. "I'm not that sort of monarch. Once I give a gift, I never ask for its return."

Leiria, Safar's guard and bedmate, stirred uncomfortably. She'd once been such a gift.

"The point is this," Protarus continued, "you have money and I don't because you have only your own household to keep up."

Protarus' hand swept across the courtroom, taking it all in. "I've got a kingdom to maintain. That's *my* household! And where does my household money go? Not for luxuries, that's for certain.

"The gods know I'm a man of simple tastes."

No one dared mention this was a great exaggeration. Protarus had long since shed his soldierly past and reveled in the comforts and pleasures of being King of Kings. He had many palaces, all fully staffed, vast stables of fine mounts of every variety and purpose, huge rooms packed with decorative weapons and armor, bulging storehouses and wine cellars, and immense harems stocked with a continuously refreshed supply of women.

The king sighed and sagged back in his throne, weary. The seven year reign had been difficult and it showed. Although he was still a man of less then thirty summers, he looked ten years older. His pride, his long golden locks, had thinned and he'd taken to wearing a jeweled skull cap beneath his crown. His beard was streaked with gray strands and his brow was plowed with worry lines.

"Tell us the problem again, Lord Timura," he said. "Lay it out fully so all can see."

Safar murmured respectful assent and rose. He strode up to Protarus' level and motioned to some men-in-waiting to pull aside the immense curtain behind the king's throne.

The wall was covered with a tremendous bas relief of Esmir. The largest features were the Gods' Divide, splitting much of the land from east to west, and the great desert, no longer forbidden, which had once separated human and demons.

Safar palmed a few pellets, hurled his hand downward in a dramatic gesture and there were several sharp retorts, drawing gasps from the court—including Iraj—and a thin haze of smoke curtained up from floor to ceiling. Behind the haze the bas relief suddenly glowed into being, causing a low chorus of amazement. They were looking at a living map of Esmir, complete with small moving figures, forests waving in the winds and waves beating distant shores.

Safar made a low bow to Iraj, with a sweeping showman's flourish.

"Behold your kingdom, Majesty," he announced.

Fari thought, I wonder how Timura does it? Not the living map...I understand that. Possibly even reproduce it, given a look at his notes. But the explosions and haze are another matter. Where was the magic? I sensed nothing!

This mystery was only one of several reasons Fari believed Safar must go.

Iraj's mood lightened. He clapped, saying, "Oh, very good, Safar. Very good!"

This was followed by a small patter of applause from the court. Luka grimly rattled his talons in false appreciation.

He thought, why all the flourishes and dramatic gestures? You would think this was entertainment instead of the serious business of administration. He's playing up to us, especially to Protarus.

Luka bitterly resented Safar's influence over Protarus. As Prince of Zanzair, Luka considered himself the second most important potentate in Esmir. He should be advising Protarus, not that commoner Safar Timura.

"Here are the locations of our most troubled regions, Majesty," Safar said.

He made another gesture and small flames flickered through the haze. There were at least two score spread out all over the kingdom. The flames were of different sizes, some minor glows where trouble was only starting, to larger spears of fire where things were nearly out of control.

"So many," Protarus murmured.

He shot a sharp glare at Kalasariz, saying, "You never told me there were so many!"

"Ah, yes, ah, I can explain, Your Majesty," Kalasariz fumbled. "Delayed reports...because of the...ah...difficulties."

Iraj gave him a cold nod and turned back to the map.

"This is the very latest information I have from our temples," Safar said. "And for the first time I think we can see just how widespread our problems are."

Kalasariz seethed anger for being upstaged by the Grand Wazier. The spy master preferred to show the king what he wanted him to know so he could control events. That damnable Timura, with his damnable network of priests, was stabbing him in the back.

Not for the first time, Kalasariz swore that some day he'd rid himself of Timura.

"The greatest problem seems to be in Caspan, Majesty," Safar said, pointing at the leaping flames near the edge of the western sea.

"Yes, yes," Protarus said. "That's why the subject of money came up. We need to send troops there and put down the rebellion. But I was informed by my treasurer I didn't have the money to pay for it. The coffers, it seems, are empty."

His gaze flickered over the map, once again noting the number. Finally he eyes came to rest on Caspan, nearly ringed with fire.

"Money *must* be found for Caspan," he said. "The question is where to get it."

"Taxes, Your Majesty," Luka broke in. "That's the answer. More taxes must be gathered. As you said, your subjects are enjoying prosperity because of your efforts. They should be willing to pay a fair price for that prosperity."

"I must disagree, Majesty," Safar said. "There is no general prosperity. A few areas, perhaps, but only those untouched by drought and plague. And, I might remind my noble friend, King Luka, these conditions have not only prevailed, but become worse over the past ten years."

Fari snorted. "Hadin, again!" he muttered.

Safar whirled on the old demon. "I've shown you the evidence," he said. "How can you deny the truth?"

"I'm not denying anything," Fari said. "Certainly there are problems. And possibly they were caused by some magical calamity in Hadin.

"What I disagree with most strongly is that these problems are necessarily long lasting. There have been calamities before. Droughts come. Droughts go. Plagues come. Plagues go. It's the gods' natural cycle. So only the best and most devout will live on to enjoy their well-deserved rewards."

"I won't quarrel with my esteemed colleague, Majesty," Safar said. "You want to hear solutions, not debate.

"I have one such solution to propose."

Protarus stirred. "Do you now?"

"I find myself agreeing with King Luka, Majesty," Safar said.

Luka frowned. Where was this going?

"Taxes are the answer, Majesty," Safar said. "Only, don't tax those who already pay. Tax those who don't."

Kalasariz' eyes narrowed. So that's his game, he thought.

"Tax *me*, Majesty," Safar said. "I not only benefited from your gifts, but I pay no taxes on them."

Safar pointed to Luka, then Fari, then Kalasariz, and all around the room, pointing at each nobleman in turn.

"We have *all* prospered, Majesty," he said. "But we pay nothing for it."

Protarus was interested. "I've often commented that generosity is my greatest virtue and flaw," he said. "Apparently I've forgiven more taxes than is good for me."

"Exactly, Majesty," Safar said. "I'm sure all of my colleagues would be delighted to share your heavy burden during this emergency."

"Ah, an emergency tax," Protarus said. "Maybe calling it that would wipe off some of the sour looks in this group." He smiled at Luka and Fari. Both forced smiles in return. He went back to Safar—"A temporary tax, lasting only through the emergency. That might go down better, politically speaking."

"I for one do not fear sacrifice," Luka said. "But I must point out that the money wouldn't be enough. It would pay for Caspan, perhaps." He pointed at the array of trouble spots on the bas relief. "But what of the rest?"

"King Luka is quite right, Your Majesty," Kalasariz said. "And I also join him in my willingness to sacrifice and share your burden.

"I also question the nature of the emergency."

He pointed at the bas relief. "This is very kind of negativism that is at the root of our problems, Your Majesty!"

Protarus lifted his head, interested.

"We are terrorizing your subjects, Majesty," Kalasariz continued, "with all this bad news. It feeds rumor that things are worse. It makes rebels out of weak men. It makes good honest subjects lie to your tax gatherers when they come to collect. And hold back vast amounts of money that rightfully belong to you.

"Vast amounts, Your Majesty. Vast."

"That's theft!" Protarus said, angered by the sudden vision of mean-spirited citizens burying huge chests of gold in their cellars.

"Exactly, Your Majesty," Kalasariz said. "Theft. "No kinder word to put on it. And I propose we end it at once!"

"How would you do this?" Protarus asked.

Kalasariz looked around at the huge assembly, then back at the king.

"I think it would be best discussed in private, Majesty," he said.

"I won't do it, Iraj," Safar said. "It may be in Kalasariz' nature to make such a great lie, but it's not in mine."

"How do you *know* it will be a lie?" Protarus said.

The two men were alone in the king's quarters. Less than an hour before Kalasariz, vigorously supported by Luka and Fari, had outlined his plan. Safar's opposition had been so heated Iraj had sent the three away so he could reason with him in private.

"Kalasariz had a good point about the effect all the negative news is having on the stability of the kingdom," Iraj continued.

"Lies won't make things better," Safar said.

"Again," Iraj said, "I don't see where anyone was proposing to lie. Kalasariz merely *suggested* we declare a national feastday. A feastday that would point up the positive, rather than the negative."

"And what of the casting?" Safar asked. "The casting that I, as your Grand Wazier, am supposed to oversee?"

"What's wrong with asking the gods when this long crisis will end?" Iraj said.

"A great deal," Safar replied, "considering that Kalasariz already had the answer he wanted me to report to all Esmir."

He held up a single finger. "One year!" He shook his head, disgusted. "One year...and the world will be well again."

"That's a good number," Iraj said, "If people believe things will be better in a year, they won't be so tight-fisted with tax money. Hells, I can even raise the taxes. An emergency measure, like you suggested."

"But on the poor," Safar said, "not the rich."

Protarus sighed. "It was a good idea, Safar. Not enough money to be gained, but a sound idea just the same.

"Unfortunately it wasn't something I could ever do."

"Why not?"

Another sigh. "These are the beings I eat dinner with, Safar. When I entertain, they are my guests. When I hunt, I hunt with them. They're my friends, after all. I don't want to sit around the table with everyone mad at me because I slapped a fat tax on them."

Safar didn't answer.

Protarus looked at him, then nodded, saying, "I suppose you're thinking if there are some things I won't do, then I should understand when you have similar reservations."

"Something like that," Safar said.

Actually he'd been thinking how revealing Protarus' statement had been. He'd rather starve the starving because he didn't want his wealthy friends mad at him.

"And if we *did* have a big public casting ceremony," Iraj said, "and you saw many difficult years ahead—rather than only one—you'd feel honor bound to report it. Is that right?"

Safar tried to lighten the situation with a smile. "Only some of it would be due to honor, Iraj," he said.

"After all, I've got my wizardly reputation at stake. When a year passed and the troubles continued no one would trust me again."

Protarus studied him for a long moment. Then he returned the smile, but his eyes were shielded.

"I can see how you might consider it too great a sacrifice to make," he said.

The meeting ended on that dissatisfying note.

Just before Safar left, the king said, "Oh, I almost forgot."

Safar was at the door. "What was that?"

"The captain of my guard says it's time for Leiria to drop by the palace for a little brush up on her training."

"I'll be sure to tell her," Safar said.

As soon as the door closed behind him Kalasariz came out of a side room. Behind him were Luka and Fari.

"I'm glad you signaled for us to linger within hearing, Majesty," Kalasariz said. "That was a most revealing conversation.

"And I must say you handled him quite smoothly, Majesty. Quite."

It was night when Safar's carriage made the approach to the grand mansion. It was raining so heavily even the Demon Moon was obscured from view.

"Who is this Lady Fatinah, Safar?" Leiria asked.

"I'm not quite sure," he answered. "Other than she may or may not be a notorious woman."

"She must be more than that," Leiria said, "to get the Grand Wazier himself to show up at her welcoming banquet."

Safar peered through the curtains, but the night was so black all he could see was his own reflection in the glass.

"It's that chief clerk of mine," Safar said. "He can't resist a bribe. I'd get rid of him, but the extra money he earns dishonestly makes him so efficient I have the best kept schedule of any administrator in Esmir."

"You could have refused," Leiria said. She gave him a teasing smile. "But I suppose you're as curious to see her as every man in the city. It's said she's quite beautiful."

"I never know when the event is the result of bribery, or duty," Safar said. "It's easier just to go to all of them. Linger an hour or so for appearances' sake, then slip off."

"And it doesn't hurt that she's beautiful," Leiria said.

Safar laughed. "And notorious," he said. "Don't forget that."

Leiria laughed with him, a lovely and exotic woman in her own right in her best dress uniform.

But Safar took note she was unusually inquisitive that night.

And her training session at the palace had been that same morning.

Interesting.

Nerisa saw him come in.

The rain had made the guests tardy but after a time she'd despaired Safar would be among the later arrivals. It had been a difficult evening, doing her best to be a charming and witty hostess to a group of strangers, while at the same time preparing herself for the moment when he arrived.

She didn't want to him think she'd come all this way because she required something. The Lady Fatinah was quite capable of taking care of herself and didn't need a man—even though he might be the Grand Wazier—to fend for her. No, she had a duty to perform. A too long delayed duty.

As for her girlish crush on Safar, it was years ago and was, after all, just that—girlish. Safar was kindly enough at the time to see it and not humiliate her.

She determined when they met she'd be as calm and cool as everyone expected the Lady Fatinah to be.

Then she saw him at the door. One minute the entryway was empty, the next a liveried servant was leading him in.

Someone pointed her out to him and he raised his head and he smiled as their eyes met.

Nerisa was lost.

His eyes were just as blue as she remembered.

Safar was stunned when he saw the woman approach. The Lady Fatinah was every bit as beautiful as people had said. Perhaps even more so in her stunning black gown, cut low to reveal a pearly bosom. The dress clung to her, showing off her long slender figure.

But her face was a cold shield when she came close, hand outstretched to welcome him. The coldness put Safar off, as did her thin smile. This was clearly a woman out for the main advantage, he thought. His clerk had taken a bribe and that was that.

Then their fingers touched and Safar felt her shiver. He looked into her eyes—saw the dancing flecks of gold. He saw her lips turn up in a familiar crooked smiled.

"It's Nerisa, Master!" Gundara hissed from his breast pocket. "Nerisa!"

But Safar had already seen and known. He was in shock, seeing little Nerisa raised from the dead to come back as the beauteous Lady Fatinah.

Nerisa gave his hand a warm, firm squeeze.

She whispered, "Don't give me away." Then, loud enough for

all to hear, "How kind of you to visit my humble home, Lord Timura."

Safar murmured a suitably polite reply.

"I fear we've started without you, My Lord," Nerisa said, pointing at the tables of food. "Why don't we dispense with formalities and join the others before you starve to death?

"Perhaps, if you are still in a generous mood, we can have a little chat later and get to know one another."

Safar came unstuck enough to make an awkward bow. In a daze he let a servant lead him over to the banquet area.

Only when he sat down did he realize he'd left Leiria in the entryway without orders. He turned his head and saw her looking in his direction, her face like stone. He whispered a message for a servant to carry to her, saying she could join the other bodyguards in the pantry. But when the message was delivered he saw Leiria give a furious shake of her head, hiss something back, then exit into the storm.

When the servant returned Safar wasn't surprised at her reply: "Please tell his Lordship thank you, but I shall wait in his carriage."

This was not good.

Then he heard Nerisa laugh—that natural earthy laugh breaking through her facade—and he forgot all about Leiria.

The rain had made the banquet late, but it also caused it to break up early. The guests streamed out, saying they had a lovely time but Her Ladyship would understand that with the storm they had to hurry home.

Nerisa murmured polite good-byes, but the whole time her attention was fixed on Safar, tarrying in an out-of-the-way corner near the verandah. It was as if all the years between them had collapsed into but a few days or weeks. Old emotions were new again, swift torrents hammering against her mature resolve.

She called herself a fool, thinking it was only the stress of the meeting churning up silly emotions. And even if she did still have tender feelings for him, Safar had never shared those feelings. He'd only been kind to an orphan waif. Kindness did not equal love.

Once again she steeled herself and when the last guest was

gone she strolled over as casually and easily as any great lady going to greet an old, dear friend.

But when she reached him he leaped to his feet, saying, "By the gods, Nerisa, I thought you were dead!"

And he crushed her into his arms.

Outside, Leiria huddled in the carriage, peering through the curtains. Even in the downpour she could make out Safar's familiar figure pacing in front of the wide glass verandah doors.

She saw another figure approach—a woman's slender figure.

Lightning crashed, momentarily blinding her.

When her vision returned she saw Safar and the woman embracing.

The last vestiges of Methydia's gentle spell of forgetfulness vanished when Nerisa came into his arms.

A thousand and one thoughts and emotions burst forward, while another thousand and one crowded behind, demanding to be heard.

But all he could say was, "Nerisa, my little Nerisa."

He kissed her hair, her cheeks, the tears flowing from her eyes, crushing her against him as if the tightness of his embrace would keep her from turning into a ghost and wisping away.

Then their lips met and the embrace become something else altogether.

It happened so abruptly there was no time for questioning, much less surprise.

Nerisa melted against him, weeping and murmuring his name. She was in a dream, an old sweet dream, and her Safar was holding her close, kissing her, whispering endearments. Passion firing them both beyond control.

She opened her eyes and saw her major domo's shocked face reflected in the glass of verandah doors. But she didn't care and she waved a curt dismissal just as Safar swept her off the floor.

And she said, "Yes, yes, please, yes," and somehow she directed him to her rooms.

Then they were in the big soft bed, tearing at each other's clothes.

***

"After I fled Walaria," Nerisa said much later, "I became a caravan lad."

She smiled at the memory, nestling deeper into Safar's arms. "I always did play a good boy."

Safar gently caressed her. "You wouldn't have such an easy time of it now," he said.

Nerisa giggled. "Actually, it became a problem fairly quickly," she said. "I suddenly bloomed, as the old grannies gently put it. One day my breeches didn't fit over my hips. The next, I was bursting the seams of my lad's shirt. I had to bind myself down and get looser clothes."

"Did no one ever suspect?" Safar asked.

She shook her head. "Never. Oh, I got a few odd looks once in awhile. But that was the extent of it. Second glances, nothing more."

Safar said, "That leaves a great leap from caravan lad to the rich Lady Fatinah."

"I suppose it does," Nerisa answered. "Although it didn't seem like it at the time. I had some money. The gold you gave me. I invested a little of it in some of the caravan goods, made a good profit and invested more."

Nerisa laughed. "I found I had a talent for merchanting. All those years as a little thief served me well when it came to picking out bargains and quality goods.

"After a time I had enough to become a minor partner of a very wealthy caravan master."

"Lord Fatinah, by any chance?" Safar asked.

Nerisa made a face. "It's true he was named Fatinah," she said. "But he was no lord. He was a merchant, nothing more. Old, fat and kindly. At least I thought he was being kindly. He treated me like a son."

Another laugh. "As it turned out, he merely had a weakness for handsome boys."

Safar stirred. "You mean, he...?"

"He...nothing," Nerisa said. "Fatinah was an honorable old man. He believed it unseemly to take advantage. I never even knew his feelings toward me...or the boy he thought I was...until just before he died. Then he confessed all. Swore he loved me. And handed me a will, saying I was to inherit all."

"That's when I became a woman...and his widow. The will would never have stood, otherwise. No one would understand, much less believe, that he'd give such a fortune to a mere boy. So I invented our marriage. Paid certain sums to certain people to draw up the necessary documents. No one ever questioned an old man would be fool enough to give his money away to a grasping young woman.

"Even so, the rumors started that I'd killed him. Especially after I purchased the necessary background to make him a nobleman."

"No one ever questioned that?" Safar asked.

Nerisa came up on an elbow, that crooked grin of hers playing on her face. A smile that brought a pang of love to Safar's heart, rather than its lesser cousin, Fondness.

"If you play the royal," she said, "and you play it well, no one questions anything. Especially if you have money.

"Besides, in these times there's so much chaos all of Esmir is turned upside down. I took advantage of that chaos, running caravans into places no one else dared go. I suppose I made a profit on the troubles of others. But I brought them what they needed. Bought what they no longer had use for. And consoled myself with the thought that I'm Misery's child.

"I believed I had a right."

"I suppose you do," Safar said. "Once I'd have said otherwise." She smiled at this. "But there are so many greater thieves in this world, thieves who will steal dreams. Thieves who break you. Thieves who would kill all you love, require you to watch, then kill you as well.

"And then steal your heart out of your body to make a sorcerer's meal."

Nerisa embraced him—twining arms and legs about him. Made her body as soft as she could for a shield that would protect him and comfort him from all the devils tormenting him.

She was Nerisa, the thief of Walaria, and she would allow no man she loved to come to harm.

***

Later she took him into the nursery to meet Palimak. The child was awake, hazel eyes reflecting the candle she carried.

Nerisa picked the child up, wrapping his favorite crib blanket close around him. He was a tubby little thing with dark hair, olive skin and pearly milk teeth.

"This is Safar," she said to the child. "The one I've been telling you about all these months."

She made a nervous smile at Safar. "This is Palimak," she said.

"My son."

Palimak turned his chubby little face to look at Safar. He kicked his feet in delight and smiled.

His eyes lit up and with a shock Safar saw the hazel turn to a glowing yellow.

Demon yellow!

Nerisa's heart plummeted when she the look on her lover's face.

Safar managed a faint smile and held out a hand. Palimak grabbed his foremost finger and squeezed.

"He's strong!" Safar said, dredging a compliment from the depths of his confusion.

Nerisa turned her face to Palimak, hiding her feelings. "Of course he's strong," she said. "Aren't you strong, my Palimak? The strongest little boy in the world!"

The child gurgled pleasure. Then he threw up, soiling himself and Nerisa's sleeping gown.

"Oh, you bad boy, you!" Nerisa scolded. "Here I'm trying to show you off and you play the little pig."

Then she burst into tears.

Safar sat beside her, putting his arms around both of them.

"Why are you crying?" he asked. "Children make messes. That's what they do! Besides making you love them, of course.

"Ask my sisters what a mess I was! No. Come to think of it, don't. They will tell you in excruciating detail what a dirty little boy I was."

Instead of calming her, the words infuriated Nerisa.

"That's not why I'm crying!" she said. "As you know very well!"

She reached into her gown, drew out an object and threw it on the bed.

"Here!" she said. "Here's your damned old knife."

Safar stared at it. It was the silver dagger Coralean had given him long ago.

Nerisa wiped her eyes, pulling herself together. "That's why I came here," she said. "To return the dagger. It's yours. It was wrong of me to keep it. And I was a fool, a stupid, weak fool, to deliver it to you myself instead of sending a messenger."

Palimak stared to cry, which made Nerisa angrier. "There, you see what you've done!"

Safar was confused. "What have I done?"

"I saw *that* look on your face," Nerisa said. "You think he's a monster! A half demon, half human freak.

"Well, be damned to you. I've had my pleasure. I've had my girlish dream. Safar Timura, my great ideal. The man who had so much kindness in him he could understand anything and anyone." She laughed bitterly. "I should have known better. And it's a good lesson for me.

"Now Palimak and I will be on our way. And to the Hells with you! And to the Hells with me for letting you make me into a fool!"

Safar started to get angry himself. "This is hardly fair," he said. "The least you could have done is warn me. At least you could have—"

A voice broke in: "Shut up, shut up, shuutt uppp!"

Safar swatted his tunic pocket. "Just stop it," he said. "I'm not in the mood to hear you argue with Gundaree."

The little Favorite leaped out of his pocket onto the bed. He put his hands on his narrow hips.

"I am *not* telling Gundaree to shut up," he said.

His eyes swept over Safar, then Nerisa, then Palimak. Back to Safar again.

"I am telling *you* to shut up, Master," he said. "And you too, Nerisa."

He sighed. "You were the first one to give me sweets in a thousand years," he said to Nerisa. "And you," he said to Safar, "have been a decent master, as masters go. Otherwise I wouldn't say a thing.

"If you both insist on making stupid human mistakes, why should I care? But I guess I do. So I'm saying, Shut up!"

"What mistakes?" Nerisa asked.

"He thought you had a husband," he said to Nerisa. "A demon husband."

"She thought you didn't want a little monster on your hands, much less a woman who would sleep with a demon."

"I don't have a husband," Nerisa said. "Demon or otherwise. Palimak is a foundling. An orphan. Like me."

"And I don't care who you slept with, or didn't sleep with." Safar said. "It's none of my business. As for me thinking Palimak is a monster because he's part demon, why nothing could be further from the truth.

"He's a child. I like children. Ask my mother. Ask my father."

"There, you see?" Gundara said. "Wasn't that easy?"

He hopped onto the bed, growing larger. He chucked Palimak under the chin. The child gurgled in pleasure.

"Why don't you leave him here with me?" Gundara said. "Go back to the bedroom and do whatever you think is necessary to apologize to each other."

The little Favorite paid no attention to the murmurs between the two lovers. Nor did he turn to watch them slip out of the room. His entire focus was on the child with the glowing yellow eyes.

"What a handsome little thing," he said. "Eyes just like mine. Do you know how to talk yet?"

Palimak burbled and wriggled his little arms and legs.

"I guess not," Gundara said.

He made himself smaller and hopped onto the child's chest. He made funny toad faces and Palimak laughed, eyes glowing brighter.

"Do you know how to say, shut up?" Gundara said. "Go ahead. Try it. Say—Shut up. Shut up. Shuutt uuppp!"

And Palimak spoke his first words, "Shut up!"

"That's my boy," Gundara said. "Won't your mother be surprised in the morning?"

"Shut up, shut up!" the baby cried, "Shut up, shuuut uuppp!"

"It's my understanding," Kalasariz said, "that Lord Timura and this Fatinah woman have been in each other's company for weeks."

"That is so, My Lord," Leiria said. She turned to Protarus. "Lord Kalasariz' understanding comes from my daily reports *to* him, Your Highness," she said. "Reports you ordered, Sire."

Protarus smiled. "I wanted to hear it from your own lips, Leiria," he said.

"Then you have heard it, Majesty," she said. "Other than for the hours of the business day, Lord Timura and Lady Fatinah have not been apart since the night they met."

"Doesn't that trouble you, Leiria?" Kalasariz asked. "It was my impression that you and Lord Timura have been lovers for some years."

Leiria shrugged. "It was my duty," she said. "The king knows that."

Protarus chuckled. "And an unlovely duty it was," he said to Kalasariz. "My friend Safar may be Grand Wazier of Esmir, but he is not so grand in bed." Then, to Leiria, "Isn't that true, my dear?"

"I have little experience with men, Majesty," she said. "But you are such a lion, sire, I was spoiled for any other."

Protarus roared laughter. "You see how it is?" he said to Kalasariz. He wiped his eyes. "When I bed a woman, she *stays* bedded, dammit! You should hear the weeping in my harem when I choose who is to enjoy my royal embrace and who must wait until another night."

Kalasariz grinned. "All of Esmir knows of your prowess, Majesty," he said.

He regarded Leiria. The moment he'd first seen her cast adoring eyes on Safar he'd known he could make use of her one day. It was his fine fortune Safar had betrayed her, giving Leiria good reason to seek revenge. Otherwise, kingly orders or not, he wouldn't have trusted her reports about Safar's activities.

"I don't think we have any further need for you at this moment, Leiria," he said, dismissing her. "You may report to me at the same time tomorrow."

Leiria touched hand to sword hilt and bowed in the military manner.

"Very good, My Lord," she said, and exited.

Protarus stared after her, thinking. Then he said, "This Fatinah must be an amazing creature to have Safar so spellbound."

"She is *quite* beautiful, Majesty," Kalasariz said. "I wouldn't mind giving her a tumble myself."

"I doubt if you'll have the opportunity," Protarus said. "Lord Timura has asked me for permission to wed her."

Kalasariz eyebrows rose. "Will you give it, Majesty?"

"I don't see how I can deny him," Protarus answered. "It's a routine request my courtiers are required to make by law. I've never said no to anyone yet."

"But we know nothing about this woman, Majesty," Kalasariz said. "This fact alone should make us be wary. My spies have sought information about her all over Esmir. To no avail. Apparently she just suddenly appeared one day. A rich noblewoman no one ever heard of before."

"And she has a child," Protarus said.

"Yes, but whose child is it, Majesty? That too is a mystery."

"I can't imagine any man wanting to wed a woman who was bred to another," the king said. "Beautiful though she may be."

"My sentiments exactly, Majesty," Kalasariz said. "Considering everything else, it tends to add to my suspicions."

"You think she is dangerous?"

"I know of no other woman like her in Esmir," Kalasariz said. "Somehow she's made herself extremely rich. From all reports she becomes richer by the day through shrewd business dealings. She answered to no man, at least until she entered Lord Timura's life. And it's my guess she doesn't answer to him either."

"Do you think she advises him?"

"That would be a safe assumption, Majesty. She's certainly a strong willed woman. And ambitious."

Protarus stirred, rapping his rings against the throne.

Then, "Yes, she would be, wouldn't she? She has my Grand Wazier in her thrall. What next?"

"Yes, Majesty," Kalasariz said. "What next?"

# 26

# WHERE THE RAVENS WAIT

The Grand Palace of Zanzair was a place of haunted chambers, cries in the night and conspiratorial whispers blowing like dry winds down the dark corridors. It reeked of centuries of intrigue and betrayal. Much blood had been shed over the years and there were places where the stone floors still bore murder's black stain.

Many kings had risen and many had fallen in that palace, but there were no noble monuments to mark their passing. Assassins were the dark messengers of each reign's end. A royal head posted at the main gates marked each beginning. And the first to praise the new monarch's name were feasting ravens.

Now Iraj Protarus was king and the intrigue and betrayal continued as before. Safar could smell the danger when he walked through the big main doors, sentries coming to attention and saluting the Grand Wazier. There was a sulfurous stink of dark magic in the air and under his formal tunic the stone idol sparked warning.

There was nothing unusual about Safar being summoned to a meeting with King Protarus, but as he strode through the palace—Leiria a few paces behind—many eyes turned his way. Some looked speculative, some glinted hatred, and some—the largest number, he hoped—appeared sympathetic.

As he approached the door of Iraj's private quarters it came open and three beings, their backs to him, bowing and humbly excusing themselves to "His Gracious Majesty" made their way out.

A sentry closed the door and they turned, each reacting in a different manner when they saw Safar standing there.

The first, Kalasariz, was cheery. "Good morning, Lord Timura," he said. "I hope this day finds you well."

"Well enough, thank you," Safar said, nodding at the hammer-faced spymaster.

The second, King Luka, was arrogant. "Grand Wazier," he said, only those two words and a nod of his demonly head noting Safar's presence.

Safar nodded in return, but said nothing.

The third, Lord Fari, was nervous. "How good to see you, Lord Timura," he said. "It's been long since I've had the pleasure of your company. Perhaps you would grace my humble home for dinner some evening?"

Safar dipped his head in a slight bow. "It would be an honor to be your guest, My Lord," he said.

Fari quivered, a jolt of alarm showing in his yellow eyes. "Quite, quite," the old demon said. "Of course, you are always so busy with your duties as Grand Wazier I suspect, alas, it will be a long time before you are able to attend."

"I'm never too busy for you, Lord Fari," Safar said. He couldn't resist the tease.

Fari clacked his talons together, distressed. "I'll have my clerk speak to your clerk," he said, "and arrange a convenient evening."

"Thank you, My Lord," Safar said, making another slight bow. "I eagerly await your kind invitation."

The sentry appeared, motioning for Safar to enter the king's chambers. He made his polite farewells to the three and went in—leaving Leiria waiting in the hallway outside.

Iraj was at his desk, looking over some reports. At least he appeared to be. His head was down, paper documents were in front of him, but his focus was on one spot instead of sweeping across words or numbers, betraying his pretense of being totally absorbed in his royal duties.

Safar cleared his throat and Iraj's head came up. He smiled. But his eyes seemed cold.

"Ah, there you are, Safar," he said. "Get a drink. Make yourself comfortable."

Safar sat and poured himself a cup of brandy from the spirits' service on the desk.

Iraj pretended to go back to the report, but his bejeweled fingers gave him away, rap, rap, rapping on the arm of the chair.

Finally, Iraj nodded, slapped the report down and raised his head to regard Safar.

"This is a little difficult for me, Safar," he said. "But I need to speak to you man to man—and as a friend."

Safar felt the stone idol glow warmer, uncomfortably so.

He smiled, saying, "Always, Iraj."

"It's about this marriage request of yours to the Lady Fatinah."

"What about it?"

"Are you sure this is wise, old friend?" Iraj asked. "I understand she is a beauty. And I congratulate you on your taste. But marriage!"

"I love her, Iraj," Safar said. "In Kyrania, marriage almost always follows love."

Iraj gave a nervous laugh. "*That* was Kyrania," he said. "You're no longer a common potter's lad. You are the Grand Wazier—second only to me in importance. You can have any woman you want. For your bed, or for marriage for that matter."

"I know that, Iraj," Safar said. "And it's Lady Fatinah I choose for both."

"But she may not be suitable for you," Iraj said, "beautiful though she may be."

"To me she's more than any potter's lad, as you put it, could possibly deserve. Meaning, she loves me too. What other requirement should I ask of a woman?"

"Here's what I think," Iraj said, leaning across the desk. "This is a mere romantic attachment. You know you have a weakness for such things. Remember Astarias? You thought the sun rose and set on her. You declared your love to the mountains. And even asked her to be your bride.

"She laughed, if you recall."

"This one didn't laugh," Safar said.

Iraj studied Safar for a moment then, "All I'm asking is that you reconsider."

Safar started to speak. But Iraj raised a hand to stop him.

"I know you're stubborn, Safar," he said, "so don't answer just now. Think on it a day or two and we'll talk again.

"I'm asking you to do this for me as a friend."

Safar bit off automatic refusal. "Very well, Iraj," he said. "I'll do as you ask."

He wouldn't change his mind, but agreement gave him time to figure out what was wrong and how to get around it.

Safar tried make a joke of the situation. "If Auntie Iraj wants a two-day cooling off period, she'll get it."

Protarus didn't respond. His eyes seemed glazed, as if he were elsewhere.

They snapped back to alertness. "Well, that's one problem dealt with easily enough," he said, forcing a light manner. "On to the next."

"Which is?"

"I'm afraid it's another delicate matter, my friend," he said. "So try to keep an open mind, as you did before."

"I will."

"It's this business about the casting," Iraj said. "Asking the gods what the future holds."

Inwardly, Safar groaned. Outwardly, he let a wry smile play across his face.

"So that's what my colleagues were doing here," he said. "Why, I'd thought they'd all gathered to sing my praises to their king."

Iraj frowned. "No one said anything against you," he said, curt. "I wouldn't allow such a thing."

Safar recognized the lie for what it was. "Of course, you wouldn't, Iraj," he said. "After all, we're blood oath brothers. And no man of honor would let another speak against his blood oath brother."

Iraj gave him the steadiest of gazes. "Never," he agreed. His cheek twitched. So he added, firmer still, "Never!"

"So what new suggestion did my friends have about the casting?" Safar asked.

"Fari proposed a compromise," Iraj said. "Make it two years, instead of one. My subjects will take just as much heart at that. Two years in not such a long time to wait for the Age of Great Blessings."

"Oh, so it's got a name now, does it?" Safar said. "The Age of Great Blessings?"

"Call it anything you like," Iraj said. "So long as it sounds positive. The point is, we want to say—quite firmly—that things will get better by and by, if only we make suitable sacrifices to the gods and be patient."

"I'll give you the same answer I gave before, Iraj," Safar said. "I won't lie. An extra year won't make it less of one. Or three, or five, even."

Protarus looked alarmed. "Five years!" he said. "You don't think it'll last that long, do you?"

"I have no idea," Safar said. "And that's the point. No one does. Not a bone caster, entrails reader or stargazer in your kingdom could say. All the signs are blank. As if there were no gods listening."

"That's ridiculous," Iraj said, features flushing. "Of course they're listening. Why else am I on this throne? Who guided me here but the gods? There's the Demon Moon. The comet ascending. Your vision long ago. All those things point to a decree from the Heavens themselves!"

Safar knew better than to argue. Iraj had fixed on this "divine destiny" idea when they were boys. To dispute it would be pointless—and dangerous.

"Whatever the reason," he said, "the gods are silent just now."

"Just say it for them, then," Iraj urged. "Say all will be well in two years. It's as good a guess as any."

"I can't," Safar said.

"It would offend your precious honor," Iraj scoffed.

"Something like that," Safar answered.

"Fari doesn't have that problem," Iraj said. "He told me he used to do such things for Manacia all the time."

"And look where that got Manacia," Safar said.

Iraj glared at him. "That has nothing to do with it," he said. "I was talking about honor, not Manacia."

"Well, if it doesn't trouble Fari to lie," Safar said, "then let him do it. He can oversee the whole thing. Feasts. Sacrifices. Prayers. Then the big lie. Let me know what date you decide on so I can be sure to be absent."

"That's damned foolishness!" Iraj shouted. "You're my Grand Wazier! Everyone will think you're opposed and are making yourself absent to show disfavor."

"That does pose a problem, doesn't it?" Safar said.

"Well, let's not have one, then," Iraj said. He'd calmed himself. He flashed his most winning smile. "Just do as I ask, Safar. A favor for a friend."

"Don't stake our friendship on this," Safar warned. "It would be a grave error to let it come to that."

Iraj trembled in fury. For a moment Safar thought he would lose his temper.

Suddenly, Protarus relaxed. He sighed deeply, emptied his cup, then sighed again.

"What a difficult man you are, Safar Timura," he said. "As immovable as the mountains themselves."

"I take no pride in it," Safar said. "It's only how I was raised."

"Then thank the gods," Iraj laughed, "that I only made one friend in Kyrania. Otherwise I would have been driven quite mad by now."

"There can only be one explanation for it, Majesty," Lord Fari said. "The Grand Wazier has clearly gone mad."

Protarus looked surprised. "Safar mad?" he said. "Why, he's always been the most stable of individuals. Oh, he has some silly flaws, of course, like that Hadin obsession of his. But madness?"

The king, led by Fari, Luka and Kalasariz, was moving along a narrow corridor toward the chambers containing what had once been King Manacia's Necromancium. The atmosphere was dank, the air smelled of embalming fluids and their bootsteps sounded unnaturally loud as they approached, making all seem very surreal.

"If I may say so, Majesty," Fari said, "madness is an affliction all wizards should guard against constantly. I am very old and know of what I speak. I've seen many a young mage overcome by the powerful forces he must reckon with. He forgets all true power resides with the king and he merely manipulates the spirit world for his monarch's benefit. After all, the king rules by Divine Decree. That is the nature of things, as the gods revealed to us long ago."

Luka snorted. "What else could you call it but madness?" he said. "Only a madman would play such a dangerous game. This is no ordinary monarch he's dealing with. But the King of Kings. Absolute monarch of all Esmir."

"What really troubles me," Iraj said, "is his attitude that somehow I want to harm my subjects. My whole purpose—my whole life—has been dedicated to the exact opposite. I want nothing but good for everyone. I truly do seek an Age of Great

Blessings. Peace and plenty for humans and demons alike.

"Why, I remember telling him something almost exactly like that years ago when we were boys. And I've certainly done nothing but become stronger in that resolve.

"I consider it my holy duty."

"The root of the problem, Your Majesty," Kalasariz said, "is that Lord Timura has become not just mad, but power mad. This is not speculation, Majesty, but fact supported by your very best spies.

"Lord Timura has said time and again that he is more popular than Your Majesty. He believes he is revered by all your subjects. And that he should be king, instead of you.

"This is why he refuses you, Majesty. He holds his own reputation as more important than your own."

Iraj was seething when they entered the Necromancium. Rather than needling that anger further, the three conspirators changed their manner, pointing out different objects of interest.

Fari, the old demon wizard, took the lead.

"You see this, Majesty?" he said, showing him a flask covered with magical symbols. "It contains a potion that would enhance even your mighty abilities with women. One drop in a glass of wine and you could pleasure a hundred maids."

Next, he displayed a small purse. He upended it and a handful of rare gems poured out. "With the proper spell, Majesty," he said, "these gems can become many. I mentioned their existence to Lord Timura, saying they would help solve your financial difficulties, but he declared them black magic, evil magic, and commanded me to say nothing."

Then he picked up a skull with the unmistakable shape of a wolf. "This is a shape-changer's amulet, Majesty," he said. "Used wisely it could give you amazing powers. Magical powers, Majesty. Which I hesitate to suggest, is the only thing Your Majesty lacks.

"Why, with magical powers, Majesty, you would have no need for wizards, other than to perform rote duties."

"Than I'd be like Alisarrian," Protarus murmured.

"Yes, Majesty," Fari said. "You would be master of both worlds. Temporal and spiritual."

"And I'd have no need for Safar," Iraj said.

Fari shrugged. "I hadn't thought of that," he said. "Lord Timura is such a mighty wizard it prevents such thinking.

"But I suppose it's true. You would have no need for him." He chuckled. "Or me either, for that matter. Except, of course, I'm more than willing to tutor Your Majesty in the magical arts."

"And Safar wouldn't?"

Another shrug. "You would be the best judge of that, Majesty," he said. "After all, you *have* been friends for many years."

Iraj pressed the point. "If that were the case," he said, "*I* could declare the Age of Great Blessings."

All three conspirators showed surprise.

Then, "I suppose you could, Majesty," Fari said.

"Indeed," said Luka.

"Why not?" posed Kalasariz.

"I must think on this," Protarus said. "I don't want to react too swiftly. That way leads to errors and disappointment."

"That is a truth that should be engraved on stone, Your Majesty," Kalasariz said. "A pause, well used, is what separates the good from the great."

At that moment a shrill noise sounded. All four heads, two human, two demon, swiveled to the source of the sound. It came from a small alembic, made of jewel encrusted crystal, which sat upon an ebony stand. The alembic had a large bulbous stopper which was flashing a purplish light.

Luka displayed his fangs in a most lascivious grin.

"Wait until you see this, Majesty!" he said.

Iraj was puzzled. "See what?"

"We had a small entertainment planned for you, Majesty," Fari said.

"Actually, it was completely unscheduled," Kalasariz added. "Everything depended upon luck. We prayed it would happen when you were here to see."

"I hate to repeat myself," Iraj said. "But...see what?"

Chuckling, the three conspirators guided the king over to the alembic. As soon as he came close the noise stopped and the flashing light became a steady glow.

"Look into it, Majesty," Fari said. "I guarantee you'll be delighted at what you see."

Iraj stared at the alembic, an expectant smile playing on his lips.

Then an image formed.

The king gasped. "By the gods," he said, "she *is* beautiful!"

Nerisa thought she heard voices. She stirred in her tub, head rising from the languorous waters. She looked around and saw nothing unusual in the huge marble bath chamber. It was hazy with perfumed steam rising from the sunken tub—large enough for four Nerisas to splay their limbs comfortably and wriggle them about to feel the water's gentle massage.

When she was certain there was no one around—and the voices were the product of her languid imagination—she eased back into her bath, breathing a long luxurious sigh.

The Lady Fatinah might have been a woman of immeasurable wealth, but she'd spent the short years of that nobility on the dusty caravan track gathering her wealth. Before she'd merely been Nerisa—a dirty orphan child who'd snatched a bath in cold rain barrels set beneath tenement gutters.

Abubensu had boasted of her mansion's view, praised the nursery he'd had remodeled to her exacting specifications, but he'd never said anything about the bath. When Nerisa had discovered it she'd whispered a fervent prayer of thanks to whatever god had sent such splendor her way.

Nerisa captured the huge sponge floating on the water. She reached over to the ledge and picked up the ornate bottle of bathing oils—one of many gifts she'd received from the guests who'd attended her welcoming banquet. The liquid inside was a deep purple, so rich in oily texture that it nearly glowed.

She withdrew the bulbous stopper, dribbled oil on the sponge, replaced the top, then smoothed the delicious, perfumed liquid over her body. Nerisa breathed another long sigh. She'd never felt so clean, so pampered, so—

The thought broke off as once again she thought she heard voices.

She let the sponge float away and looked up. Once again there was nothing and no one to be seen.

Then she heard a high-piping voice and smiled.

A moment later Scani came in, Palimak perched on her hip.

"Lord Timura is here, My Lady," the nurse announced.

"Thank you, Scani," Nerisa. "Tell him I'll be with him when I've done with my bath."

Scani bobbed a curtsy. "Yes, My Lady."

Nerisa smiled up at the child.

"And how is my darling Palimak?" she said.

The child's finger jabbed out—pointing directly at her.

"Shut up!" he said.

Scani was shocked. "Don't speak to your mother like that," she scolded.

Again, Palimak pointed, but his finger was at a lower level.

"Shut up!" he said again. He sounded angry.

"Hush, child!" Scani said. "Young lord or not, old Scani will peel your hide if you keep talking like that."

"Pay him no mind," Nerisa said. "He's just trying to get attention. If we ignore him he'll stop."

But Scani was upset. This was a blow to her skills as a nursemaid. "I don't know where he got such language, My Lady!" she said. "Those are words I most certainly never use."

"Shut up!" Palimak broke in.

Then he wriggled and kicked so fiercely Scani was forced to lower him to the floor and let him go.

"Stop that, Palimak!" Scani cried.

But the child paid no attention. On his hands and knees, he skittered across the wet marble floor. He stopped at the edge of the bath.

His eyes glowed yellow as he regarded the bottle of bath oils.

"Shut up!" he demanded.

He slapped at the bottle, rocking it.

"Shut up, shut up, shuutt uppp!"

And then, to the shocked amazement of the two women, he gave the bottle such a blow that it slammed against the edge of the tub.

Glass shattered in every direction.

Iraj reeled back as the image exploded in his face.

"The little whore's son!" he shouted.

Then he looked at the alembic, saw it was quite whole, and realized no harm was done.

He laughed mightily, slapping his thigh in glee. "It was almost as if the little bastard knew we were spying on his mother," he chortled.

His three new friends laughed with him.

"Tell me, Majesty," Kalasariz said, "wasn't she as beautiful as you've heard?"

Iraj glanced at the alembic again. His mouth suddenly went dry as he recalled the vision of Nerisa floating naked in her bath. He could almost taste her woman's scent rising on the perfumed steam.

"Yes," he said, voice rough.

"Even I was moved, Majesty," Luka said. "And I'm a demon and have little appreciate for the female human form."

"She seemed a dish more fit for a king," Fari said, "than a man of such common breeding as Timura."

Iraj's eyes narrowed. "What are you suggesting?" he asked.

"Suggesting? Why, nothing, Majesty," Fari said. "I was only commenting on the obvious."

"Lord Timura *does* claim to be His Majesty's most ardent friend and supporter," Kalasariz said to the others.

"That's certainly true," Luka said. "He's told us all that often enough...When it suits his purpose."

"Perhaps it's time you tested that friendship, Majesty," Kalasariz said.

"See how deep his feelings for you really are."

Protarus licked dry lips. His fingers rapped against the alembic's stopper—thinking, rap, rap, thinking.

Then he nodded—hard. His decision was made.

"As I see it," he said, "Safar's left me with no other choice."

"In the past," Safar said to Nerisa, "Iraj always listened to what I said. He didn't necessarily take my advice, nor did I always act as he wanted, but there were no hard feelings over it. At least none he showed."

It was night and the two were curled up on Nerisa's bed, the sleeping Palimak between them. The child had been restless since the incident in the bath the previous day, his sleep plagued with nightmares. At Safar's urging Nerisa had brought the child into their bed and now he was sleeping peacefully, thumb stuck firmly in his mouth.

"We don't *have* to become man and wife, Safar," Nerisa said. "I'll be your concubine, if you like. Or, since I'm a woman of means, you can be mine."

Safar smiled, but the smile didn't linger long.

"There's much more behind this than our nuptials," he said.

Nerisa nodded. He'd told her about the great lie Protarus was demanding of him, and the conspiracy he suspected was being hatched by Luka, Fari and Kalasariz.

"I was just making a silly jest," she said.

"For some reason," Safar said, "he's taken a sharp turn off the road we were both traveling on. And I don't know how to move him back."

Nerisa shivered. "I feel like a devil just perched on my grave," she said. "When I was girl on the streets of Walaria I always took that feeling as a warning sign. I don't know how many times I bolted—for no reason other than that shivery feeling—then saw the thief catcher creeping down the alley."

"Gundara has been howling danger since I left the palace," Safar said. "He advises me to flee."

"Then let's do it," Nerisa said, suddenly fierce. "Leave everything behind us and flee immediately. We won't lack for money. I have gold cached all over Esmir."

"I can't," Safar said.

Nerisa peered at him. Then, "I suppose it'd be pretty difficult giving up being Grand Wazier," she said. "It's hard to imagine having so much power."

"That means nothing to me, Nerisa," Safar said. "It was never anything I wanted, much less sought. Why, my fondest boyhood dream was to succeed my father some day as the greatest potter in all Kyrania."

"Then let's go to Kyrania," Nerisa said. "You talked about it so much in Walaria that it seemed a paradise to me. We'll go together. I'll be your wife, a simple village woman, with Palimak on my hip and his sister growing in my belly."

Her eyes glistened. "That was always *my* fondest dream, Safar," she said. "So why don't we both make those dreams come true?"

He took her hand and said, "I wish I could, but the Fates have decreed otherwise."

And then he told her the tale of two women—one a vision in Alisarrian's cave, the other a living woman, Methydia, a powerful witch and visionary in her own right.

When he was done he said, "Both insisted Iraj and I must travel the same path together. And at the end of that road is the answer I seek. The answer to the riddle of Hadin."

"Well, I'm no witch," Nerisa said, "and I'm certainly no vision in a cave. But it's plain to me Protarus has strayed off that path. You said it yourself. You said he'd taken a sharp turn and you didn't know how to get him back on the same road again.

"Did you ever think that maybe the road has ended? For the two of you, I mean? And *you* must go on, leaving Protarus behind in whatever madness he makes for himself?"

"Yes," Safar said, almost a whisper. "I'd thought of that."

Then he said, "But Iraj isn't mad. He's only king, which is a kind of madness in itself, I suppose. I remember I told him that a long time ago."

"Still," Nerisa. Then firmer, "Still!"

Safar thought a moment, then said, "I'll try one more time. We're supposed to meet again tomorrow. I owe him that one last chance."

"You don't *owe* him anything," Nerisa said. "It's the other way around, Safar. I wish you could see that."

Safar shrugged. "I can't help how I feel."

He looked down at Palimak, then back at her, brow furrowed with worry.

"What disturbs me most of all," he said, "is that both of you are in danger because of me. If Iraj acts badly he'll come after you as well as me.

"I think you should leave first thing in the morning."

Nerisa, a sensible woman, agreed. She had the responsibility of Palimak after all.

"There's a village at the crossroads about twenty miles outside of Zanzair," she said. "I'll have Abubensu get a carriage ready. I can tell him I'm considering an investment in the area, which isn't far from the truth. It looks to be a promising place."

"I know the village," Safar said. "If all goes well I'll send a message for you to return. And if doesn't, I'll meet you there."

"One of my caravans—bound for Caspan—will be crossing the desert in a day or so," Nerisa said. "We can go with it."

Palimak stirred. His eyes came open, a golden glow in the dim light.

Suddenly he screwed up his face and started crying.

Nerisa comforted him. "Everything's okay, little one," she cooed. "Mother's here.

"She won't let anyone hurt you."

Outside the mansion, Leiria crouched in the shadows watching the house.

She heard a flutter of sound and her head snapped around to mark it.

It was a raven on the prowl, big wings spread to catch the evening air. The raven circled the mansion grounds, then it turned and flew off toward the palace.

It soared higher and higher until it disappeared in the red glare of the Demon Moon.

Leiria's eyes returned to the house. Deep inside she heard the child cry.

She thought she'd never heard such a lonely sound.

# 27

# ESCAPE FROM ZANZAIR

Iraj paced the royal chamber like a captive lion, golden hair flowing from under his crown like a mane, beard jutting forward like a lion's snout; his eyes were narrowed, lips stretched back over his teeth as if in a snarl.

Safar stood in the center of the chamber watching him pace, feeling the anger build.

"I could command it," Iraj said. "I could require you to make the casting."

"Yes, you could," Safar said.

"Would you obey?"

Safar breathed in deeply. Then let it out. "No."

"Even if the penalties were most severe?"

"Even so."

"I could strip you of your title and fortune," Iraj said.

"I understand that."

"I could even take your life," Iraj said. "Are you so set in your refusal that you'd risk it?"

"Let me answer this way," Safar said. "If you were in my boots and felt your honor was at stake, how would you answer such a threat?"

Iraj paused. "I didn't threaten," he said. "I was only pointing out a fact."

"Still," Safar said, "how would *you* answer?"

"It's not the same. *I* am Iraj Protarus!"

"And *I* am Safar Timura!"

It was not an answer sculpted to please. Iraj glared at Safar, who stood there calmly, manner mild, but will just as strong. The king broke first, spooked by the strange glow in Safar's eyes.

He resumed his pacing, saying, "I'm told you think you are more popular than I am."

Safar lifted an eyebrow. "I'd brand that a lie," he said, "but it's too stupid a charge to deserve the name."

Iraj whirled. "What? Now you dare to insult me?"

"I don't dare anything," Safar said. "But if you believe such a claim, it's no insult, but the truth."

Iraj's fury suddenly turned to anguish. Tears welled up. "Why do you insist on defying me, Safar?" he cried. "We are friends. No, more than friends. More even than blood oath brothers. I swear that I love you more than my mother, more than my father, more than any son born to me."

"I can only answer that with another question," Safar said. "If you love me, why are you pressing so hard to make me violate a thing I hold most sacred?"

The anguish reverted to fury. "Because I am your king!" Iraj thundered. "And I find it necessary to ask this of you for the greater good of Esmir!"

Safar said nothing—there was no reply to make.

Iraj's manner returned to normal. He shook his head, as if saddened. "And still you refuse," he said.

"I do," Safar answered.

"What if I made this a matter of friendship?" Iraj asked. "You pleaded with me not to before. But we *do* have a blood bond between us. We swore we would give the other anything that was asked—freely and without hesitation.

"If I asked out of friendship, would you comply?"

"Whatever I did," Safar said, "it'd be the end of our friendship. If I agreed, it would my last act as your friend. If I refused, you'd consider our bond broken. Either way it would be over.

"Are you willing to risk that, Iraj?"

Protarus laughed bitterly. "It would be the only thing in my life I haven't risked," he said.

"Family? Hah! I killed my uncle. And slew his wives and his children too so they wouldn't sprout into enemies.

"The honor of my clan? Yes, I risked that from the very beginning. For if I had ever stumbled and fallen, the name Protarus would have been shamed for all history.

"Fortune? Bah! I am like you in that, Safar. I know I tell little lies to myself now that I am king and can have anything I want. It's habit, like drinking too deeply and too often. But I risked one fortune after another on the road to Zanzair. Every palace I looted I risked in the next toss of the dice to win another.

"Life itself? No one would deny that I've proved my willingness to cast it down as the price of a challenge. Why, I've nearly thrown it away many times just for the thrill of it."

Safar suddenly remembered Iraj's headlong race down the Kyranian mountainside to confront the demon raiders. It seemed like such a pure act at the time. The act of a storied hero. And for what? To save a merchant's caravan? A caravan carrying not a soul Iraj knew or cared about. And there was not an innocent among them—not a babe, not a maid, mother, granny, or man who if you met them would wring pity from your heart.

Then he remembered his own mad dash in Iraj's wake. He saw it clear. Saw the snow crusted boulders leaping up in his path. Saw the demons with fangs and talons and terrible swords. Saw their steeds who fought like great cats. And he felt it. Felt the fear icing his veins. Felt the demon magic crackling with power he never knew was possible. Felt the anger when he saw Astarias being dragged through the snow by her long black tresses. Felt the cold, distant satisfaction of his first kill.

He looked at Iraj and for the first time truly understood the man he'd been following for all these years. With that knowledge came a small understanding of himself. It arrived with a pang of disappointment. Like Iraj, he'd been a creature of events. A creature who'd cried holy purpose when there was only self at heart. Made himself a man who stretched his head above others, falsely ennobled by the vision of Hadin.

For the first time since this confrontation had first roused itself, Safar wavered. What did it matter? In a world of lies, what was one more? Magic was no holy thing. He was no priest with a godly cause. He had no temple, no altar. And the gods themselves were silent on the matter. Why *not* do as Iraj asked and declare an Era of Great Blessings? He could say it, then work like the devils from the Hells to make it so.

Then it came to him to do otherwise might destroy the man he'd called friend. A man who had only one thing left to risk in the chest that made him human—Iraj's claim of friendship with Safar.

He almost said it, almost relented, almost opened his lips to speak.

But Iraj said, "And finally, there's friendship. My love for you. That I haven't risked. Am I willing? I can't say. The first question I have to ask myself before I do, is if that friendship, that love, is returned? Is it real?

"Or have you been playing me false all these years?"

"You know I haven't," Safar said.

"Do I?" Iraj asked, an awful smile growing on his face. "Do I now?"

"Of course, you do," Safar said. "So we're arguing. We've argued before. We'll argue again. We're different men, so we hold different opinions. But they are merely differences between friends."

"I tested you once long ago," Iraj said. "If you recall, you didn't do well at that test."

Safar shrugged. "I was a boy in lust," he said. "It meant nothing."

"I also said someday I might test you again," Iraj went on. "I think that day has finally come."

"You mean the casting?" Safar asked. "You want me to lie to prove my friendship?"

He was about to say, very well, then, I'll do it. But Iraj shook his head, cutting him off.

"No," he said. "You claim that as a matter of honor. I won't ask you to soil it. A man of equal honor would never require such a thing of his friend."

The statement caught Safar by surprise. Was it over? Had he succeeded?

"So here is the test, Safar Timura. The man who claims to be my friend. It's a small test. One that should give you no trouble."

"And that is?" Safar asked, alarm rushing back.

"I gave you a woman once," Iraj said. "A virgin I greatly desired for myself. Astarias.

"And now I ask the same of you, although she is no virgin and is therefore the lesser gift."

Iraj looked deep into Safar's shocked eyes.

"Give me Lady Fatinah," he said. "I want her for myself."

"How can you ask that?" Safar said, dumbfounded. "You *know* she is to be my wife."

Iraj shrugged. "You can have her back when I'm done with her," he said. "And still marry her if you like. There's no shame in following a king in his pleasure.

"You liked Leiria well enough. Now that I think of it, that's two women I've given you. Two, Safar!

"I ask only one in return."

"This is foolish, Iraj!" Safar cried. "Even if I would consider such a thing—which I wouldn't—she's not mine to give. She belongs to herself."

"I imagine Astarias and Leiria felt the same way," Iraj said. "But that didn't stop you."

Struck to the quick, Safar struggled for an answer. Before he could, Iraj drew an object from his pocket.

"Here," he said, "I'll even sweeten the bargain, although why this should be a bargain is beyond me. Our oath was to give freely, no questions asked."

Iraj dropped the object into Safar's open hand. He glanced down and saw a small golden amulet. A wondrously formed horse dangling from a glittering chain.

"Coralean gave me that a long ago," Iraj said. "It was my reward for saving his caravan. You remember, don't you? You received a magical dagger at the same time."

Safar remembered very well. That same dagger, whose image was Nerisa's crest, was tucked in his belt.

"Coralean said someday I would see the perfect horse. A warrior's dream of a horse. And all I had to do was give this amulet to its owner and he would not be able to refuse me.

"Well, I never found that horse, Safar. But never mind, I'm sure it's there."

He clasped Safar's numb hand around the amulet.

"This is yours now, my friend. I give it to you for the woman. Why, it isn't even an equal exchange.

"For what mere woman could ever match such a wondrous steed?"

Silence followed. A silence where murder crept out of the shadows. Safar had anger enough to call it closer. He had the opportunity—they were alone in the royal chamber. And he had the weapons, the dagger in his belt, the blasting magic at his fingertips. He fought down the violence, nearly gagged on it. If he did act, terrible reprisals would certainly follow.

And at this moment Nerisa and Palimak would be making their way to the village at the crossroads, and safety. If Safar slew Protarus they'd never reach it. He had to play for time. It was the only way.

Before he could stumble out some sort of answer, Iraj said, "I'm afraid you've waited too long to reply, Safar.

"You failed the test."

Protarus abruptly turned away and strolled toward a small private door leading out of the chamber.

He paused at the door. "But I'm not so hard a man that I won't give you another chance," he said.

"Send Lady Fatinah to me tonight. And all will be forgiven."

Then he was gone.

As soon as he'd cleared the palace grounds Safar ducked into an alley and shed his cloak of office. The rich costume, emblazoned with the symbols of Esmir's Grand Wazier, was kicked into a dung heap. Beneath the cloak he'd worn the plain rough tunic and breeches of a common soldier. Then he hurried off, head low, trying not to move so fast he'd draw stares. Even so, he soon came to the vast demon quarters that sprawled all the way to Zanzair's rear gates. Demon females peered up from their washing to watch him go by. Demon kits shouted insults, or crowded close to beg. And big demon males loomed out of taverns to issue drunken challenges at this human worm who dared walk their streets alone.

Safar paid them no mind, averting the eyes of the females, shaking off the young beggars and sidestepping the challengers.

His goal was a small shabby stable near the rear gates. He'd risen before dawn that morning, made a few hasty additions to the plan he and Nerisa had discussed the previous night, then gone home to pack some necessities before his servants arose. Afterwards he'd taken his best horse to the stable by the gates. He'd left it with the sleepy-eyed stablemaster, along with enough coins to ensure the animal's care, but not so many as to arouse suspicion.

The whole time he'd prayed luck would be with him and the preparations would be unnecessary. He'd thought the first sign of that luck was Leiria's absence either at the mansion or his home. He'd assumed she was attending one of her "training sessions"—the transparent ruse Protarus and Kalasariz had used so their spy could report to them and receive her instructions.

As he approached the stable he thought at least that one bit of luck had held. If it hadn't he would've been forced to incapacitate Leiria in that same alley where he'd shed his cloak. Or, worse, be required to slay her. Safar had strong doubts he'd be able to do such a thing, no matter what the cost. Spy or not, Leiria had crept into his heart long ago and held a small piece of it.

There was no one about when he entered the ramshackle

building. He called for the stablemaster, but no one answered. So he fished out a few coins, laid them on a work bench within easy sight and picked his way to the back where his horse and gear waited.

He froze in front of the stall. His horse was already saddled, bags strapped to the back, sheathed sword hanging by its belt from the pommel. On either side of his mount were two others—both saddled and ready. But ready for whom? He moved closer and suffered another jolt. Both horses were his!

Straw rustled and he whirled, dragging out the only weapon he had, the small silver dagger.

Leiria stood there, mailed and fully armed. He nearly lurched at her with the dagger, but pulled back in time. Just as he'd feared he lacked the necessary hate.

"What are you doing here?" he demanded.

Leiria held out her hands to show they were empty. He looked down and saw her sword was still in its sheath.

"I'm here to help you, Safar," she said.

Safar barked laughter. "So I see," he said with heavy sarcasm. "But to where? My grave?"

"I don't blame you for thinking that," she said. "But you've got to believe me when I say I've never done or said anything to harm you. I told you once long ago I'd never betray you, Safar Timura. And I never have."

"What do you call spying?"

Leiria's eyes were pleading. "If I didn't give the king and Kalasariz what they wanted," she said, "they would have replaced me with someone else. Someone who didn't love you, Safar. And you know that I do. Even now, when your heart is with another woman."

Safar thought he saw truth, but he was desperately afraid he was seeing what he wanted, not what really existed.

"Besides," Leiria said, "you never did anything wrong. You've never been a traitor. Never conspired. What did it hurt to tell them about your innocent excursions, friendly meetings, or all the long nights you spent studying books of magic? There's one thing I didn't tell them, however. I said nothing about the child. About Palimak."

"What are you saying?" Safar said. "They know he exists. It's no secret."

"They don't know he's part demon," she said. "You kept it from me but I saw, Safar. I saw his eyes. What do you think Iraj would've imagined if he'd known that? His Grand Wazier in the arms of a woman with a monster for a child? Palimak's no monster, but that's not what Iraj would've thought. Especially after Kalasariz and Luka and Fari got to him. Whispering all kinds of disgusting things."

"I thank you for that, at least," Safar said. "But it doesn't matter anymore. If I were you I'd get away from me just as fast as you can. Iraj and I are finished!"

"I know that, Safar," she said. "You were finished before you met this morning. It'd all been decided. Iraj never had any doubt you'd refuse him. He just needed an excuse to bring you down. To declare Safar Timura a criminal. To blacken your name. He's afraid of you, Safar. He thinks you are his rival for his kingdom and the love of his subjects.

"But most of all, my dear, dear Safar, he's afraid and jealous of your magic."

She paused a moment. Saw the suspicion vanish from his eyes. Saw those eyes turn from icy blue to the color of the lake in far Kyrania.

He said, "I'm sorry about Nerisa." He shrugged. "I never meant it to happen."

"I know that," Leiria said.

"I thought she was dead."

"I know that too."

"I'm ashamed to admit that I've treated you badly."

"Never mind," Leiria said. "There's no time for apologies or remorse now, my love."

She took a deep breath, then said, "Hold on tight as you can while I tell you what's happened. I would have said it first, but I knew you'd think it was a trick. A trap.

"Nerisa and Palimak never left. They are still in Zanzair."

"What?" Safar's voice came like a cry.

"She was betrayed by Abubensu," Leiria said. "The carriage never arrived. He delayed her with lies until it was too late to find another. Now there are guards outside her home. Not many, but she knows they're there so she doesn't dare leave."

"How much time do we have?" Safar asked.

"I don't know," Leiria said. "A few hours at most. They would've moved sooner but it's you they want most of all. Besides, they have to gather their nerve and their forces to oppose you. You can be sure when they come it'll not be just with soldiers, but with Fari's best wizards and witch sniffers.

"That's how much they fear you."

Leiria indicated the horses. "Everything's ready. We have only to ride."

And ride they did. A mad clatter of iron hooves, shouted curses and cries of alarm as they dashed through the streets. They burst through the busy market place, scattering shoppers and knocking over stalls. They tore through parks, leaping hedges and showering mud. But when they came to the hill leading up to Nerisa's mansion they hauled the horses in, dismounted as quietly as they could, and hid them among some trees.

Then they crept up the hill in full daylight, using every rock and stump and bit of brush for cover. A young nurse with two young charges in tow saw them and hurried away. A gardener came on them while they were lying in a hedge and Leiria took him captive as gently as she could and bound him with leather laces from her harness.

There were four guards patrolling the grounds. Three demons and a hulking brute of a human.

They killed all four, quietly and efficiently.

Then they were at the door.

"I'll get the horses," Leiria said and she turned and ran back down the hill.

The door came open and Nerisa rushed into Safar's arms.

"I was afraid you'd never come," she said. "And I was more afraid you would. It's you they want, not me."

"I wish that were true," Safar said. "But when the king condemned me he condemned you as well.

"Now, quick! Get Palimak. We have to flee!"

Then they were out on the broad lawn and Leiria was thundering up, leading two horses behind her.

Safar took Palimak while Nerisa mounted. The child was

silent, trembling. Eyes flashing from yellow to hazel and back again.

Then Nerisa was fully mounted and she reached down to take the child.

Safar was handing him up when Gundara suddenly shouted, "They're coming, Master! They're coming!"

He whirled, clumsy with the child still in his hands. Down the hill he saw helmed demons and humans kicking their mounts up the road. Then he heard the bay of the witch sniffers and saw the devil hounds bounding in front of the troops. He felt a blast of magic and reeled back, stumbling against Nerisa's horse, which shrilled and shied away. He heard her shout to him to hand up the child.

But there wasn't time, there wasn't time.

Another blast, stronger than the first, came at him like a great wind, shriveling the grass with its heat.

He managed a blocking spell, but diverted only part of it. He turned to protect the child, catching the force with his back. He felt it sear through his clothes, gritted his teeth against the pain and he heard Gundara shout, "Shut up!" and Palimak echo, "Shut up!" and then the pain was gone.

He set the child down and came about, clawing at his pocket. The witch sniffers were almost on him now, but he had time to hurl the pellets and they exploded, sheeting fire and smoke.

The devil hounds were scattered by the blast, shrieking in fear and pain.

Smoke clouds—red and green and yellow swirled all around.

Then he heard the thunder of the approaching troops and through the smoke he saw Leiria, sword in hand, charge into the mass, cutting left and right, leaving demon howls and human screams in her wake. She broke through, then wheeled her horse and came crashing back, her killing sword releasing rivers of blood.

And now Nerisa was off her horse and beside him, armed with nothing but a whip. A witch sniffer leaped out of one of the smoke columns, slavering jaws yawning. It came so fast it almost had him, but Nerisa lashed out with her whip, slicing through those open jaws and the creature's face became a gory mask and it slammed to the ground. So close that Palimak hit it with his tiny fist, crying, "Shut up! Shut up!"

Nerisa scooped Palimak off the ground. Slinging him on her hip, she held him with one hand while she whirled the whip with the other.

Then the air shrilled and a dark swarm of arrows came lofting towards them.

But they were slow, so very slow. They reached the apex of their flight then down they came, down, down and down.

Just as they struck, Safar hurled himself on Nerisa and the child. His body, not magic, was their only shield. He heard them strike all around him, thought for an instant they'd been saved by a miracle or incompetence. Then he grunted as one buried itself in his thigh. Grunted again when another struck his shoulder. He hurt, by the gods he hurt, but he didn't care because he could feel Nerisa's warmth against him. Hear Palimak crying beneath her. And he knew they were safe.

He rolled away, purposely and painfully breaking off the arrows against the ground.

Safar came to his feet, calm and strong and gathering more power with each breath.

He slipped the dagger from his belt. Casual, as if he had all the time in the world. With cold interest he noted Leiria savaging the soldiers. She was here, there, everywhere, darting in and out, dealing out death as if it were the sweetest of gifts. But she was tiring, as was her horse. He saw the animal stagger once, saw her sword arm droop and the effort on her face as she forced it up again.

Then the great spell came, just as he knew it would. He could smell Fari, that damned old demon, behind it. Ah, and there was a little bit of Luka there. A whiff of arrogance. And Kalasariz? Where was he? He sniffed again, caught the sewer stench of conspiracy. There you are, you whore's son. But Fari would need more for this spell.

He'd need Iraj.

Safar imagined them tucked safely away in some dark room of the palace. The Necromancium, most likely. Fari was a cautious old fiend and wouldn't trust his wizards to drag Safar down. So just in case he'd create a mighty spell. He'd take a drop of blood from each. And build on the innate power all conspiracies hold. He'd take one from Luka for his poisonous hate of his father. One from Kalasariz, to confound. One from himself for real magic. And finally, one from Iraj, for there is nothing as deadly as friend against friend.

Asper had taught Safar that.

Then Fari would mix the blood in a potion. A potion he would've labored long and hard on well before this conspiracy had come into the open. And then they'd drink. Each passing the cup on to the other.

Poor Iraj, Safar thought. He probably didn't know the potion would seal him to the others forever.

Then Fari would cast the spell. But what spell would it be?

Ah! What else?

The Force of Four!

Another lesson learned from Asper.

He shouted for Gundara who leaped out onto his shoulder.

The little Favorite chattered a spell, head darting this way and that, looking, looking...

He jabbed a finger to the east. "There, Master!" he cried.

At first all he saw was the glare of the Demon Moon above the palace. Then he saw a shape take form. It looked like a wolf's head. A wolf with long fangs like a demon's. Baleful eyes moving. Searching.

Then the wolf saw him. It bayed in hellish joy and shot forward, head growing larger as it came.

But it wasn't the head Safar feared. It was the killing spell coming like a desert storm behind it. So strong it was impossible for him to stop.

Safar pointed the dagger at the wolf's head, the tip glittering blood red from the moon.

He made that his center. Then he cut to the side, once for Luka. Another slice. Twice for Kalasariz. Again. Thrice for Fari. And then the fourth—for Iraj.

Then he aimed the dagger at the center again. Right between the wolf head's glaring red eyes.

He felt the force of its gathering hate. Felt the first buffet of searing magical winds.

He put all of his might, all of his will behind the dagger tip.

And he shouted—"*Protarus!*"

There was a clap of ungodly thunder and the wolf head shattered. He heard a distant howl. And then the sky was empty and the air was still.

He looked around and saw the troops fleeing down the hill. Leiria was coming up to him, leading her horse, which was bleeding heavily from many wounds.

"There's more of them, Safar," she said. "You can see from the edge of the hill. Hundreds of soldiers. They're milling about now, gathering their nerve. But they'll come soon enough. This isn't over yet."

"I couldn't kill him," Safar said. "I hurt him, but I couldn't kill him. There wasn't time."

"Iraj won't give you another chance," she said.

"Then let's not give *him* one," Safar said.

He turned to find Nerisa, saying, "We'll head for the village just like we—"

Nerisa was sprawled on the ground. There was an arrow through her breast, blood stain creeping across her tunic.

Palimak was kneeling beside her, weeping and blubbering over and over again—"Shut up, shut up, shut up!" as if he were trying to silence Death himself. And perhaps he was.

Safar felt nothing. He was too shocked to grieve, too numb for thought. The only sensation was the cold stone in his chest where his heart had once lived.

He felt a tug at his sleeve. "We have to go, Safar," Leiria said. "I'm sorry she's dead, but there's nothing we can do."

Her voice sounded distant—like a gull crying above a great sea.

Then it came closer, clearer. "Safar! They'll be here any minute."

Still, he did not move.

Leiria rushed over to Nerisa's body. Gently she picked up Palimak, soothing him, but awkwardly in a soldier's manner.

She carried the child back to Safar and pushed him against his chest. Safar didn't react and so she grabbed each arm in turn and folded them across the boy, forcing an embrace.

"They'll kill the child, too, Safar," she said. "Nerisa's child!"

Safar came unstuck and clutched the weeping Palimak tight.

"I won't let them," he said. "I'll kill that whoreson, I swear I will!"

"Killing will have to wait, Safar," Leiria said. "We have to get away first."

And so that is what they did. They rode off the hill, Leiria leading the way and Safar carrying Palimak. Exactly how they escaped, he'd never be able to recall. He remembered only the shouts of soldiers behind and to the side of them. The sound of shutters and doors slamming as they clattered through the streets. Screams and blood at the city gates. The countryside whipping past. Switchback trails, splashing in creeks, hiding in woods.

Finally they arrived at the village where Safar and Nerisa had planned to meet.

There Safar came alive again. His heart was still stone, but he felt a growing heat.

It was hate that brought him alive, desire for revenge.

He sent Leiria on with Palimak. Perhaps she argued, he couldn't remember. There was only a vague recollection she'd return on a certain date. Soon as she was gone he forgot the date.

There was a large stream running through the village. Safar searched the banks until he found a small clay bed of the purest white.

He gathered what he needed and mounted the hill that rose above the village. He could see Zanzair from that hill. See the palace where King Protarus sat on his throne and ruled the land.

Safar spread out the things he needed. He gathered wood and lit a small fire and when it'd burned out he stripped to his loin cloth and covered himself with ashes.

He cut the first slab of clay with his silver dagger and started on the model of Iraj's great palace.

And there he sat, day into night, and night into day, mourning Nerisa and planning his revenge.

# Epilogue
# THE RECKONING

The spell was ready.

All his hate was gone. Contained, now, in the model of the Grand Palace.

He'd conjured up every bit of bitterness and made each into a monster. Some he enclosed in the gilded turrets. Others in the smooth domes. Each parapet bore a devil's visage. Anger, betrayal, murder and lust, on and on until the whole palace was ringed with the faces of hate.

In the bowels of the palace, deep, deep within, where the only sounds were the cries of tortured things and the clank of the chains that bound them to their pain, he placed the greatest hate of all. And that was what had been done to Nerisa.

Satisfied, he looked up from the model. Shimmering under the Demon Moon he could see the real Zanzair, the real Grand Palace where Iraj Protarus sat upon his golden throne. He wondered what Iraj was thinking, what he was seeing as he looked out over his teeming court. Who were his friends, now? Which were his foes? Iraj could hurl the greatest army at the gates of that riddle and never seize the answer. All the mailed men, all the horned demons, could not bring it down.

Safar recalled a riddle from Asper's book:

*"Two kings reign in Hadin Land,*
*One's becursed, the other damned.*
*One sees whatever eyes can see,*
*The other dreams of what might be.*
*One is blind. One's benighted.*
*And who can say, which is sighted?*
*Know that Asper knocked at the Castle Keep,*
*But the gates were barred, the Gods Asleep."*

Safar took one last long look at the gleaming city and glorious palace that had been another man's dream. He turned away.

And would not look again.

Only the final touches remained to make the spell. He surrounded the model with the dried branches of a creosote tree. They had an oily smell, not pleasant, but not unpleasant either. He sprinkled powders all around, concentric circles of red, green, yellow and black. He made a wide patch of all the colors just in front of the gate. And in that patch he first pressed the silver dagger, making the impression firm and deep. Next, the horse amulet, pushing hard so the stallion seemed to rear up from the mark of the blade.

When he was finished he cleaned the dagger and amulet, scouring until every speck of powder was gone. Then he put them carefully away in his saddle bags.

At the crest of the hill a spring trickled from beneath a large boulder, making a shallow pool where the boulder's weight leaned hardest. He stripped and washed himself, ash-colored rivulets coursing off until the pool was black.

He stepped out, skin gleaming in the morning sun, the pool a dark mirror of sorrow he would leave behind.

Then he dressed with care, clean tunic and breeches and a wide leather belt cinching his waist. He stamped on his boots, buckled on his spurs and then looked around to see what he should do next.

But there was nothing to be done.

So he sat on the boulder and waited, although he couldn't remember exactly what he was waiting for.

He thought of Kyrania. It came to him on a fresh breeze of imagination, blowing off The Bride's Veil, clean and full of spring's promise. He saw the valley's broad thawing fields with green sprigs bursting through white. And the orchards shaking off winter, swelling knots on the branches where clusters of cherries and peaches and apples would soon appear. He saw the sleepy-eyed boys leading the goats to pasture, the pretty maids giggling and posing as they passed, the watchful grannies grumbling warnings as they knocked winter's grime between the washing stones. Out on the lake the birds were returning, filling the skies with the sound of courting and challenge. He saw the hearth smoke pouring from the gray-slated rooftops and smelled roasted lamb, picked with garlic, and bread from the oven and toasted cheese crusting by the fire. His saw his family at table, mother, father and all his sisters laughing and gossiping and spooning up his mother's thick porridge to gird them against the day. He heard Naya bleat that she wanted milking and his mother shouting—

"Wake up, Safar, you lazy boy!"

Safar's head jolted up. He heard the sound of horses approaching and he smiled when he saw Leiria riding up the path, leading another horse behind her. She had a sword at her hip and Palimak strapped on her back, cooing and gurgling at the world from his little basket stuffed with soft blankets.

Leiria's brow was creased with worry, but when she saw his smile the creases vanished and she smiled back, sweet hope blooming in her dark eyes like the buds bursting from the fields of Kyrania.

She cantered up to him, smile widening.

Then she looked over at the model of the palace, surrounded by dry brush and voltive powders, and the pearly smile melted away.

"Are you ready?" she asked, a tremble in her voice.

Safar answered with a question. "What day is it?"

"Why, the day I said we'd return. The day of the feast when Iraj declares the Era of Great Blessings." She gestured down the hill. "All the villagers are talking about it."

Safar nodded, remembering his final instructions to Leiria. This was the day she was supposed to return if she could.

"Then I'm ready," he said.

"It's a good thing," Leiria said, "because if you weren't I would've knocked you on the head and taken you away tied to the back of the horse."

Safar could see she wasn't joking.

"He still hunts me?"

"All of Esmir hunts you," she said. "His troops are scouring the countryside dreaming of the fat purse your head will fetch."

Safar laughed. "I've been here all along," he said. "Twenty miles from his gates."

"Don't feel so clever," Leiria replied. "On my way I saw a patrol heading for the village. I rode with them for awhile. The sergeant told me there's rumors of a mad priest living in these hills who is none other than Safar Timura in disguise."

She shrugged, the smile coming back. "Fortunately he didn't think much of the rumors and was going to inspect a few other places before coming here."

Safar looked up at her, searching—for what he didn't know.

"Are you certain you want to do this?" he asked. "You could leave now. You could give me the child and ride on and find a much better life."

"Shut up!" Palimak cried. He was looking at Safar, hazel eyes turned to demon yellow in his delight at finding him here. "Shut up, shut up, Shuuut Uppp!"

And Safar heard Gundara answer from the nested blankets. "Shut up yourself! I'm tired of shut up! All the time, shut up, shut up, shuuttt upppp!"

Leiria laughed, horse skittering to the side at the loud sound of it. "There's your answer, Safar Timura!" she cried.

And so he broke a jar of oil over the palace model and surrounding brush. He lit the brush, blew the fire into life until it roared.

Then he leaped on the horse and they rode away.

As they clattered past the startled villagers there was a thunderclap from the hill. A moment later there was another clap—from a great distance, but louder, as loud as if the gods themselves had awakened.

Then the whole northern sky was a sheet of flame so hot the Demon Moon vanished in the brightness.

But they didn't look back. They didn't pause and wait for the sky to clear and see the molten place where the Grand Palace of Zanzair had once stood. Where kings had come and kings had gone since times most ancient.

And where the last king—the King of Kings—Iraj Protarus, Lord Imperator of Esmir, greater even than the Conqueror Alisarrian, abode his destined hour and went his way.

Home was a thousand miles or more distant. But Safar could see it beckoning, a hazy, welcoming vision hanging just before his eyes.

He led them hard and fast across deserts and grasslands and wide rocky plains sprawling to the mountains of his birth.

To far Kyrania.

Where the snowy passes carry the high caravans to clear horizons.

The place he should never have left.

The place where this tale ends.